THE GOLDEN FLUTE

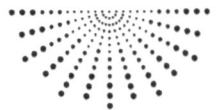

ROSALIE OAKS

Parkerville
PRESS

eBook ISBN 978-0-6453005-2-9
Print ISBN 978-0-6453005-1-2

CONTENTS

IN WHICH CARRIAGE TRAVEL IS HAZARDOUS

*L*ord Beresford's crested carriage rumbled away from the London townhouse, the lamplight gleaming weakly through the window. Elinor arranged her skirts neatly and pulled the blinds down. For tonight's little lesson in Musing they needed privacy.

Beresford was driving up front; they had decided that the coachman would think it odd to be directed to drive slowly and randomly through the streets of London. Beresford, becoming immune to his beloved's eccentricities, was happy to oblige. Besides, he was a very good driver, and they needed a steady hand for their experiment.

Elinor sat up straight and eager, glad that her mother had finally decided to share her knowledge of Musor magic rather than hide it. Of course, if the Avelys were to open a school for Musors, Mrs Avely would have to become accustomed to the role of teacher, and Elinor had to learn all she could.

Mrs Avely sat opposite Elinor, her hands primly clasped in her lap, already looking the part of teacher and instructor. Perry sat next to his mother, nibbling his lower lip. Aldreda, in bat form, hung from the roof, somehow conveying her scepticism by the angle of her wings.

"Is this really necessary?" asked Perry. "Surely I won't have to Travel from a moving object very often."

"One hopes not," agreed Mrs Avely. "Yet it is best to be prepared for all eventualities, as we have seen."

Elinor nodded. "And it will give me a chance to practise finding you, brother dear." After all, there was a good chance that Perry would get himself lost, with his newfound ability to Travel anywhere at the drop of a glove.

"And I, too," said Mrs Avely. She unfolded a large map of London and spread it across her lap. "Though finding lost items is not a branch of Discernment in which I excel."

"You did it before," Elinor reminded her, though of course her mother's talent lay (unfortunately or otherwise) in Truth Discernment. Elinor peered at the map; it was difficult to see in the dim light of the carriage. Fortunately, map divination did not require one to see with the eyes, but with the mind.

Perry sighed. "Very well. Can I go anywhere in London?"

"Not too far," warned his mother. "You don't have a vampiri companion yet, and we don't want you too Bemused. And remember, it is better to wait at least ten minutes before you can Travel again, to ameliorate your Bemusement. Though I suppose if you find yourself in trouble you may vanish away again."

"Ten minutes!" said Perry. "That is an age." He lurched to his feet as the carriage rumbled on, his back curved under the roof. Elinor was glad to see he was gaining more ease with his injured shoulder, for only a couple of weeks ago he had been knifed by a villain. Thankfully, a Healor had been on hand to help mend the wound, but it had been a deep injury. It had caused Elinor worry and guilt, for she was the reason Perry had Travelled into danger.

"Be careful," she told him now.

Perry winked, then vanished.

Elinor rolled her eyes. She could guess where he had gone, even without a Discernment. Jaq's hotel was nearby and Perry would snatch at any chance to spend ten minutes in Jaq's company.

Her mother shifted the map so that it lay across both their laps. "Are you ready, Elinor? We shall Discern together, though I imagine you will be more adept at it than I. Map divining is a subset of Discernment closer to jewel divining."

Obediently, Elinor closed her eyes and raised her hand. Trying to quieten her mind, she focused her attention on her fingers, gloved but cold, hovering above the map. Her breathing slowed and she reached with her other hand for the lapis lazuli pendant that hung on her bosom. She had not owned the Talisman Stone long (a thank-you gift from King George), but she had immediately found that the stone assisted her Discernment. She was already very fond of the deep-blue pendant with its slivers of gold.

Where is Perry? she asked, feeling with her inner senses.

An image came to her mind's eye of her brother falling clumsily onto Jaq. She smiled, but wondered if her own ideas were intruding and waited for an unequivocal sense to guide her finger. She returned to the question, pushing away thoughts of Jaq's surprised face. *Where is Perry?*

"There." Mrs Avely put her finger down before Elinor. However, her voice lacked its usual ring of authority.

Elinor squinted down and saw that her mother had landed on a corner of Hyde Park. Yet Mrs Avely withdrew her finger and bit her lip.

"You are not certain," observed Elinor.

"No," said Mrs Avely. "Where would you suggest?"

Elinor closed her eyes and stuck out her hand again. After a few moments, she dropped it, a finger pointing to Grenier's Hotel. Jaq's quarters: a fashionable and extravagant residence that the Regent had recommended to him.

She sighed. "I'm not certain either."

Mrs Avely opened the shutter and told Beresford to drive to

Grenier's. Beresford laughed, Aldreda sniffed above them, and Elinor smiled in the darkness.

Mrs Avely turned to Elinor. "What is so amusing?"

"Jaq is staying at Grenier's."

"Oh." Mrs Avely paused. "Perry is very close to Jaq, isn't he?"

Elinor did not want to inform her mother that Perry had captured the romantic interest of a selkie prince, as she was not sure how Mrs Avely would take the news. After all, such liaisons were harshly punished in England, and Perry and Jaq had to keep their courtship very discreet. Elinor was glad Perry was now a Travellor, for if he was ever discovered in a compromising situation, he could simply disappear into thin air.

Now she merely observed that Grenier's Hotel was reasonably close and a wise choice, since Jaq was well accustomed to Perry appearing out of nowhere. It was a safe place to spend ten minutes in the privacy of a hotel room – with extra delights such as holding hands with a gorgeous rascal, though Elinor did not mention that part.

Soon they reached the grand facade of Grenier's, suitably elegant for a prince, though Elinor thought it was probably too far from the sea for a selkie who couldn't spend long out of water. She unlatched the window. It was time for Aldreda's part: to fetch Perry.

Aldreda's small black shape dropped from the roof and glided into the night. Elinor leaned out of the window, trying to follow her progress, but it was impossible in the darkness.

Beresford, keeping the horses reined in, turned his head to address her. "My love, you ought to display a little more decorum, not stick your head out of the carriage like a hoyden." But his voice was warm. He smiled down at her, his thick chestnut hair crammed under a curly-brimmed beaver and his broad shoulders enclosed in a double-caped driving coat. Elinor stared at him with longing. She wished she could Travel into Beresford's room without anyone being the wiser. The wedding was still weeks away and he was being annoyingly protective of her virtue.

"I was admiring Grenier's Hotel," she replied.

He grinned. "Even I could have divined Perry was here."

"Yes," she agreed. "Which makes it more difficult to know if I divined right."

She shrieked as Perry appeared in the carriage behind her and knocked her into her seat. "Perry!"

"Be careful!" retorted Perry. His blond hair was dishevelled, his cheeks flushed. He smiled sweetly and sat down next to his mother. "You knew I'd be back; it behoved you to stay on your side."

Mrs Avely took in his rosy appearance and foolish smile. She frowned. "Are you so Bemused already?"

Elinor giggled. "Perhaps something else has flustered your senses."

Mrs Avely's frown deepened. "Have you been drinking, Peregrine?"

Perry darted Elinor an admonishing glance. "No!" He cleared his throat. "To Travel while moving is taxing, mother dear."

"You weren't moving just now," Elinor pointed out.

Mrs Avely leaned forward anxiously. "How did you find Travelling from out of the carriage?"

Perry shrugged. "I did land with rather a bump."

Elinor poked him. "You do that anyway. Did you land on Jaq?"

"No!"

Elinor narrowed her eyes. "Are you certain?"

"Yes."

"More's the pity," said Elinor.

Mrs Avely tutted. "You are both Bemused."

"I am not!" declared Perry.

"You are," said Elinor. "Admit it, Perry, you simply aren't as Gifted as I am, and you need a vampiri companion like Aldreda to keep you lucid. Just as Mother does."

At that moment, Aldreda herself flew back into the carriage. Elinor closed the window behind her in a pointed manner. Mrs Avely tapped the front shutter and Beresford set the horses in motion again.

"I admit no such thing," said Perry, sinking back in his seat. "I don't hold with carrying a naked miniature person in my pocket." He frowned at Mrs Avely. "Even if Mother thinks it appropriate for a matron of her age."

Mrs Avely bristled. "You will observe that I do not have Pagrilliard with me today."

"Where is Pags?" asked Elinor. Above them, Aldreda cocked her head, listening.

"Never you mind," said Mrs Avely. "Perry, let me know when you are ready for the next attempt. As for you, Elinor, do not become complacent. You have a long way to go before you are as accomplished a Discernor as your father."

Perry folded his arms. "Ten minutes, Mother, I believe you said. Meanwhile, I think it is high time you told us what happened to Father."

Elinor's eyes widened and she leaned forward. "Yes, indeed! You promised you would."

"Did I?" Mrs Avely looked shifty.

"Yes!" Elinor tried to keep her tone reasonable. "After all, it is partly due to Father's services that we have been granted Lanyon Castle. It is only right that we know what happened to him."

Mrs Avely sighed and settled back in the dark of the carriage. After a pause, she spoke. "Very well. Though I only divulge his story so you can learn from it."

Outside, link boys called, and another carriage rattled past. Elinor found she was clasping her hands tightly together.

Her mother shifted on the seat. "Truth be told, I don't know all the circumstances, as I only heard the story from his superior."

"We understand," said Perry impatiently. "Tell us what you *do* know."

Mrs Avely drew a breath. "It was in France, in the city of Turcoing, in 1794 during the Revolution. Your father was serving as a Royal Discernor, deployed with the British troops in the north of France. He was there to detect spies and assist the general and officers, though of course he was not open about his Gift."

Perry and Elinor leaned forward.

Their mother continued. "One day in May, the British troops left their position to cut off a French line. At the last minute, your father Discerned that it was a trick: an ambush. He rode with all haste to warn the officers, but he arrived too late. He died in the crossfire." The words were bare, unadorned, as if repeated verbatim from her source.

"How could he be so foolish?" Elinor exclaimed. "If Father knew the French were there, how could he ride straight into harm's way?"

Mrs Avely's voice became stern. "It was noble, not foolish. Your father was trying to save his men. Perhaps he felt to blame for not Discerning the ambush sooner. You ought to know, Elinor, that Discernment often gives you dangerous information and moral obligations. If you are the only one who knows of a danger, often that requires you to go towards it. That is why I did not want you to become a Musor in the first place!"

Elinor bit her lip. Her mother had always discouraged her jewel divining. Mrs Avely had even kept her own Gift from Elinor, and stayed away from the Musor circles in London after her husband's death. Elinor could understand only by stretching her own empathy, as the magic and power of Musing was too intriguing for her to relinquish.

Perry spoke at last. "Discernment seems a burden," he pronounced. "Always knowing things you oughtn't."

"Exactly," said his mother, with approval.

"Travelling, however, is great fun."

His mother frowned. "Travelling is even more dangerous. You don't know what you might land on."

"Like Jaq," said Elinor, giggling.

Perry raised his eyebrows but grinned.

Mrs Avely sniffed. "Better to bump into Jaq than Travel straight into a knife, like you did in that hayloft."

Perry's hand went to his shoulder, still bandaged under his coat, and his lips twisted in acknowledgment.

Their mother continued. "Elinor, you are equally reckless, chasing after anything you happen to Discern. You both need to learn maturity with your Gifts. Such power requires responsibility." She looked around austerely. "Are you both ready to try again?"

They nodded meekly.

Perry made two more attempts: one to Drury Lane, which Elinor managed to Divine without too much trouble. The second time, she had barely put her finger over the map when Perry's form reappeared and collapsed in a pale heap on the carriage floor, crumpling the map beneath him.

Elinor gasped and bent over him. "Perry? Are you all right?"

Mrs Avely put a hand to her son's brow, her lips tightly compressed. "Foolish boy! What shall I do with a Bewildered child? He has returned far too soon."

Elinor's eyes widened. "Surely he will not become Bemused past hope, just from Travelling so quickly?"

Mrs Avely said nothing and felt along his arm. Then she looked up at Aldreda.

Aldreda nodded and fluttered down. She landed by Perry's hand and began drinking from his wrist.

Elinor sank back against the seat. "Thank goodness Aldreda is here."

After a few moments, Perry's eyes opened and he sat up abruptly, causing Aldreda to tumble away. "Oh, thank God," he said, clutching at his head. "I thought you were the lion."

"A lion?" said Elinor in astonishment. "Oh, did you go to the Tower's menagerie?"

"Yes. Didn't expect to land that close. I could see the marks on his nose." He shuddered. "A sight one might see in hell: the pattern of a lion's nose as it contemplates eating you."

Elinor raised her eyebrows. "Did you land *on* the lion?"

Perry shook his head. "That might have been preferable."

Mrs Avely heaved a deep sigh. "You're Bemused. Please be more careful!"

Perry settled himself on the seat, looking abashed. "Yes, Mother."

Elinor frowned. "I'm certain I would have found you, if you had just managed to entertain the beast a bit longer."

Mrs Avely folded up the map. "You are improving, Elinor. However, it might be more difficult to find something less familiar to you than your brother."

"Like a vampiri roost," agreed Perry.

"She can but try," said Mrs Avely. "Tomorrow night, Elinor, you can attempt a map divination. Let us hope you can determine the location of the missing queen."

2

IN WHICH NEGOTIATIONS ARE CONDUCTED

*T*he following evening, Elinor crept into Beresford's library before everyone was due to gather there. As she had hoped, Beresford was behind his desk, writing in his decisive scrawl. He had not heard her enter and was frowning.

Elinor cleared her throat. Beresford looked up, and his stern visage was replaced by a smile that transformed his face into something approaching handsomeness. He stood up and came around the desk to clasp her hands in his own. "You are early, my love."

She was having none of this hand-clasping nonsense. She leaned in to kiss him, sighing with pleasure as his arms slipped around her and drew her close.

A little while later Beresford drew back, looking just as flushed as Perry had in the carriage. "Elinor, my heart, we must be married as soon as possible."

"I agree," sighed Elinor. Yet they both knew it was a vain hope. Their mothers were determined to have a very exclusive and respectable wedding, which took some planning. The Countess of Beresford claimed it was necessary, after all the scandal Elinor had caused, to eliminate any gossip. Or to replace it with gossip about Elinor's wedding guests, who would include the Prince Regent himself.

Beresford groaned. "Four weeks still to go! How shall I endure it? Do not forget that I have consumed too much of that plum jam in my lifetime. I have excessive levels of zest to contend with."

Elinor chuckled. "I think your zest was excessive anyway." She ran a hand over his chest. "James, what were you writing with such a frown?"

"Oh, just a letter to my steward."

Elinor stilled, her head tilted to the left. "That is not true," she said slowly.

He stiffened. "Elinor, are you Truth Discerning me?"

She bit her lip and nodded.

He stepped away from her, a frown darkening his features once more. "I wish you would not."

"I cannot help it!" she replied. "If it comes to that, I wish you would not lie to me!"

"You can most certainly help it," he snapped, folding his arms. "I would appreciate some privacy. If I choose not to tell you something, I have my reasons."

"What reasons?" demanded Elinor.

"I do not wish to say."

Elinor ground her teeth. "Then simply *say* that you wish not to tell me," she said tartly. "Do not lie! A marriage cannot be based on lies."

"If it comes to that, a marriage cannot exist without basic privacy of mind," said Beresford. "It is well known that white lies smooth the path of matrimony." His tone became aloof. "I must ask you not to use your Gift on me."

Elinor suddenly deflated. He was right; it was unfair to keep watch on him like that. She ought to trust him unconditionally and indeed she did, though she felt a little hurt. "Very well," she said. "I am sorry. It is just a habit of mine to practise my Truth

Discernment, since I want to be as good as Mother. However, I shall endeavour to respect your privacy."

"You should consider excluding the rest of your family too," said Beresford, allowing his folded arms to loosen. "It is an uneasy feeling to know that someone is looking to catch you in a lie."

"Yes," said Elinor, a little dourly. She eyed the letter on the table, her curiosity now well and truly piqued.

Beresford smiled at her, reading her thoughts – which was both ironic and extremely annoying. However, he drew her back into his embrace and lifted her chin to kiss her again.

A minute later, Perry's voice came from behind her. "I say, you two! Not the thing! Not married yet!"

Elinor spun round, hastily stepping out of Beresford's grasp. Perry was leaning against the fireplace, having appeared without a sound: he must have Travelled there. "Perry! Don't sneak up on us like that."

Beresford sighed. "You two are as bad as each other."

Perry put his hands in his pockets, looking as scandalised as Elinor. "*I* was just practising. Aren't we having a meeting?"

"We are," said Elinor, brushing her skirt down and tucking a curl behind her ear. "I am going to do my map divination shortly."

She hoped she was capable of it. His Majesty King George had been impressed with her abilities in Discernment, especially when she managed to uncover a treasonous plot against him, and he had entrusted her with this quest. She nibbled her lip nervously. Such a nebulous task was quite different to finding a missing sapphire or some pearls.

The roost, led by its queen, had fled France during the Revolution twelve years ago, when King Louis XVI lost his head. The Revolution, Elinor had learned, had fomented violence not only towards the aristocracy, but also toward the Musors and vampiri who had been feted in the French royal court. Fearing for their lives, the queen's roost had gone into hibernation.

Elinor could not blame the queen for hiding. It had been a time of violence and death, by all accounts. England had managed to avoid similar tumult only because King George had instituted oppressive laws to keep the vampiri and the Musors secret. That was why Elinor had grown up with no idea that there were others like her, with a range of Gifts.

The Musor Edicts were still in force, forbidding open fraternisation between Musors and vampiri. Elinor disliked the Edicts; she thought they were oppressive and unfair to vampiri, for all that Aldreda said she was accustomed to keeping in the shadows.

Elinor sighed. She had (carefully) voiced her more liberal opinions to the king. He had stood firm on the Edicts but admitted a compromise might be necessary: a school for Musors, discreetly located in the wilds of Cornwall, where vampiri and Musors could associate and learn together. After the decimation of the Revolution, it was crucial to protect the remaining knowledge of Musing. His Majesty now possessed the Moria Pearls, with all their embedded scholarship on the subject, but it was clear they also needed practical knowledge. The French vampiri queen and her fellows could provide that, as well as vampiri companions to the Musors of the school.

So before the Avelys could begin a school, they needed the roost. King George had made one dependent on the other, promising the Avelys land for the school at Lanyon Castle, along with a suitably noble title, if they should manage to find the roost.

Elinor went to Beresford's desk and spun the globe that stood there, and the carefully etched shapes blurred into brown. The crucial question remained: where had the French vampiri queen taken her people? Pags himself had seen them flying off the northern coast of France ten years ago, before he retired to the wilds of Dartmoor to lick his own wounds. However, the northern coast of France was a large area to search. A map divination might help narrow it down. One hoped.

Elinor stopped the spinning globe with a fingertip. "Beresford, do you have the requisite maps of France?"

He nodded and set about laying them out, though Elinor noticed that he put his own letter away first. As he worked, the others arrived: Mrs Avely, with Pags in her pocket, and Jaq with Aldreda on his shoulder. Elinor was glad to see that Aldreda was at last friends with Jaq; he had finally managed to dissolve her long-held prejudice against selkies.

Jaq was ravishingly handsome as always: his black hair thick and shining, his cheekbones impossibly sharp. Aldreda, also with burnished black hair, was a miniature version of beauty on his shoulder. It was unfair that supernatural creatures were so gorgeous. No wonder Perry was so smitten with Jaq, though Elinor preferred the rugged good looks of her own fiancé. She smiled at Beresford and he smiled back, straightening the papers.

"All present?" asked Mrs Avely. "Shall we begin?"

"Not before tea," declared Elinor. "A Discernor needs the divine liquid to divine." This wasn't strictly true, but tea *did* help, for Discernment was assisted by the element of water.

Jaq deposited Aldreda on the chair behind the desk, where Elinor now sat in the place of honour, the letter a few infuriating inches away in the drawer. Beresford rang the bell for the butler, so Aldreda slipped under the table and Pags hid in Mrs Avely's shawl. The servants, of course, did not know of the vampiris' existence or their free association with humans – or at least they were good at pretending they did not, under the Royal Edicts.

Once the tea arrived, the vampiri re-emerged and conversation became serious. Elinor wanted to know where Pags had been.

Pags, less classically handsome than Jaq, nonetheless had a virility to his presence that made him supernaturally attractive despite his large nose and unruly hair. He had only recently deigned to wear clothes, having spent the better part of ten years on the moors of Devon, feeding from horses and abjuring human company and customs. Elinor privately thought that Aldreda's presence had civilised him, though of course he had been a dukel in France before his time of wilderness.

He leapt from Mrs Avely's shawl to a side table, a huge jump which he managed with aplomb. There he struck a pose: legs wide, arms folded. "I have been to the palace. I have troubling news."

"Oh?" said Aldreda sceptically from her perch. She knew Pags' tendency to melodrama better than all of them.

Pags ignored her. "The king sent someone else to find the roost before us," he announced. "One Lieutenant Chaboot was directed to investigate in secret." He paused dramatically. "Chaboot has not returned."

Elinor was affronted. "I thought *we* were to be entrusted with this quest."

"A Musor?" asked Aldreda.

Pags shook his head. "A vampiri. He is one of a secret military contingent called the Vilitia, which King George commissioned. Though it is few in numbers, it consists of vampiri loyal to the English crown. Chaboot was sent on this quest alone."

They stared at each other in the candlelight of the library. It made sense: a lone vampiri could search quietly and unobtrusively for any likely hibernation places. It also meant that the Avelys were still the first Musor party to investigate.

Yet Elinor felt uneasy: vampiri were not safe in France. Nor, come to think of it, were Musors. The Revolution had stirred hatred against all things magical.

Jaq pursed his lips, leaning back in his armchair. "And this vampiri has not returned?"

Perry was standing next to Jaq's chair, his hand resting on the back, almost but not quite touching Jaq. "Is this Vilitia fellow still searching for the roost, do you think?"

"We don't know." Pags strode back and forth on his side table like a general instructing his troops, and Elinor smothered a smile. "No reports or sign of Chaboot for the last two months. He should have returned a month ago, or at least sent word. His Majesty says we are to seek him as we look for the roost."

"Certainly," said Elinor dubiously, tapping her finger on the desk. "Though how shall we know if it is he? I imagine Chaboot will keep hidden. If he does show himself, he will not announce his real identity as a lieutenant in the Vilitia."

Pags paused in his pacing. "Apparently he has distinctive light-brown colouring," he said. "And either in bat or human form, he has a streak of grey over the top of his head. He will confide in me, I am sure," he added, puffing out his chest. "Especially if I tell him I am aware of his service."

Aldreda raised her eyebrows at this arrogance. "More likely he will confide in me, as a sympathetic feminine ear."

Pags frowned but had no rebuttal for this claim. After all, Pags himself had confided in Aldreda, or so Elinor had gathered. Perhaps he didn't like the notion that Aldreda had that effect on all vampiri males.

Jaq spoke quietly. "You are assuming this lieutenant is still alive. I remind you that vampiri haven't been seen in France for a long time."

Elinor attempted a cheerful tone. "It has been twelve years since the violence of the Revolution. It may be that a lone vampiri will not be targeted."

Pags nodded. "Perhaps you, Miss Avely, can Discern his whereabouts."

Elinor's lips twisted. She doubted she would be able to find a bat she had never met – though she had not met the roost either. She interlaced her fingers nervously; they were all relying on her to guide them, and she might well lead them astray. "I am not at all confident that I shall be able to find the roost, or this Chaboot."

"Ah," said Pags, "I have something to assist you, Miss Avely, borrowed from the king's library." He pulled from his pocket a small golden object that shone in the candlelight. Elinor decided not to ask whether 'borrowed' meant 'stolen'.

Pags held the object aloft. "This is a Viveroust flute."

Aldreda leaned forward in sudden interest. "A Viveroust flute? To wake the queen?"

Pags nodded. "We are to play it when we find the roost."

"It is a rare instrument," said Aldreda, "crafted to play at a very high frequency. As far as I know, the only surviving examples were made by a German artisan in the sixteenth century: a vampiri by the name of Edeltraud Tanzer. Myth has it that only a female vampiri can play it, and that its notes will rouse a queen out of roost hibernation."

Pags bowed. "Yes, it is tuned to waken the queen first. It might help to guide you, Miss Avely, as it is so closely connected with Her Majesty's existence."

Elinor was not so certain, but Jaq carried it to her. The tiny golden instrument was exquisite, with flourishes engraved around the holes and mouthpiece. She had to squint to see the pattern: delicate whorls dancing around stars, like the path of a bat in flight. Only a vampiri hand could have fashioned it, rendered so small as it was. Elinor admired it for several moments, delaying the moment of truth.

Eventually, her mother spoke. "Shall we try the maps?"

Elinor nodded, and Aldreda hopped onto her lap in support.

A silence fell over the company. Elinor took a fortifying sip of tea and held the Viveroust flute in the centre of her hand. Then she put her teacup down and reached for her lapis lazuli pendant. She needed all the help she could muster.

Curling her fingers around the flute, she held it over the maps and closed her eyes. Taking a deep breath, she hoped devoutly that the flute's connection with the queen might guide her Discernment.

Where is the vampiri queen's roost?

The quiet in the library was absolute. Elinor felt tense as the collective expectation pressed upon her. She let her breath out, trying to soothe her heightened nerves. *Where is the missing queen?*

Her hand, holding the tiny flute, quivered above the maps. She tried to remain calm, as if she were just finding Perry in London, not a colony of bats hidden somewhere in the depths of France. It didn't matter that the bats were unknown to her, small, and concealed. The vampiri population was decimated, and England without a queen. Elinor was supposed to be gathering the remnants of Musor knowledge, and for that she needed vampiri. She simply *had* to find the roost. So where in all of cursed France was it?

Her finger wobbled, then dropped. Her eyes snapped open and she leaned forward with everyone else.

Her fingertip seemed to have landed in the middle of the sea. She felt her heart sink and lifted her hand with a sigh of despair, but underneath was a tiny speck of an island, vanishingly small.

Aldreda jumped onto the map. "Sark," she read out.

Beresford, standing behind Elinor, hummed under his breath. "Quite possible," he said. "Sark is off the northern coast of France. Culturally, it is quite French – French speaking, I believe – but in fact it is a British dominion, granted by Queen Elizabeth as a royal fief in the sixteenth century. Clever of the vampiri to seek shelter there, out of French territory."

"I've been there," put in Jaq. "A beautiful island. Plenty of seals."

Perry raised his eyebrows. "Selkies?"

"Just seals," said Jaq. "Selkies keep to Skerry, away from human domains. Except me, of course." He smiled up at Perry.

Elinor let out a breath of relief. She had found a reasonable starting point, at least. Better not to mention that time when her map divination for the Moria Pearls had taken her to Pags instead.

Perry spoke up. "Didn't your map divination for the Moria Pearls take us to Pags instead?"

Elinor gave him a cross look. "That was a while ago. I've had more practice since then. I found you in London, did I not?"

Aldreda tapped her foot on the map. "Still, we won't assume anything. It will be an interesting trip; Sark is somewhere to start."

Beresford took a step away from Elinor. She realised why when he suddenly spoke to the group, his eyes avoiding hers. "It will indeed be an interesting trip – for Jaq and me. The rest of you will not be coming; I have been composing a letter to His Majesty to that effect. Once we have a direction, there is no need for all of us to undertake this quest."

Elinor's mouth fell open. "Pardon?"

Beresford adopted his most forbidding tone. "Sark, though English, is too close to France. It is too dangerous. We are at war with France, I remind you."

Elinor drew in her chin with an outraged huff. "I am appointed as a Royal Discernor – of course I'm coming with you! You need me to find the vampiri."

"Sark is small," argued Beresford. "If we know the roost is there, it shouldn't take us long to find them."

Jaq grinned from his armchair, but wisely said nothing. Perry frowned.

Aldreda rustled her skirts indignantly. "The roost is hidden," she pointed out. "Furthermore, Elinor's direction is not certain. Once she is closer to the island she might have a better reading. Besides, traditionally the Viveroust flute is played by a female vampiri, so you need me. You will offend Her Majesty if Jaq plays it. If, indeed, he *can* play it, with such large lips." She stuck her nose in the air.

Jaq pursed his luscious lips and twinkled. "I'd be happy to play the flute, but I agree that I may have difficulty, being both male and selkie."

Aldreda nodded, for once in accord with him. "You need my feminine presence," she declared.

Pags nodded reluctantly from his table. "It is true, I'm afraid. And as I was the last person known to see the roost, I must go too. Not to mention that I know the queen personally and my presence will reassure her."

Beresford looked sceptical at the unruly Pags' claim that he would reassure Her vampiric Majesty. He folded his arms. "Well, if you two bats keep out of sight, I suppose you may attend. At least you can fly off if there is trouble. The rest of you will stay behind."

Elinor was speechless. She realised she was gripping the Viveroust flute tightly and put it down on the table with a small click. Its tiny golden form looked like a matchstick about to light, the golden swirls glinting in the candlelight.

Perry shook his head. "Won't fadge, Beresford. I'm a Travellor. You might need my particular skills."

"And mine!" spluttered Elinor.

"No," repeated Beresford stubbornly. "I won't have my future wife venturing near France in the middle of a war."

"But the king ordered me to go!" shouted Elinor.

Mrs Avely sipped her tea, watching them. "His lordship is right about the danger, Elinor, especially if you are known to be a Discernor. If someone doesn't want the roost found, you might be a target of malice."

Elinor glared. "I refuse to be left behind! This is outrageous!"

A heavy silence fell in the library. Beresford looked mutinous, but Elinor felt even more rebellious. She sat stiffly in her chair and glowered at him. It appeared they had reached a stalemate of stubbornness.

Perry pulled at his lower lip. "You know what we need," he said, slowly. "We need a subterfuge."

Everyone turned to look at him.

"No," said Beresford pre-emptively. "Absolutely not."

Perry ignored him. "We don't tell anyone that Elinor is a Discernor. I can say *I'm* the Discernor. If anyone tries to murder me, I can just vanish out of harm's way."

Elinor sat up. "That's brilliant, Perry!"

"Furthermore," Perry continued, "we need not say that we are looking for vampiri. We tell everyone that I'm divining for gold or minerals, or some such thing." He waved a hand carelessly.

Beresford shook his head. "That could be just as inflammatory."

Jaq disagreed. "At least it doesn't raise the political problem of the vampiri."

"Yes," said Elinor eagerly. "And I can pretend to be married to you, Beresford: a mere diplomat's wife. No one will look twice at me."

Beresford gave her a sceptical glare.

"What about me?" asked Mrs Avely. "Who shall I pretend to be?"

Beresford looked hunted.

Mrs Avely laughed. "I am jesting. I shan't join this expedition; I'll go ahead to Castle Lanyon and prepare it for our new guests. I'm sure His Majesty will be pleased to open it to me on the presumption of your success. No doubt the cellars need cleaning if they are to host a whole new roost."

"Yes," said Elinor with enthusiasm. "Mother can oversee the castle arrangements, but you need me, James!"

Beresford's shoulders drooped. Then he straightened them with a new resolve. "If Elinor is to come, she will be my wife in reality. I shall write to the Bishop and obtain a special licence."

Elinor smiled up at him. "If you wish, my lord."

Mrs Avely shook her head. "I'm afraid not, my lord. Your mother has already arranged the date and time of the wedding with the Bishop. The invitations have been sent out and a special gown commissioned. You cannot undo an event of these proportions."

"Never mind Elinor's gown, what of her reputation?" persevered Beresford. "We shall be living as husband and wife, without you to chaperone her."

Mrs Avely gnawed at her lip, conflicted between her desire to prevent a quick wedding at the registry, avoid scandal, maintain propriety before the wedding night, and ensure that Elinor followed the king's orders. Everyone waited with interest to see where the penny would fall.

Finally, she spoke. "Miss Zooth can serve as chaperone," she announced. "She will live in your room, Elinor, and be ideally situated for the task. Your quest will be undertaken in secrecy, far away. No one in London need know of these ... less than ideal circumstances."

Elinor nodded demurely. "Yes, Mother."

Beresford's fists clenched. "Absolutely not," he said, his brow thunderous. "I refuse to embark on such terms – unmarried, yet travelling with Elinor into danger. She and Perry will stay in London." He glared around at everyone. "And that is the end of it."

3

IN WHICH CUPS OF TEA ARE
CONTENTIOUS

A week later, Elinor and Perry sat on the quarterdeck of the *Crescent* and admired the sunlight sparkling on the sea off the Devon coast. Seagulls swooped low over the water, following the glint of tiny fish.

"Well, Chief Mineral Discernor," said Elinor to her brother, "how do you find this weather? Lovely sunshine, wouldn't you agree? Perfect for a picnic on the deck."

"Delightful, Lady Beresford," said Perry, grinning. "I'm sure you are a dab hand at pouring tea while beset by waves."

Elinor was enjoying her pretence of being a happily married woman. Her beloved husband leaned against the railing gloomily, staring at the sun-drenched sea as if it spoke of storms and shipwreck. He did not look as if he were basking in newly wedded bliss. To be fair, he was not. Mrs Avely had insisted that the wedding date remain fixed, and when Prince George himself said that he was looking forward to attending the august event, Beresford was given no choice but to acquiesce. A royal presence at the wedding was not to be lightly tossed aside.

With her mother's support, Elinor was determined to attend the quest to Sark. She had overridden Beresford's objections by threatening to tie herself to the mast, or failing that, tie him to the mast.

"This is not a pleasure trip," he growled now, "but a dangerous mission into foreign territory. I'll thank you to remember that."

Perry shaded his brow from the warm sun. "I thought you said Sark was British land?"

"Yes, but it is near French waters."

"How did it become British?" asked Elinor curiously.

"It was part of the Duchy of Normandy," said Beresford. "Therefore it passed to England with the Norman conquest in 1066. However, for a long time it was little more than an outpost for pirates. Difficult territory, stuck out there in the ocean." He glowered at them. "When we begin sailing, cups of tea will not be tolerated."

Elinor sniffed. Cups of tea were always more than tolerated.

Jaq was frolicking in the water as a seal while they were becalmed. Beresford frowned at the horizon. "A wind would be more to the point."

A faint touch of breeze soothed Elinor's brow, but apparently it was not enough to sail by. "While we wait," she said cheerily, "let us plan our approach. Perry, we need a code."

"We do?" Perry leaned back against the railing, watching Jaq fondly.

"Yes, if you are to play the role of Discernor and protect me. I need a way to communicate any Discernments to you, especially if any Musor attempts to test you."

Perry's hazel eyes widened. "Do you think that could happen? What do you suggest?"

"I can burble along in the background – a running commentary, if you like – as I play the role of chatty wife." Beresford snorted, but she continued blithely. "As I chatter, I'll offer my own guesses as to where the object may be. For example, if you are looking for a lost book, I shall say" – she put on a light airy tone – "Oh, do you think it could be under the *armchair*, or perhaps it *could* be in the desk, or perchance it fell down behind the *sofa*!"

Perry and Beresford stared at her. She grinned back.

Perry frowned. "And? Where is it?"

"The second suggestion!" Elinor said triumphantly. "People will pay attention to the first thing I say, and the last, but they won't notice the middle one. That is the one you have to remember, Perry."

Perry looked impressed, running a hand through his blond hair. "That is quite clever, Ellie."

Elinor preened, though Perry's use of her childhood name made it sound as if they were planning a biscuit raid, not an important quest to recover a queen.

Beresford shook his head. "This is not a chance to play parlour tricks. People may be watching you closely, Perry. Rather say that you can only Discern silver, to avoid any other tests of your ability. Or claim you need to reserve your strength, or some such excuse."

Perry wrinkled his nose. "I shall look like a sop."

Elinor giggled. "Think of it as a play where you are performing a part. Just like I shall be, as Lady Beresford, loquacious wife to the stern Lord Beresford." She displayed her left hand, where a gold wedding ring glimmered in the sunlight, a little too big for her finger. Her mother had given it to her, but Elinor loved the sight of it on her finger regardless.

The stern Lord Beresford gave her a reproving look. Elinor nodded in admiration. "Very good, my love: you are playing the part to perfection."

Perry was struck by a new idea. "If you are Lady Beresford, why can't I be Lord Avely?"

Beresford threw his hands in the air. "Why not, indeed! Or Your Grace, the Duke of Avely."

After a moment's reflection, Perry drew the line there. "Oh, but the islanders might well know the ducal titles, if Sark is an English territory. I can't claim to be a duke."

"Lord Avely has a nice ring to it," said Elinor. "Though one day you will be the Marquis of Lanyon, if all goes to plan." The title of Marchioness of Lanyon was to be bestowed upon Mrs Avely with the acquisition of the castle in Cornwall, in retrospective acknowledgement of her husband's services to the Crown.

Perry sighed. "Very well, Lord Avely will do."

"Good of you," said Beresford sardonically. "However, as much as I hate to dispel these delightful fancies, a royal letter of introduction has been sent ahead of us. I believe that already describes you as Mr Avely, Chief Mineral Geologist."

"Oh, pooh," said Perry. Then he looked worried. "Geology? I know nothing about geology." A gull hopped onto the deck and looked around hopefully, its grey feathers gleaming in the sunlight.

Beresford shrugged. "Just make vague remarks about the Diluvian formations — theorised by Abraham Werner. Or you could make learned comments on Hutton's opposing theory of Plutonism."

Perry gave him a dark look. "Diluvian," he muttered anxiously. "Werner. Plutonism. Egads, I don't know if I can do this. Much better pretend I'm a duke. Can we change our story?"

"The Seigneur of Sark will have already received the king's letter," replied Beresford unfeelingly.

"Who is the Seigneur of Sark?" enquired Elinor.

"The current owner of the royal fief of Sark," Beresford replied. "A woman, as it happens: the Dame of Sark, so I suppose I should call her the Seigneuresse. She has a house on the island, but I believe she mainly resides in Guernsey and leases Sark out. Apparently there are forty tenements."

"She owns the whole island?" asked Perry.

"Yes," said Beresford. "One hopes our royal letter of introduction will clear the way for us, for she could very well refuse us landing rights."

Elinor sat up straight. "She can try; we are travelling by royal command!"

A breeze suddenly ruffled the water, creating little peaks in the waves and twirling Elinor's hair around her ear. Beresford tilted his head with interest. "We have to sail there first," he said. "Then we can come up with a plan."

Elinor nodded. "Let us have more tea while we wait." A new thought occurred to her. "Do you think they will have soufflés on Sark, being so close to France?"

Perry put his hands behind his head, leaning back against the railing. He closed his eyes against the sun. "You mean those puffy cakes?"

"I do hope so," breathed Elinor. "We shall have to drop a hint to the Dame of Sark that we are desperate to sample some French cuisine."

～

Three days later, Elinor had rejected all the contents of her stomach several times (it seemed she had drunk *far* too much tea) and lay limp on the cabin bed, desperate never to sail again in her life. She didn't even want to look at a soufflé.

She had been anticipating sharing the cabin with her 'husband', but her hopes for a romantic interlude at sea had been cruelly dashed – unless one called it romantic for Beresford to hold back her hair as she hung over the washbasin. True, he had tenderly wiped her forehead with a cool cloth, but he had also wiped her chin. She only hoped he hadn't decided that he'd rather marry someone with better sea legs.

Fortunately, he had to spend most of his time captaining the ship, so he hadn't had too much opportunity to witness her disgrace. Now, though, the ship was no longer being tossed about like a giant's plaything on the waves, and the terrible lurching seemed to have stopped.

Perry stuck his head round the door. "Ahoy!"

"Don't look so cheerful," she moaned. "How can you still be standing?"

"I've been part of the crew," said Perry. "No time for lying about; Jaq has been showing me the ropes, and even Rusty says I have a knack for it. I'm here to tell you that we have arrived. The isle of Sark lies just a few miles off our port side."

Elinor raised her head tentatively. "What time is it?"

"Seven in the evening. The sun will set soon." Perry widened his eyes meaningfully and tapped the side of his nose. "I've come up with a plan."

Gingerly, Elinor pushed herself to a sitting position. "You have?"

"Well," said Perry, "the ship's company includes vampiri, a selkie and a Travellor, so we can approach Sark by stealth. I propose that tonight we send Aldreda and Pags to reconnoitre by air, Jaq by sea, and I can pop over to have a look too. No one will even know we are there."

Elinor blinked. "What about me?"

Perry strode into the room with enviable vigour. "Beresford won't want you going anywhere."

"So I am to stay here like a lady?" She frowned crossly. "Is Aldreda awake?"

Perry knocked on the cupboard set into the wall above Elinor's bed. After a few moments, Aldreda stuck her head out, yawning.

"Sark ahoy," Elinor told her. "And dusk approaches."

"Oh good," replied Aldreda. "I'm desperate to stretch my wings above land."

Elinor observed the vampiri a trifle bitterly. "You seem to have weathered the trip well."

Aldreda yawned prettily again. "I slept the entire time, except when I practised with the flute. It is so delicately wrought, with such a lovely sound."

"Hmph," said Elinor. "I didn't hear it."

"You were otherwise engaged," observed Aldreda.

Perry grinned. "Yes, you are looking rather green about the gills, Elinor. Should I fetch you some tea?"

Elinor closed her eyes. "Even tea has no allure!"

Lines of concern creased Aldreda's brow. "Oh dear. Rest a bit, and see if the longing returns."

Perry grinned and left, and Elinor turned to look up at Aldreda. Lately there had not been much opportunity to talk properly. "Aldreda, is everything all right with Pags?"

She had noticed that Aldreda had been quite short with Pags when they boarded the ship a week ago. Pags had been relegated to sleeping belowdecks in a sea chest, which though very proper (Pags could hardly sleep in the same room as Aldreda) must also be uncomfortable. Elinor dared not suggest that Pags and Aldreda pretend to be married as well. Aldreda might bite her ear off.

Aldreda wrinkled her pert nose. "Why don't you ask him? If you are worried about his sleeping arrangements, I can tell you that he is quite accustomed to barbaric conditions."

"Oh," said Elinor, feeling both rebuffed and rather sorry for Pags. She swung her legs out of the cabin bed. "I thought there might be some argument between you."

After a moment, Aldreda cleared her throat. "Well, there is one troubling matter. Are you aware that Pags has not formalised his bond with your mother? He told me that for this trip he is reverting to the title of Dukel and a diet of horses."

"Oh." Elinor knew Aldreda disapproved of both. "Could they be expedient measures?"

Aldreda shrugged. "Measures that align with his preferences. I am concerned that he is having second thoughts about becoming civilised again."

"Hm." Elinor privately thought that Pags preferred Aldreda to both his title and horses, but the vampiri spinster had difficulty believing it. Or perhaps Aldreda herself was unsure of her own affections, and was using this matter as an excuse to put distance between them. "Well, time will tell. It is good of him to join us; he might be useful, especially if he knows the queen."

Aldreda sniffed.

"This cursed ship is still moving," moaned Elinor. "I thought Perry said that we had stopped." Her stomach felt as if it might heave up its contents again and it was proving difficult to dress herself.

An hour later, however, she was feeling much restored. She had come on deck and managed two cups of tea, as well as jam on toast and a few sips of the prize cognac that Beresford kept on board. The orange glow of the sun was fading and a gloomy dark settled over the sea, for clouds hung low over Sark and the stars were invisible. She could not make out the island, but Beresford assured her it was there, a few hundred yards to their left.

The rest of the company were dining more heartily on a beef and bean cassoulet, which was creamy with melted cheese. Rusty, one of Beresford's crew from Devon, was keeping lookout on the foredeck, which still heaved slightly. Elinor shuddered and took another delicate sip of tea.

"Right," she said. "Has Perry told you all his excellent plan?" Everyone nodded. "Aldreda, see if you can find the Dame of Sark's residence and look inside. Pags, I suppose you will fly over the island and spy the lie of the land? And Jaq will circle it by sea? Perry, where are you going to land?"

Perry swallowed a mouthful of food. "It will be tricky, as I have never been to Sark before." He put his fork down and stared into space. "I shall envisage a lonely Sarkian hilltop."

Jaq frowned. "Sounds risky."

"It does," said Elinor. "What if you land on top of a sheep? Or worse, a farmer?"

"*Lonely* hilltop," said Perry. "I shall leave sheep out of the picture."

Elinor's brow furrowed, but Beresford interjected. "The main thing is to keep out of sight and simply observe. After one hour, return to the ship. If you don't, I shall come looking for you."

"Yes, sir," said Perry.

"Ha," said Jaq. "You won't be able to find me; I'll be a flicker in the waves." He took a large mouthful of cassoulet.

"Well, Aldreda and Pags," said Elinor brightly, "if you find the roost, bring them back here! We might be in and out in a night."

Pags was leaning against the cognac bottle, a thimble full of the liquid in one hand, and scowling. "You are assuming that the roost wants to leave. They might like it in the wild."

Elinor turned to look at him, eyebrows raised.

"Nonsense," said Aldreda sharply. "You are thinking of yourself. The queen will be very pleased to remove to a proper castle, as befits her rank."

Pags shrugged and sipped from his thimble. "I'm not the only vampiri who enjoys a simpler life. We must at least consider the possibility that the roost has gone feral, or that the queen has decided to stay on Sark. If I found myself a nice little island, I might consider it home."

"*You* would," said Aldreda, "But this is the French queen. She is accustomed to human companionship and a life of luxury, like most sensible vampiri."

"She may have acquired a distaste of it," snapped Pags. "Like me, of course."

Aldreda folded her arms. "Don't let us keep you at a civilised table, then." She gave a pointed look at the thimble in Pags' hand.

There was an uncomfortable pause before Elinor spoke. "I know the Troubles must have been difficult for the queen, as it was for you, Pags. However, we must at least present King George's offer to her."

Aldreda turned her head away. "We must find her first. Then we shall see who is right."

Pags said nothing; he had made his point, and managed to aggravate Aldreda even more, which had probably been his desired aim. Elinor wondered why.

After dinner, the company deployed one by one. Elinor's stomach was still roiling a little: perhaps from nerves, despite her confidence in her companions.

As Pags and Aldreda took flight, Elinor went to stand beside Beresford at the deck rail. Inky water slapped against the ship and cold air brushed her cheeks. She turned her face towards Sark, but could only see a distant dark mass, shrouded by fog. She slipped her hand into Beresford's and watched Jaq's seal form slip between the waves.

Perry, the last to leave, studied them. "What will you two be doing?"

"Keeping watch," replied Beresford.

Perry looked hesitant. "I ought not to leave you unchaperoned for a whole hour."

Elinor rolled her eyes. "This is not the time to develop brotherly concerns! Besides, we are married, if you recall."

"You are not married *yet*."

Beresford coughed. "I won't forget it, Perry."

Perry pursed his lips. "It's not *you* forgetting that I'm worried about," he said. "Elinor has a very selective memory when it suits her."

Elinor blushed. "Shoo! Off you go! Rusty will be here to keep an eye on us." Though she had just seen the red-haired sailor retire belowdecks to his hammock for a well-deserved rest.

"Righto. Lonely Sarkian hilltop, here I come." Perry closed his eyes and stood before them, the ship's lamp making his hair shine gold. Elinor felt a pang of guilt, remembering his healing shoulder, the muscle still knitting over the knife wound. But before she could stay him, Perry vanished.

She turned to Beresford, biting her lip. "Will they be all right?"

"I hope so." He stared into the dark, one hand gripping the rail tightly. "I should be the one out there, not Perry."

Come to think of it, this *was* a very good opportunity for some marital intimacy. Elinor sidled up to her fiancé and tentatively put her hands around his waist. Of course it would be more proper to wait until Church, God and relatives had been pacified with a ceremony, but she was feeling rather bold, which she put down to the fresh sea air and being so far from London. "Shall we repair to the cabin, my dear?"

Beresford let go of the rail and turned to kiss her. After a while, he drew back and smiled at her. "I just gave my word to your brother that I would protect your virtue."

Elinor huffed and snuggled in closer. "If we are to be married in three weeks, it scarcely matters!"

"I want to do things properly," said Beresford. He seemed about to say more, but went quiet.

Elinor looked up at him. "You do *want* to go to the cabin with me, do you not?"

"Of course I do."

She stiffened. "James!"

"What?"

"You're lying!" She gulped back the words, but they were out. She stared at him in apprehension.

His eyes narrowed. "Are you Truth Discerning me again? Elinor, I specifically requested that you do not—"

"I'm sorry, I can't help myself!" Elinor knew she ought to be more remorseful, but she was mortified: she had brazenly attempted to drag him into the cabin and he wanted none of it. She pulled away from him, her cheeks ablaze.

"Elinor…" He groaned. "I don't want to go into the cabin because I don't trust myself. Once there alone with you, I might forget all my principles."

"Oh." Elinor hesitated, shyly. "Is that really true?"

Beresford gripped her arms. "I swear it." He kissed her. "Thank you for not Truth Discerning me again."

Elinor returned to his arms with one last wistful glance at the cabin door. She supposed that a ship's cabin wasn't proper enough for him, though she wasn't quite certain why. Something to do with her cursed honour, no doubt. There was also, admittedly, the risk that Perry would reappear at any moment.

She sighed. "Well, I insist that you spend a good part of the hour kissing me."

"That I am very happy to do," said Beresford, and bent to claim her lips with his own.

4

IN WHICH STEALTH IS EMPLOYED

*A*ldreda battled the uplift of wind over the waves as she winged her way to the island. Pags, ahead of her, did not seem to have as much trouble, but he was larger. She wondered what size the missing Lieutenant Chaboot was, and if he had managed to find his way to Sark. He could be anywhere in France, though, as he didn't have the advantage of Elinor's Discernment.

Aldreda repressed her doubts about Elinor's map divination and focussed on the task at hand. A murky fog obscured any sight of land. Fortunately, Aldreda had her bat senses, which she followed through the mist. The sound of the waves became louder, swirling and crashing against rock. Finally, she crested the cliff face. Pags cocked a wing and veered to the left, while she continued, flying directly over the island.

Once flying over land, she swung lower to find patches of clarity in the mist. Fields stretched out, full of cows and sheep. A broad ribbon of road ran through the middle of the island. Assuming it led to something important, Aldreda followed it, skimming above the hedgerows.

An owl hooted in the distance, which reminded Aldreda to look for cover. Just as she made it to a blackthorn hedgerow, a silent shape swooped past her shoulder. She watched, cringing, as a white owl snatched a mouse from the ground. When the menacing shadow vanished, she carried on more cautiously.

She hoped Pags was being careful, though it would serve him right if he were gobbled up by an owl: *that* would prove to him the benefits of civilisation. How could he suggest that the queen might rather stay on this lonely, wild island? It was merely a reflection of his own desperado inclinations. She quite expected that all these sheep would tempt him to return to his former savagery. Still, it was none of her concern where Pags decided to live. It would only be a shame if Mrs Avely had to find another companion.

Small buildings began to appear, then a cluster. Was this the village? Did Sark even have a village? Continuing her policy, Aldreda followed the biggest road that led onwards, north, through the mist that hung low over the island.

The road led to a house larger than the others, built of grey stone and set with mullioned windows. Flying higher, she circled the building, noting the extensive walled gardens, the broad driveway, and the plenitude of old trees populating the grounds. This was no farmhouse. It must belong to the Seigneuresse whom Beresford had mentioned: the Dame of Sark.

Aldreda cast her mind back. Beresford had said that the Seigneuresse effectively owned the island but did not generally live here. Yet there were lights on, trickling from behind closed curtains. Servants?

She flew closer, hovering by the shallow eaves. Then she swung in to hang from a window cornice where light seeped out.

The curtains were too tightly shut to see anything. Aldreda tried the next window, but the same problem greeted her: windows and curtains closed against the fog. She could hear voices, however, speaking in French. The sound was dull through the walls, but Aldreda could hear that one voice was masculine, one feminine, and both speaking with upper-class inflections.

These were not servants. Could they be guests of the Seigneuresse?

Aldreda decided she must see for herself. She needed to have something of interest to report back, especially if Pags was fetching all sorts of information from his trip around the island. Circling the house once more, she saw that the scullery door was open a crack. That would have to do. She inched her way in and found herself hovering above a housemaid, who fortunately had her head down scrubbing dishes. Aldreda flew out the scullery, arriving in a dark hallway.

The hall was well swept and narrow. Light and voices came from further in, so she followed them, keeping to the ceiling. Slowly, in the dim light, she made her way to what must be the dining room.

She held her breath. Trusting that no one would be watching the door, especially the ground, she skimmed low and entered. Quickly, she slipped behind the wooden door and peered out.

The warmth of a fire blazed through the room. A long dining table was set out with the remnants of a large meal. At the head of the table sat an elderly woman, with gaunt, elegant features and steel-grey hair arranged in fashionable ringlets. She wore an expensive gown of green brocade, decorated with gold epaulettes, and she was toying with the remains of her food.

To her right sat a young man with a similar cast of features: dark and angular, with an impatient expression. Aldreda would gamble that the two were related.

Her guess was confirmed when the young man spoke. "The new guests are not arriving for another day, Mother," he said, his voice low. "Why are we here so soon?"

His mother laid down her fork. "We must ensure everything is in order. This Chief Mineral Geologist is acting under His Majesty's direction, after all, and he is a Discernor. We do not know what other instructions he has been given. We must present a good appearance."

There was silence as the son digested this. Then Aldreda had to leap backwards to avoid being run over as the door was pushed further open. A round figure bustled into the room, staunch in proportion and clad in housekeeper's garb.

"Madame." The housekeeper curtsied. "The rooms have all been cleaned and the bed linen aired. Is there anything else you would like me to do?"

"Hide the silver," said the Dame of Sark.

"The silver, madame?"

"I want to test out this Chief Mineral Discernor," she replied. "He can give us a demonstration of his Musor skill. Make certain you hide it somewhere one would not expect to find it."

"But where, madame?" asked the housekeeper, looking confused.

The Dame of Sark waved a hand impatiently. "In the cellar, near Lilian's quarters."

Aldreda pricked up her ears. Who was this Lilian, who lived in the cellar? Then she saw what she had not observed before, hidden from her view by the angle of the table. A side-cart was pulled up to the dining table beside the Dame of Sark, and on it sat a vampiri lady. She was perched on a book and bent over a human-sized handkerchief, placing tiny stitches with her needle.

The vampiri was dressed austerely: her dark hair pulled back from her face, her gown simple and her face plain. She was small for a vampiri, with very pale skin. Aldreda frowned. It looked as if this companion was not being fed properly.

The Dame turned. "Lilian, you must not show yourself. If they go hunting in the cellars for my silver, you must keep yourself hidden. You know what the English rules are on the subject of Musor-vampiri fraternisation."

"Yes, madame," Lilian replied quietly, without looking up. "Will this stitching serve?"

The Dame leaned forward for a cursory examination. "Yes, neat enough."

Aldreda, watching, wondered that Lilian was so openly displayed. Perhaps the Dame thought she was exempt from the king's decrees, being so far from London. Or perhaps it was simply that in the privacy of her home, with minimal staff, she felt she could do as she pleased. Elinor would probably sympathise.

"Oh, one more thing, Mrs Sidgemoor." The Dame turned back to the housekeeper. "Give the attics a good clean tomorrow." She paused. "Our guest might bring his own vampiri companion and we shall need somewhere to house him."

"Yes, madame." The housekeeper bobbed another curtsy and left.

Well, thought Aldreda, *that makes two pieces of useful information: one, where the silver will be hidden, and two, that Lilian's quarters are in the cellar.* Perhaps she could arrange to meet Lilian at some point, away from the overbearing presence of her mistress.

In the meantime, since the cellars were busy, it was a good opportunity to inspect the attic before it was cleaned on the morrow. Waiting until the Dame was engaged in eating a piece of fruit, Aldreda slipped from her hiding place and flew out, keeping low.

The stout housekeeper was in the kitchen, talking to a male servant who was equally stout and dressed in footman's livery. Yet he could not be a footman, or he would have been serving in the dining room. He looked awkward in his clothes. Aldreda guessed he must be a caretaker or groundskeeper, pressed into service while the mistress of the house was in residence.

The housekeeper spoke in a cheery voice. "Off you go. She'll be waiting for her coffee."

The caretaker-footman cleared his throat. "I wish she had brought her people with her. What if I spill it?"

"You won't spill it," said the housekeeper briskly. "Simple as child's play, my dear Sidgemoor. We have to do our best while she is here without her usual staff."

Aldreda didn't wait to see if dear Sidgemoor could manage the coffee tray. She whisked past the kitchen door and flew upstairs to the attic.

At the top of the narrow staircase was a locked wooden door. Around the doorknob hung a red ribbon with a key dangling from the end: brass, simple but heavy. With some difficulty, Aldreda managed to lift the key and slip it into the lock. Even more difficult was turning it, but eventually she heard a loud click. Drawing a deep breath, she swung on the knob and pushed with all her might.

The door swung open, scraping a path over a dusty floor. No wonder the Seigneuresse had ordered the housekeeper to clean the attic. The room looked as if it hadn't been touched in months.

Large chests lined the left side and cupboards stood on the right. The middle of the room was cluttered with mysterious cloth-draped objects. On the far wall, a little window was thickly curtained.

It would be difficult for the poor housekeeper to navigate all this clutter. Fortunately, Aldreda had the advantage of flight. She winged slowly around the room, aware of a sense of disappointment. Some part of her had hoped to find the missing roost comfortably ensconced in the attic.

Could the vampiri nonetheless be here, in less comfortable arrangements? Aldreda examined the cupboards and chests, wondering if they would serve for hibernation. At least the window was tightly blocked against daylight. Ordinarily, attics would have too much human passage, yet this one was clearly undisturbed. If the queen had an arrangement with the Dame of Sark then she might have chosen such a place to sleep.

Aldreda went to the largest cupboard and hovered by the keyhole. A jumble of crockery greeted her eyes. No space for a roost in there.

The next cupboard contained folded linen. Between the cupboards, however, was something else entirely.

Aldreda halted in mid-air, her eye caught by a small bundle tucked against the wall. If her eyes did not deceive her, it looked like vampiri clothing.

She edged between the cupboards, her wings cramped in the narrow confines. Then she vaulted to the floor in her human form, so that she could use her hands.

Flicking her hair over her shoulders, she stepped through the dust and bent over the bundle. It was indeed a pile of vampiri clothes: masculine ones, neatly folded. They were certainly not Lilian's clothes. Did they belong to some long-ago guest? In which case, why would the clothes have been left behind? Aldreda fingered the plain cloth, frowning. On looking up, she saw a wing tip protruding from behind the cupboard.

She jumped back, stifling a gasp, aware of her own immodesty and flinging her long black hair over herself. Yet even as she did so, she realised it was unnecessary. She came to a standstill, her breath catching in her throat.

The wing was motionless and paper-thin. It would not lie at that angle if the owner of it were sleeping, hiding, or merely resting.

Cautiously, her fingers wound tightly through her own hair, Aldreda crept forward to peer behind the cupboard.

A vampiri lay there, dead. His wings were furled, his eyes closed. His body was hollowed out, gaunt and empty.

Aldreda swallowed. It looked as if he had starved to death: he was a frail husk of a bat. It was several moments before she saw the distinctive streak of grey running over the top of his head.

She backed away, hands trembling. *Lieutenant Chaboot.* What was he doing here, dead of starvation in the Dame's attic? She looked around wildly. Could he not escape? Was it an accident? Or had someone locked him in?

Aldreda became a bat again, wings fluttering rapidly, and lifted into the air. When she had arrived, the door had been locked from the outside with the brass key that hung on the ribbon. What about the window? Surely *that* could not be locked from the outside. She flew to the thick red curtain and shouldered her way past it.

A small dark window looked onto the fog. Four thick panes of glass, set sturdily in wood. An iron latch held the window closed. Aldreda grasped it with her claws and lifted it. The metal hook moved and she dropped it onto the sill. Frowning, she pushed with all her might against the window.

It wouldn't budge.

Shoving and pushing again, she grunted with the effort. Abruptly, she stopped, realising with a sickening lurch that the lieutenant must have tried this, endlessly. The window was not going to open.

She drew a shuddering breath and landed, clinging to the curtain. Outside, the view was blurred by the heavy blanket of grey. Behind her, the attic lay dusty and devoid of life. Suddenly, she desperately wanted to leave. What if she were to be trapped here, too? Could someone return, see the key in the door and turn it once more? With clumsy movements, she freed herself from the curtain and flew with all haste to the exit. She darted into the stairwell with a sigh of relief.

Aldreda turned to look at the door, still partly open: a telltale sign that she had been inside. Pushing with all her might on the frame, she shut it with a clunk. She did not stay to turn the key in the lock. Somehow, she couldn't bring herself to do it.

Slipping down the stairs, her pulse still fluttering, Aldreda made her way back through the scullery, past the housemaid, and flew outside. Only when she felt the damp mist on her skin did the tension in her wings ease.

It was time to report back.

5

IN WHICH THREE IS A CROWD

*L*eaving the house behind, Aldreda decided to fly directly back to the *Crescent* rather than follow the winding road, for she longed to return to the familiarity of friends. She set off across the fields, careless now of owls and eager to feel the warmth of the ship's cabin. The night air felt colder now, the mist thicker.

A forest loomed to her right, the trees still and gloomy in their shroud. She veered further to the left, over an empty field, and quivered with surprise when Pags swept up alongside her. His large wings flapped briskly, then he went into a glide and dipped below her. Aldreda narrowed her eyes – would he *dare* to presume a mating dance again? As if sensing her disapproval, Pags merely twisted into a spin and shot off into the air above her.

Another shape moved in the darkness on her other side. There was another bat with them. A male, from the length and breadth of his body: he was almost as big as Pags. The new bat also flicked away in a spin, imitating Pags, but then zoomed to cut him off in mid-air.

As Aldreda watched, Pags darted to the right in an impressive swerve. The other bat followed and Pags did a strange flip, an acrobatic move that Aldreda had never seen before. He sped out of the pathway of the other bat.

His shadow copied him, with an extra twist, then tapped Pags on the side and fell away into the sky. The manoeuvre looked like an arrogant taunt.

Aldreda watched with interest as, quick as a snake, Pags followed the other male, tapped back, and spun away.

She rolled her eyes. They were like a pair of puppies frolicking in the night. Pags had found someone to play with: a vampiri, as she doubted a mundane bat would be capable of such devilry.

She made her own pace decorous and stayed on course for the ship. The two males kept diving and darting, attempting all manner of ridiculous tricks. The other bat matched Pags in flight skills, and Aldreda tried not to look impressed. Both were clearly pleased to have a feminine spectator, so Aldreda ignored them.

However, she didn't want to lead this stranger back to their ship, even if he were Pags' new best friend. When a barn appeared in the fog, she made a show of fluttering down towards it. She landed on an eave, and waited.

Soon the males realised she was no longer watching and came back to find her. When she saw them hovering, she dropped off the eave and looped into the barn. It was slightly warmer inside, from the bodies of two horses sleeping in the stalls. The wooden beamed roof was low and functional; this was a farmer's barn.

After a moment, Pags followed her in alone.

Aldreda transformed and tumbled into a pile of hay. As usual, she flicked her long black hair over her body, to provide some modesty. She had not been able to bring a gown on a reconnoitre like this.

She stood up and put her hands on her hips. "Found a playmate, have you?"

Pags also fell out of the air. He landed with more grace and style than she, and also put his hands on his hips. Unlike her, he didn't bother with any attempt at modesty.

His black eyes gleamed. "I found him in the forest. He is a wild fellow, like me."

"He seems glad enough of your company," she said dryly. "But do you think we ought to lead him to our ship?"

"I wasn't going to lead him to our ship."

"You led him to me."

Pags shifted uncomfortably. "I didn't intend to. You flew past us; he saw you and followed. I thought you might want to be introduced." He paused. "I didn't want him to surprise you."

"I am more than capable of handling wild bats, as you well know."

Pags folded his arms. "True. You are a headmistress in training. Next time I shall discard my chivalry."

"A headmistress still merits chivalry," said Aldreda. Then she shook her head crossly. "Anyway, I am not going to be headmistress."

"Who else will teach the vampiri at the Lanyon school?" Pags enquired. "Perry? No, my dear, you have just the right manner of reserved imperiousness for the task."

"We are becoming distracted," said Aldreda severely – perhaps with a modicum of reserved imperiousness. "Does this other bat have a name?"

"Durl," said Pags meekly. "Thomas Durl. He was happy to share a sheep with me and even offered me some sloe gin. You'd be welcome to some too, I'm sure, if you could so lower your tastes."

Aldreda frowned. "No, thank you. Did you ask if he has seen a roost anywhere?"

Pags raised his eyebrows. "Of course I did. He said no, not in the twenty years he has lived here in the woods."

Aldreda pressed her lips together, for this was not promising news. Perhaps Elinor was wrong about Sark. She had been wrong before.

Pags jerked his head at the door. "Do you want to ask him yourself, headmistress?"

Aldreda folded her arms. "In this state?"

"I've never seen you look better." Pags grinned at her. "Gowns are overrated, in my opinion."

Aldreda ignored this scandalous remark by making a show of looking around the barn. She pointed, imperiously. "I'll be in that blanket. Bring him in."

"Yes, headmistress," said Pags, and sauntered out.

A few minutes later, he strolled back in. Behind him was a vampiri almost as tall and broad as he. The new vampiri's hair, however, was a thick tangle of brown instead of Pags' black wildness. The newcomer's face was bearded, but in a neater fashion than when Aldreda had found Pags on the moors. Perhaps this vampiri had not regressed as much as Pags had in his lonely sojourn. His face was apprehensive and he kept his hands clasped in front of him.

Aldreda was wrapped in an old, rather smelly horse blanket, a far cry from her usual attire. She gave a polite curtsy to set the tone.

The other vampiri bowed in return, red creeping into his cheeks. He was well fed, then, even if it were on sheep. "Madame, I apologise for my state." He was, of course, naked, but Aldreda kept her eyes fixed on his attractive face. His voice had a low timbre, warm and uncertain. "I wasn't expecting company."

Aldreda tried to put him at his ease. "Pagrilliard *was* expecting it and, as you can see, he remains unconcerned."

Pags tossed his black mane and grinned. He made the introductions, presenting Miss Zooth with a bow to Mr Thomas Durl. One of the horses woke and clambered to its feet to peer curiously over the stall.

Mr Durl shuffled from one foot to the other, glancing at

Aldreda every so often from his downcast eyes. "A pleasure to meet you. What brings you to Sark, Miss Zooth, if I may ask?"

"I am travelling with my companion, Mr Avely, who is a Mineral Discernor. He has come to see if there are any mineral deposits on the island." It was better they kept to the official story.

Durl scuffed the floor thoughtfully. "Minerals, you say? Like gold? There is talk of pirate gold hidden on the island, though I've never seen any. Though I keep to myself and wouldn't know if a pirate came calling."

"Prefer your own company?" said Pags. "I know the feeling."

Durl shrugged his broad shoulders. He glanced at Aldreda, then hastily dipped his head and stared at the floor.

Aldreda realised her blanket had slipped to reveal one bare white shoulder, and yanked it back up. "Well, I hope you don't mind *our* company for a short while. We shall not stay too long on the island, and we beg permission to fly in your territory."

"Of course," said Durl quickly. "A little bit of company is pleasant. I would find a whole roost too much, though. You're not planning on bringing one here, are you?"

Aldreda shook her head. "No, you need not fear that."

As she said the words, she wondered. Could Pags possibly be right? Could the roost like Sark enough to stay? Then Durl's peace would be disturbed. However, it was unlikely. The French queen ruled an urban roost, used to the comforts and bustle of Paris. They would be pleased to remove to London rather than stay on a draughty, misty rock.

Pags coughed. "We must return to our ship. Thank you for the sheep and the gin, my good fellow."

Durl dipped his head again. "You're welcome." He looked back at Aldreda. "Charmed to meet you, madame."

Aldreda found that she was rather charmed to meet him, too.

Pags, watching him leave, narrowed his eyes. "I'll just follow him for a while and see where he goes. Then I'll finish my circuit of the island."

The horse whickered again. It was the first time Aldreda and Pags had been alone for a while. The last time had been in a London townhouse, when he had taught her the latest dances to the distant sounds of a quartet. She dismissed the memory of his warm hands on her waist, but nevertheless found herself wanting him to stay.

"Wait," she said. "You must be careful. I didn't want to mention it before, but I found Chaboot – dead." She was annoyed to hear her voice quiver on the last word.

Pags took a step closer, his gaze softening. "Where? How?"

Aldreda explained.

Pags raised a hand and moved towards her, then paused before he could brush her arm. "All the more reason for me to finish the circuit." He dropped his arm. "You must return to the ship without delay."

She nodded, wishing suddenly that they were back in London about to attend a revel, instead of this grim investigation. Pags gave her one last bow, somersaulted into the air, and swept out of the barn.

Slowly, Aldreda flew back towards the ship.

6

IN WHICH PERRY IS OFFENDED

*T*he deck rail pressed into Elinor's back, but she barely noticed it. She was too caught up in the feel of Beresford's arm around her waist, his other hand cradling her neck, his lips warm on hers …

Beresford groaned. "You intoxicate me even on a cold ship's deck, my love." Now his hands were in a rather scandalous place, and Elinor wriggled happily as she kissed him.

A crack came over the water from the direction of the island. The sound was muffled, but still recognisable.

She drew away from Beresford, who lifted his head in sudden enquiry. "Was that a gunshot?" she asked.

"I would say so," he replied, grimly.

There was a moment of silence as they considered it. "Perry," they said together.

Elinor swung round to peer through the fog. "What shall we do, row ashore? What if he is hurt?"

Beresford had turned to face the deck. "Wait."

He was right. Within seconds, Perry popped into existence on the quarterdeck. His arms shielded his face as if warding off a blow, but he lowered them, looking pale and flustered. With a rush of relief, Elinor saw that he was unhurt, though he was still standing on the balls of his feet as if ready to run.

"Damn rascals!" exclaimed Perry, fending off Elinor's hug. "Someone shot at me!"

"Yes, we know," she said. "You must be more careful!"

Perry looked affronted. "How could you know? They might have been shooting at anyone!"

Elinor rolled her eyes. "It is rational to suppose that some poor islander received the fright of his life when you appeared out of nowhere."

"That is not what happened!"

Beresford nodded. "You've been gone too long for that."

Elinor realised he was right, but at that moment Jaq vaulted onto the deck, stark naked and dripping wet. He strode forward. "Perry, are you hurt? I heard the shot."

Perry glared. "Not you too!"

Jaq looked surprised. "I have good hearing."

"And you just assumed they were shooting at me?" Perry snapped.

"Well, yes." Jaq shrugged his bare shoulders and grinned. "Who else would they be shooting at?"

Elinor tried to intervene, even though she was politely looking away. "It is a fair assumption, Perry. Who else would they be shooting at?"

Perry folded his arms. "A bird. A smuggler. It could have been a duel, for all we know!"

Jaq struck a pose as if duelling with a sword. "Ah, yes, I forgot to mention I was meeting a seal at dawn." Elinor let out a giggle, for she couldn't help but glance at his posturing form; he was like a Greek sculpture on the deck.

Beresford frowned. "Jaq, put some clothes on, for heaven's sake. Perry, tell us what you saw."

Before Perry could answer, Aldreda tumbled onto the deck in her naked, womanly guise. "Perry, are you all right?"

Perry swung around. "Argh!"

Aldreda draped her hair over herself. "I heard the shot."

"I know you did," said Perry bitterly.

Elinor cleared her throat. "Perhaps they were shooting at Pags?"

Aldreda gestured for Elinor's shawl. "Of course not. No one would even see him to shoot at him."

Perry harrumphed. "I was a silent shadow in the night, I tell you—"

"Let's repair to the cabin and we can each make our reports," interrupted Beresford. "We can start without Pags."

Perry huffed his way past them. "You will not have much to report, Elinor," he snapped.

Once they were all in the cosy confines of the cabin, Elinor insisted that Aldreda dress herself and they all have more tea. "My nerves are on edge," she admitted. "I don't like people shooting at my brother. Now tell us what happened, Perry."

Once the tea was poured, Perry demanded a fortifying splash of brandy in his and then began his story. "I arrived on an empty hill, just as I planned – or at least, it appeared to be empty. I could hear nothing except waves and the bleating of sheep. *Distant* bleating," he emphasised, at Elinor's quick look of enquiry. "I couldn't see much because of that cursed fog. I walked carefully, I can tell you, away from the sound of the waves. I didn't want to fall off the cliff."

Elinor shuddered. "How frightening, to make one's way in the dark and fog in an unknown land."

Perry looked a little cheered. "Yes, well, eventually the fog cleared slightly, and I saw a stone building. There was a faint light coming from it, so I thought I'd better investigate."

"Was that wise?" asked Aldreda, now gowned, slippered, and perched on the sill of the porthole, sipping her own thimbleful of tea.

Perry took a gulp of his doctored brew. "Anyone inside

wouldn't be able to see out in the dark, so I crept up and peered in. It was just a funny little shepherd's hut. Two men were hunched around a small fire, talking and playing cards. I listened, but my French isn't good, so I didn't understand much of it. They were speaking quietly, too. They had rifles next to them."

"Did they spot you?" asked Jaq.

Perry sat up straighter and gave his beau a cross look. "No, they did not! The shot came from behind me. Gave me a damn fright. The bullet landed in the stone, inches from my arm." He ran his hand down his left arm as if he could still feel the bullet whizzing past it. "The men inside shouted and leapt to their feet, but I didn't stay to greet them. I popped myself back here before I could see who had the nerve to take a shot at me."

Jaq shook his head. "Thank the goddess Amphritrite he missed you."

Beresford was frowning. "Someone must have thought you were an intruder."

"He *was* an intruder," said Elinor.

"But why would they assume that?" asked Beresford. "Surely you'd ask questions first if you saw somebody outside your hut."

"It's a small island," Aldreda pointed out. "Perhaps everyone knows everyone. Maybe Perry's blond hair was instantly recognisable as alien."

"Or they were hiding something," suggested Jaq.

"The roost!" cried Elinor.

Perry scowled. "Don't be ridiculous, Elinor. There was no room in that stone hut for a roost of vampiri."

There was silence as they all wondered why an islander had been so eager to shoot at Perry.

"Well, if Perry is unharmed, I'm afraid we have other things to worry about," said Aldreda. Everyone turned to look at her. "I found Lieutenant Chaboot. He is dead."

"What?" exclaimed Elinor.

Aldreda explained how she had sneaked into the Dame of

Sark's house and unlocked the attic to find the hollowed-out figure of Lieutenant Chaboot. "He was behind a cupboard, in his bat form, very thin and brittle. The grey streak over his head was quite apparent. He was locked in the attic: I could not tell whether by accident or design. I tried the window myself, but it would not open."

Elinor eyed her. She could sense that despite Aldreda's calm tone, the vampiri was shaken by her discovery. "If he were locked in, could he not have hibernated to give himself more time?"

Aldreda warmed her hands on her thimble. "We require a large feed before hibernation. I assume he was hungry already when he found himself trapped."

At that moment Pags sauntered through the cabin door, trousers hastily donned and a cloak around his shoulders, though he was shirtless. Aldreda frowned disapprovingly.

"Are you all right, Perry?" he asked. "I heard the shot."

Perry just glowered.

"Perry is fine," Elinor said hastily. "An islander shot at him when he was investigating a shepherd's hut, though we are not certain as to why. Did you see anyone with a gun, Pags?"

"A few," said Pags. "At lookout points stationed around the island. It seems they are guarding the place well."

"Hm," said Beresford. "I believe that was a condition of the original tenements: that each tenant provide arms to guard the island."

"I saw them too," said Jaq. "It looks as if they are expecting trouble."

"Oh," said Elinor. "So any one of them could have spotted Perry and decided he was a threat."

Beresford nodded. "Fulfilling their duty to protect the island. They probably thought he was a pesky Frenchman."

Perry looked affronted. "Do I look French to you?"

"No, no," said Jaq soothingly. "As English as a rose."

Perry smiled reluctantly.

"Anything else, Pags?" asked Elinor.

"Some lovely woods," said Pags, "with lots of tree hollows for bats. I even found a vampiri in one of them."

"Alive or dead?" asked Elinor anxiously.

"Alive," said Pags, "but a little wild."

Everyone cocked their heads with interest, except Aldreda, who took a sip of tea from her thimble.

"Were you right, Pags?" Elinor demanded. "Has the roost gone feral?"

"Oh no, he claims he doesn't belong to a roost," answered Pags. "He is a lone wolf."

"A kindred spirit, in fact," observed Aldreda tartly.

Elinor let that remark pass without comment. "What was his name?"

"Durl," replied Pags. "Thomas Durl."

Elinor tapped her finger meaningfully on her lapis lazuli. "I shall have to question him."

"It will be interesting for you to question the Dame of Sark too," said Aldreda. "I saw her and her son in the house, ordering it to be prepared for us. She was quite particular about cleaning the attic."

"Hm," said Elinor.

"Oh yes, and she sent the housekeeper to hide the silver in the cellar. She wants to test Perry's Mineral Discernment."

Perry bit his lip nervously.

Elinor put down her teacup with a clatter. "How dare she test him! Well, we shall be ready for her. What about you, Jaq, did you see anything of note in your circuit?"

Jaq leaned his elbows on the table in a rather unprincely fashion, resting his chin on his hands. "Lots of lovely treacherous cliffs. Other than that, just seals and puffins. There are a few places I might climb up, but I didn't attempt it tonight."

Beresford stretched his legs out. "I'm glad you didn't.

Tomorrow we shall approach in daylight, waving a white flag if we must, to avoid being shot by these overzealous tenants."

"Yes," said Elinor. "It is high time that Beresford and I investigated for ourselves."

She said the words firmly – perhaps even pugnaciously – but internally she felt a tingle of apprehension. Lieutenant Chaboot was dead, locked in an attic to starve. Even if it were an accident, it was a horrible way to die. Elinor shivered. Yet she was human-sized, and a Discernor to boot. It would be far more difficult to lock *her* in the attic. And she would keep a very sharp eye on Aldreda and Pags.

7

IN WHICH ELINOR PLAYS A WIFE

*a*t dawn, Beresford hoisted the anchor and they sailed towards the main harbour of the island, the flag of England fluttering at the mast. The fog slowly cleared and the sea lay blue and sparkling. The sky was dotted with white clouds, and Elinor could see the cliffs of Sark rising out of the ocean, a wall of dark green and purple.

After a hearty breakfast, Beresford tied a white flag to a stick and gave it to Elinor. She was to wave it from the back of the jolly boat, to forestall any more bullets. She sat holding it aloft, enjoying the sensation of the sun on her face and hoping she cut a wifely figure. Aldreda was asleep in the cabin, of course, and Elinor assumed Pags had retired to his sea chest. Jaq was in the water in seal form, just in case. Rusty was staying behind to guard the ship.

Beresford and Perry took up the oars and rowed, while Elinor waved her flag diligently. The white cloth was almost too bright in the sunlight, so she was certain it would be visible from the shore. Jaq was keeping below the waves, for once happy not to draw attention to himself.

As they drew closer, she saw a man stand up at the top of the dunes and stare down at them. His silhouette was distorted by the shape of a gun hanging by his side. As Elinor watched, he began to make his way down the steep slope.

Beresford's shoulders were straining under the task of rowing, and Elinor smiled at him with approval. He was taking most of the weight, in consideration of Perry's weak shoulder.

Beresford frowned back at her. "Remember, Elinor, you are my wife."

"I am glad to hear it, husband dear."

"And remember you are *not* a Musor, and be as inconspicuous as possible."

Perry snorted, but was too preoccupied with rowing to comment further.

"Yes, dear," said Elinor. "Indeed, I shall be quite thankful to let you two do the talking. It will give me time to Discern."

Perry grunted. "Don't overreach yourself. Aldreda won't be there to stop you being a fool."

Elinor gave a particularly brisk wave of the flag but spoke sweetly. "I am *meant* to be a foolish, chattering wife, if you recall. And you, Perry, would do well to remember our code, and all about Diluvian formations."

A bead of sweat appeared on Beresford's brow. "This is not a game," he snapped. "Chaboot is dead; Perry was almost shot. I don't want you in the line of fire, Elinor. That is the whole point of us conducting this deception."

"Yes, dear," said Elinor meekly and waved her flag.

Jaq gave a splash of his tail from the water and glided off, a dark-brown shape vanishing into the green-blue depths.

They were close to the landing point. By the time the boat touched sand, the man from the dunes was there to greet them. He was a stocky fellow, wearing farmer's clothes and a broad-brimmed hat. The well-oiled rifle rested on his shoulder. Elinor examined the gun dubiously, wondering if it might be the one that had shot at Perry.

The farmer, likewise, was examining them suspiciously. His

gimlet eyes were set deep in a weathered face, taking their measure. Elinor tried to look as guileless and wifely as possible.

"*Bonjour.*" The man continued in a dialect of French. "Who might you be?"

Beresford jerked his head towards Perry. "This is Mr Peregrine Avely, Chief Mineral Geologist, sent by King George to investigate for Sark reserves. I am Lord Beresford and this is my wife. I believe we are expected?"

Perry, pink and sweating, did his best to look like an important dignitary and respectable scientist. Elinor put down her white flag and smiled. It was thrilling to be announced as Beresford's wife, even if it wasn't yet true. It would be true soon enough. She gave a sigh of happiness. The fact that Beresford was still over-protective was delightful, not annoying, and only to be expected from a husband. Well, a future husband.

"My name is Hedley," said the farmer. "I own one of the tenements here. I can take you to *la Seigneurie.*"

"The Seigneurie?" asked Elinor brightly.

"The main house," replied Hedley. "Where you are to stay."

He held out a hand to steady the boat as Beresford leapt out. Beresford nodded at the rifle. "Expecting trouble?"

"Not from you," replied Hedley. "*Les Français.*" He seemed a man of few words. Then he smiled, transforming his face with sudden humour and the glint of white teeth. "Though we speak something like their tongue."

If the Sarkees all spoke French, Elinor wondered, were there any Napoleonic sympathisers? She dared not ask the question outright. She smiled at him. "I am glad Sark is so diligently guarded."

An unreadable expression flitted across Hedley's face. "Yes, Lady Beresford."

Elinor forbore to mention that she'd prefer it if they didn't shoot at Perry. Fortunately, Hedley didn't seem to be taking undue interest in her brother, therefore he probably hadn't seen Perry's blond head the night before.

Hedley nodded at the *Crescent*, which lay gleaming out in the bay. "Have you any luggage, my lord? I can fetch the horses."

Beresford said he would row back for their trunks, so Elinor and Perry were left to wait in the sun until Hedley rejoined them, driving a chestnut horse pulling a cart for the luggage. Beresford returned, his coat removed after the effort of rowing, and loaded the first of the trunks onto the cart. He swung himself up next to Elinor, while Perry sat opposite them.

The drive through Sark was delightful. After the steep laneway up from the cove, they left the plunging cliffs behind them. The land rolled gentle and verdant, dotted with sheep, cows, and goats. A breeze blew, softening the heat and rustling the leaves of the hedgerows. Occasionally they passed farmhouses, with chickens pecking in the dirt and washing hanging in the sun. The sea shone blue on the horizon.

"So," said Hedley, casting a backwards look at Perry, "are you examining the lay of the land for minerals already, Mr Avely?"

Perry shaded his eyes. "Er, yes. Excellent Diluvian formations, I see." He cleared his throat. "Yet it is too soon for such examinations. I need a good meal first."

Hedley nodded as if he quite expected such laziness from a Royal Geologist.

Elinor, sitting behind, thought it was an excellent idea – both the good meal, and trying an initial Discernment. She tightened her hands on her reticule, wherein lay the tiny Viveroust flute, like a golden needle hidden in her spare gloves. Could she find the roost right now? Closing her eyes, she reached out with a question.

The undulating hills of Sark gave her no answer.

Elinor sighed. Perhaps she hadn't asked in quite the right way. Besides, with Aldreda back on the ship, it was better not to

Discern too much. She did not want to become Bemused: not when she was about to meet the Dame of Sark.

The horse trudged slowly, but quite soon they were plodding up the drive of the Seigneurie, past a heavy gate that scraped along the ground. It was a lovely old house, and just as big as Aldreda had described: three storeys high, with jutting attic windows. It was built of grey and white stone, square and imposing, with large mullioned windows set at intervals. Green ivy crept up the walls, contrasting with the white window frames. Leafy trees surrounded the house, and a stone wall marked off part of the gardens.

They drove up to the turning circle outside the front door, and a round, cheerful woman bustled out to greet Hedley. She curtsied to the rest of the company, her eyes curious and assessing. "This way, this way, please do come in. Sidgemoor, help Hedley with the bags."

Sidgemoor, an awkward servant, sidled up and began unloading the luggage. Beresford stepped down and helped Elinor dismount. Once she descended, she perceived a tall figure in the doorway of the house, watching them.

The figure moved forward into the light: a woman, wearing a high-necked gown of expensive green silk. A closed expression guarded the dark, crisp features that Aldreda had described.

The Dame of Sark spoke in English "Good morning. I am Lady Orlend."

A young man stepped out from behind her. He had the same cast of countenance, though unmarred by the lines and hollows that characterised his mother's face.

Lady Orlend gestured to him. "This is my son, Chester Orlend. You must be the party sent by the king. Welcome."

Chester gave them an uncertain smile, and Elinor smiled back in a friendly fashion, keeping her fingers tucked into Beresford's elbow like a good wife.

After curtsies, bows, and introductions, Lady Orlend led them into the house. It was gloomy after the sunlight, and Elinor felt a sense of oppression which seemed at odds with the stately appearance of the exterior. She wondered if her own worry about Chaboot was weighing her down, for he lay dead in the attic above them.

She could not see much in the gloom until they came to the drawing room. It was well used and well furnished, with thick curtains and carpet. A serviceable chandelier hung from the ceiling. The curtains were open, letting in squares of sunlight and showing the pretty gardens.

Elinor smiled. "I see you live in comfort out here."

"Of course," said Lady Orlend coldly. "Why would we not?"

"Indeed," said Elinor, flustered. "I merely assumed, with such a lonely island…" Embarrassed, she comforted herself with the fact that she was *meant* to appear foolish.

Lady Orlend turned to the housekeeper. "Mrs Sidgemoor, please bring tea and refreshments. We must show these Londoners our hospitality." She took a seat in one of the comfortable-looking green armchairs and nodded for them all to sit.

Elinor and Perry hastened to do so; however, Beresford made his excuses and said he must return to help see to his ship. Before he departed, he gave Elinor an admonitory look. She smiled sweetly at him and put her reticule next to her chair.

Beresford spoke. "Don't begin any work yet… Mr Avely."

Perry nodded. "No fear of that! After all, we've only just arrived!"

Beresford bowed and left. Lady Orlend watched him go with a thoughtful expression, perhaps observing the hierarchy of their party. Or perhaps she was admiring Beresford's broad shoulders, Elinor thought complacently.

Once the refreshments were served, including some delightful tarts and cheeses, Elinor decided to ask questions. That would forestall any being directed at Perry, and also establish her as a burbling, loquacious woman.

"Such a lovely place to live!" she began. "I declare, I am quite envious. Such a romantic locale! And you are the queen of it all, Lady Orlend. I see you rule in splendour over your island refuge." She glanced around to ensure that the servants had withdrawn. "I assume you are a Musor?"

Lady Orlend's hands twitched a little at this directness. "Yes," she responded, after a moment. "I am. Only an insignificant Gift, unfortunately."

"I could tell you were a Musor!" announced Elinor. "You have that indefinable air of magic about you. Which Gift, may I ask, are you so lucky as to possess?"

Lady Orlend gave her an appraising look. "I am certain you must already know, if your party is in the king's confidence. I am Gifted in Impacting. Though, as I say, it is not very strong."

"Impacting?" asked Perry. "Defensive measures and strength?"

Lady Orlend gave a tiny, regal nod. "Not very feminine, I grant you. It is much better expressed in my sons."

"Oh!" Elinor turned to Chester. "Are you Gifted, too?"

Chester flushed slightly and shook his head, shifting in his chair.

His mother answered for him. "Not this son. My other sons: I have three more. Unfortunately, their Impacting Gifts mean that they are required to serve as Musor agents in the war – though, of course, we simply say they are serving in the army. Chester is all I have left. I am so glad that he has no Impacting talent, as it means he stays by my side."

There was a note of irony in her voice, and Chester reddened further, shoving his hands in his pockets.

Lady Orlend turned mildly to Elinor and offered a plate of pastries. "What about you, Lady Beresford? Are you Gifted?"

"Oh, not I!" exclaimed Elinor at once, taking a custard tart. The drawing room, despite its elegance, still felt oppressive to her, though perhaps that was Lady Orlend's forbidding presence. "My brother is a Discernor, and he has quite enough talent for both of us." She beamed at Perry, who tried to look nonchalantly brilliant as he chewed on his piece of cheese.

"I thought you might be siblings, from your looks," observed Lady Orlend. "Mr Avely, as Chief Mineral Discernor you must be very Gifted to hold such a position. I have not met many Discernors. Could we hope for a demonstration of your skill while you are here?"

Perry nodded benignly. "Certainly. It would be my pleasure."

Lady Orlend leaned forward. "Then I am sure it is a trifle for you to tell me where my silver cutlery is kept, for example. A simple question for such a bright talent!"

Perry gulped, then waved a hand negligently. "I believe it is below us. Perhaps in a cellar?"

Lady Orlend looked taken aback, and Elinor felt rather cross that Perry had not put on more of a performance. He ought to have made Discernment look more difficult – now they would expect him to find minerals immediately! What if she could not find the roost at once, and they were forced to prevaricate? Perry must simply invent vast stores of silver somewhere on the island, she thought.

Lady Orlend sipped her tea. "Very impressive, Mr Avely. Do you have a vampiri to assist you?"

Perry's eyes widened, then he coughed. "Oh yes, I do. Miss Zooth, a delightful creature. She is back on the ship, though I am sure she will fly here once it is dark."

Elinor bit her lip. Aldreda had deigned to pose as Perry's companion and Perry had deigned to go along with it, though so far he had expressed a disinclination for vampiri companionship. She hoped they could play their roles properly.

She thought of another question. "Do you have suitable quarters for my brother's companion, Lady Orlend?"

Lady Orlend took another sip of tea, as if to delay her answer. "Certainly. She can sleep in the attic."

Elinor repressed a shudder and smiled. She told herself again that no one would dare lock Aldreda away, especially not with Perry and herself around. "Perhaps, after this delightful tea, we can inspect the attic to ensure it is suitable."

Lady Orlend looked down her nose at Elinor. "I assure you that it is suitable. It was cleaned this morning."

"How kind!" exclaimed Elinor. "Could I put Miss Zooth's basket in there, and her little trunk?"

Lady Orlend nodded. Good, thought Elinor. I can stumble across poor Chaboot, if they have not already tidied him up.

She took another bite of the tart, but somehow, the custard was tasteless.

8

IN WHICH LACE IS SHUNNED

*E*linor and Lady Orlend left Perry in the drawing room, making awkward conversation with Chester. On the way to the attic, Elinor chattered glibly about the voyage and how awful it was to be seasick. Lady Orlend listened in silence and only commented that she never experienced seasickness. When she pushed the attic door open, Elinor followed her in, noting that Lady Orlend took the brass key out of the door and slipped the ribbon around her wrist.

Clean floorboards greeted them, swept free of dust. The far window was open, a small aperture allowing a breeze to finger the curtains. By the walls stood the cupboards and chests Aldreda had described, but the cloth-covered shapes she had mentioned had been moved to another location. A table stood in the middle of the room, a heavy cream tablecloth covering it to the floor.

Lady Orlend pointed to the table. "You can put Miss Zooth's bedding and trunk under there. The cloth provides extra protection from sunlight."

Elinor frowned. She did not like the idea of Aldreda sleeping on the floor, relegated to beneath a table. Yet such measures were in line with the royal edicts. "Thank you, Lady Orlend." She went further into the room, making a show of inspecting it. In reality, she sought the second cupboard from the far-left corner. That was the one Aldreda had described as hiding the body of the unfortunate Lieutenant Chaboot.

Elinor tripped over to it. "This room will serve very well indeed. What a lovely attic! I am certain Miss Zooth will find it most commodious. Do you often have vampiri staying here, Lady Orlend?"

"Not often, no."

Elinor stared into the gap between the cupboards. There was nothing to see. The pile of clothes and the protruding wingtip were gone.

She glanced at Lady Orlend's impassive expression and realised that she could not say a thing about it.

She cleared her throat. "No vampiri visitors? That must be a shame for your own companion. Does she not feel lonely for her own kind? I know Miss Zooth was glad to find the London circles."

"We have a few vampiri in Guernsey, kept reclusive," replied Lady Orlend.

"So she will be glad to meet Miss Zooth, I do not doubt."

Lady Orlend's eyes narrowed. "How do you know I have a companion, Lady Beresford, or that she is female?"

Elinor blinked and cursed herself. "Oh, is she not? I simply assumed that, as Dame of Sark and a Musor, you must have a companion, and since you are of the feminine persuasion ..."

"Yet Mr Avely does not have a male vampiri companion."

"True!" Elinor floundered. "Yet he is an exception to the general rule. Am I to assume that you are an exception also, Lady Orlend? I do apologise for jumping to conclusions."

Lady Orlend regarded her for a long moment. "No, my companion is female."

Elinor laughed in a somewhat brittle fashion. "Well, then she *will* be glad to meet Miss Zooth. What is her name?"

"Miss Lilian Reed."

Elinor went to the window, glad to escape that penetrating gaze for a moment. A chest was set under the sill and she leaned against it, looking out over the paddocks to the gleaming blue sea in the distance. The sight was soothing, and she drew a deep breath. "What a lovely view! Such a shame that vampiri cannot see it in the daylight, with that wonderful ocean sparkling in the sunlight... Is this window usually locked at night? With Miss Zooth here it must be left open, of course."

"I have undone the Defence that locked it," said Lady Orlend.

Elinor turned. "The Defence?"

"The Impactor spell that keeps it closed against intruders. We have such spells on all the windows – my sons set them up before they left. When the spell is operating, you would not be able to open that window for the world. Only one of the family can undo them. Or my housekeeper, if need be, as I have given her a special key."

"Oh." Elinor blinked. That must have been why the window would not open for Aldreda, or for the unfortunate Chaboot. She shivered. "That sounds... wise."

"My sons worry unduly," replied Lady Orlend. "It is an unnecessary precaution, I assure you; there is no danger here on Sark. Mr Avely will be able to work untroubled."

"Of course," said Elinor. "Dutiful sons must be a delight."

Lady Orlend turned abruptly. "I shall show you to your own room now."

Elinor trailed after her with a last glance around the tidy attic. Where had the body of Lieutenant Chaboot gone? And who had moved it?

Elinor and Beresford's room was on the eastern side of the house on the second floor. Like the rest of the rooms, it was well furnished, with a large four-poster bed. The bedlinens and curtains were cream and rose, with bows, lace, and furbelows. Elinor's eyes widened. What would Beresford say about *that?* Yet of course they would share a room – and a bed – as husband and wife. She was rather looking forward to it. She clasped her hands together and exclaimed that it was delightful. Lady Orlend announced that she needed to rest, and retired to her room.

Elinor spent the rest of the day on a tour of the house and grounds, conducted by the housekeeper. Once outside, the stifling atmosphere of the house lifted a little. The sunlight and the reprieve from Lady Orlend probably had something to do with it, Elinor reflected.

Mrs Sidgemoor led her into the walled gardens, which were fragrant with flowers. "Sidgemoor's work," said his wife proudly, putting her hands on her rounded hips. "He and I look after the place while the mistress is in Guernsey. He is a dab hand with the plants, though not so good indoors."

"Beautiful," said Elinor. "You two must be kept busy, running this place by yourselves."

"We have a few maids to assist us," admitted Mrs Sidgemoor. "Mr Hedley helps as well."

"Ah, the helpful fellow who drove us here?" asked Elinor.

"Yes, he is the Dame's right-hand man," said Mrs Sidgemoor, leading the way to the herb garden. "How will you manage, Lady Beresford? We were expecting you to bring a maid. If you like, I can arrange for one of ours to assist you."

Elinor reflected that it would be useful to question a maid, and agreed to the plan. She chewed her lip, wondering if she could accuse Mrs Sidgemoor of disposing of a vampiri corpse, and decided she couldn't. Even if Mrs Sidgemoor had swept him away, she would only have been following Lady Orlend's instructions.

Whoever had done the deed was keeping the matter quiet; Lieutenant Chaboot had been denied a proper burial and his death was a secret. It was possible that Mrs Sidgemoor had thought the body merely that of a mundane bat, but presumably she knew of Lilian's existence, and might suspect it was a vampiri. However, it was too risky to announce Elinor's own knowledge of it.

She turned the conversation to safer ground. "Tell me, Mrs Sidgemoor, do you cook soufflés at all? Even in Devon, we have heard of this famous French dish."

Mrs Sidgemoor bent to pick some chives, breaking the thin green sheaves at the base. "Not usually, Lady Beresford. Not soufflés. I confess I haven't had much success with them."

Elinor could hear some reserve in the housekeeper's voice. "Well, you will have an appreciative audience if you should be tempted to try again."

Mrs Sidgemoor straightened up, shaking her head. "You'd be better off visiting Little Sark, to the south of the island. The mistress of the tenement there has a knack with soufflés. Or the Fittens, in the west."

That sounded promising, and Elinor decided that Little Sark warranted a visit as a matter of priority.

Just then she saw Beresford returning on Hedley's cart, bearing the last of their trunks. Mr Sidgemoor hurried up to help unload them, and Elinor led the way upstairs.

Once the trunks were deposited and Sidgemoor dismissed, Elinor turned to see how Beresford would respond to the ruffled glory of the four-poster in the centre of the room.

Beresford took one look at it and strode briskly past it to look out the window. "Nice view," he observed, with his back to the bedroom.

Elinor, rather disappointed, walked over to the bed and sat down, hoping to draw his attention to it. He turned around but stayed where he was.

She twinkled at him. "What do you think of our sleeping arrangements?"

"Rather frilly."

She bounced a little. "Fairly comfortable, I think."

"I hope you will sleep well in it."

She smiled. "Do you think you will have trouble, my lord?"

"I won't be sleeping in it at all," he replied. "I'll sleep there." He nodded towards a stiff-backed, firmly cushioned settee. It looked as if its thin legs would barely support a child, let alone his bulk.

Elinor frowned. "Don't be silly." She patted the bed next to her. "Try it out."

Suddenly, in a few hungry strides, he was in front of her. He did not sit down on the bed; instead he dropped to his knees and placed his hands so that one strong arm rested on either side of her. It felt indecently intimate. She blushed, and laid a hand on his chest.

"Miss Avely," he said, and his voice was husky, "I remind you that your chaperone is asleep at the moment."

"True," she murmured. "It seems that for us the daytime hours are more amenable to scandalous trysting than the evening."

She ran her tongue over her bottom lip and he leaned in to kiss her. Her arms crept around him and his body pressed into her, warm and demanding. Thrilling sensations swept through her. After a few moments, a moan of pleasure escaped her lips.

Abruptly, he drew back. She kept her hands clasped around his neck so he could not go too far, but his expression was now guarded, his grey eyes opaque. She bit her lip, embarrassed. Oh, *why* had she moaned?

"I'm not sleeping on that bed," he said. "Miss Zooth will not countenance it, and I don't trust myself not to ravish you as soon as I lie in it. Especially if you make sounds like that."

Elinor's eyes widened. "Oh." Ravishing *did* sound good. She would simply have to convince him to lie in it. "In that case, if anyone is sleeping on that settee, it should be me. I am smaller and lighter. You sleep in the bed." Then she could creep into it later, when his defences were down.

Beresford cast her a suspicious look; he was too much of a

strategist to be caught like that. He ducked out of her embrace and waved a disparaging hand. "I refuse to sleep in that pile of lace. I shall lie on the floor if I must."

"You are infuriating, my dear." She sighed. "Why don't you just accept that we are man and wife now?" She fluttered her eyelashes in what she hoped was a seductive manner.

"Because we are not!" He disentangled himself from her hands and stood up. "Stop looking so adorable and intoxicating, we have work to do. Besides, I'm starving." He stepped away, settling his coat in a businesslike fashion.

Elinor's shoulders drooped. Clearly, food was more appealing than her efforts. She would have to work on her eyelash batting. However, she would be the first to admit that the thought of food was alluring. Lady Orlend had promised an early dinner and Elinor *was* feeling hungry, especially after the privations of the sailing trip.

"Yes," continued Beresford thoughtfully. "I wonder what they serve for dinner out here? Grilled fish with marinated vegetables? Lobster? Cheese soufflés?"

Elinor brightened. "Do you think so? I do smell something delicious, now that you mention it." She stood up and led the way out, following her nose.

Only afterwards did she realise that Beresford had masterfully outmanoeuvred her.

9

IN WHICH AN ITEM IS RECOVERED

*a*fter an early, delicious dinner of soup (liberally laced with cream), baked fish and marinated lobster, Elinor realised that she was exhausted. The sailing voyage and the excitement of landing had quite taken it out of her. Beresford and Perry went to see how Jaq and Rusty were faring, but she made her excuses and retired to the bedroom. Perhaps a little nap before nightfall was advisable. The sun was setting late, so Aldreda would not arrive for a while yet.

Elinor had already placed Aldreda's little trunk and a basket in the attic. It could be a decoy vampiri bed if Aldreda wished, and would give credence to the idea that Aldreda was sleeping in the attic, even if she could not abide it. Elinor had covered the attic basket with one of Mrs Avely's shawls, patterned in matronly deep blues and reds and complete with tassels. Aldreda's other bedding was still on the *Crescent*, but perhaps the ornate shawl would tempt her. Elinor slipped under her own rose-patterned bedcovers and fell asleep immediately.

When she awoke, the room was dark with night. The curtains were open, and in the dim light she could see a black bat hanging from the lace above her head. She muffled a shriek and Aldreda blinked at her. Elinor put a hand to her heart. "You startled me!"

Aldreda transformed and landed on the pillow, her black hair contrasting with Elinor's golden curls. "My apologies. I thought you were asleep for the night."

Elinor's eyes narrowed. "You were keeping watch."

"I have strict chaperone duties," said Aldreda, with sublime unconcern for the fact that she was stark naked. As an afterthought, she pulled a piece of lace over herself.

Elinor sat up and folded her arms. "Aldreda, this is ridiculous. Beresford and I are to be married in a month; we can afford to be a little lax." She put on a wheedling tone. "Mother need never know."

"*I* shall know," said Aldreda. "You mustn't undermine the sanctity of your wedding night."

The sanctity of her wedding night was fast making Elinor cross. "So you are going to hang there like something out of a Gothic novel and scare Beresford away? Then you'll be pleased to know that he won't be sleeping here. He says he will take the settee, though it will serve him right if it breaks in two in the middle of the night."

"Hm," said Aldreda, considering the settee. "It does look rather spindly."

Elinor flung the rose-patterned quilt aside. "Let me show you to *your* quarters, Aldreda. You have been relegated to the attic, under a table. I am starting to see the sense in such an arrangement."

She passed Aldreda a gown that she had kept aside. While the vampiri dressed, Elinor crossed to the window and saw that once more fog clouded the night. She closed the curtains. "I wonder where Beresford is at the moment."

Aldreda announced that he was in the book room, reading.

"Reading? I would have thought he'd be exploring the island in the dark, looking for who shot at Perry. That would be far more in character."

Aldreda tied up her gown. "It is quite late, you know; people would ask questions if he went out. And you may find that, for this trip, he is indeed an assiduous reader."

Elinor frowned and put her hand out for Aldreda to climb aboard. If it were that late already, and people were abed, it might be a good time to investigate the house.

They ascended to the attic, with Elinor explaining in an undertone what she had discovered that day: that Chaboot had been removed, but she had been unable to ask about it. When she opened the wooden door, Aldreda shifted on her shoulder, then remarked casually that the room had certainly been cleaned well.

Elinor felt immediate remorse. "Of course you will not really sleep here," she said. "Your basket is under the table to make it appear so, but you may sleep in my room if you wish. We can make a space in the wardrobe, though you might prefer your basket." She pulled the tablecloth aside to show the basket with its tasselled shawl covering.

"This will suffice," said Aldreda calmly.

"I should warn you that Lady Orlend has the key to the door. I saw her take it."

"Then you know whom to ask for it," said Aldreda. "Does the window really open now?"

Elinor went over to the window to demonstrate, and explained about the Defence spell that had prevented it earlier.

Aldreda pushed it open with her own tiny hands, frowning. "Oh yes, I should have thought of that. My mind was probably addled with the shock of finding the lieutenant. Poor Chaboot. He certainly wouldn't have been able to break the window if there was a Defence upon it."

"The question is whether Lady Orlend or her servants knew the lieutenant was here."

Aldreda turned on the sill. "He might have crept up here, like me, and been trapped by accident."

There was silence as they dwelt on this awful thought.

Outside, a shred of moonlight fought its way through the fog to glimmer on the windowpane.

"Perhaps we should question this Lilian, the vampiri companion," said Elinor. "She might be able to cast light on the matter."

"Yes," said Aldreda thoughtfully. "I shall have to introduce myself."

They shut the door behind them and went down to the cellar, Elinor's footsteps light on the stairs. The rest of the house was quiet, everyone seemingly in bed, except for the light from the book room. They crept past it, in the assumption that Beresford's presence would not put Lilian at ease. However, at the cellar door, Aldreda whispered that Elinor too should stay outside, and leave the vampiri to introduce themselves to each other.

Elinor reluctantly put Aldreda on the floor and watched her slip out of sight. Then she reflected. This was a perfect opportunity to do her own investigating: time for a divination or two.

She returned to the ground floor and pushed open the door to the empty drawing room. Inside the furniture loomed in unfamiliar shapes. She took possession of an armchair, lounging in it and preparing to open her mind – though it was unlikely that the vampiri roost would be conveniently hidden next to the main house.

She closed her eyes to begin, and a tentative voice broke the silence. "Excuse me, Lady Beresford, are you all right?"

Elinor's eyes shot open. "Quite well, thank you." She sat up straight and looked round. Chester was peering at her from the window alcove. Had he been hiding behind the curtains? She could have sworn that he had not been there when she entered. He looked sheepish, too, blinking rapidly as he lit a candle on the cabinet.

"Are you lost?" he asked. "I can show you to your room, if you like."

Elinor shook her head. "I couldn't sleep. I thought I would just come down to, ah, stretch my legs." Never mind that she was sitting in an armchair.

Chester took a tentative step forward. "Were you worried about Mr Avely? He has not yet returned from his evening stroll. I cannot think it advisable to be walking around after dark."

Elinor caught her lip between her teeth. Perry was probably spending time with Jaq, perhaps on the ship. She was not *too* worried, but she couldn't explain that to Chester, who was giving her an anxious look. However, she could take the opportunity to question him. "Oh?" she said. "Is Sark dangerous?"

Chester hesitated. "To someone unfamiliar with the territory, perhaps. There are cliffs, rabbit holes, and loose rocks."

"Perry is sure-footed," lied Elinor. "Though we did hear a gunshot last night," she added. "Why was that?"

Chester's gaze shifted to the wall behind her. "Rabbit hunting, I imagine."

"In the dark?"

"That, or hunting Frenchies," admitted Chester. "The locals are hoping to shoot a few in the line of duty."

Elinor pursed her lips. "I hope they would not mistake Peregrine for a Frenchman."

"One hopes they would not," said Chester dubiously. Then he leaned forward. "Lady Beresford, could Mr Avely Discern the location of gold?"

Elinor did not want to deny it, for Perry was meant to be Chief Mineral Discernor. Gold was surely the chief mineral of interest. She nodded cautiously.

Chester continued. "There are old stories of pirate gold hidden on this island, you know." His eyes lit up. "Gold coins which have remained undiscovered for centuries. Do you think Mr Avely will find treasure?"

Elinor kept her expression bland, though she felt uncertain. Her talent was for divining jewels, not gold or silver. She had managed to extend her Gift to pearls and plum jam, however, so gold might not prove too difficult. She would have to practise at once. A pirate hoard was an enthralling thought, though it could be merely a boy's fancy. Chester, kept at his mother's side, might be looking for adventure where there was none.

She kept her tone light. "If there is buried treasure, I am sure Perry will discover it. That is, if he is not too busy looking for copper or silver. We did not expect to find gold here, and we were not going to search for it."

Chester took an eager step forward, his dark hair shadowing his face. "You must tell Mr Avely of the possibility. Or I shall, so that we make the most of his Gift while he is here."

"Certainly," said Elinor. An uneasy feeling gripped her. If treasure were indeed hidden on Sark, someone might not want it to be found. Besides, she had enough to concern herself with in finding the vampiri. Recalled to a sense of her responsibilities, she smiled wearily at Chester and told him that she would return to her bed. He nodded and watched her leave the drawing room.

Once in the passageway, she stopped and closed her eyes. *Where is the queen? Where is the vampiri roost?*

Without much hope, she waited for any glimmering sense to answer her. She was surprised when the answer came quick and strong. Something was pulling at her senses from directly beneath her.

For a moment she was filled with excitement. Her breath caught in her chest and her eyes flew open in the dark passageway. The vampiri roost might be hidden below this very house! Could their search be almost over?

Then she remembered that indeed there were vampiri below, and her shoulders drooped. Aldreda, visiting Lilian in the cellar. Lilian, as companion to the Seigneuresse, was the highest ranking vampiri on Sark, so perhaps that was why Elinor's senses had been drawn to her in lieu of the queen.

Elinor sighed in disappointment and leaned against the wall. Then she turned, aware of eyes upon her again. Chester was at the door of the drawing room, staring at her. "Lady Beresford, are you well? Do you need assistance?"

Elinor shot upright. "Oh! No, indeed. I was feeling a little faint, but I am better now." She hoped he hadn't been watching her too long. However, he would not have seen much: simply Elinor closing her eyes and standing still. Would he know enough to suspect that she was Musing? She licked her dry lips. "I bid you goodnight."

"Wait," he said. "Is this yours?" He held out a large reticule: the one she had carried ashore that morning. Belatedly, she realised that she must have left it in the drawing room earlier in the day.

"Why, yes. Did I misplace it? How silly of me."

He came to her side and gave her the reticule. She took it and smiled. "Thank you."

"Good night." He bowed, and Elinor could feel his eyes on her as she made her way upstairs.

IN WHICH A CUPBOARD IS
COMMODIOUS

*A*ldreda, slipping past the cellar door, took a moment to orient herself. The room was much bigger than the small stone cellar of the Avelys' cottage in Devon. This one went right back, like a cavern, and was lined with chests and barrels. No attempt had been made to beautify it, as Elinor had done at the cottage when Aldreda had been forced to occupy the cellar. It was dim and the floors were grimy.

One single candle burned in a lantern, set on a wall above a big cupboard carved of pale pine. Aldreda narrowed her eyes. Surely the candle would be close to Lilian's quarters, yet it was in an odd place, located as it was above a cupboard.

She glided silently forward, listening intently, but she could hear nothing. Perhaps Lilian was with her mistress; perhaps they had a more convivial relationship than had first appeared. Aldreda paced around the cupboard, wondering if a bed or basket lay behind it.

Footsteps clattered outside the cellar door. Aldreda ducked behind the cupboard just as the housekeeper swung the door open and barrelled in, muttering under her breath. "Oh, and now I must fetch the silver, must I? What's the point in hiding it down here in the first place then, I ask you? What strange, distempered thing will she do next?"

She strode over to a chest and snapped open the lid. Gathering up a large, heavy bundle, she put it on top of a keg to close the chest. "Lilian!" she called, her tone a warning. "Stay hidden. I saw one of our guests wandering about." She paused. "Her ladyship says please may you work on those sleeves while you wait."

No answer came, but Mrs Sidgemoor appeared satisfied. She marched out of the cellar bearing her burden and the door closed behind her with a thud.

So Lilian was here somewhere. Aldreda looked about her by the light of the candle far above and realised that a rope hung down behind the cupboard, with knots tied into it.

She gazed upwards. Was Lilian's residence on the roof of the cupboard? There was one way to find out. Wishing to remain clothed, Aldreda placed a slippered foot on the bottom of the rope and swung herself up.

With her supernatural strength, it was fairly easy to pull herself up the rope, even with her skirts hampering her. She tried to be quiet, to mask her approach. When she reached the top, she peered over cautiously.

The roof of the cupboard had been removed. The top shelf made an open room and a door had been cut into the middle board, marking two rooms in the little house that lay before Aldreda. A bedroom formed one side, with blankets laid in a small basket and a bedside table made from an overturned cup. On the other side was a sitting room with two Vember chairs, lit by the candle glowing above.

On one of these chairs sat Lilian, her plain face smooth and her dark hair pulled back. She was still pale, despite the flickering warmth of the lantern. She did not notice Aldreda, as her gaze was bent on some sewing. This time she was doing intricate lace-work on a sleeve. A human-sized sleeve, noted Aldreda. Once again, Lady Orlend had her vampiri hard at work: a servant more than a companion.

Aldreda cleared her throat.

Lilian looked up, but she seemed less startled than Aldreda would have expected. Then her dark eyes widened.

Aldreda smiled. "I am sorry to disturb you. I thought I should introduce myself; I am visiting Sark with my Musor companion, and I was not sure that we would be given formal introductions. My name is Miss Aldreda Zooth."

Lilian stood up gracefully, putting her sewing aside. "Please, do come in. I am Miss Lilian Reed. So pleased to meet you."

Aldreda heaved herself over the edge and dropped to the wooden floor. The rope was cleverly hidden on this side by a ream of cloth that hung down the back wall, adding a touch of ornament to the bare room. Dusting her hands off, she curtsied. "You are the companion to Lady Orlend?"

"I have that honour." Lilian dipped her head and sat down, nervously picking up her sewing again. "Please sit. You must excuse me; I am unused to company. I do not have much to offer in the way of refreshment."

"That is quite all right," said Aldreda, taking the other chair. "Do you not meet with many vampiri?"

"Oh, there are some living on Guernsey," said Lilian, "but vampiri society is quite limited in this part of the world. I was not expecting to see a face such as yours on Sark; we do not receive many visitors."

"Oh?" asked Aldreda curiously. "I am staying in the attic." She paused, wondering if she could ask Lilian about Lieutenant Chaboot, but decided against it. How else could she lead the conversation that way? "Is the attic often used as a guest room?"

"Sometimes." Lilian bent her head to her sewing. "Lady Orlend used to allow parties from the mainland – wedding parties, and such like. Sometimes Musors would attend with their vampiri. But I am kept quite separate from the attic, as you see."

"Ah," said Aldreda. "English law now expressly forbids our open fraternisation, which makes things difficult. I suppose your mistress follows those decrees, as she should."

"Yes, indeed: I am kept apart." Lilian placed another tiny stitch, keeping her eyes lowered.

Aldreda cast a look around the bare room and reflected that it was little more than a prison. "When was the last party from the mainland?"

Lilian did not have to search her memory. "Before the Troubles," she replied. "Since the war, we have been very quiet."

"I have just come from London," said Aldreda, and began talking of the roost revels of London and Paris. Lilian was fascinated and wanted to know all the details of the last revel. She even put down her sewing, her face lighting up as Aldreda described the latest fashions and the new dances.

"How wonderful," said Lilian, and paused shyly. "And what of a queen? Do you have a vampiri queen in London?"

Aldreda explained that there was no London queen, only a duchessel, for King George's vampiri was still too young to rule. "And the French vampiri queen has been missing for years," she added. "Did you ever meet her?"

"No," sighed Lilian, her head drooping back to her needlework. "I hardly meet any vampiri at all, let alone the queen."

Aldreda was just about to risk mentioning the lieutenant by name when the cloth on the back wall quivered. She watched it curiously and it moved again. Someone was coming up the rope. Surely Lilian had noticed this when Aldreda had climbed it, unless she had been too absorbed in her sewing.

A minute later, Durl's curly brown head popped up. "Good evening," he said cautiously. Lilian seemed unsurprised, turning with a smile to greet him, which rather gave the lie to her statement that she did not see any vampiri. Durl must be the person she had expected to see when Aldreda showed herself.

Durl pulled himself over the edge and landed with an easy grace. He was dressed this time, in breeches, shirt and coat. However, there were patches on them, well darned with tiny stitches. Aldreda rather thought she detected Lilian's handiwork. So the vampiri did not only do Lady Orlend's work.

Durl stood with his hands clasped behind his back. "I just thought I'd see how you fared, Miss Reed," he said tentatively. "I gathered you had company." Aldreda wondered how much of their conversation he had overheard.

"I am well, thank you," said Lilian. "I have just met Miss Zooth. Miss Zooth, this is Mr Thomas Durl. He lives on Sark, in the woods." A touch of hauteur entered her tone. Aldreda wondered if Lilian was defensive of Durl's wildness, or embarrassed by it.

"Indeed, I have met Mr Durl," said Aldreda. She did not want to mention the flying display to which she had been treated, but Lilian gave her a curious, questioning glance. "We met when I flew in last night with another vampiri friend of mine, by the name of Pagrilliard Deponzel."

Curiosity flashed across Lilian's face. No doubt she recognised Pags' ducal name, for the Deponzels had been famous in France. She was not to know that Pags was considering becoming a companion to Mrs Avely, in which case he would forfeit his ducal title. "How delightful!" she said. "I shall pour some port for you both; Lady Orlend allows me a small bottle."

She moved around, suddenly elegant in her role as hostess, fetching thimbles and an old medicine bottle into which port had been decanted. Durl stood awkwardly by the wall, as there were only two chairs, and asked Aldreda if her companion had found any minerals yet.

It took her a moment to remember that he was referring to

Perry, not Elinor. "Not yet: he only came ashore today. He has been settling in and recovering from the journey."

"Do you think he will look for pirate gold?" asked Durl. "They say that a hundred years ago or more this isle was a pirate haunt, full of wild ruffians who were the menace of the northern coast. Surely they buried treasure here."

He had an eager look in his eye, and Aldreda smiled, reflecting that Durl seemed to identify with the pirates. She was intrigued by the story, and thought to herself that Elinor would not be able to resist looking for pirate gold. However, she merely observed that Mr Avely was expert in mineral deposits, not treasure, and she could not say whether he would be able to find a pirate chest.

Durl looked disappointed and Lilian smiled fondly as she poured the port into the thimbles. She passed one to each of them with a stately nod. It was clear that she was happy to have guests for once, in her isolated little cabin, and she was making the most of it.

Aldreda took a sip of the sweet liquor and decided it was time for a direct approach. "Have either of you ever met a vampiri by the name of Chaboot? We heard that he came to this part of the world recently. I hope to hear news of him."

Lilian shook her head, holding her thimble carefully. "No, I have not met any Chaboot." But it was possible Chaboot had assumed a different name. Aldreda wondered how she could describe him without it sounding odd.

However, Durl looked up, frowning. "I met him." He seemed reluctant to say more.

Aldreda leaned forward. "Oh yes? How was that?"

"He visited Sark a few months ago," replied Durl. "He only stayed a while, then left without saying goodbye. I do not know where he was headed."

Lilian looked concerned. "Were you expecting him back in London by now?"

Aldreda debated whether to mention that she had found Chaboot's corpse in the attic. Looking at Lilian's pale face, she decided not to distress her. "Do you know where he stayed?"

Durl looked embarrassed. "He slept in a crevice in a cliff, I believe. I'm afraid I am not too hospitable in my part of the woods, having been alone for so long."

"He did not sleep in this house?" Aldreda asked, looking from one to the other.

They both shook their heads. That made sense, for if Chaboot had been known to sleep in the attic, they would have also known to look for him there. Could he have grown tired of his crevice in the cliff and sought a more civilised shelter, only to find himself locked in? Aldreda shivered.

Durl took a final gulp of his port and put his thimble down. "Thank you, Miss Reed. Mr Deponzel is meeting me soon, so I'd best be going. Good evening, Miss Zooth."

Lilian's hands fluttered nervously as she reached for his cup. She looked wistful as Durl hauled himself over the wall and disappeared, then she sat down again with a sigh.

Aldreda, somehow annoyed that Durl was going off to play with Pags, stood also. "I must depart as well. It was lovely to meet you, Miss Reed. I hope I may call again?"

"Of course," replied Lilian, picking up the lace sleeve. She smiled. "I would be delighted."

More awkward than Durl, Aldreda pulled herself over the edge and clambered down the rope. Once on the stone floor, she looked around at the empty cellar. No one would guess that Lilian was perched above them. Still, it was strange that Lady Orlend would keep her vampiri companion so far from her.

She walked and hopped briskly back up the flights of stairs. In the hallway she met Beresford, coming out of the book room. He was frowning, but made a small bow. "May I carry you to the bedroom, Miss Zooth?"

She nodded and he dropped to one knee for her to walk into

his cupped hands. Carefully, he rose and lifted her to his shoulder. She sat down and held onto his coat. This was the first time she had ridden on Beresford's shoulder. He was being a gentleman about it and walked in slow, even strides.

He spoke quietly as they went upstairs. "May I enquire as to your presence in the corridor?"

"You may." Aldreda paused. "I called upon Miss Lilian Reed, Lady Orlend's companion. She lives in the cellar, treated little better than a servant. She seemed to know nothing about Chaboot, even when I mentioned him by name."

"Hm. Odd, when he was found in the house. What is she like?"

Aldreda considered. "Reserved. Lonely, I think. Quick to occupy herself with Lady Orlend's needlework; she seemed nervous, perhaps afraid."

When Beresford pushed the bedroom door open, Aldreda saw Elinor fast asleep on the bed, a candle still burning on the dresser.

Beresford gave a heavy sigh. He deposited Aldreda on the dresser and retreated to the settee by the window. Before Aldreda blew out the candle, she saw him settle himself into the hard couch, pushing his broad shoulders in and folding his arms across his chest. "Good night," came his low rumble.

"Good night," said Aldreda. She felt a twinge of sympathy, seeing his large form squashed into such a small bed. Yet she undressed, transformed into a bat, and took up her perch in the lacy awning above Elinor. A wedding night was sacred. Elinor was not going to rush the event under *her* watch.

11

IN WHICH ELINOR DIVINES A DIRECTION

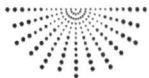

The next morning, Elinor woke early. She sat up in bed and saw that Beresford was still fast asleep, lying on a rug on the wooden floor. He did not look at all comfortable. She frowned; he could be so stubborn sometimes!

A faint light was creeping around the edges of the curtain yet the room felt stuffy, especially since she was surrounded by drapery. She looked up to see Aldreda hanging sleepily above her. "You've done your duty," said Elinor, quietly but crossly. Then remorse shot through her, for Aldreda was only following Mrs Avely's strict instructions. "You should sleep now. The sun is rising."

Aldreda yawned a pretty little bat yawn and flew down to her spare basket without a word, transforming into human shape and reaching for her silk dressing gown. Elinor flung her own blankets back, shooting a glance at Beresford. His eyes remained tightly closed.

Slowly, she dressed herself, wondering if she could try a divination while everything was quiet and Aldreda was near. Perhaps she needed to broaden her question to increase her chances of success: the exact location of the vampiri queen might be too much to ask at this point.

In which direction should I search? she asked. *North, south, east, or west?*

She sank onto the bed, waiting. Silence, both inner and outer, greeted her senses. The morning was still and quiet, apart from birds beginning to twitter outside. She sighed and ran through the directions once more in her mind, lingering on each with a faint question.

This time, there was a glimmer of an answer. 'South' glowed a little more brightly in her mind. She sat up with renewed cheer, then recalled that Mrs Sidgemoor had mentioned the south as a location of soufflés. Perhaps she had allowed her innermost desires to distort the direction?

Looking around, she saw that Aldreda had tucked herself into bed and pulled the shawl across the basket. She must be tired, but Elinor could still take advantage of her proximity. The golden flute might give the divination even more certainty. She stepped over to her reticule and rifled through its contents.

It took her a moment to realise that the flute was missing. Its delicate shape was not among her gloves and fan and other trinkets. Elinor turned her bag out on the table, but nothing golden clinked onto the wood.

She clutched the bag, her heart suddenly racing. Good Lord, how could she have lost it? The tiny, precious implement was crucial to the whole undertaking. How would she awaken the vampiri queen without it?

She searched through the reticule's contents again with shaking fingers. Could it have fallen out? Or worse, had it been stolen?

Her reticule had been left in the drawing room a good part of yesterday. There had been plenty of opportunity for someone to look through it and remove the flute. Chester himself could have done it – perhaps that was why he had lingered in the drawing room so late. Or his mother had had the opportunity, or indeed any of the servants.

Elinor cursed herself for being so careless. She sat back on her bed and put her head in her hands, sending out a wild question, seeking the flute.

The inner silence this time was deafening.

How was she to find it again? She straightened her shoulders. She could learn to divine gold. She had learned to divine pearls; surely it was a similar matter. She and Aldreda would have to practise. In the meantime, she had at least a glimmer of a direction for the vampiri – or soufflés. The south of the island was as good as any other direction to begin their search during the day. Even if they found the roost, they had until nightfall to find the flute.

Now she just had to communicate all that to Perry over breakfast. Beresford was still fast asleep. She crept up to him, kneeling by his side and smoothing a lock of hair away from his brow. What would he say when he learned that she had lost the flute? At the moment, his face rested in noble splendour in the dim light, his strong jaw relaxed.

At her touch, his lips parted and a sigh escaped them. She bent down to place a kiss on his mouth, her hand caressing his shoulder.

"Elinor Avely," said Aldreda sharply.

Elinor spun round. Aldreda's head was poking out of her basket, a dire frown on her face. "Just *what* do you think you are doing?"

"Er, nothing," said Elinor. "That is to say, just a kiss. I'm allowed to kiss him, Aldreda, he is my fiancé!"

"Hm," said Aldreda. "Kisses can lead to more. You had better put me in the attic, then go straight down to breakfast."

Elinor glanced down at Beresford, whose eyes remained steadfastly closed, though a faint red had stolen into his cheeks. She huffed and stood up. "Very well, you staid old spinster. Let us put you in the attic." She debated whether to tell Aldreda about the flute, but she couldn't bring herself to do it. Why disturb Aldreda's sleep with such worrisome news?

Aldreda pulled the shawl back with a swoosh.

Carefully, Elinor carried the spare basket upstairs and put it next to the one in the attic, under the covered table. She backed away, feeling reluctant to leave Aldreda there. Yet it would raise questions if a zealous maid found Perry's alleged vampiri companion sleeping in Elinor's room.

She made her way down to the breakfast parlour, where Lady Orlend and her son were already eating. Mr Sidgemoor stood by the door with his hands clasped behind him, doing his best impression of a butler but falling short, perhaps because his eyes darted around nervously.

Elinor helped herself to a plate of toast and pound cake. She was accepting a cup of hot chocolate when Perry came into the room. He had dark circles under his eyes, and when Lady Orlend enquired after his rest, he admitted he had not slept well. "There was a scraping noise outside my room," he explained. "Like a shovel scraping earth away. Was anyone gardening last night?"

Lady Orlend's nostrils pinched together. "I should think not. Sidgemoor, were you gardening in the night hours?"

"No, madame," squeaked Sidgemoor from his post.

"Well, I could swear it was someone digging a hole," said Perry. "Most distracting."

Elinor's eyes widened. Had Perry heard someone burying the body of Lieutenant Chaboot? Perry cast her a glance, as if the same thought was in his mind.

Lady Orlend shook her head. "I shall talk to Mrs Sidgemoor. She might know what it was."

Elinor considered trying to Discern the whereabouts of Chaboot's body. However, she could scarcely order Perry to dig in the light of day – and perhaps it was best not to expose a dead vampiri to sunlight. Such investigation would have to wait for nightfall. No, she decided, the day would be devoted to the south of the island, just as her divination had suggested.

Beresford finally appeared, looking tired, but she had no patience with that. It was his own fault, after all.

She turned to Perry, who was moodily sipping his coffee. "Are you ready to begin work today?" she asked him brightly, and chattered on. "It looks as if it will be a lovely day; I am sure I see a hint of blue sky. Perhaps the clear air will assist your geological explorations. Do you think a fog would confuse the matter? A walk would be delightful. Perhaps we can explore the northern end of the island, or the lovely southern reaches, or indeed the middle grounds near this house ..."

She continued to rattle on, but when she eventually paused for breath, Perry had picked up her hint. "We shall investigate the south today," he announced. "You are welcome to join me, Elinor."

Elinor smiled broadly. "Oh, I *will* enjoy a walk through the fields."

Beresford gulped down his coffee. "I shall join you too. Let us start soon, Mr Avely."

However, they were not allowed to wander off unattended: Lady Orlend insisted that Hedley drive them in his cart to their suggested destination. "I have told him you are a Discernor, Mr Avely, so there is no need to pretend you are simply a geologist," said the Dame. "He will be happy to guide you around the island as you undertake your divinations."

"Er, yes, thank you," said Perry, looking relieved that he didn't have to make any more remarks about Diluvian deposits.

They could not refuse Hedley's company without rousing suspicion, so after breakfast they had to wait for him to be fetched. It was after ten o'clock before they climbed into the cart, with the same chestnut horse waiting patiently at the heavy gates that guarded the driveway. Hedley informed Elinor that the horse's name was Pumpkin-Pie, and a steady, reliable mare. Elinor could see no added hostility in Hedley's face, now that he knew Perry for a Musor; but Hedley was a rather inscrutable fellow.

It was indeed a fine day. The sun was warm on Elinor's cheeks and a brisk wind had cleared the fog away. She could smell rich, loamy earth and hear the sheep bleating in the fields. Above them, the sky stretched blue and clear. Bright yellow toad-flax dotted the edge of the stony road, and the clip-clop of Pumpkin-Pie's hooves was a comforting sound.

It was so lovely that she quite forgot to Discern, and occupied herself with slipping her hand into Beresford's. His palm was calloused from sailing, but warm and firm. He ran his thumb over her own palm and she shivered with pleasure. It was so delightful to be able to be publicly linked in affection at last.

Hedley drove them up a lane and pulled Pumpkin-Pie to a stop. Around them, the vivid green of the fields was broken by a speckling of white daisies. A cream-coloured butterfly wafted past Elinor's nose, its wings laced with delicate black and dabs of blue. In the distance, the sea gleamed bright azure.

Hedley sprang off the cart. "We walk from here along the edge of this farmer's property. The path leads all the way to Little Sark, so you should be able to cover quite a stretch of ground for your Discernments."

"Excellent," said Perry. He jumped down and rolled an expressive eye at Elinor.

Beresford helped her down and they set off, Perry marching ahead as if leading the expedition and Elinor holding Beresford's arm in a wifely manner.

She did a Discernment immediately. It would not matter if she became a bit Bemused out here, in front of Hedley. After all, she was meant to be a silly, chattering matrimonial accessory. So she sent her senses out, searching for the vampiri, feeling another stab of worry that she no longer carried the golden flute to help her.

No sense of the queen or of vampiri answered her.

The wind tickled the hair on her neck as she walked. Every forty yards she attempted another Discernment as Perry trudged on ahead. Every now and then he would pause dramatically and close his eyes, holding up a hand for the benefit of Hedley, who was bringing up the rear.

At one of these theatrical moments, having just completed another Discernment herself, Elinor used the opportunity to snuggle closer to Beresford. They watched as Perry thrust his brow into the breeze with his eyes squinted perspicaciously.

"I'm afraid I have rather bad news," she muttered.

Beresford glanced down at her. "Oh?"

She bit her lip. "I've lost the Viveroust flute, or someone has taken it. I'm afraid I left my reticule in the drawing room yesterday for several hours, and now the flute is missing – taken or lost."

Beresford's eyes narrowed. "Who would do such a thing? That implies someone knows our purpose and wants to forestall it."

"Or perhaps they thought the flute was valuable in its own right," she suggested. "It is golden and finely wrought."

"Let us hope that is it," said Beresford grimly. "Perhaps you should tell Lady Orlend that it is missing, and create a stir."

Elinor shook her head. "I might be able to divine it if I can just practise a little. Aldreda can help me." She changed the subject, for she did not want to dwell on her own carelessness. "Did you sleep well last night, my dear?"

Beresford gave her a wry smile. "Well enough. The floor is a little uncomfortable, I admit."

"You are being ridiculous," she murmured to him. "But I adore you anyway." She stretched up to sneak a kiss onto his cheek.

Then she heard low muttering behind her. Another farmer

had joined them. His hat was pulled low on his head and he was communicating something to Hedley which was clearly of a private and imperative nature.

Hedley looked resigned. "No, Fitten, I won't come and look." He gestured towards Elinor and Beresford. "I am showing these folk around; I don't have time for your nonsense."

Fitten nodded his head in a perfunctory greeting. In an audible aside, he asked Hedley if the Dame were hosting wedding parties again.

Elinor blushed. Were she and Beresford so obviously a newly married couple? At least their act was convincing.

Hedley cleared his throat. "This is no wedding party," he said. "These are the folk sent by King George to test the area for silver and copper. Mr Avely over there is the Chief Mineral Geologist."

"Oh?" said the farmer. "Well, they'd better be careful round my part of the island." After a few more low words – with Hedley vehemently shaking his head – he turned and left.

"Goodness," said Elinor. "Why should his part of the island be any different?"

Beresford frowned. "Was he threatening us?"

"Oh no, my lord," Hedley hastened to say. "Fitten's tenement is in the west, and he has a fondness for sloe gin. I wouldn't listen to him if I were you."

Beresford thoughtfully watched Fitten retreat. "Would there be resentment towards a wedding party?"

Hedley shrugged. "We're a bit close to France and their notions for our liking, Lord Beresford. I do my best to reduce tensions, but they are suspicious of noble visitors."

Beresford nodded. "Lady Orlend is lucky to have your loyalty, Hedley."

Hedley went slightly pink, which Elinor thought was sweet. "Well, then," he said, "shall we continue?"

Perry nodded, and grandly led the way.

The path left the fields for the headland. An ocean breeze buffeted the cliffs and Elinor pulled her skirts closer, staring over the choppy blue waters.

Ahead of them lay a narrow isthmus of land leading to the southern headland. The bridge of land was only ten feet wide, like the stem of a flower with the headland as a huge bulb at the end. On either side of the isthmus, rocks plunged down almost three hundred feet.

Elinor shivered a little as she examined that drop. This, then, was the southern headland. Birds wheeled above and she could see puffins dotted on the cliffs, their gentle, funny faces turned towards them in curiosity. On the narrow strip of sand below, a couple of seals lay in the sun. Not selkies, she assumed, as they were smaller than Jaq appeared in seal form. This was just the sea-life of Sark, seemingly undisturbed and innocent.

She closed her eyes, reaching with her senses for the vampiri queen.

Nothing answered, and Elinor heaved a sigh. Perhaps asking for the queen might lead her astray if the queen had been killed or separated from her roost, though she didn't like to think of such possibilities. Maybe she should try for a general direction again. It had worked last night, and might guide her closer.

This time, Elinor sought the direction of the hidden roost itself, though her mind was starting to feel a bit woolly. *North, south, east, or west?*

And this time, an answer came. It whispered across the isthmus from the headland beyond.

Elinor stilled, catching her breath. She grasped Beresford's elbow tightly and sent her question again with renewed vigour.

A faint tug pulled her towards Little Sark.

"I feel something!" she said, quietly and urgently.

Beresford had halted, warned by her tight grip on his arm. "Where?" he asked.

"Over there, across the isthmus. It is just a general direction, however: nothing specific."

Beresford shielded his brow from the sun and surveyed the dramatic landscape, as if appreciating it. "I am not certain we should cross; the path looks dangerous."

She pulled on his arm. "We must cross! I cannot tell anything from this distance."

The bridge of land stretched hundreds of feet before them, narrow and rocky. On either side, the vast blue ocean narrowed to this intersection of perilous cliff, and Elinor experienced a flash of vertigo as she looked down at the steep descent.

Hedley was approaching. "Let us tell Perry," said Elinor quickly in an undertone, then she burbled on loudly. "Such a lovely view. Just look at the sea: it is so large. I feel quite small in this wonderful landscape! Like a snail in a field!" That didn't quite seem to do it justice. "A star in the sky!"

It was also true that she was a little Bemused from all the divining. Beresford gave her arm a warning squeeze and she fell silent.

"Aye, the tide is rising," observed Hedley. "The sea always looks bigger in the high tide."

Elinor nodded eagerly. "And the brisk wind is so invigorating! Or should I say refreshing? What sweet puffins! Do tell me – what lies over there, on the headland?"

"Little Sark," said Hedley. "A few tenements, that is all. La Coupee – that's the crossing – is dangerous in a high wind. A couple of years ago we lost a man over the edge when he tried to carry his tithe of corn across. I advise you to stay here, Lady Beresford."

Even more intriguing, thought Elinor, though she gave a tiny shudder. "Mr Avely will want to investigate, and we shall simply follow," she said firmly. "Silver deposits do not take human preferences into account!"

As she prattled on, Beresford began walking towards Perry.

He was pacing out the cliffs further to the east, with occasional theatrical pauses. Elinor paraded along the eastern cliff with Beresford, feeling a renewed sense of excitement. The vampiri might be very close – they might achieve their quest soon! Perhaps she would not need the golden flute after all; she could shake the queen awake herself, if necessary.

Below them, the ocean swirled against the rocks in a violent onslaught. She gazed at the white spray on the cliffs, marvelling at the movement and noise, and glad they were at a distance from it. Then she saw something that made her heart clench.

A seal was clinging to the side of the cliff, bleeding. It was larger than the two seals sunning themselves, and its chocolate-brown colour was terribly familiar.

Even as Elinor watched, the seal shuddered and became human. It was Jaq.

He was about halfway down, his pale body distinct against the harsh, grey rocks. A splash of red on his back stood out even more against the muted colours of the land. Without meaning to, Elinor let out a small cry of protest.

Beresford's grip on her elbow tightened, then he followed her gaze and his breath also caught.

Hedley hurried up. "Lady Beresford, is something wrong?"

Elinor was filled with rage at the sight of Jaq's poor defence-less body. She whirled round, twisting out of Beresford's arm. "One of Lord Beresford's crew is hurt down there – I suppose your men had to shoot him too! How dare you! You know how dangerous these cliffs are!"

Perry hurried over, then strode to the edge of the cliff and stared down. Elinor gulped and went to his side, regretting her outburst. His fists clenched and his blond hair whipped in the wind. His face was pale with shock.

"Don't Travel to him," she hissed. "Don't show Hedley your Gift! Look, Jaq is moving. He will pull himself up, you'll see."

She wasn't as certain as she sounded. However, as they

watched, Jaq did indeed claw his way a little further up the rock, though angry waves beat below him. It must be too dangerous for him to go back into the water, even as a seal. Or perhaps he was aware of his audience.

Beresford's voice was grim. "I shall climb down."

12

IN WHICH THERE ARE CLIFFSIDE DRAMATICS

*U*nder Elinor's horrified gaze, Beresford began taking off his coat.

"Are you mad?" She racked her brains for another solution. "Hedley, for God's sake, fetch a rope and your cart!"

Hedley turned and ran.

Elinor faced Beresford. "You can't go down there! Remember, Jaq has supernatural strength. If he is having trouble, imagine your own plight!"

Beresford ignored her, throwing his coat aside and walking to the edge. "Perry, stay your hand in case we need a Travellor. In case I fall, too."

Elinor swallowed her angry retort and glanced at her brother. Perry was white-faced and frozen, his eyes pinned to Jaq as if he could hold him safe by the force of his gaze. Realising that Perry was restraining himself, she pulled herself together too. If her own brother could stop himself from rash action, so could she.

Beresford knelt at the edge of the cliff and cautiously swung himself down. He went backwards, reaching with his feet for the next foothold.

The next ten minutes were ghastly. The thunder of the waves and the nip of the breeze faded from Elinor's consciousness, for every move Beresford made demanded her full attention. Every now and then she shifted her gaze to Jaq. The selkie seemed motionless.

"Catching his breath," she muttered to Perry.

Perry didn't say a word, but his fists were still clenched by his sides.

Slowly Beresford inched his way down the cliff, heading diagonally towards Jaq. When he was almost there, Elinor heard the welcome sound of Hedley's footsteps pounding across the gorse.

She turned. Hedley was panting and waving a thick rope, and he was accompanied by the other farmer, Fitten. They reached the cliff edge, took in the situation, and set about tying the rope to a boulder. When it was fastened, Hedley heaved it over the edge with all his might.

Agonisingly, Beresford, almost at Jaq's side, had to retrace his steps to reach the rope. Once he had it, he climbed back to Jaq and looped it around his waist. Jaq raised his head and clasped a hand on Beresford's shoulder. Beside Elinor, Perry's breath came out in a whoosh, and his fists uncurled with a tremor.

With the rope as extra support, Beresford escorted Jaq up the cliff. Going up was a slow process, as Jaq seemed to be in pain. However, when his pale face finally showed above the edge, he smiled weakly. The smile faded when he saw Perry standing over him.

Perry's voice was harsh. "What the hell happened? How badly are you hurt? For God's sake, man!"

Jaq hauled his naked form over the cliff. "Only a graze," he said, with an attempt at a grin. "And maybe a few broken ribs."

He stood up shakily and Perry raked him with his gaze. Jaq's side was splattered with bright-red blood, oozing from a wound in his ribs. His black hair was plastered to his face and a bruise bloomed on his shoulder. He looked like a wreck, albeit one in the style of a naked Greek god.

Hedley cleared his throat. "Where are your clothes, sir?"

Jaq passed a hand over his brow. "I went for a swim and my clothes were swept away. The waves were too rough for me."

Elinor had already removed her cloak. Wordlessly, she handed it to Beresford, who wrapped it around Jaq, untying the rope and hiding the battered body.

Perry stepped forwards and offered a gentlemanly arm to Jaq, though Elinor knew he would rather have picked the selkie up and carried him tenderly to the cart while scolding him. The presence of Hedley and the other farmer meant he had to restrain his natural inclinations, and he stood stiff and frowning, his arm out like a tin soldier.

Jaq took it gratefully and stumbled towards the cart. "I think I need to lie down," he announced and collapsed into the back of it.

Hedley and the other farmer went to untie the rope from the boulder. Quickly, while they were thus occupied, Beresford, Elinor and Perry crowded around Jaq, prostrate upon the cart.

Perry leaned forward and brushed a damp lock from Jaq's brow. However, his voice was still rough with anxiety. "What happened? Tell us quickly."

Jaq opened one eye. "I think I found the vampiri cave." He closed his eye again as everyone stared at him.

"Where?" demanded Elinor.

"A hole in the cliff, on the other side of the headland. There is a ledge and a long passageway. And a cave, if I'm not mistaken, at the end of it."

Beresford frowned. "And you had to attempt it by yourself, immediately."

"Of course," said Jaq. He opened his eye again. "The rising tide made it difficult. I was injured and tried to swim back. Then I decided to rest a while on the cliffs."

Beresford muttered something rude and Jaq grinned at him. "I'll recover. I'm a selkie, remember. Superior healing powers."

Elinor had already recalled this and was feeling less panicked as a result. Jaq would be better within a few hours, unless his injuries were very bad indeed.

Perry, however, shook his head in disapproval. "Superior healing powers won't help if you're dead."

"I'm not dead."

"You looked as if you were," observed Elinor tartly.

"I'm sorry," replied Jaq, but he was looking at Perry.

Hedley and Fitten returned with the rope, watching them suspiciously. Their conversation turned to how they could best transport Jaq. Perry insisted on sitting in the back of the cart too, providing his lap as a pillow for Jaq's head. That left Beresford and Elinor in the front, with Hedley driving. The other farmer reluctantly bade them farewell and watched the cart until it disappeared.

The journey back to the main house seemed to take much longer than the trip out. Clouds were sweeping across the sky with a chill wind, and every bump and rattle exacted a toll on their passenger in the back.

Elinor frowned over her shoulder at Jaq's pale face. His stoic silence was somehow worse to bear than if he had groaned and complained. Perry tried to distract him with a firmly worded lecture on swimming by cliffs like an idiot, but that lasted only so long before he fell silent in sympathy.

Elinor stepped into the breach with her burbling prattle, but even she could not long maintain chatter about the ominous-looking clouds.

However, nearing the end of the drive – which in truth was not very long – she looked back to see that the silence had taken on a different tone. Jaq was now sitting up and kissing Perry rather thoroughly.

Elinor cleared her throat loudly. She was extremely glad to see Jaq was getting better, but his quick recovery might raise an eyebrow – as might his current activity.

The two men reluctantly let go of each other and Jaq winked at Elinor. "Taking my medicine, Lady Beresford."

"You seem *at death's door*, my poor boy," said Elinor. She widened her eyes meaningfully and cocked her head towards Hedley.

Jaq nodded and lay back down, settling his head comfortably in Perry's lap. He raised a hand artistically to his brow and rolled his eyes back in his head. Elinor sighed. At least he was more himself again.

When the cart stopped in front of the Seigneurie, Perry made a show of helping Jaq out. Beresford and Elinor hovered anxiously, but she could see that Jaq was standing with more ease and only leaning on Perry because he rather liked that arrangement.

Hedley, standing back, also watched Jaq closely.

Elinor stepped forward and muttered in Jaq's ear. "*At death's door*, for goodness' sake."

Jaq clutched at Perry and groaned. Beresford, his lips a grim line, stepped forward to take Jaq's other arm. Thus disposed, they proceeded to the front door, Jaq limping ostentatiously and moaning.

The door opened and Mrs Sidgemoor came out. She halted when she saw the tableau, a hand to her mouth, perhaps because Jaq's naked thigh was visible beneath Elinor's cloak. "Oh Lord," she exclaimed. "What has happened here?"

Hedley answered. "The young fellow was injured while swimming by the south-eastern cliffs. We found him on the rocks by Triton's Wall, near La Coupee."

Mrs Sidgemoor let out an exclamation of horror and rushed back into the house. A minute later, Lady Orlend appeared. Her eyes narrowed, she examined Jaq. "Who are you, and why were you swimming in such a dangerous place?"

Jaq took one look at her austere features and promptly fainted. He did it in a very lovely fashion, swooning delicately on the spot, his long lashes against his pale cheeks. He also managed to collapse into Perry's arms.

Perry supported Jaq's weight and tried to retain his stoic facade, but Elinor could see that he was worried. Beresford, on the other hand, looked irate, and Lady Orlend raised her eyebrows.

Elinor took charge. "Mr Delquon is a member of Lord Beresford's crew. He needs to lie down. Lady Orlend, may we carry him into my brother's room, so that we can tend to him there?"

"Of course," said Lady Orlend. "What a singularly beautiful young man."

Jaq's head rolled a little more, so that his black hair fell across a muscled shoulder. Elinor frowned; Jaq was already vain enough without Lady Orlend admiring him.

Beresford also looked unimpressed. He heaved Jaq's legs up and, together with Perry, bodily carried him upstairs.

Lady Orlend gestured to Elinor. "Mrs Sidgemoor says you have no maid, so one of mine will serve you while you are here," she said. "If you need her to help tend to the young man I am sure she will be happy to assist you."

She took Elinor inside and introduced her to a competent-looking young woman named Dinah, with dark skin and curly black hair. Her white cap and maid's apron were neat, her gaze businesslike. Elinor wondered if she would be open to gossiping with visitors and graciously accepted her service.

She made haste to assure them both that Mr Avely would look after Jaq. It would not do to have curious servants around to see Jaq's condition restored within the hour. She left Dinah to sort through her own trunk and hurried to Perry's room.

Jaq was sitting up cheerfully in bed, now clothed in one of Perry's shirts. Perry sat by his bedside and Beresford stood by the window.

Elinor sighed with relief. "You gave us quite a scare, you wretch. Thank goodness you seem all right now."

"Yes," agreed Jaq, "Yet my wounds require me to rest here, I think." He patted the blankets. "It is much more comfortable than ship's quarters."

Perry was still anxiously inspecting Jaq. "It is comfortable only if you can ignore the scraping noises at night."

"You will have to stay at least a night, to allay suspicion," said Beresford. "Meanwhile, tell us more about what you found."

Jaq shrugged. "A tunnel into the cliffs on the far side of the island, about a quarter of the way up. When I first saw it, the ledge at the entry was just under the waterline, so I thought it best to enter in human form. I was so intrigued that I forgot to take account of the tide coming in. It rose rapidly, and made the tunnel very dangerous. I retreated, but not before sustaining an injury."

"How long was the tunnel?" asked Elinor. "How far in did you go?"

"It was dark and narrow," said Jaq. "I went in at least twenty yards, but I could not see in the gloom. The water picked up quite a speed as it was forced along the tunnel, like a horizontal water-fall. I think the tunnel must angle downwards. I couldn't be sure, or I would have continued."

Elinor clasped her hands together. "There might be a cave in there! I sensed something too."

"You did?" asked Perry. "When was this?"

"When we were at the top of the cliffs. I was Discerning for the vampiri and I felt a faint pull to the south." She did not mention that it might have been the possibility of soufflés that had drawn her.

However, Beresford also had his doubts. He spoke from by the window. "It might not be the vampiri."

"It's not soufflés," said Elinor defensively.

Beresford raised an eyebrow. "I never said anything about soufflés. But didn't you say something about gold?"

"Oh, that's right!" she exclaimed. "It could be the pirate gold! Could the tunnel lead to a pirate's cave, Jaq?"

Jaq looked thoughtful. "It is set into the cliff and accessible to humans at low tide. It is possible, though dangerous."

"Whether it is gold or vampiri," said Beresford, "we must proceed with caution, as Jaq has demonstrated."

At that moment they heard a soft knock at the door, followed by the new maid's voice. "Can I fetch anything for you, Lady Beresford?"

Jaq wriggled down in the blankets. "Some fish soup would be good."

Elinor frowned at him, but asked Dinah if she could fetch any broth for the invalid.

When the maid's footsteps had retreated, Elinor spoke in a lower tone. "We shall reconvene tonight. And we must make a plan!"

13

IN WHICH COGNAC AIDS DISCLOSURES

*L*ater that evening, Beresford was in the dining room having a drink with Chester Orlend. The ladies had retired to the drawing room and Perry was upstairs with Jaq. The official story was that Perry was tending to Jaq's injuries, but in fact he was probably tending to something else. Possibly Jaq's ego, or his lips.

Beresford sighed. He could easily have been alone with Elinor in their bedroom now. No one would blink twice at a husband and wife retiring together. It was only his overly refined sense of honour that prevented him from taking advantage of the situation.

Frowning, he turned the glass in his hand, watching the candlelight refract through the cognac and make it glow golden red. In one sense it was true; what did propriety matter if they were to be married within a month? Yet Beresford did not want to deny Elinor a proper wedding night, in the full sanctity of marriage. And what if he were to die, in some awful accident of fate, before then? Heaven forbid that Elinor be left unmarried and with child.

Chester sat down opposite him, nursing his own drink. The cognac was so good that Beresford suspected it came from a similar source to his own stash back home: smuggled in from France. It would be an easier task here, in Sark, to receive such goods from the northern coast.

Beresford realised he had been silent for a while, brooding about his wedding night. Yet Chester too was quiet. A shy young man, perhaps, or worried about something. His angular features, so like his mother's, were set in thoughtful lines.

Chester looked up as if he could sense Beresford's examination. He flushed a little and laughed. "I apologise for my abstraction, my lord. I was regretting again that I cannot be out fighting with my brothers. Instead, I am tied to my mother's apron strings."

Beresford smiled in sympathy. "You need not be Gifted to fight," he pointed out. "Could you not sign up in another capacity?"

"You need not tell me!" Chester took a gulp of his cognac. "I wish I could. Mother is convinced that she requires a masculine presence on the island."

"Yet she has all her tenants to protect Sark," observed Beresford. "What about the tenants themselves – does she need protection from them? I gather there has been trouble."

Chester shifted awkwardly in his seat. "A little. We have a feudal system here which is quite unique, so there was bound to be some sympathy with the Revolutionary ideas in France. Mother soon put a stop to all that."

"How did she accomplish that?"

"Oh, she built a school." Chester took another swig. "To demonstrate that noblesse oblige is a good thing."

Beresford raised an eyebrow. "It worked?"

Chester turned his glass in his hands. "With many. And Mother was quick to follow King George's decree about the vampiri. Lilian is usually kept out of sight and out of mind. Mother is the only one who is even allowed a vampiri companion." Chester looked up and met Beresford's eyes squarely.

"Given that her Gift is so weak, you understand. My brothers, who are stronger, are not permitted vampiri assistance while here unless they are serving the Crown."

Beresford reflected that this was an interesting approach to the problem of vampiri relations. It also meant that Lady Orlend, as the only Musor with a vampiri, had an advantage over other Musors, even if her Gift was weak. He wondered what she would do if she was suddenly presented with a whole roost.

He swirled his drink thoughtfully. "Were there many vampiri on the island before the war? I imagine there might be a few caves or trees to house them."

"Oh no, just Thomas Durl," said Chester. "He has been here for decades, but he keeps to himself. Mother doesn't concern herself with him."

"He likes his own company?"

"Yes: he says he doesn't need a Musor."

"So you've spoken to this Durl?"

Chester's face closed. "Once or twice, when I was younger. He is polite enough for all his separatist ways." Beresford wondered if this had been when Chester still nurtured a hope that he would develop a Gift like his brothers, and had sought a vampiri to assist him.

"I can see why Lady Orlend wants support," said Beresford. "Sark is a bastion of English territory close to France. You mustn't let the French get hold of it."

"Of course not," said Chester. "No chance of that."

Beresford saw that the boy was staring fixedly into his cognac. He took an appreciative sip. "The French are good at liquor; at least we can say that about them. Do you keep trade going for such things?"

"Oh, I don't know about that," said Chester, embarrassed. Beresford, feeling weary, did not bother to explain that the same arrangement held sway in Devon, England.

When he thought enough time had passed, he made his

excuses and went upstairs. He pushed the door open to Perry's room.

There he was greeted with a cosy scene. Perry was sitting at the foot of his own bed while Jaq lay in state, fully recovered and devouring a piece of trifle someone had smuggled up for him. Jaq was artistically bandaged, a white cloth wrapped around his head and another around his shoulder. He looked the part of a wounded hero, not a foolish selkie who had tried to swim down a horizontal waterfall.

Aldreda was sitting on the windowsill with the window open slightly, no doubt in preparation for Pags. Elinor was sitting beside her, but stood up and went to Beresford, leaning in to kiss him on the cheek.

Beresford breathed in her soft scent and resisted the urge to pull her into his arms. This marriage charade was hell. It would be hell anyway, but it was made damn near impossible by seeing a ring on Elinor's finger and her lying in their bed. Maybe he could sleep in Perry's room tonight, with Jaq, though the new maid might think it odd in the morning.

Elinor took a step back, her brow furrowed. "I've been trying to Discern where Chaboot's body has been placed, but I'm afraid I have no answer. I don't know if that is because I can't Discern him, or because he has been buried beyond the reach of my divination."

Perry grimaced. "I swear I heard someone digging a grave last night."

"Maybe they were burying the flute," said Jaq, around a mouthful of trifle. "Elinor told us that it is missing."

By the window, Aldreda shook her head disapprovingly. "Such a treasure – an irreplaceable antique – and you've lost it!"

Elinor rubbed her forehead. "I might be able to find it again. Perry has just hidden my gold chain in the room, but I haven't managed to Discern it yet," she explained to Beresford. She sighed. "I think I am becoming confused between trying to divine the roost, the queen, Chaboot, the gold, the flute, and soufflés. It is all too much!"

Aldreda folded her hands in her lap. "You had better focus on one location Discernment from now on. I suggest that the roost is our priority."

"Not soufflés," put in Perry.

"What of the pirate gold?" wailed Elinor, pacing back and forth. "And the flute? Shall we have to whistle instead to wake the queen? I warn you now, I cannot whistle, and neither can Perry!"

"Can't you?" asked Jaq, with interest.

"Like fish, both of us," said Perry cheerfully. "I don't think the queen will appreciate it."

"I like fish," said Jaq.

Beresford saw Elinor's troubled face. "Is the Viveroust flute the only way to wake the vampiri, Aldreda?" he asked.

Aldreda considered. "They will be deep in roost hibernation, which is different to the sleep of a single vampiri. We *could* try to rouse them by more prosaic means – shouting or shaking or, heaven forfend, Elinor's whistling – but the Viveroust would wake the queen first, as is proper. Safer, too, to ensure the cohesion of the roost, as the queen then plays the flute to wake her subjects." She paused. "We could risk it, of course. But I don't know the full power of the Viveroust or how it works."

"We may not have a choice," said Beresford dryly. "Jaq, can you whistle?"

Jaq grinned. "Like one of those English tea kettles."

Aldreda was not impressed. "A selkie should not be the one to wake the queen." She turned to the open window. "Here come Pags and Durl, climbing up the vines."

"Fully dressed?" asked Elinor. "Thank goodness." She sat down on the bed with a thunk.

Pags' head popped over the sill. "Lady Beresford, I am not a complete barbarian."

Aldreda sniffed. "Are you not?"

Pags ignored her. "Good God, what happened to Jaq?"

Jaq touched a hand to his ornate bandaging with a grin. "Don't worry, this is all for show. Earlier today, however, my investigation into a cliff tunnel was trickier than expected."

Pags raised his brows. "I see." Then he leapt up to the sill, gave an all-encompassing bow and flung out an arm. "I have company. May I introduce Mr Thomas Durl, a local vampiri?"

Beresford watched with interest. This must be the vampiri whom Chester had mentioned: the one who lived in the woods.

A head of brown curly hair poked over the sill, and the vampiri looked around rather apprehensively. His unruly hair was not tied back, but as he pulled himself up Beresford was relieved to see that the allegedly wild vampiri was suitably clad in breeches, shirt and coat, with a neatly trimmed beard. A thin rope hung from his belt, the only sign that this vampiri lived by his own resources. Beresford wondered if he became lonely, despite Chester's assurances that Durl liked his own company.

Durl gave a stiff bow and Pags grinned as if he had produced the other vampiri out of a hat. Then Durl smiled tentatively at Aldreda, she smiled warmly back, and Beresford saw that Pags' satisfaction dimmed a little.

Elinor, always civilised, stood and curtsied in response. "Ah, another Sarkee vampiri! We are very happy to make your acquaintance. We wish to ask you a few questions."

Durl straightened his shoulders uneasily. "Yes, my lady. I am sorry to hear of your Lieutenant's death; Deponzel told me that you found him in the attic. I only wish I had been in the habit of visiting that part of the house, as I might have found him in time. He was a good vampiri."

His sincerity seemed real, but Beresford saw Elinor tilt her head to the left. She was using her Truth Discernment to test his words.

Elinor sat down on the bed and regarded Durl, wide-eyed. "You knew Lieutenant Chaboot?"

"I wouldn't say I knew him well," Durl replied, shifting on the windowsill. He shot Aldreda a sideways glance. "We shared wine together. I thought he just made a passing visit, though it was odd he did not say goodbye."

Elinor nodded. "Did Chaboot say anything of his reason for being here?"

Durl chewed on his lip. "He was looking for a roost, my lady – as I suspect you are. He asked everyone about it, just as you have asked, though with less discretion."

"Everyone?" Elinor leaned forward. Beresford wondered that a vampiri trained for the Vilitia would not employ more circumspection in his enquiries.

"Ay. He asked the Seigneuresse, the servants, Mr Orlend – even the tenants, though Lady Orlend forbade it."

Elinor's head tilted so far that her ear almost touched her shoulder. "Why did she forbid it?"

"The laws, my lady," said Durl. "They say we are not to show ourselves." His gaze dropped, but not before Beresford had seen the flash of disapproval. "Though the Orlends are happy to have Miss Reed sewing in the dining room like a slave."

"Oh?" said Elinor. "Do you disapprove of the Orlends' treatment of Miss Reed?"

"I do indeed," said Durl, and everyone, not just Elinor, could hear the righteous anger in his words. "Miss Reed is not meant to be kept as a servant." He cleared his throat. "None of us are."

Elinor nodded. "Is that why you abjure human companionship? Fear of slavery?"

"All vampiri should be free," said Durl quietly.

"I quite agree—" Elinor began.

"I am not sure that you do agree," Pags interjected, pacing on the windowsill. "Durl means that vampiri should be free of *any* human bond. Don't you, my good fellow?"

Durl shuffled his feet. "Er, well…"

Pags grinned. "You have Rofanite sympathies, I suspect."

Durl looked up, taken aback. Then he dropped his gaze again and shrugged, looking amused.

Elinor frowned. "What are Rofanite sympathies?"

"Rofan was a vampiri who made a philosophy of wildness," said Pags. "Even before the Revolution he set up his own sect, preaching vampiri independence. Are you a convert, Durl?"

Durl blinked. "Oh no, not really. I just think that vampiri ought to have freedom to choose. And if we bond with a Musor, we should be treated as equals."

Aldreda sighed. "Quite, but we are becoming distracted by Pags' fixation on the appeal of the wild. The important question is where we might find the missing queen."

Durl nodded. "I shall do my best to assist you, Miss Zooth."

Pags lips pursed. "Assist all of us, you mean."

Durl did not reply.

Elinor's hand crept to her heart, where her lapis lazuli stone lay hidden within her bodice. "Did Lieutenant Chaboot discover anything of interest when he questioned everyone?" she asked.

Durl seemed to guess that he was under interrogation, and shifted nervously again. "I was not in his confidence, my lady."

Elinor raised her eyebrows.

Pags coughed in a significant manner. "You can tell us, my friend."

Durl cast him a look, then faced Elinor again. "He did pay particular attention to La Moinerie, I know."

Jaq sat up with interest, having polished off his trifle. "What is La Moinerie? A monastery? Not in the south, by any chance?"

"No," said Durl. "It is a very old monastery, in ruins now, built by Breton monks hundreds of years ago. The Seigneurie was built on some of the ruins, but more lie west of the house."

Elinor leaned forward eagerly. "Durl, do you know why the lieutenant was interested in La Moinerie?" Beresford saw that her eyes were narrowed and her hand was still clasped to her bosom.

"No, my lady," said Durl.

Elinor glanced meaningfully at Beresford. Her implication was clear: Durl was either lying, or uncertain of the words he spoke. Beresford took a step closer. "You cannot guess?"

"No," said Durl, and pressed his lips together.

"Hm," said Pags. He sat down on the windowsill and swung his legs in a rather unseemly fashion. "It is in ruins, you say? What is it used for now?"

Durl gave a small shrug. "Human matters do not concern me. I know there is a dam there, constructed by the monks, and a water mill. I know the Orlend boys used to play there, as it is so close to this house."

Jaq stroked his chin with interest. "I wonder if the boys found anything there." Beresford reflected that he could ask Chester about it over their next brandy.

"Well," said Durl, reluctantly. "I did hear that a boulder moved and no one could say who had done it or how. Chaboot was curious about it, too."

"A boulder moved by itself?" asked Jaq.

Durl shrugged as if to say that such was the way of large rocks on Sark.

Elinor was staring intently at Durl. Beresford joined her, placing a hand on her shoulder. "We can investigate La Moinerie and this boulder tomorrow. Now, I think we should retire for the night. Thank you for your assistance, Mr Durl."

Elinor looked mutinous but took the hint. Graciously, she bid Durl goodnight and Pags held the window open for him to depart. Durl bowed and made his exit, disappearing over the sill. Pags followed, winking at the remaining company and closing the window tightly after him.

It was several moments before anyone spoke. "Was Durl lying?" asked Aldreda.

"I'm not sure," mused Elinor, standing up and going to look out of the window. "Something wasn't quite right about his talk of the monastery and the boulder. I suspect he knows more than he is saying." She turned to the group. "I am not certain whether we should investigate it tomorrow or go to the south where I felt something, not poke around in silly old ruins. If anyone asks what we are doing, we can claim Perry believes there is a mineral deposit on the headland."

Beresford frowned, but before he could speak, Jaq broke in from his position of honour on the bed. "We should go back to the entrance in the cliffs that I found. *That* is the most intriguing discovery. As soon as the tide goes down, I can investigate again more safely."

Perry, perched on the end of the bed, shook his head. "You're not going anywhere near that place again. I, however, can pop in and out in a trice. You said there was a ledge, didn't you? I can Travel to it with ease."

Aldreda patted her hair. "I can fly down there, and what is more, I can do it right now. I can find the roost while you sleep."

Beresford cleared his throat. "I am glad to see that you are all eager to help. However, the southern cliffs are too dangerous tonight, and tomorrow Jaq must stay in bed to keep up a pretence of injury. I say we leave the cliffs for now and start with the boulder tomorrow. After all, Chaboot was asking questions about it and ended up dead. It behoves us to look into it."

Elinor nodded reluctantly. "I suppose so." She brightened. "I know! We can ask Lady Orlend to help us move the boulder, since she has a small Gift in Impacting. We can tell her that Perry senses minerals behind it. If she is reluctant, it might indicate that she had something to do with moving it in the first place."

Perry looked apprehensive, but after a moment he nodded. "Very well. I can make a show of finding something at La Moinerie tomorrow, if you like."

"Are we agreed?" asked Beresford.

Jaq settled his shoulders into the pillows. "I must spend all day in bed? Certainly, my lord."

Briefly, Beresford imagined what it would be like when he could spend all day in bed with Elinor. Then he shook the thought off. "There is one more thing," he said. "Considering the matter of the missing flute, I think we should announce its absence; it will look more suspicious if we say nothing. We can use the opportunity to gauge people's reactions. We need not say anything about the vampiri, simply that it is Aldreda's much-treasured instrument."

Aldreda sighed. "Flute playing is now to be one of my talents, I suppose?"

Beresford nodded. "Elinor was carrying it for you during the sea voyage, and now you are deeply chagrined at its loss."

"I *am* deeply chagrined at its loss," said Aldreda crossly.

Elinor looked despondent. Beresford wished he could gather her up in his arms and kiss away the downturn in her lips. He sighed. "I am tired now. I shall go to bed."

Aldreda coughed delicately. "You go ahead; we shall follow later."

Jaq and Perry looked amused, so Beresford frowned at them as he left. "No funny business, you two. And no gallivanting off to the cliffs together. Jaq must stay in bed."

"Certainly," said Jaq with alacrity. He winked at Perry, who blushed.

Beresford returned glumly to the frilly bedroom and lay down upon the cold floor. He was still awake when the ladies slipped in, and he listened as Elinor undressed and climbed into bed. From under his eyelashes he could see Aldreda take up her post as a bat on the bed hangings.

He sighed to himself, cursing his own good name.

14

IN WHICH UNCOUTH HABITS ARE USEFUL

*A*ldreda had no intention of playing duenna all night. She waited an hour or so, by which time Beresford's chest was rising in gentle, even intervals, and Elinor had long fallen asleep. Seeing that Beresford's form had at last relaxed, Aldreda swooped from the lacy canopy and wriggled her way through the window.

The night was blustery. It was squaring up to a storm, the trees waving wildly in the wind and the air damp with impending rain. She must hurry, though she would not mind if she were soaked. It was only that a storm gale might make the cliff more treacherous to navigate.

It was hard work flying against the wind. However, Aldreda was unsurprised when Pags appeared next to her. He must have suspected she would make her own investigations tonight. Despite her irritation with him lately, she was glad of his company, his silent form joining her battle against the headwind. They flew low along the road, trying to keep beneath the worst of it, and scooted along the isthmus that led to Little Sark.

What she had not expected was that Durl would follow them too. When she finally landed on a gorse bush on the southern tip of the island, his brown form swung into another bush nearby.

He had a cloak hanging around his neck, along with a rope. Upside-down, he hooked both with his claws to keep them from falling around his ears, so he looked like a sack hanging from a branch. Perhaps he was trying to be more civilised for her sake.

Aldreda hated gorse: it was so prickly and difficult to perch on. Yet Durl seemed unconcerned by it, as indeed did Pags. She guessed that came from living in the wild for so long. Or perhaps that was why Durl had brought a cloak, not because he had hoped to protect his modesty in the event of seeing her again.

Aldreda shrugged the thought away. It was more likely that Pags and Durl were becoming best friends, with their equal tendencies to Rofanism, or whatever Pags had called it.

They all kept their bat forms and eyed each other. Pags gave an expressive shrug. Perhaps he had invited Durl along for the adventure, or at least did not mind his presence. Aldreda decided she would have to ignore him too.

She let go of the prickly gorse and lifted into the air again, preparing to sweep over the side of the cliff and search for the passageway Jaq had described. The strong wind buffeted her, tossing her up like a kite. She clenched her jaw and fought her way back down. She would have to stay low and close to the rocks. It would be dangerous, but less embarrassing than being wafted around like a butterfly.

The sharp, briny scent of the sea assailed her nostrils as she edged over the cliff and began searching. The tide was at its midpoint, and the vortex of water that Jaq had described might well have subsided. Waves splashed against the rocks, the water gleaming and lurching below. Even if the entrance was still covered, there could be another way in, less obvious to a human or selkie eye – especially if the entrance led to the hiding place of a vampiri roost.

Aldreda searched, hovering close to the ground as she combed the cliff face. Pags, she saw, was following her example, but he had started from the bottom, where the waves met the rocks. Of course he *would* choose the most challenging – or exciting – task. Durl, not knowing what they were looking for, chose a ledge to hang from and watched curiously, wrapped up in his cloak.

After a while, a strange smell wafted past her. It was familiar but it took her a moment to recognise it, being so out of place on the cliff.

Blood. The smell was rich and tangy on the wind. Then she remembered that it must be Jaq's blood, spilled on the cliffs as he climbed up from the tunnel. It had the fragrance of the sea in it, and of selkie.

Aldreda wrinkled her nose, but the scent would provide a clue as to where Jaq had been exploring, and therefore where the entrance lay. The wind threw the smell towards her, and soon she navigated to where it originated.

A dark stain marked the grey rocks. Waves hurled themselves against the cliff below, their spray wetting Aldreda's wings. Narrowing her eyes against the wind, she saw that something was clinging to the blood.

Or someone.

It was a small bat. The black figure huddled into the rock, presumably attracted to the smell of blood even though it was selkie blood. Aldreda hovered closer, cautious yet concerned. What bat would be so hungry as to want to feed from Jaq?

The figure did not respond to her low whistle, so she landed and inched closer. It was too small to be a grown vampiri. A child, then, lost and hungry. Her heart contracting, Aldreda reached over a wing and touched the figure gently, praying this wasn't another corpse for her to discover.

The bat stirred. The head came up, eyes widening in shock. Aldreda murmured quietly in bat frequency, aiming to soothe.

Behind her she sensed Pags landing, then Durl. Between them they could help the little one, who was obviously starving and very weak.

Aldreda transformed, her naked human form shivering in the icy wind. She was well aware that she had two males watching her, but now was no time for maidenly reserve. "A sheep," she said, over her shoulder. "We need a sheep."

Pags nodded. "There are some nearby."

Durl watched, eyes narrowed, in his human form, his arms crossed over his chest. With gentle fingers, Aldreda prised the little bat off the rock and heaved him into her arms.

Durl stepped forward and laid down his rope, his cloak billowing around him. "I can carry him on my back as I fly."

Aldreda nodded, glad he had offered, for she was not certain the little bat would follow them easily.

Durl transformed and lay upon the rock. Gratefully, she placed her burden on his cloaked, broad back.

Durl lifted into the air, tenderly carrying the child, his cloak fluttering around them both. Pags flew at his side, ready to catch the boy if it came to it. Aldreda became a bat again and followed.

She was relieved to leave that bloodied cliff-face behind. The wind still blew viciously, but Durl flew to a field with a copse, the sturdy tree trunks providing a modicum of shelter. More to the point, it also sheltered a flock of sheep, huddled together under the branches.

Durl landed carefully on the back of a sheep and slid the child off his shoulders. Aldreda landed too, after transforming again. The wool was soft and warm under her bare skin. The sheep twitched but did not otherwise protest.

Aldreda inched towards the child and put an arm around the little wings. It was a boy, she could see now, less than half grown. "You must feed," she said gently. "You can drink from this sheep."

She had not fed from ruminants very often. She turned to look for Pags, but it was Durl who transformed again. He took off his cloak and placed it over the little bat. Aldreda was glad, though it meant Durl's large masculine form was in full view, rather close to her.

He smiled at her. "I'll look after him now, Miss Zooth."

"Thank you, that is very kind." She hastily slid off the woollen back, smelling the rich scent of sheep dung as she did so.

Durl pulled the smaller vampiri up to the sheep's ear and showed him how to grasp it. The little bat followed Durl's instructions and was soon drinking deeply. Aldreda sighed with relief. At least these wild bats were good for something.

She turned away with a blush from the sight of Durl's well-shaped derriere and saw that Pags was watching her with narrowed eyes. Durl was murmuring something soothing as the boy clung to the sheep, so she stepped away to give them more privacy.

Pags became human, somersaulting to a stop in front of Aldreda. He folded his arms over his hairy chest. "Your blushes are unexpected, my dear."

"I was not blushing!"Aldreda said. Irksomely, she felt her face heat up. "You know I don't approve of these barbaric practices."

"Is it the savage feeding or the lack of clothes on a fine specimen that is putting a bloom in your cheeks?"

"Pardon me!"

Pags winked. "You know I'm always happy to oblige with the latter."

Aldreda spluttered. "You are shameless!"

"Merely without civilising influence," replied Pags. "As you are always so quick to point out."

Aldreda glanced back at the sheep. "That is a poor substitute for Musor blood," she snapped.

Pags raised an eyebrow. "It is necessary in this case. Do you think the child was drawn to the cliff by the smell?"

"It seems so. He looks malnourished." Aldreda bit her lip. "I hope he has not been mistreated."

They waited in silence until the boy had taken his fill. High above them, clouds raced across the sky and Aldreda felt the first specks of rain on her bare skin. She called up to Durl, "Please ask him to transform, if he can. We must question him."

Durl relayed the request, and the little bat looked down at them with huge eyes. Durl kept talking quietly. After a few minutes, the bat let go of the sheep. In a blink, a small, pale body tumbled onto the ground, tangled in Durl's cloak.

A scared face looked up, dirty and childish. His eyes were too large for the rest of his features and his brown hair hung lank around his shoulders. He wiped the blood from his mouth.

Aldreda cleared her throat. "What is your name, little one?" She spoke in French, assuming that was his language.

After a long pause, the boy said, "Raddle, Mademoiselle."

Pags spoke, also in French. "Good evening, Raddle. I am Pags and this is Miss Zooth and Mr Durl. Where do you hie from?"

"Hie from?" Raddle blinked.

"Where do you live?" asked Aldreda patiently. "Before you found the food on the cliffs, where were you?"

Raddle frowned, as if trying to recall. "I was sleeping. Then I was hungry. So I went looking for something to drink." His French was Parisian, with no hint of the Sark dialect. Perhaps he was a refugee from the mainland. His little arms were skinny and he shivered in the bitter wind. Aldreda felt a rush of disapproval towards whoever had left the child so needy.

"Where? Were you sleeping somewhere on the island?" If so, she was willing to bet it was with Lady Orlend's knowledge.

His answer, however, was a surprise.

"With the roost," said the boy. "I was sleeping with the roost."

Aldreda stared at him and her heart beat faster. Could it be? Little wonder the boy looked so skinny and underfed, if he had been in hibernation for several years. And he spoke with a Parisian accent. If he had been sleeping with he roost, it would explain why he was so desperately hungry and a little groggy.

She exchanged a glance with Pags, who snapped his mouth closed. Durl looked from one to the other, frowning.

Pags took a step forward. "Where is the roost?"

The boy shrank away and said nothing.

Aldreda tried a softer tone. "Where is your roost, young man? Could you take us there? We are looking for one, and yours might be the roost we seek."

Raddle blinked rapidly, pulling the cloak closer around him. "I don't know where it is."

Pags was struggling to keep his tone calm. "What do you mean, you don't know where it is? You just flew from it!"

"I can't remember," said the boy nervously. "I was hungry and half asleep. I just followed the smell of blood."

"How far did you fly?" demanded Pags.

The boy chewed on his lower lip. "I don't know. A long time? It seemed long, but I was hungry."

Aldreda shook her head in despair. It was possible the boy had flown quite a distance before smelling the blood. He could have come from anywhere. Yet if the blood had woken him, the roost might not be too far from the cliffs. Her pulse quickened.

Durl put a protective arm around Raddle's thin shoulders. "Perhaps, once you are properly awake, you can look around the island," he said. "You might recognise something."

"Good idea," said Pags. "Give him an hour."

Aldreda could understand his impatience, but she shook her head. "Not in this weather, with a storm blowing. We need shelter."

Pags glared at the hurrying clouds. "Where should we take him now?"

Aldreda considered. Perry was a Musor without a vampiri companion, though she didn't want to mention that in front of Durl as *she* was meant to be Perry's companion. "Perhaps Perry will not mind feeding him."

Durl looked taken aback at her willingness to share her bonded Musor. "That won't be necessary, Miss Zooth. The boy will do well enough with sheep for now. I can take him to Lilian. She ought to look after him."

Aldreda wondered why Lilian should be the one to look after him. Perhaps Durl's Rofanite sympathies made him reluctant for Raddle to feed from Perry. But Lilian could indeed share her quarters in the safety of the cellar. Would she be happy to receive a bedraggled little boy into her rooms, though? It was worth a try. They did not want to lose the little bat on the cliffs again.

She nodded. "Very well. Raddle, would you like to meet a nice lady vampiri called Miss Reed?"

Raddle glanced at Durl and nodded slowly.

"Tomorrow, at dusk, the tide might be low again, and we can return," said Aldreda. "Don't you want to find your roost again? We can help you."

Raddle nodded again, but uncertainly.

Durl patted his shoulder. "Come with me. I shall take you to Miss Reed, who will look after you."

Aldreda smiled. "Thank you, Durl."

Durl smiled back at Aldreda, tucking a brown curl behind his ear. Then he took the cloak from Raddle, hunched into his bat form and rose into the air. Raddle hastened to follow suit and the pair flew off into the restless wind, small black figures buffeted in the night.

Pags folded his arms as he watched them leave. "I don't trust that fellow."

"Who, Raddle?" asked Aldreda.

"No, Durl."

Aldreda raised her eyebrows.

"I don't think he is telling us everything he knows," grumbled Pags. "He has been on this island a long time; he was bound to see the roost if they landed here. They would have had to feed before hibernating. It's pretty difficult to miss a whole cloud of bats."

Aldreda bit her lip. "That is true. Yet Durl has been helpful."

She frowned at Pags. "And you seem to like his company, for all that you say."

Pags shrugged. "I'm keeping an eye on him."

Above them, huge dark clouds gathered. The wind tossed Aldreda's curls. "Or you like being out in the wild with him."

"That too," admitted Pags. "The night sky is refreshing. I'd rather be out here than in that attic."

Aldreda agreed, though she wouldn't admit it. "Are you sleeping in the woods?"

Pags nodded. "Close to the stars."

"Close to your dinner, you mean."

Pags winked at her. "Is it not romantic to dine in the moonlight, Miss Zooth? I'd be happy to share a sheep with you one evening."

Aldreda grimaced. He was being deliberately provoking – or worse, returning gladly to savagery. There was an amused glint in his eye, however, and she decided not to rise to the bait. She was also careful not to look at his nether regions, bare as they were. He seemed to have no such compunction, and traced his eyes down her shivering form. "You are cold," he observed. "I must not keep you dallying here, much as I enjoy our raillery. Goodness knows what Miss Avely and his lordship are doing without your eagle eye upon them."

Aldreda started. It was true: she was neglecting her duties. Pags grinned at her obvious flash of guilt.

She lifted her nose into the air. "Yes, I must go." She paused, looking at the branches waving wildly above in the gale. "You should find shelter too; don't be swept up in this storm."

Pags bowed, but did not move as she transformed and rose into the gusty air.

The strong wind blew Aldreda home. As she flew, she told herself that Pags would manage perfectly well; indeed, he would probably enjoy the unfettered storm. She hoped Elinor would find the roost quickly on the morrow – or perhaps she, Aldreda, could accomplish that task.

Rain was falling properly by the time she returned to Elinor's window. Aldreda closed the panes against the cold and turned, shaking out her wings. That was when she saw Elinor fast asleep on the bed – in Beresford's arms.

He was awake, and watching Aldreda.

She became human in a flash and snatched at a curtain to protect her modesty, opening her mouth to give him a scolding. Then she saw he was fully dressed and his body was above the blankets, while Elinor was tucked into bed, her golden head resting on his broad chest. Beresford's chestnut hair was somewhat tousled, but his eyes were wide open and apologetic. "Forgive me, Miss Zooth. She threatened to sleep on the floor. I had no choice."

Aldreda shut her mouth with a snap. She could well believe that Elinor had lain down beside Beresford and attempted to seduce him. "My apologies," she muttered, pulling the curtain closer around herself. "I shouldn't have left you alone and subject to her advances."

Beresford let out a faint huff of a laugh. "I can look after myself – though I admit she is making it damn difficult." Carefully, he extricated his arm from underneath Elinor and laid her tenderly back on the pillows. Her face was soft and open, and he heaved a sigh. "I assume you went to look at the cliffs. Did you find anything?"

Aldreda nodded. "A young vampiri."

15
IN WHICH A BOULDER IS
MYSTERIOUS

*E*linor woke feeling beautifully rested. It took her a moment to realise that Beresford was no longer in her bed, with that ridiculous blanket as a barrier between them, but back on the hard floor, his hand under his cheek and his brown hair falling over his eyes.

She sighed fondly at his sleeping form and squinted up at the bed hangings. Aldreda hung there, black and sharp against the pale rose. Then the bat blinked blearily and transformed into her human form, landing with a thud on Elinor's pillow.

"Good morning," said Elinor cheerfully, though quietly. "You went out last night, did you, in that gathering storm?"

Aldreda ignored the question and shook her hair off her face. "You must not make things difficult for Beresford," she said, in a scolding whisper.

Elinor widened her eyes. "I'm sure I don't know what you mean," she murmured. She did: she had cajoled him into her bed and thoroughly enjoyed the snuggling, kisses and low-voiced conversation that had followed. It hadn't quite been the seduction she had hoped for, though. Beresford had been annoyingly strict about blankets, and had started a long conversation about soufflés and ices.

Aldreda tutted. "You should only celebrate your wedding night once you are properly married in the eyes of church and law. He is trying to do the right thing, and you are being troublesome."

Elinor's shoulders sagged. "He doesn't seem to find it difficult to resist me."

Aldreda rolled her eyes as she put on her silk dressing gown. "Go down to breakfast. You have a long day ahead and you must prepare yourself. I found a young member of the missing roost last night."

Elinor gave a tiny squeal, then looked guiltily at Beresford. "Where?" she whispered.

"By the cliffs," said Aldreda, smugly. "Drawn out of hibernation by Jaq's blood. Unfortunately, he could not tell us where he had flown from: he was confused and hungry." She hopped onto Elinor's lap and jerked with her chin to indicate that she was ready to be carried out.

Elinor obliged, slipping a cloak over her shift and tiptoeing out of the bedroom with Aldreda on her shoulder, hoping that no one was about to catch the vampiri *en déshabillé*. "Where is this vampiri now?" she asked, as they headed for the attic.

"With Lilian, I hope: Durl took him there. His name is Raddle. He seems very young."

"How exciting!" exclaimed Elinor, in full voice now that they had reached the attic. She went to check that the windows continued to open, as she still harboured uneasy feelings about leaving Aldreda there. Outside, grey clouds hung low in the sky and the ground was wet from the night's rain. "Our first recovered vampiri – we must be close! Well done, Aldreda!"

"It was nothing," she replied modestly. "If you can, return to Little Sark soon, after you examine La Moinerie today."

Elinor nodded, breathing in the fresh air streaming from the window. "I shall insist upon it. Who knows what we shall accomplish while you sleep!" She carried Aldreda to her basket under the table, draped in Mrs Avely's shawl. "Are you certain that you want to sleep here?"

Aldreda twitched the red tasselled cloth aside and shrugged. "Everyone knows I am here; I can be in no danger."

Elinor frowned, then her expression cleared. "You know what else I shall insist upon? A soufflé. It has been two days and not a soufflé in sight."

"Shocking," agreed Aldreda tiredly, and swept her curtain shawl closed.

~

Once dressed in her primrose gown (with Beresford's eyes still tightly shut), Elinor made her way down to breakfast. Toast, cold meats, and tea awaited – no soufflés – and Elinor seated herself gladly, nodding her thanks to Mr Sidgemoor as he pulled out her chair.

Lady Orlend was at table, with Chester next to her. Perry was still abed, no doubt making the most of Jaq's invalidism. Elinor repressed an envious sigh and turned her attention to the food.

"Ah, this looks like a good English breakfast," she remarked. "Yet dare I hope to try a soufflé one day, as we are so close to France?"

Lady Orlend frowned. "No: we do not serve soufflés here."

Feeling somewhat rebuffed, Elinor sipped her tea and wondered how she could announce their interest in La Moinerie today. "The Chief Mineral Geologist will return to the southern part of the island this afternoon," she announced, thinking it was better to warn everyone in case they shot at Perry again. "Little Sark, is that what you call it? He says that the southern headland gave some promising hints of minerals before his search was interrupted by that terrible accident. He will have to go back to be certain, however."

Lady Orlend put down her toast. "Good, then you can rest and recuperate today."

Elinor nodded, warming her hands on her cup. "Actually, Peregrine wanted to look closer in the interim. Perhaps we could explore La Moinerie, the remains of the old monastery."

Lady Orlend tensed. "La Moinerie? Surely there will be no minerals there."

"Minerals can be anywhere!" said Elinor brightly.

The lines on Lady Orlend's brow deepened. "It will be unfortunate if they are found so close to the Seigneurie. It is a short walk, though; we can arrange a picnic there for lunchtime. I shall be happy to accompany you."

Elinor dabbed at her mouth with her napkin. "How lovely." She was not sure she wanted Lady Orlend in attendance, though, and now they would have to wait until luncheon to go. She cleared her throat. "By the way, there is another, more troubling matter: I seem to have misplaced a little golden flute. It is Miss Zooth's prized instrument and it was in my reticule for safekeeping, yet now it is gone! Have you seen it anywhere?"

As she spoke, she glanced over the assembled company. Sidgemoor looked wooden: the most impassive she had seen him. Perhaps he was finally accomplishing the demeanour of a butler. Chester looked up from his plate and shook his head.

Lady Orlend was also impassive; she simply raised an eyebrow. "How dreadful. I shall tell the servants to keep an eye out for it. Is it very small?"

Elinor held out two fingers indicating the length and realised anew that the flute was very small indeed. It would be cursedly difficult to find. Her heart sank again, but she nodded briskly. "It is made of gold, with an intricate design etched upon it. I do hope it will turn up. Aldreda is distraught at its loss."

Elinor finished her breakfast before Perry or Beresford showed their sleepy heads. Leaving the dining room, she paused in the corridor. She was extremely curious about the little vampiri whom Aldreda had rescued. Perhaps she ought to ascertain that he was indeed safely installed with Lilian.

Checking that no one was watching, Elinor slipped down to the cellar. The old wooden door swung open noiselessly, as before, and she peered inside a dim and cluttered room. She had not looked within when Aldreda had entered, and now her eyes ran over the rows of chests and kegs, and the cupboard by the wall with the candle glowing above it.

She took a few tentative steps, and her eye caught movement in the corner.

"Please," said a small voice in French, "shut the door!"

Elinor realised guiltily that daylight was filtering through the doorway. It was only dim, but to a young bat just out of hibernation it might seem harsh. Quickly, she shut the door behind her, bracing herself for the darkness. Her eyes adjusted to the faint glow of a candle.

"Good morning," she said. "Are you Raddle?"

A small, grubby, naked boy stepped out from behind a keg. "Yes, mademoiselle." His tiny face was thin and white, his eyes wary.

Elinor dipped a curtsy. "How do you do? We are very pleased that you woke up to join us. Should you not be sleeping now?"

The boy gave a solemn bow, seemingly unaware of his nakedness. "I am not tired, mademoiselle. It feels as if I have been asleep for years."

In fact, it *would* have been years: the twelve years the roost had been hibernating.

Elinor nodded. "One can only sleep so much. Are you hungry?" She wondered if she ought to feed him with her own wrist, but hesitated to do so without Aldreda's agreement.

Raddle leaned forward. "Gorged myself on sheep," he confided.

Elinor raised her eyebrows.

"Don't be vulgar, Raddle," reprimanded a soft, feminine tone above them. "Apologise to the lady."

Elinor looked up to see a neat, plain lady vampiri peeking over the roof of the cupboard. She smiled. "That won't be necessary; I have a brother myself. You must be Miss Lilian Reed, companion to the Dame of Sark?"

Lilian nodded, watching Elinor carefully.

Elinor introduced herself as Lady Beresford, then turned to Raddle, for he was far more interesting to her at present. "Where did you have your long sleep, Mr Raddle? Can you recall?"

Raddle's face was wooden. "No, my lady."

"Not at all?" pressed Elinor. "How long did you fly before you reached the cliffs?"

"I can't remember," said Raddle. "It seemed like an age, but I was befuddled at the time and cursed hungry. I'm sorry, my lady," he added. "I wish to find my family, too."

Elinor smiled. "Perhaps tonight we can find them together."

"You would go out in the night, Lady Beresford?" exclaimed Lilian. "Surely that is a task for your brother."

"Oh, not I," Elinor said hastily. "I'm sure Pags and Aldreda will assist you, Mr Raddle, along with my brother, who can Discern. Or we might even find your family during daylight hours. We have plans to investigate those cliffs and the old monastery. Could you smell the sea or the forest from your hiding place?"

Raddle chewed on his lip. "Just blood, my lady."

For some reason, the words sent a chill through Elinor. She tried to shrug it off. Blood was merely sustenance to vampiri; there was no need to be melodramatic. Though it had been Jaq's blood upon the cliffs.

Raddle glanced at Lilian and spoke apologetically. "It was a very faint smell of blood, but it was all I could think of, being so hungry."

Elinor was disappointed but tried not to show it. "Well," she said calmly. "I am disturbing your repose, Miss Reed, as I know these are your sleeping hours." She gave a parting curtsy. "Mr Raddle, please stay with Lilian and do not wander off again. I might even be able to find you a Musor to bond with, so that you have no need for any more sheep."

"Yes, my lady," said Raddle, wide-eyed.

"Good rest to you both," said Elinor. She blew out the candle and was careful to open the door only a fraction as she left.

~

Beresford and Perry finally came down for breakfast, and Elinor left to while away the morning in the walled gardens at the Seigneurie.

The flower beds were awash with colour: white foxgloves, apricot roses, and the purple of dog violets peeping below. The grey stone walls must keep the sea winds out, allowing the plants to flourish. The house had been built over a hundred years ago, but Elinor wondered if the gardens were even older.

She found an old stone bench, mounted it, and stood on tiptoe to peer over the wall. The remaining ruins of the old monastery were close by, partly hidden by old trees. Elinor tried to reach out with a few divinations for both a golden flute and for vampiri, but with no success except for the sense of Lilian below the house and Aldreda in the attic. She stepped down and sat on the bench before anyone could witness her indecorous behaviour. Perhaps she should try to divine the location of Chaboot – but she was meant to limit her quest to the roost, to avoid confusing her Discernments.

Elinor sighed impatiently. She would much rather be exploring Little Sark, with its intriguing call and mysterious tunnel entrance in the cliffs. Surely, if Raddle had been woken by the smell of blood, his sleeping place was near Jaq's accident. Why must she waste time with an old monastery? It was all on the say-so of Durl, who claimed a boulder had moved: a silly story if ever she heard one. Maybe she should have mentioned the boulder at the breakfast table when they announced their intention to explore La Moinerie, to see their hostess' response.

She leaned against the warm stone bench. At least she could enjoy the sunshine and the gardens, out of the wind. The walled stillness might account for why she still felt a faint sense of oppression, as if something weighed upon her, even outside the house. Her worries, perhaps.

Her gaze found the attic window where Aldreda slept. How had Chaboot been trapped there? It did not bode well for their quest, since he had also been searching for the roost. The curtains were shut now against the sun, guarding Aldreda's sleep. Briefly, Elinor wondered where Pags was sleeping; some tree hollow deep in the woods, most likely.

When the company finally assembled on the driveway at lunchtime, Chester Orlend joined them, though he hung back behind his mother as if he hoped no one would notice. Perhaps his mother had requested his company, for he appeared uncomfortable.

Perry also looked nervous: this was the first time he had been required to demonstrate his alleged Discernment to a crowd. He pulled at his cravat, then clasped his hands firmly behind his back. Elinor gave him a reassuring smile, but he avoided her gaze.

They cut through the gardens to the ruins, Hedley accompanying with a large basket for the picnic, and Sidgemoor trailing behind with a blanket. This was not to be a discreet outing, by any means.

La Moinerie lay in shadows cast by large fir trees. The old stone walls were built of granite and covered in moss and lichen, with some lying in what looked like long-standing disarray.

Elinor looked eagerly for signs of a significant boulder. How would they know which one had been moved? Durl had not given them any further clues. If she found one that was free of moss, though, that might indicate it had been shifted recently.

Meandering among the stones, she came to the old mill: a creaking, wooden contraption whose wheels still spun gently in the dappled light. The stream burbled calmly below. An ancient wall of rocks held up a bank. No boulders seemed to be displaced, however, and they were all mossy with age.

In front of the wall were the remains of an old fire, grey ashes scattered in a small stone circle. Elinor wondered how long that had been there and whether it hid the vacant space of a missing boulder. She turned and saw that Hedley had put down the picnic basket. The taciturn farmer was standing with his arms folded in the middle of the ruins, watching them all suspiciously as Sidgemoor laid out the blanket.

Perry had his back to them all, apparently in deep contemplation of a tree, and thus avoiding Hedley's watchful eyes. He shaded a hand to his brow artistically, and Elinor took the opportunity to do her own divination for the roost.

Nothing whispered to her senses. She turned away from the stream and retraced her steps, going deeper into the ruins. The granite floor seemed to sink further into the earth and an ancient, low wall, overgrown with ivy, stood crumbling behind it.

Elinor wondered if the lower gradient indicated an old cellar. That would be a promising hiding place for a roost. She came to a halt before the grey and green wall, and saw the boulder.

It lay on the floor, its uppermost face clear of both moss and earth.

For some reason, she had expected it to be round. It was not: it was a huge, square granite block. She could not tell whether it had been hewn or naturally shaped. What was clear was that it was nestled in the ground, and an enormous gap lay in the wall where it had stood. It would have been very difficult for a single person to move it by physical strength alone.

Elinor walked around the boulder thoughtfully. She looked across at Beresford, eyebrows raised, and he came to join her.

"This must be the agile boulder," she murmured. "Why was it moved, do you think?"

Beresford considered it. "It certainly looks like a fairly recent event." He turned to Perry and spoke in a louder voice. "How goes it, Mr Avely? Any luck?"

Perry turned from the tree and Elinor added her own wide-eyed look, tapping the boulder meaningfully.

Perry considered the boulder, then cleared his throat. "I think I sense some minerals here." He strode forward. "It is difficult to say for certain, but it emanates from under this rock. I would be able to achieve a better sense if it were moved."

Elinor clasped her hands to speak her lines. "Oh, Lady Orlend, do say that you can use your Impacting to roll it out of the way!"

Lady Orlend, unlike the others, had not moved any closer. "My Gift is weak, Lady Beresford. I do not think I would be able to do so."

Elinor batted her eyelashes. "I would so love to see a demonstration of Impacting. I look forward to telling King George of how you assisted our enquiries so graciously."

Unexpectedly, Chester spoke up. "No. Mother must not exert herself with such a task."

Lady Orlend looked suddenly cross. "I can try if I like, my son, though I warn you all that I may not succeed." She stepped forward with a pugnacious lift of her chin. "Move back, everyone."

"Mother—" said Chester, but she glared at him.

The rest of the party obliged, stepping away from the block. Lady Orlend took a few steps forward, closed her eyes and held out her hands – in a way rather reminiscent of Perry's act, thought Elinor.

All eyes turned to the boulder, Elinor with eagerness, as she had never seen someone perform the art of Impacting. After a long, tense moment, the huge rock groaned and shifted to the right. Then, with a sudden thud, it tipped onto its side.

The chatter of birds in the trees halted. Not content with that feat, the boulder flipped again, like a domino falling. A collective gasp went up as it subsided into the ground.

Elinor's eyes widened. "Goodness me, that was impressive!"

She turned to see Lady Orlend looking pale and tottering on her feet. With a flutter of her eyelashes, the Dame of Sark gently collapsed into Chester's arms.

"I warned you!" he scolded. "You must not overdo it, Mother!" It was doubtful that Lady Orlend could hear him, though. She was crumpled in his arms, looking far less austere and suddenly vulnerable.

"Smelling salts!" cried Chester, his gaze intent on his mother's face, his hand coming up to feel her brow. "Hedley, fetch them, please."

Hedley turned and fled.

Elinor was far more interested in the boulder. She ran up to the ground that had been revealed. Raw earth, in a dark square. She frowned: could someone have buried something and used the boulder both to hide and mark the spot? And who was capable of that but Lady Orlend – or her sons?

Elinor turned to examine Lady Orlend. "Will she recover?" she asked. "I do apologise; I did not realise it would tax her so much, especially as she has a vampiri companion."

"She will recover," said Chester grimly. He half-carried his mother over to a rock and sat down, still cradling her in his arms. Elinor thought she saw Lady Orlend's eye glimmer beneath her lashes – but she must have been mistaken, for the Dame's form was still limp.

Beresford came to Elinor's side and drew her away. "Can you sense anything?" he asked, under his breath.

Elinor shook her head. "No, but there could still be a roost below us. The old monastery may well have had cellars, long since blocked up."

"Indeed: a perfect hiding place for vampiri," Beresford replied. "Use this opportunity while they are engaged to do your own divination, my dear."

Elinor was glad that he trusted her ability. She let go of his arm and took a deep breath. So far, she had sensed nothing as she looked for the roost. A new thought arose: perhaps she should try her old trick of looking for a secret. That was broad enough to cover all sorts of possibilities: a flute, a roost, or something nefarious that might explain why a block of stone had been mysteriously relocated.

A secret, she murmured in her mind, with some apprehension. *Where is something secret?*

After a moment, a clear tug came from the wall. Elinor, feeling a surge of triumph, followed it, trying to stroll as if she was simply admiring the scenery. She brushed past Perry, who was still eyeing Lady Orlend's inert form. Beresford went to greet Hedley, who had returned with the smelling salts, to distract him from Elinor.

Elinor reached the end of the old, crumbling wall, and a pulse of secrecy vibrated at her. She stared at the stones, her gaze drawn to a round object wedged between the rocks. It looked different to the other stones: it was smoother, darker, and smaller, no bigger than a robin's egg.

Taking off her gloves, she pulled it out. It was heavy in her hand, and she turned it over. It seemed it was simply a rock: cold, damp, and unremarkable except for its smoothness, which might just be from the passage of time. Perhaps the secret lay hidden behind it. She tossed the stone to the ground, her gaze returning eagerly to the wall.

A noise loud as a gunshot thundered through the clearing. Elinor didn't even see the explosion that threw her sideways: she only felt the whoosh of its impact.

16

IN WHICH A CHOICE OF WORDS IS APPRECIATED

*E*linor was flung into the wall with surprising force, as if a large dog had cannoned into her. Fragments of rock pelted through the air, biting into her skin. As she fell forward, her head thudded against stone.

There was pain, then blackness.

When she opened her eyes, she was in Beresford's arms. She clutched at his coat, feeling blood trickle down her forehead. Looking down, she saw cuts on her forearms and hands. She felt shaky, befuddled, and sore.

"Elinor!" Beresford pulled her closer, his gaze anxious. "What happened?"

Perry was standing at her side. "Good God," he said, "why did you fling yourself at the wall, Ellie?"

"I didn't fling myself," she muttered. "I was thrown, as if off a horse."

Beresford looked around angrily. "Someone explain to me how my wife was injured!"

Elinor smiled mistily: she rather liked it when Beresford called her his wife in such possessive tones. She looked around to see what everyone would say. She was rather interested to find out how she had been hurt.

Across the clearing, Chester was still holding his mother and waving smelling salts beneath her nose. He did not speak, merely stared at Elinor. Hedley's lips thinned and he shook his head disapprovingly, but neither did he say anything. Neither of them, however, looked shocked enough for Elinor's liking. They ought to be aghast, not merely disapproving.

Lady Orlend chose that moment to open her eyes. She sat up, pushing herself off her son. "What happened? Did I faint?"

Beresford snapped. "Something exploded next to my wife – that is what happened!"

Elinor smiled fondly again. She would have to be injured more often, if it effected such an admirable change in his vocabulary.

Lady Orlend froze. "Exploded?"

Elinor raised her head. "I think it was a rock. Black, smooth, round, and as small as an egg. I found it in the wall and tossed it aside."

There was silence.

"Hm," said Lady Orlend. She exchanged a glance with Hedley.

"Hm, what?" demanded Perry. He came to stand next to Elinor. "Tell us what it was, Lady Orlend. I insist."

Lady Orlend's features were more gaunt than usual, perhaps because of her recent fainting spell. She spoke slowly and reluctantly. "It is possible that it was a shatterstone, though I do not know how one found its way to La Moinerie."

Elinor frowned. "A shatterstone?"

Lady Orlend folded her hands in front of her. "A device constructed by Impactors. We have a few stored in our cellar in case of attack, made by my sons. They are rare and difficult to make: a round rock imbued with Impaction power. I do not know why one should be in this wall, but you are lucky that it was black; it is the grey ones you need to watch out for."

Beresford growled. "Are you saying there was a magical bomb near my wife?"

Elinor grinned and snuggled closer to him. "Perhaps your sons left it there, Lady Orlend?"

Lady Orlend nodded slowly. "They were accustomed to using this abandoned clearing to practise. This boulder has been moved before: my boys were extending their skills, in training for their military work." She waved a casual hand. "It must have been they who left the shatterstone behind. I do apologise."

She spoke with calm authority, but Elinor was not convinced. Chester sagged on the rock, his gaze cast down. Hedley's arms were folded, his face impassive under his straw hat.

"Mr Orlend," said Elinor. "Did you practise with your brothers?"

His mother answered for Chester. "No, he did not. I have told you that he has no such Gift."

"Did anyone else have access to the store in the cellar?" asked Beresford.

Lady Orlend said nothing.

"I should think everyone had access to the cellar," Elinor observed. "Your servants, certainly. Even Hedley here could have walked in without comment, I imagine. In fact, I myself was in there this morning."

Lady Orlend's eyes narrowed. "Were you indeed, Lady Beresford? Why did you pay a visit to my cellar?"

Elinor blinked, realising that she had blundered. "I was looking for Mrs Sidgemoor; I wanted to ask her about soufflés."

"We don't make soufflés here," snapped Lady Orlend. "I'll thank you to stop harping on about them and to leave my cellar alone." She glared at Elinor. "And how *did* you stumble across the shatterstone, Lady Beresford? I would have thought it would draw Mr Avely. There is silver embedded within them which he might have Discerned."

Perry gulped and looked around, as if there might be another one waiting for him. Elinor shrank before Lady Orlend's sudden hostility, glad that Beresford was with her.

"That is quite enough," said Beresford. "Elinor is hurt and shaken; she must return to the house and rest. Later we can investigate how the shatterstone came to cause such harm. I warn you, Lady Orlend, that King George will be made known of this event in our report."

Lady Orlend nodded coldly. She turned and swept out of the clearing, her son and her right-hand man following without so much as an apologetic glance.

Elinor rather thought that the Dame of Sark had forgotten to totter.

∿

Beresford carried Elinor into the house. It was as if he were carrying her over the threshold as a bride – but the Seigneurie, with its oppressive, heavy feeling, was not at all the same as airy Beresford Manor in Devon. She let out a sigh of homesickness. The explosion must have taxed her nerves more than she realised; she was starting to feel melancholy.

Beresford hauled Elinor to her room and rang the bell. When Dinah appeared, he asked if she could run a bath and assist Elinor into it. First, though, he cleaned her brow with his own hand-kerchief.

Elinor waved him off, promising to rest. He gave her an anxious look, but departed to hunt down Perry, who had disap-peared soon after they returned to the house.

As the maid heaved buckets of water into the room Elinor undressed herself, tutting at the blood that speckled her primrose gown. "I'm very sorry to pass you such a stained garment," she said. "I'm afraid I had an accident today: something exploded next to me. Can you imagine?"

Dinah looked up, eyes wide. Elinor could only imagine what her forehead looked like, despite Beresford's ministrations. She looked down and saw that her right arm was already starting to show bruises.

"Exploded, ma'am?" said Dinah, tipping hot water into the tub.

"A shatterstone," Elinor replied. "Have you heard of such a thing?"

"No, ma'am. Is it some devilish toy that the Orlend boys made?"

"I believe so. Are they known for such sport?"

Dinah shrugged expressively. "They've caused trouble before on Sark with their pranks." She left to fetch another bucket of water.

When Dinah returned, Elinor picked up the conversation. "What sort of trouble, if you don't mind me asking? I feel an interest, you see, having become a victim myself."

"Rocks moving in the night, tenants being locked out of their homes, digging holes in the fields. That's why Lady Orlend was glad to send them off to war."

Elinor cocked her head. "I thought she didn't want them to go. Isn't she keeping Chester back?"

"Oh no," said Dinah. "Chester stays of his own accord."

"Oh!" Elinor tried to remember where she had gained the impression that Lady Orlend had tied Chester to her side. It had been Lady Orlend herself, she thought, who had said something along those lines. Elinor frowned. "The Dame said she didn't want Chester to join his brothers."

Dinah's expression suddenly closed. "That may be the case, ma'am."

Elinor regarded her thoughtfully. "These pranks... did Chester join in, too?" She recalled the remains of the fire she had seen in the ruins. She could imagine young boys around it, plotting mischief.

Dinah paused before she poured the water in. "Most likely,"

she said. "He is the second-youngest son, so he would be dragged into it."

She trudged off for more water. Pouring in the next bucket, she asked if Elinor had seen the special bar of soap which was usually left with the bathtub.

"A bar of soap? I don't believe so," replied Elinor, untying her shift. It would be so much nicer if Beresford helped her bathe. She sighed the thought away.

"It's from King George," explained Dinah. "A gift for Lady Orlend, bars scented with lavender, rose, and orange flowers, and made out of olive oil in the new fashion. I thought you'd like to try one, but I can't find them in their usual place."

"I can do well enough without lavender soap," replied Elinor, running her fingers through the hot water with appreciation. "By the way, I have lost something else: a tiny golden flute. If you could find it, I would be most grateful."

Dinah nodded, gathering up Elinor's gown and backing out of the room.

Elinor stepped out of her shift and into the bath. The warm water was soothing, and she sat down, closing her eyes with a sigh. For just a little while, she let problems and mysteries recede.

Unfortunately, the image of Lieutenant Chaboot soon rose in her mind, dried out and dead in the attic. Could that have been a prank gone wrong? Dinah had mentioned tenants locked up by the Orlend boys, so maybe they had tried the same trick on a visiting vampiri. Surely, however, they would not have left him to die.

There remained the possibility that her own injury hadn't been an accident at all. Perry had suffered the indignity of being shot at, and now she had been hurt. Was someone trying to drive them off the island? But why?

Could something be hidden which someone wanted to remain undiscovered? But whom, and what? Briefly, Elinor considered the tales of pirate gold. Old tales only, most likely, and why would Chester have mentioned it if there was a conspiracy to keep it hidden? Unless he was not part of the conspiracy ...

Or was there some kind of smuggling going on? Elinor was familiar with such things, having spent time in Devonshire, where it was common practice among the villagers. Perhaps here the trade took on a more sinister expression, if it were trade in weapons: a more dangerous prank to entertain the Orlend boys. Could that shatterstone have been left there for someone to pick up? God forbid if it were to be sent to Napoleon's troops.

Elinor pushed the thought away as she sank deeper into the bath. More likely, there was a monetary relationship with the French traders for cognac and the like. Beresford himself had undertaken such negotiations. The trade was alive and well, though the two countries were officially at war.

She wrinkled her nose as she washed herself with the soft soap Dinah had found as a replacement for the royal gift. Her bruises would certainly colour up beautifully tomorrow. She had probably been pelted with bits of silver as well as rock, if that was how the shatterstone was constructed.

Then she froze. Lady Orlend herself had pointed out that such an item would draw a Mineral Discernor. That meant that the shatterstone might have been intended for Perry.

Shivering, she washed the last of the soap from her skin. If Perry was in danger, Elinor had to sharpen her attention and her Discernments. If she found the vampiri quickly, they could leave Sark to its secrets and its problems, and return to England on the next tide.

She stepped out of the bath, reaching for the thick towel that waited ready for her. A last reluctant thought occurred to her: if Lieutenant Chaboot had been murdered for approaching those secrets, they would have to bring the murderer to justice. Especially if the same person had planted a shatterstone for Perry to find.

On these conflicted contemplations, she finished dressing.

Just as she put on a fresh pair of gloves, a piercing scream vibrated through the house.

Elinor's heart leapt into her mouth. The ghastly sound immediately conjured the worst: Perry's body, lifeless on the floor. Instinctively, she knew the scream had come from his room. She ran down the stairs.

When she reached Perry's room, the door was open. Mrs Sidgemoor had beaten her to the scene, but Elinor pushed past the housekeeper's broad back. Inside, a scene of disarray met her eyes.

Perry was in the corner: dripping wet and bleeding. Not dead, however, and Elinor let out a gasp of relief. He was sitting in an armchair, clutching his leg, looking very pale and startled.

Next to him stood Jaq. He, too, was dripping wet, and wearing only a pair of breeches. Elinor bit her lip.

In front of them stood Dinah, looking even more shocked than Perry. Her hand was over her mouth, and Elinor guessed it must have been she who had screamed like a banshee.

"What happened?" demanded Elinor, though she had an inkling. "Perry, what have you done to yourself? How did you get so wet?"

"Twisted my leg," said Perry. "I fell down near the cliffs. The waves drenched me, as you see. Damned ocean." He coughed, and Elinor realised he was Bemused. "I was soaked and hurt, and it was cursed difficult to walk back." He widened his eyes at her. "If you know what I mean."

Elinor ignored the implication and tutted loudly, as if this were nothing unexpected. "Dear me, Perry, you do find yourself in trouble. You would give anyone a fright; I can quite understand Dinah's dismay. Jaq, where are the rest of your clothes?"

For once, Jaq looked as if he would rather be dressed. "I ... I wished to borrow a shirt from Perry. My spare ones are, er, back on the ship."

Elinor had to give him credit for quick thinking, but that

didn't explain why he was wet, too. She handed Jaq one of Perry's shirts. He hastily slipped it on and backed out of the room, past Mrs Sidgemoor's bulky form, his long lashes lowered.

Dinah had her gaze fixed on the ground, for which Elinor was also inclined to give credit. Jaq's masculine form, half-clothed, was a sight to draw the eye.

Elinor cleared her throat. "I cannot excuse Jaq's behaviour, but I am also sorry that my brother is so untidy, Dinah. It seems that we are all having accidents today! These cliffs must be quite dangerous." She nodded to the maid. "You can leave us now. Perhaps fetch Mr Avely a spare blanket, however. He looks cold after his long walk back from those treacherous cliffs."

Dinah bobbed a curtsy, her face expressionless. "Yes, ma'am."

"Yes, long walk back," said Perry. "It was very long. A good walk. Saw some puffins. Funny looking things, puffins."

Elinor frowned at him, then turned to Mrs Sidgemoor, who stood with her hands folded across her generous bosom. "You too, Mrs Sidgemoor. We apologise if Perry startled anyone."

"Just popped in!" said Perry brightly. "Sorry to startle you!"

Mrs Sidgemoor gave Perry an appraising look before following Dinah. She shut the door with a measured click.

Elinor hurried to Perry's side. "How bad is it?"

"Bad, very bad." Perry heaved a gusty sigh. "Not my leg. That'll mend, though it damned hurts." Elinor saw he was also holding his old knife wound, but he gloomily waved off her concern. "I've mucked it up now, Ellie. That nosy maid saw me materialise with Jaq and screamed like a bloody cat on fire."

"With Jaq?" Elinor stared at him. "You Travelled together?"

"Yes." Perry looked at the ground. "It works if he holds me very tightly."

Elinor clutched her head in dismay. "So the maid saw the two of you appear out of nowhere, locked in a close embrace? Let us hope that she holds her tongue. What possessed you to Travel together?"

"I couldn't walk," said Perry, sulkily. "I can't put weight on my foot. And I didn't want to leave Jaq there. He pulled me out of the water."

"I suppose you were looking for the tunnel?" she asked with resignation. She couldn't really blame him; she probably would have done the same.

"Yes — I thought my Travel would give me a handy shortcut to Little Sark, bypassing La Coupee. But I slipped and toppled off the ledge in the cliff. Jaq dived in to pull me out. It would have taken too long to hobble back, so I decided to Travel us both." Perry groaned. "And now I've ruined everything. Can't believe I was so cursed clumsy." He looked shaken and remorseful. No doubt the fall had given him a shock, and Dinah's greeting had probably not helped matters.

"Well, the harm is done now," said Elinor briskly. "We shall just have to make the best of it; I shall think of an explanation. You dry yourself and change into fresh clothes." She laughed. "Perhaps we shall have matching bruises."

Indeed, a lump had formed on Perry's brow. Despite her laughter, Elinor considered it crossly. One bruised Avely forehead was bad enough; two were beyond the pale. She would have to do something about it.

Perry nodded and reached for a towel. "Sorry, Ellie."

Elinor's own head was aching as she left the room, and it threatened to worsen when she saw Mrs Sidgemoor conferring with Lady Orlend at the end of the corridor.

The two women stopped talking when they saw her. She hoped she might pass them without any comment, but Lady Orlend barred the way.

17

IN WHICH ACCUSATIONS FLY

*L*ady Orlend spoke, her voice hard. "The maid swears that Mr Avely appeared out of nowhere."

"It does seem he gave her quite a fright," agreed Elinor. "He has very quiet footsteps; he has startled me in the past."

Lady Orlend pinned her with a penetrating gaze. "She says that he materialised out of thin air, with Mr Delquon wrapped around him like a worm on a hook."

"Goodness," said Elinor faintly. "Really? Does she, er, have a vivid imagination?"

Lady Orlend ignored this pitiful parry. "Your brother's predilections are none of my business," she said coldly. "However, I find it strange beyond belief that he should have two such disparate Gifts as Discernment *and* Travel."

Elinor cursed inwardly, then assumed a penitent expression and sighed loudly. "Oh dear. I see you have guessed it! You must understand, being a woman, how it is."

Lady Orlend narrowed her eyes. "No, I do not see how it is."

"Well," said Elinor, adopting a confiding air. "It is I who have a talent in Discernment. Perry, as you have deduced, is a Travellor. As a woman, however, I could not be appointed to the royal position of Chief Mineral Geologist and Discernor, so my brother pretends to have my Gift. He also likes the idea that he is protecting me, so we persist in our little charade. I do hope you forgive us, and forgive him for startling your maid."

She smiled benignly, hoping this blithe explanation would suffice. However, Lady Orlend and Mrs Sidgemoor simply stared at her.

"Protecting?" said Lady Orlend. "Why would *you* need protecting?"

Elinor realised she had made an error. "Well, Discerning can be quite dangerous, as we saw today. You were right, my lady, when you guessed that I found that shatterstone not by accident, but by Discernment. You see where it got me!" She touched her brow delicately.

"Yes," said Lady Orlend thoughtfully. "Sometimes people don't want things to be found."

Elinor, feeling rather cross, decided it was time to take the offensive. She let her hand drop and glared at her interlocutor. "And why would that be, Lady Orlend? Is something hidden on this island?"

The Dame of Sark's gaze narrowed, and Mrs Sidgemoor dropped her eyes.

"You know all about hiding a Gift, do you not, my lady?" continued Elinor hotly. "Your own Gift is more than you admit."

"No, it is not," snapped Lady Orlend.

"You moved that boulder with ease."

"I fainted from the exertion!"

"Did you? Or was that a little performance?" pressed Elinor. "Or perhaps you are hiding your son's Gift, just as Perry hides mine. Chester is Gifted, is he not? I sense it."

She was bluffing, but the sudden chagrin on Lady Orlend's face told her she had hit the mark. "I knew it!" she said triumphantly. "He is an Impactor like you, is he not? Perhaps *he* moved the boulder, and you put on a show to persuade us otherwise."

Lady Orlend's features tightened and her hands trembled. "I'm sure I don't know what you are talking about."

"Did he put the boulder there in the first place?" demanded Elinor. "Why would he do that? Was he looking for gold?"

"Nonsense," said Lady Orlend. "If he did move anything, it was just harmless practice. He wishes to join his brothers, much as I resist the notion."

Elinor lifted her chin. "Not so harmless, if he leaves shatter-stones lying around." She held up an imperious hand. "And if he *is* up to anything else, I will discover it, being a Discernor!"

She stalked past the women, this time with no trouble, for Lady Orlend seemed to have become lifeless. Elinor walked away, hoping she had managed to turn the tables: away from questions about her Gift and why she must hide it, and towards the suspicious nature of the Orlends' own activities.

Shaking a little, she marched downstairs. Beresford was nowhere to be seen; he was most likely still looking for Perry. Elinor went and paced in the lane beyond the gate. She needed to soothe her nerves, though she had promised Beresford she would rest.

The lane was edged prettily in white daisies and pink thrift, bright and cheerful in the daylight. It was a relief to be outside the oppressive Seigneurie, but her dark forebodings were not entirely eased. With Jaq, herself, and now Perry injured, she was anxious to lay eyes upon Beresford and reassure herself that he was still whole and safe.

When Beresford's broad-shouldered figure came over the hill, she let out a sigh of relief and hurried to meet him.

He caught her in his arms. "Why are you outside, my love? You ought to be in bed."

"Perry has been hurt," said Elinor and found she was close to tears. "And I am discovered as a Discernor." Blinking the moisture away, she explained what had happened.

Beresford's jaw tightened. "Damn Perry." He sighed. "This calls for a council of war. This time it will take place in your room, and you are not to move out of it all day."

∼

Accordingly, soon after dusk and dinner, Jaq sidled into Elinor's room, fully dressed now, with his arm and head bandaged once more. Elinor, sporting a compress on her forehead, smiled at him, folding her hands on the cream and rose blanket. "We make a fine matched set, do we not?" she said.

Jaq did not return her grin. "I am sorry about today, Miss Avely, and also to hear that you were injured."

"Lady Beresford to you," she reminded him. "That, at least, remains a secret, I hope."

Perry, limping behind Jaq with his leg and head bandaged, also looked sombre. "The game has become serious, sister dear."

They sat down, pulling up a chair each on either side of the frilly bed, and gazed at Elinor sorrowfully, looking slightly tragic in their bandages.

Beresford leaned against the windowsill, his legs crossed in front of him. "Good God, look at you three. It's like a hospital ward in here."

Jaq grimaced. "The third time makes us fools, I have to say."

Beresford nodded. "Your accident and Perry's could be put down to rank stupidity" – Perry looked affronted, but Jaq grinned — "but Elinor's brush with violence is more suspicious."

Perry shrugged. "I'm happy to admit it was my own cursed fault on those damned slippery rocks, though I can't think why I was so muddle-footed. But I was close to the queen, I swear it. I could smell something sweet, like lavender and roses. Did you smell it, Jaq?"

Jaq tilted his head. "Why, yes, I believe so. I thought it must be some odd species of cliff-sage at the time, but you are right: it was lavender. The scent of the queen, perhaps, floating out of the tunnel?"

"Don't be ridiculous," said Elinor, twisting her hands. "I'm sure the vampiri queen doesn't smell of lavender and roses; dust and mould, more likely, if she's been asleep in a cave for twelve years."

"She might smell of roses," argued Perry. "She's a queen, isn't she? And if it wasn't the queen I smelt, what was it? I definitely caught a whiff of something as I toppled off that ledge."

"Roses and something else," agreed Jaq. "Juniper?"

Something tingled at the back of Elinor's mind and she sat up suddenly. "Lavender and roses? It was *soap!*"

"Soap?" They all stared at her.

"Someone *was* trying to kill you, Perry – the soap was missing today from my bath! Dinah, the maid, told me it was a special gift from the king, scented with lavender, rose and orange flowers."

"Orange flowers," said Jaq. "That's it."

"I didn't smell orange flowers," objected Perry.

Elinor drew an impatient breath. "Don't you see, Perry? Someone put soap all over the ledge so that you would slip. Or whoever investigated the cliff next would fall to their death – perhaps Jaq."

Jaq nodded. "The question is whether it was done to eliminate Perry or me, or simply to guard the tunnel in the cliff? I confess that I am becoming more and more intrigued by this cliff."

Perry's eyes were wide. "Who would resort to trickery with soap?"

Elinor bit her lip. "Everyone knew you would return to the cliff, Perry – I announced it at breakfast this morning." Her heart sank. "If I had said nothing, you might not have been injured."

Jaq folded his arms. "I object that Perry is considered the only target. Don't forget I was by the cliffs too; the soap may have been intended for me."

"You didn't need soap to injure yourself," Elinor snapped, and he pulled a face.

Beresford spoke from the window. "Perry was playing the Discernor. Of course he would be targeted, if there is something to hide."

Elinor nodded. "The shatterstone was most likely intended for Perry, if it contained silver." She paused. "At least I took that blow for him," she added, faintly.

Perry patted her hand. "You should have seen yourself fly through the air, Elinor. Glad it wasn't me." It was her turn to pull a face.

Beresford frowned. "That shatterstone may have been intended for Perry, but now Lady Orlend knows that Elinor is the Discernor."

Jaq winced. "And of my affection for Perry."

Beresford thrust his hands in his pockets. "Indeed. And while society is more lenient in France, we are still in English territory. Jaq, you must remember that this is not Skerry and it is dangerous to be open about these matters here." He sighed. "At least try to wear more clothes next time you publicly embrace Perry."

"We simply Travelled together!" said Perry. "And *I* was wearing lots of clothes."

"More's the pity," said Jaq, then held up his hand in acknowledgement. "Yes, we will be more careful."

Elinor leaned back, a dull ache gathering behind her eyes. "Lady Orlend seemed more concerned that you are a Travellor, Perry. I'm afraid she will inform the household of *that*."

Perry sighed. "If not, then Mrs Sidgemoor or that cursed maid most certainly will."

"Well," said Elinor guiltily. "I discovered that Chester is a Musor too. So there was a point for each of us."

"Chester?" demanded Jaq. "An Impactor?"

Elinor nodded. "Kept home to keep his mother safe." She frowned. "Though I'm not certain if that is his or her decision."

Perry narrowed his eyes. "Do you think Chester moved the boulder and set off the shatterstone today?"

"Possibly," said Elinor. "Though he doesn't seem a violent type. Lady Orlend did *appear* to be deeply affected by her endeavours to move the rock." She pursed her lips. "It could have been an act, so that she was conveniently comatose when the shatterstone exploded."

Perry looked thoughtful. "They all kept their distance from the wall, even Hedley."

Beresford shook his head. "That is not conclusive. The shatterstone could have been placed there at any point, knowing it would draw a Mineral Discernor's hand. It is almost a point in her favour that Lady Orlend attended today."

"Chester, then," said Perry. "Why was he there? Perhaps he attended to make sure his mother was not caught in the crossfire, because he knew what would happen."

"Or Hedley," said Elinor. "He could have accessed the shatterstones, as I pointed out. Or Durl could have flown it there the night before; he is a frequent visitor to the cellar. Don't you think it suspicious that he directed us to La Moinerie in the first place?"

Perry considered, then shook his head. "Again, it isn't conclusive, as that morning you told everyone we were going to La Moinerie. Chester asked me about it himself when I came down for breakfast."

"Yes, and Lady Orlend was quick to arrange a luncheon picnic," said Elinor.

There was a silence as they all contemplated the possibilities.

At last, Beresford spoke. "What interests me is the motive. Why do they want to rid the island of a Discernor? Are they hiding the roost from us, or something else?"

Perry stood up and walked to the window. "I don't care what they are hiding; I just want to find the roost and leave as soon as possible. Where is it, Elinor?"

Elinor sighed and moved restlessly in her blankets. "I don't know. I feel it is in the south, but I am not certain. Where is Aldreda? Can someone fetch her from the attic, if I am to be kept to this silly bed?"

Jaq leapt up and hurried to obey.

Elinor rubbed her head, trying to think what she could accomplish while bedridden, with Beresford watching over her like a hawk. She considered Perry, who was staring moodily at his feet, and a thought came to her. "Perry, have you heard that Aldreda discovered a young vampiri bat by the cliff?"

Perry nodded. "Beresford told me."

"Well ... he was a very hungry child, by all accounts. He has partaken liberally of sheep, but I am certain Musor blood would benefit him."

Perry's head drew back. "You mean ... ? Oh no. I've told you before that I don't need a vampiri hanging about me. Especially not a little boy."

Elinor sighed. "You *do* need one. Look at what happened today. After you startled the maid, you began blathering on about puffins. You might not have made the idiotic decision to Travel into your room with Jaq had you not been Bemused!"

"Idiotic?" said Perry hotly. "Where else was I supposed to land? How was I to know there'd be a wretched maid in there?"

Elinor considered. "Yes, why was Dinah in there, I wonder?" That point had yet not occurred to her.

"It was unfortunate," said Beresford. "But Elinor is right, Perry: pairing up with Raddle might help you both. God knows we need every advantage we can find, especially if Elinor is subjected to any more violent attacks."

Perry, his chivalry thus appealed to, muttered something about the excessive bossiness of big sisters. Then he sighed. "Very well. While we are on the island, I will feed this little bat. But you will have to find a new owner for him when we remove to the castle."

"Not an owner, Perry, a companion!" snapped Elinor. "Please be more thoughtful. And yes, when we return to the castle we will be preparing to host many Musors, and you can slink off to Skerry."

"I never said I was going to Skerry!"

Elinor gave him an exasperated look. "Jaq will be going, no doubt, and you two are inseparable. It is probably safer for you both there, too."

Before Perry could respond, Jaq himself returned, bearing Aldreda on his shoulder. They walked into a tense silence, which faded when Aldreda leapt gracefully onto the bed, roundly scolding Elinor for being injured.

Elinor bore this in good part until Aldreda paused for breath. "Yes, Aldreda, but now you must take Perry down to Raddle. He has agreed to bond with him temporarily." She sat up, flinging her blankets aside. "I will come too, to oversee proceedings."

As she suspected, this convinced Aldreda to hastily take charge of Perry. He bore Aldreda downstairs, leaving Elinor and Beresford alone with Jaq.

"Jaq," said Elinor briskly, "can you make enquiries among your own people? You are fully recovered despite your contretemps today?"

Jaq nodded. "Fit as a dolphin."

"Please go and ask the selkies what they know of Sark. Any information will do, but be sure to ask about any rumours of hidden gold. And vampiri, of course."

"Yes, my lady," said Jaq. He stood up and clicked his heels together, bowing in his showy manner. "Now?"

"Yes, now," said Beresford wearily.

"Should I leave you two alone," enquired Jaq blandly, "while your chaperone is downstairs?"

"Out!" snapped Beresford. "Make enquiries in Skerry, but do not return to that cliff until I am there to keep watch."

"Yes, sir. I will just check in on Perry first, to see how he fared in his experience as a vampiri dinner," said Jaq. At the door, he turned with a beatific smile. "Don't eat any plum jam while I'm away!" He slipped out before they could answer.

"Cheeky rascal!" said Elinor. "As if we have plum jam lying around, when you have expressly forbidden it."

Sighing, Beresford took two strides to the bed and gathered Elinor close. "Alone at last," he muttered into her hair.

She turned her face up for a kiss. "Stay with me tonight, my love. Who knows, you might not have another chance."

"Don't say such things." He kissed her gently; at first, at least. "Aldreda will return, and you are injured. You must rest, so that you are fully recovered by our wedding day." He paused. "Would you like some leftover pie?"

Elinor sighed. "I am hungry, but don't think I haven't noticed your ploy!"

Beresford extricated himself from her arms. "I'll return shortly, bearing pie. Do not move!"

18

IN WHICH PIE IS INSUFFICIENT

*A*lone now in her room, Elinor put her hand to her bandaged head. She had not liked to admit it before everyone, but she was feeling sore, tired, and a little frightened. Her realisation about the missing soap made it quite clear that there was malevolent intent behind Perry's accident. It also implied that the shatterstone had been planted on purpose.

She tried to soothe her panicked thoughts. There was another possibility: that someone had put the shatterstone there to be discovered by Perry, not to injure him but to expose its existence. After all, it had not exploded when she picked it up. If she hadn't been so foolish as to toss it aside like an old apple, she would not have been hurt. Could someone wish to inform their party that the Orlends were making and keeping shatterstones?

Or it could be Chaboot's murderer trying to drive them away – or worse.

She sank back on her pillows, gnawing on a fingernail, until her reflections were interrupted by Perry at the door, Jaq at his shoulder. "I can't feed Raddle," he said triumphantly, "because he has disappeared."

Elinor sat up abruptly. "Disappeared?"

"Well, gone off on his own little jaunt," said Perry. "Probably looking for a sheep."

"But I told him strictly to stay with Lilian!"

"Well, you do not have sovereignty over everyone," said Perry pointedly. "Didn't you say that Raddle is a young boy? It is entirely natural that he would want to escape Miss Reed's watch."

Elinor threw off her blankets. "Where are Pags and Durl? They must look for him! What if we lose him? He is our likeliest lead to the roost! I'm going to the cellar to question Lilian." She paused defiantly. "I'm not staying abed when I might be able to discover something."

Perry threw up his hands. "I'm not preventing you."

"Neither am I," said Jaq. "I'll go outside, see if I can spot the little fellow."

"Good." She frowned at Perry. "You can tell Beresford where I am."

"I don't think so," said Perry promptly. "I'll come with you and guard you. I'm sure that is what Beresford would want, what with bombs being in the cellar."

Elinor gave him a cross look, threw on a shawl and marched downstairs. Perry limped behind her.

When she opened the cellar door, her eyes sought the keg behind which she had last seen Raddle. The floor was dusty and empty. Quickly, she shut the door behind Perry, who planted his feet and folded his arms, taking his duties seriously.

Lilian's soft voice came from a dark corner, where a broad chest sat. She was standing on it, as simply dressed as before. "Lady Beresford, do you know where Raddle has gone?"

Elinor strode into the room. "No. When did you last see him?"

"When you last saw him," Lilian replied. "After you left us this morning, I fell asleep again. Raddle said he would stay awake a little longer, exploring the cellar, and I had not the heart to stop him. When I awoke, he was gone." Her face was pale and frowning.

"Could he have opened the cellar door?" asked Elinor. "Surely it is too heavy."

"Yes," said Lilian. "I suspect that Mrs Sidgemoor came in and Raddle used the opportunity to slip past her."

Elinor paced around the cellar, glancing into the corners as if she might find Raddle playing a joke on them. The stone floor remained as empty and grimy as before.

Perry also looked around curiously. "Where's Aldreda?" he asked. "I left her here."

"She went to look for him," replied Lilian. Her hands twitched in her skirts, showing her perturbation. "Perhaps I should look in the house for him too."

Elinor tilted her head to the left, suddenly wondering if Miss Reed knew more than she was saying. "This is most unfortunate. Do you have any inkling of why Raddle left, Miss Reed?"

Lilian shook her head and Elinor cursed inwardly; head-shaking was beyond her powers of Truth Discernment. She reached for her lapis lazuli pendant, feeling the shape of it beneath her bodice.

Perry, watching, helpfully repeated her question. "Raddle didn't say anything that might give us a clue?"

Lilian shook her head again. Elinor pursed her lips crossly. Above them dust motes danced in the candlelight, and she could hear a rat scratching somewhere. Lilian cleared her throat, seeming to realise that more was expected of her. "I'm sorry, Lady Beresford." She spoke with a touch of hauteur. "Raddle didn't say much at all. He seemed quiet, for a little boy. And I was asleep, I'm afraid."

This sounded all too true to Elinor. She sighed. "What did Durl tell you of the circumstances of finding him?"

Lilian's gaze relaxed and she carefully sat on the edge of the chest, crossing her ankles neatly. "Durl said that Raddle was found by the cliffs, hungry, after hibernating. Do you think it means there is a roost nearby? Thomas said you were looking for one."

Elinor nodded, letting go of her lapis, but noting that Lilian was on first-name terms with Mr Durl. "Yes, and it is of the utmost importance that we find this roost. I hoped Raddle would lead us to it."

"Why is it so important?" asked Lilian cautiously. "What do you know of this roost?"

Before Elinor could answer, a scratching noise came from behind the chest. A moment later, a head popped up. It was not Raddle, however, but Durl.

Elinor jumped. "Goodness me! Were you there all the time, Durl?"

Durl hauled himself onto the trunk, looking abashed even though he was fully clothed. "No, my lady. I have a little entrance to the cellar down there: a rat hole I have rebuilt so that I may come and go as I please. I am sorry to interrupt."

Lilian had stood when he first appeared, and she flushed at this evidence of his courtship of her. "Raddle has gone missing."

Durl's eyes widened and he took a step forward, staring intently at Lilian. "Since when?"

"We don't know when," said Elinor. "It must have been in the last hour, as he was afraid of the light. Mrs Sidgemoor or someone else must have let him out, unknowingly. Or could he have found your tunnel, Durl?"

He frowned. "Perhaps. If he left recently, there is a chance that we can still find him." He began to remove his jacket. "I'll be quicker as a bat."

"Tell Pags as well, if you see him," begged Elinor.

She turned away as Durl stripped off, noting that Lilian also averted her face, her pale cheeks reddening.

"Let's go," Elinor said to Perry. "We can look in the house while Durl and Jaq search outside. Aldreda is probably looking there, too."

"Can I help, please?" asked Lilian.

Elinor gave her an appraising look. "I don't see why not. As a bat, you might be able to search corners that we cannot reach."

Durl paused in his undressing. "No, Lilian. You stay here, where it is safe."

Lilian lifted her chin and her gaze became aloof again. "You presume too much, Mr Durl. I am tired of being kept in this cellar. If Miss Zooth may assist, then so may I."

Durl shook his head. "What will Lady Orlend and Chester say if they find you gone?"

Elinor raised her eyebrows at him, heedless of the fact that he was now shirtless. "Shame on you, Mr Durl," she said. "I thought you were in favour of Lilian's freedom? Lady Orlend and Chester can have no objection if Lilian wishes to stretch her wings beyond this musty cellar."

"Quite right," said Lilian, though she blinked apprehensively.

Durl said nothing, but he did not look happy, which Elinor thought rather contradicted his proclaimed sympathies with independence.

"Very well," said Elinor. "We shall depart, Lilian, leaving the door slightly open so that you can follow us once you are, er, disrobed. An extra pair of eyes will be most useful."

Elinor and Perry retreated from the cellar, leaving the door ajar as promised. They made their way slowly upstairs, but did not make it far. Beresford was glowering in the passageway outside. "Where have you been?" he barked. "Won't even the promise of pie keep you in one place for ten minutes? For God's sake, Elinor! How am I supposed to keep you safe as your husband if you won't listen to me?"

"Shh!" said Elinor. She could hear sounds from the kitchen

and looked over his shoulder nervously. "You'll bring Mrs Sidge-moor down upon us."

"Good!" growled Beresford. "Maybe she'll convince you to stay abed."

"I like that!" Elinor put her hands on her hips. "You won't even get *into* the bed!"

"Hush!" hissed Perry, looking embarrassed. "Beresford, Raddle is missing; that's why we came down."

"Raddle?" Beresford frowned. "The little boy?"

Perry nodded. "Probably just out having a lark. Nothing to worry about, but Elinor insisted on coming to see for herself."

"Of course she did!" snapped Beresford.

Elinor shook her head. "Raddle knows where the roost is, so we must find him without delay." She did not want to admit her own increasing doubt that she could find the roost by herself. "Aldreda is already searching, and we have others to assist us. Durl, Pags, and even Miss Reed will look for him." She cast a glance behind her, but could not see Lilian hovering in the shadows.

"Good," said Beresford. "That means *you* can return to bed. The vampiri are better equipped to find him, and you are injured." He glared at her bandages.

Elinor scowled back. "You are forgetting my map divination. I can use it to try to find Raddle, though I have only met him once." She did not know if one meeting would be enough, but it was more times than she had met the vampiri queen, so it was worth a try. "My divinations for the roost have only told us to go south, but perhaps I shall have a better chance with Raddle and he can lead us to the roost, if only he can remember where it is. Perhaps he is looking for it now."

"And then what?" demanded Beresford. "Once you have a point on a map, I suppose you will want to charge off into the night!"

Elinor did not deny it. "I promise to eat some pie first."

Beresford folded his arms in a menacing fashion. "No. I shall not fetch you a map unless you promise to stay in your room. Be reasonable, Elinor."

Perry gave a snort. "Not much chance of that."

Elinor slayed her brother with a glance, then she heaved a sigh. "Very well. Map and pie in the bedroom, as soon as possible. And tea!"

19

IN WHICH THERE IS A WILD BAT CHASE

*N*ot so long before, Aldreda had left the Seigneurie by the servants' entrance.

When Lilian told her that Raddle was not in the cellar, Aldreda knew he could not have gone far. The sun had only set an hour before. Raddle, fresh from hibernation, would not be accustomed even to the fading light of dusk. He would have waited until it was dark before he dared venture forth.

Aldreda flew slowly around the house, trying to catch a scent of the young bat. The night was calm this time, thankfully, the air clear and fresh after last night's storm. It should be fairly easy to track him if she could just find a starting point.

The kitchen was still busy, with Mrs Sidgemoor clattering pots and the smell of human food lingering in the air. Aldreda flitted past, but could catch no trace of Raddle.

She would be inclined to put his disappearance down to boyish irresponsibility, except that Raddle had seemed biddable, even frightened, and glad of the refuge of the cellar. It seemed strange for him to wander off without a word. Had he felt a higher responsibility to his roost and been drawn back to it? Yet he claimed he had no idea where the roost lay. No, it was more likely that something else had pulled him out of the house.

167

Having circled the eaves with no luck, Aldreda widened her scope to the gardens. She saw Jaq poking around in the ivy along the walls, and gave him a wide berth. Perhaps Raddle was hungry, and she should try the stables.

She darted through the trees, her senses alert. Insects hummed, and the new moon shone like a curved talon in the sky. She was just about to fly into the stables when a movement caught her eye from the driveway.

It was a human figure. Aldreda hovered under the eave of the stable, trusting that she would not be seen. As the figure drew closer, she saw that it was the servant, Sidgemoor. He was keeping to the shadows and walking quickly. Aldreda hung from the eave to watch him.

Sidgemoor, oblivious to his audience, nonetheless put on quite a display. As he reached the head of the driveway, he paused and looked around furtively. Then he edged through the shadows and with one last glance over his shoulder, disappeared down the side of the house towards the servants' entrance.

Aldreda clicked her teeth together with interest. Clearly, Sidgemoor had been on some dubious expedition. It behoved her to find out what he had been doing.

What of Raddle, however? After a moment's inner conflict, Aldreda abandoned her quest to find the little bat. He was most likely chasing a sheep, while Sidgemoor's activities were suspicious. She dropped low to the ground at the spot where Sidgemoor had paused so nervously, trying to catch the scent of him.

Ah, there it was: a mixture of boot polish, cooked meat, and sweat. Wrinkling her nose, she followed the smell, winging her way along the path he had trodden, trying to discover where he had been.

The trail passed through the gates at the end of the drive, then turned sharply to the right and plunged through a field. The long grass made the trail more difficult to follow, but Aldreda clung to the scent, still fresh.

Beyond the grasses stood a ruin. She had circled back to La Moinerie. At least, so she supposed, from what Elinor had told her about the place.

Sidgemoor's scent stopped at an old water mill. Around the mill were old stones, tumbled and covered in moss, just as Elinor had described. Fir trees stood on the outskirts, casting shadows over the stones and the remains of a fire.

This must be the old monastery that Durl had mentioned, which Chaboot had investigated before he died. And it was also where Elinor had been injured that very day.

Aldreda cautiously rose into the air. Why had Sidgemoor come here? From his trail, it seemed that he had simply rested upon the millstone, then returned the way he had come. Had he met with someone?

Aldreda fumed that she had not arrived earlier. Then she saw a bat, darting from one fir branch to the next.

A small bat.

Aldreda flung herself after him, hurtling through the cool air. She caught up quickly and cut in front. It was a move rather reminiscent of Pags' tricks, and the little bat reared up in fright.

Aldreda dropped onto the stone, transforming into a woman. She flung her long black hair over herself and put her hands on her hips. "Raddle, is that you?" She spoke in French, as before.

The little bat drifted down, transformed, and sprawled on the stone in an ungainly pile of arms and legs. "Yes, mademoiselle," said Raddle, peering up at her. "Pardon, mademoiselle."

"What are you doing out here?" Aldreda put out a hand to help him up.

Raddle swallowed. "Exploring, mademoiselle."

"Whatever for? You were meant to stay in the cellar."

The boy looked down and did not answer. Aldreda sighed, then a thought occurred to her. "Did you see a man come here earlier?"

Raddle looked up again. "Yes."

"What did he do? He is a servant from the house, and it is strange that he was out here in the night."

Raddle heaved himself onto a higher rock and sat with his legs dangling. "It wasn't him that I saw first. It was the lady."

"What lady?" demanded Aldreda.

Raddle shrugged. "She came into the cellar, you see, but she didn't know I was there. Largish lady, with an apron."

"Mrs Sidgemoor," supplied Aldreda. "What did she do?"

"She pulled a chair over to look into Miss Reed's house, but she didn't call out to Miss Reed, so it seemed to me that she didn't want to disturb her. Then she crept to the other side of the room and tied up a small sack of rocks."

"A sack of rocks?" Aldreda stared at him.

Raddle nodded. "I thought it odd, too. Round rocks, black and grey. Heavy, too, by the look of it. She tied the sack up carefully, then slunk away with it, trying to be quiet, though it looked very cumbersome. So of course I followed, and slipped out before she shut the door."

"Of course," said Aldreda. "Though you were supposed to stay in the cellar."

"Was I?"

"Yes, but I'm glad you didn't. What happened next?"

Raddle leaned forward, grinning. "The lady took the sack to the side door and gave it to the man. They were both acting all secretive, and they had a whispered conversation which I couldn't catch, for all it seemed to be in some kind of French. I know she told him to be quick, though. So of course, I followed him."

"And he came here? What did he do with the sack?"

Raddle's chin jerked. "He tied it to a rope and lowered it down behind the old mill."

Aldreda turned to look at the mill. The old wheel spun placidly in the night, the water gleaming with a faint reflection of the moon. Sidgemoor must have hidden a whole sack of shatterstones, but why? And at whose direction? It must be Lady Orlend, she thought, eager to hide any evidence of the bombs. Perhaps then she would not be blamed for Elinor's accident.

Or perhaps they had been placed there to cause another, more serious accident.

Aldreda turned back to Raddle. "You did well to discover this; the objects in that sack are very dangerous. You must not go near them."

Raddle nodded, looking attentive, and Aldreda hoped she had not achieved the opposite of her purpose in warning him.

"And now," she said firmly, not one to let an opportunity pass, "you must lead me to your roost."

Raddle's face changed, tightening with – was that fear? "Oh no, mademoiselle."

"Why not?"

"I don't know where it is."

"Nonsense," she replied. "You must have an inkling, now that you are rested and more yourself. It is imperative that we find your vampiri family. I can lead you towards the southern cliffs and then you can look around. You might see or smell something you recognise, or your memory might return."

"I'd rather not—"

"You must at least attempt it. You owe me a favour for rescuing you from the cliff face."

Raddle's expression became sullen, but he followed her lead in transforming into a bat. Aldreda led him cautiously across the fields, following the hedgerows as he flapped close behind her. It would not do to lose her charge to an owl. She hoped Perry was not worrying unduly about Raddle's whereabouts, and trusted to her to find him.

She was thankful for the still night, as it made the flight less onerous for both of them. When they reached the southern part of Sark, she climbed higher and gestured for Raddle to take the lead.

He did so slowly, drifting in a meandering circle. Below them lay fields, trees, and sheep, all sleepy in the quiet darkness. Further out was the sea, vast and seething. The only sounds were the hypnotic rolling of the waves against the cliffs and the occasional call of a night-bird.

Raddle hovered above a flock of sheep in a suggestive manner. Aldreda shook her head and flicked her wing again.

The little bat seemed to heave a sigh. He wandered on and then, suddenly decisive, shot off to the east.

Aldreda simmered with excitement. She sped after him, hoping he had seen something recognisable, for he was flying with purpose now. She might find the roost this very night, before Pags, Elinor, or Jaq. The thought gave her some satisfaction.

At the south-eastern cliffs, Raddle pulled up. He hovered for a moment, then flew a slow arc over the bay and back again, as if searching for something. Then he shot off to the south.

Aldreda followed eagerly again. The same performance occurred twice more: once on the southern tip, and once in the middle of Little Sark, where Raddle flew in a perfect spiral around an unremarkable rock.

She began to feel resigned. When he charged off to the north, she flapped after him wearily. This time, as he drifted in a wide circle over the isthmus that joined Little Sark to the mainland, she became human and landed on a patch of sand.

"Raddle!" she called. "Are you prevaricating?"

Raddle flew back and tumbled into his human form in front of her. "Prevaricating? What does that mean?"

"Are you playing?" she snapped. "You are wasting my time. You are not looking properly."

"I am looking!" he said nervously. "I just can't find it. I told you, I don't know where it is."

Aldreda frowned, uncertain whether to believe him. Perhaps he had been trying to please her in a misguided way. "Well, I don't want to fly in circles all night, so we might as well return. Miss Reed is probably concerned for your whereabouts."

"Yes, mademoiselle," muttered Raddle.

Before she could transform, another vampiri landed with a thump on the ground next to her. She turned and saw Durl, who for once was unabashed in his nakedness. He strode forward and picked up Raddle, shaking him roughly. "Where have you been?" he growled.

Raddle quivered in his grasp, eyes wide. "Nowhere, sir! Just for a little fly around!" He gulped as Durl's hands tightened on his arms. "Miss Zooth wanted me to look for the roost, but I couldn't find it."

Durl gave him another shake, then put him down. He did not let go entirely, however. Grasping the child by an elbow, he turned to Aldreda. "No luck?"

Aldreda grimaced. "No. Raddle seems quite unable to remember."

Durl seemed to recall his state of undress and shoved Raddle in front of him. "Well, it is time this boy returned home. Everyone is in an uproar."

Aldreda looked startled. "They should have known I would find him."

Durl smiled. "I have complete confidence in your abilities, Miss Zooth, but Pags and Lilian are searching too. Even Lady Beresford, I believe, is out looking."

She drew a breath. "Oh dear, she ought to be in bed. Let us return with all haste."

Aldreda, thoughtful, led Durl and a sullen Raddle back to Elinor's room. As she had hoped, Elinor was there, guarded zealously by Beresford and sitting petulantly on her bed. She had a map spread out on her lap and a plate of half-eaten pie and a cup of tea next to her, but she was regarding the map disconsolately. Perry, Jaq, and Pags were absent.

Aldreda flew through the open window and catapulted onto

the bed behind Elinor. "My gown!" she demanded. Then she noticed Lilian sitting demurely at the end of the bed, regarding her with interest. She was wearing one of Aldreda's cloaks, so she must have had wings recently too.

Elinor cast the map aside and rushed to fetch Aldreda a gown from the spare basket. "Aldreda! You found him!" She had seen the other two bats, who were now hanging from the windowsill. "I'm so glad! My map divinations were not working at all and Lilian could not find Raddle anywhere in the house."

Aldreda, dressing, suggested that Durl and Raddle be given some handkerchiefs to allow them to join the conversation. Beresford whipped out one of his and laid it upon the windowsill, and Elinor hurried over with her own. Then they all turned their backs while Durl and Raddle became human and made themselves decent.

Aldreda finished doing up her ties. "You were trying to find Raddle with the map?" she asked, noting that Elinor had ceased to keep her Discernment a secret in front of Lilian or Durl. Of course, it would only be a matter of time before the gossip reached the vampiri through Mrs Sidgemoor or Lady Orlend.

"Yes, I was," said Elinor. "It was terribly confusing. I kept pointing to different spots all over the island."

"That is because Raddle was flying all over Sark," said Aldreda dryly. "He led me on quite the wild-bat chase."

Elinor looked at Raddle. "What were you doing, young man? I told you specifically to stay in the cellar."

Raddle muttered something and Durl loomed direfully over him.

"Raddle was trying to find the roost for me," Aldreda said hastily. "Without success, I might add." She did not want to mention aloud her suspicion that Raddle had not been trying very hard, but she gave Elinor a meaningful look. "We went searching in Little Sark but he could not recall anything – despite flying with great purpose all over the cliffs."

Elinor's eyes narrowed and her hand found her lapis lazuli, hidden beneath her gown. She turned to the little bat, huddled in her handkerchief on the windowsill, the cool night air seeping into the room. "Raddle, do you know the location of your roost?"

"No, madame," said Raddle in a low voice.

"I knew it!" said Elinor. "You are not telling the truth. I can tell," she added, leaning towards him. "Why will you not tell us, my dear boy? We only wish to help."

Raddle looked up with scared eyes and said nothing.

20

IN WHICH A SECRET SURFACES

*E*linor stared with frustration at the little boy. She had heard the tinny echo of the lie in his voice. He *did* know where the roost was, so why was he keeping it from her? Did she look like a person of ill intent?

Raddle dropped his gaze to the windowsill and silence held sway over the room. Beresford, standing by the door, folded his arms.

Elinor sat on the bed in an attempt to look less threatening, crossing her ankles and smoothing her skirts. "Please, Raddle. We have come all the way from England just to find your roost. We wish to tell your queen that she may return with us to escape any further danger."

Still the boy said nothing.

Aldreda stepped forward. "I suspect – I am afraid – that Durl has threatened Raddle to ensure his silence."

Elinor drew in a startled breath. She looked at Durl, who stood just behind Raddle, towering over the boy. Now she saw that one of his hands gripped Raddle's shoulder hard. "Durl, is this true? Let go of Raddle, please."

Durl raised his eyebrows and shook his head forcibly, his

beard bristling. He let go of Raddle as if he had been holding a hot coal.

Elinor began to feel annoyed. "What can you mean, Aldreda?" she asked, turning back to her. Behind Aldreda, she could see Lilian looking very pale, her hands clasped tightly in her lap, her eyes fixed on Durl's face.

Aldreda folded her arms, her black gown serving only to emphasise the formidable frown on her face. "I was there when Durl found Raddle this evening. He picked him up and shook him, and only let go when he learnt that I had not been shown the roost." She paused. "Furthermore, Durl was first to speak to Raddle when we initially discovered him. He had plenty of opportunity to scare Raddle into silence, under the guise of soothing utterances. Pags and I could not hear what he said while he helped Raddle to feed."

Beresford walked over and shut the window behind Durl, and the vampiri stiffened. Beresford stepped back, letting his hands rest by his sides. Raddle gave a frightened glance over his shoulder. It was unclear whether the boy was looking at the window or at Durl, who still loomed menacingly behind him.

Elinor observed Beresford's pre-emptive measure approvingly, then she sharpened her gaze on Durl. "Is this true?" she demanded again. "Are you hiding the roost from us? You may as well tell us the truth, as I shall know if you are lying."

Durl stared back aggressively, then his head drooped. "Yes, Lady Beresford."

Beresford glared at him. "Yes, Lady Beresford, what?"

"I am hiding the roost."

Elinor's mouth fell open. "But why?"

"I am not at liberty to say," said Durl, addressing the windowsill, and affording her a view only of his curly brown hair. "I shall not tell you where it is, so you may as well cease to ask me."

Elinor scrutinised him. "I did find it hard to believe that it had escaped your notice all these years. Did you stumble across it in your adventuring?"

Durl pressed his lips together and remained silent.

Beresford stepped forward. "Speak up, man. We need to find that roost before anyone else is hurt. Today my wife was injured – and it had better not have been you who caused it."

Elinor smiled at Beresford, but his statement reminded her of Chaboot. Durl could be refusing to speak because he was guilty. She stood up and took an angry step forward. "Did you put the shatterstone where I would find it, Durl? Have you been so eager to keep us away?"

Durl's eyes widened but he clung to his silence, his hands stiff by his sides.

This time, Lilian spoke gently into the fraught atmosphere. "Tell them, Durl. It can do no harm now. You may as well tell Lady Beresford the truth." She turned to Elinor. "Durl came with the roost all those years ago. He is a royal guard."

Elinor felt the truth of Lilian's words, and her eyebrows lifted. She stared at Durl, who raised his eyes to meet her gaze. A hardness was there that she had not seen before.

He folded his arms. "Her Majesty gave orders to be very careful as to who woke her. You have by no means proven yourself to be a worthy custodian of the roost."

Elinor sank back onto the bed. Suddenly, it all made sense. No wonder Durl lived wild on the island, in the solitary, thankless task of guarding his queen and her roost. No wonder he had lied to protect the roost, threatening Raddle to keep him quiet and misdirecting them to La Moinerie.

Would he have planted a shatterstone there to scare them away? Elinor could not believe it, though she reluctantly conceded to herself that he was right to be suspicious in the current climate of fear and secrecy around vampiri – especially as their party was sent by King George, who had instigated the repressive Edicts.

"Oh dear," she said weakly. "I do assure you that you can trust us. We have the queen's best interests at heart. King George has decreed a safe place in Cornwall for Musors and vampiri. We even have a castle awaiting her."

"Oh!" said Lilian, from the end of the bed. "A castle? How lovely! See, Durl, it may be time to end your vigil."

Elinor did not want to admit that the castle might be draughty and dusty. "Surely it is time to wake the roost?" she asked Durl. "You must at least ask Her Majesty if our offer pleases her."

Durl pressed his lips tightly together and glanced around uneasily at the earnest feminine faces regarding him.

Beresford, Elinor noted, had not adopted such a conciliatory expression, but looked stern. "If you are guarding your queen's interests, Durl, then it is your duty, not your preference."

Durl nodded slowly, glancing at Lilian then back to Elinor. "Very well. You may ask Her Majesty."

Elinor clasped her hands together. "Wonderful! Will you lead us to the hiding place?"

Durl's expression became sardonic. "You already have a good inkling, do you not? One of your men found a tunnel in the cliff despite my efforts to lead you to La Moinerie – though I hasten to add that I did not intend you to come to any harm, Lady Beresford."

Elinor could hear the truth in his words, and waved the matter away. She could solve the mystery of the shatterstone later; now she was determined to know where the roost was. "So Jaq did find the entrance?"

Durl nodded. "It will be challenging for your men to breast it. I insist that I accompany them."

"We shall rely upon you," said Elinor, ignoring the implication that she would not be present. "Raddle can stay with Lilian." She smiled at the little boy, who looked relieved that the subterfuge was over, though he still clutched his handkerchief close with white fingers.

Durl held up a hand. "The entrance can only be accessed by humans when the tide is low. Vampiri can only use it when the sky is dark. It will be difficult to find a suitable window for both. You must not attempt it in the daytime without me."

"Of course," agreed Elinor. "We do not want to wake the queen without her guard." She reflected that Durl's steady presence might help soothe the queen, as well as provide a guide into the cave.

Beresford cleared his throat. "Aren't you forgetting something, my dear?"

"What would that be?"

"We still lack the flute."

"Oh." Elinor's shoulders sank. "Durl, do you know how to wake Her Majesty? We brought a flute for the purpose, but I seem to have mislaid it."

Durl's frown deepened. "Mislaid? Do you mean a Viveroust flute?"

Elinor nodded guiltily.

"That was careless," he said. "Fortunately, I have one. They are rare instruments; not many exist."

Elinor agreed meekly. What a pity that the royal guard should form such a terrible impression of their party. She hoped Durl did not have too much influence over Her Majesty. "We shall have to use your flute," she said quietly. "Aldreda can play it, if you will allow it."

Durl's eyes shifted to Aldreda and he nodded slowly. "I permit it."

Aldreda nodded graciously. Behind her, Lilian opened her mouth then shut it again.

"Very well," said Beresford. "Tomorrow evening we shall reconvene, and attempt to breach the cave if the tide is right."

Elinor sat up. "Why not now?"

Beresford shook his head reprovingly. "Hedley informed me earlier that the tide is high again tonight. Moreover, we need a day of rest to gather our forces after your accident this afternoon."

Elinor took the hint. "A splendid idea. Shall we all retire to our beds? I confess I am in need of a rest after all the excitement. Goodnight, Durl, and thank you for taking us into your confidence, however reluctantly. We shall see you tomorrow evening for our presentation to your queen!"

Durl bowed, the linen handkerchief billowing around him. "I hope you prove worthy of my trust," he said. He put a hand on Raddle's shoulder. "Come, lad, you can sleep in the woods with me tonight."

He leapt into the air and became a bat, abandoning Beresford's handkerchief. Raddle followed suit with less dexterity. Beresford unlocked the window and the two bats flew off into the night.

Elinor let out a deep sigh, putting a hand to her head. "Goodness me. My head aches again."

Beresford pulled the curtains shut and came to sit beside her on the bed. He took her hand. "You must rest now."

Elinor gave him a gimlet stare. "If you think to keep me from joining the expedition tomorrow night, you are sadly mistaken."

"We can discuss it tomorrow," said Beresford, then spoiled it by adding, "though I do not see the need for your presence." He held up a hand at her look of outrage. "We shall not require your divination if Durl takes us there."

Aldreda had been silent, but now she stirred. "Do you trust Durl entirely, Elinor? Was he telling the truth?"

"As far as I could tell," said Elinor. "Why, what is in your mind?"

Aldreda gave a tiny shrug. "Merely that he may have been wild on this island for too long. Perhaps he doesn't wish to leave."

She gave a sideways glance at Lilian, who still sat on the end of the bed.

Lilian caught Aldreda's look and blushed faintly. "Oh, I am certain that Durl would not put personal interest ahead of his duty," she said. "I have only known him a little while, yet I know enough to say that his is a noble soul. He will do the right thing by the roost."

"If he is convinced we *are* the right thing." Elinor said morosely.

Beresford squeezed her hand and stood up. "We should ask Pags' opinion: he may have more insight into Durl's character. Perhaps Durl enjoys being wild more than he would admit to us. After all, twelve years of solitude may have permanently altered his tastes."

Elinor tapped her chin. "You fear that he wants to keep the roost asleep on Sark, James?"

"It is possible." Beresford put out a hand for Lilian. "Miss Reed, allow me to return you to the cellar," he said. Lilian daintily stepped onto his broad hand, keeping Aldreda's cloak pulled tightly around her. He turned to Elinor. "Elinor, if I come back and you are not here then I shall not answer for the consequences."

"Yes, husband dear."

Lilian gave a small curtsy. "Thank you for allowing me to participate this evening, Lady Beresford. I am glad it has all turned out well."

Elinor nodded and curtsied in return. Yet as Beresford left, she could not shake off a feeling of foreboding.

21

IN WHICH MUNITIONS ARE EASIER TO MANAGE THAN MEN

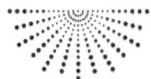

*P*ushing the cellar door open, Beresford saw that the room was lit by a single candle. It seemed rather bleak quarters for a young woman. Perhaps vampiri had different tastes – though Aldreda seemed to like her luxurious basket in the attic, with its richly tasselled shawl.

"Where should I put you?" Beresford asked, feeling Lilian's little feet on the palm of his hand. He hoped he wouldn't drop her, though she seemed to be standing at ease, as if she were well accustomed to such transport.

"Up there." Lilian pointed in a rather imperious fashion. Beresford wondered how such little people had so much self-possession. "You are tall enough to lift me to the top of that cupboard, I believe."

He did so. Lilian stepped over the edge and disappeared. Then Aldreda's cloak was thrown over the edge and Lilian gave him some prim words of thanks. Reaching for the tiny cloak, Beresford realised that he had been dismissed.

As he came out of the cellar he saw Chester on the stairs. The boy started guiltily and muttered something about fetching another bottle of cognac. Beresford refused his offer of a drink and went on his way. He ignored Chester's curious gaze on his back; he had learned long ago not to explain his actions and simply act as if he had every right to be leaving the cellar at night.

He headed back to the bedroom feeling as though he had to gird his loins. Almost literally: a chastity belt for himself would be useful where Elinor was concerned. How would he survive another night in that bedroom with her? At least now they knew where the roost lay. They might be done with this charade by tomorrow, and then he wouldn't have to endure the torture for much longer. Only three more weeks until his wedding night, thank God. That cursed plum jam had ruined him – though he suspected that even without its continuing effect, Elinor's curves and soft invitations would still be driving him wild.

Thankfully, when he went into the bedroom Aldreda was awake. Though she looked tired from her adventures with Raddle, she was nonetheless constant in her role as chaperone. Elinor was sitting sulkily in her big bed now, the maps put away, her head adorably bandaged, the pie finished, the tea cup emptied. She, too, had shadows under her eyes. Beresford pressed his lips together grimly. Today's events had shaken them all, but at least they had also shaken out some revelations.

He laid himself gingerly on the settee and Aldreda told them about her discovery in La Moinerie: a sack of shatterstones left unattended. They all agreed on the likelihood that Lady Orlend had ordered the Sidgemoors to hide the shatterstones.

Elinor nibbled on her lower lip. "Did you see the stones inside the sack?" she asked Aldreda. "Apparently the grey ones carry more Impact than the black. I do not like the idea of Sidgemoor dragging such power about."

"I did not see the sack at all, but we can ask Raddle," said Aldreda. "Regardless, our position on Sark is precarious now. I do not know if it is wise to confront Lady Orlend. She could in turn accuse us of treasonous behaviour in hiding Perry's Gift from the king."

Beresford nodded. "Not to mention that Jaq and Perry have been seen embracing in Perry's room."

Elinor rubbed her forehead crossly. "Could we explain to Lady Orlend that it was due to the logistics of Travelling together?"

"Jaq was not wearing many clothes," Beresford reminded her dryly.

She sighed heavily. "It is all very awkward."

Beresford stared up at the ceiling. "Awkward, and dangerous for Jaq, too. I wish he would remember that his status as a royal selkie won't necessarily protect him here."

Elinor's voice quivered. "It is not fair for them. Maybe we should send them to Skerry, out of harm's way."

Aldreda shook her head. "Running away now would look like guilt."

Beresford considered the risk, his fingers laced behind his head. "We don't know yet what Lady Orlend will do with her new knowledge. The most important thing is to fetch the roost: that is our primary purpose. We don't want to provoke a confrontation which could endanger Perry or Jaq before that. Not when we could be on our way tomorrow."

Aldreda shifted restlessly on the rose-coloured pillow. "Yet the shatterstones remain unaccounted for. I think it is too risky to leave them there."

"Yes," said Beresford. "I shall have to move them."

Elinor sat up so suddenly that Aldreda tumbled off her pillow. "No, James! It could be dangerous."

"Not as dangerous as leaving them there," he replied. His plan also had the advantage of removing him from this bedroom. He swung his legs over the side of the settee and it creaked in protest. "I'll go now. Aldreda, where precisely was the sack?"

"I'll go with you," Aldreda offered. "After all, I've been asleep all day."

"No!" Elinor huffed. "Well, if you are both going, I insist that you take Jaq as well, if he hasn't already left for Skerry. Aldreda will not be much use if Sidgemoor leaps upon you."

Beresford strode to the door. "Fine, I'll take Jaq." It was a good excuse to remove Jaq from Perry's room, if indeed he was there.

Aldreda's hands moved to her ties. "You fetch Jaq; I'll fly ahead to read the lay of the land."

Elinor watched them leave, the mournful expression on her face emphasised by her bandage. "Don't be long!"

Beresford paused outside Perry's room and listened before knocking softly. He couldn't hear anything within, but he certainly didn't want to interrupt.

After a few moments, footsteps sounded and Perry opened the door a crack. "Oh, it's you," he said, with relief. "Come in."

As Beresford entered, Perry went to his wardrobe and opened it. Jaq tumbled out in a swirl of dressing gown.

Beresford sighed. "You two are playing a dangerous game. I hope you realise that."

"Of course we do," Perry snapped over his shoulder. "And I, for one, find it very tiring."

Righting his dressing gown, Jaq put an arm around Perry's shoulder. "It is odd that you humans have such prudish notions and barbaric customs."

Perry slipped his arm around Jaq's waist and laid his head on his shoulder. Then he pushed himself away and sat down on the bed with a sigh. "We weren't doing anything untoward, just talking," he said defensively. "If this carries on, I'm starting to think that Elinor is right, and we should run off to Skerry."

Jaq stilled for a moment in the act of tying up his dressing gown, then he pulled it tight. "Run off to Skerry?"

Perry raised his eyebrows. "Yes. The selkies are more understanding, are they not? We could live in peace there."

Jaq's arms dropped to his sides, but Beresford could see that they held a sudden tension.

"Skerry is tolerant," said Jaq carefully, "when it comes to selkies. It is true that we have all sorts of romantic and sexual arrangements. But it may not be quite so accepting of you as you imagine."

"Why?" Perry's eyes clouded. "Because I am human?"

"Yes, and because you are mine," said Jaq. "I left Skerry under a cloud, remember."

"I don't care about that!" Perry frowned. "Unless you are suggesting that my presence will undermine your return?"

Beresford wondered if he should make a discreet exit, for Perry looked like a kicked puppy, and Jaq's jaw was clenched. Before he could carry out this plan, however, Jaq turned to him in appeal. "You know how it was, Beresford! My mother sent me off in disgrace; her kingdom reviles me. I've been gone a while, but it is not long enough for everyone to forget what I did. I have to be careful how I return. In fact, I am not certain that I even *want* to return."

Beresford shrugged. "In any case, neither of you can go to Skerry now. We have work to do." He was trying to change the subject before this conversation became more difficult. He did not want to see Jaq and Perry fight; Jaq had been much happier since Perry came into his life.

Perry's hands clenched into fists. "It sounds as if we can *never* go to Skerry, since I am not welcome there, either."

Too late. Beresford sighed.

Jaq jammed his hands into the pockets of his dressing gown. "That's not what I said! Skerry traditionally shuns humans. We have gone to great pains to keep ourselves secret, as you well know. My mother did a radical thing in making me Beresford's ward: she took a risk. If I go home with a human in tow, people might think I've been corrupted."

It was the wrong thing to say; even Beresford could have told

Jaq that. Perry was already discouraged by English society's view of him as aberrant; the last thing he needed to hear was that the selkies might also scorn him.

Perry's spine stiffened. "Well, I do not want to corrupt you, Your Highness," he snapped. "You won't have to *tow* me to Skerry."

Jaq stared at him, his cheekbones somehow sharper than usual.

In the tense silence, Beresford cleared his throat. "Let's not be discomposed by what happened today; it may all blow over." Two pairs of eyes, one hazel, one dark, looked at him, but he could tell that neither man was really listening. "Right now, Jaq, I need your help. We need to secure a sack of munitions."

As he had hoped, this announcement distracted them. Perry tilted his head in sudden enquiry and Jaq raised an eyebrow. "Shatterstones?"

"Yes, carried to La Moinerie by Sidgemoor earlier this evening."

Perry's hands unclasped and his shoulders relaxed a little. "Is he our villain? I thought he looked shifty."

Beresford shrugged. "Sidgemoor could be following orders," he replied. "Either way, I don't like leaving the bombs there. I'm going to move them and I want to be prepared for trouble. Jaq, come with me." He was pleased that Jaq obeyed without question, flinging off his dressing gown and reaching for his clothes. Though the selkie was no longer technically Beresford's ward, he was still part of his crew and owed him allegiance. And perhaps, also, Jaq wanted to escape the accusation in Perry's gaze.

Perry sat slumped on the bed, and stared broodingly before him. Beresford backed towards the door. "I'll wait in the corridor for you, Jaq."

As he closed the door, he heard Perry speak. "You issued me a standing invitation to try Skerry's wines, Jaq. Didn't you mean it?"

Jaq's voice was subdued. "I was flirting with you, Perry; I didn't think it was really going to happen. Why can't we just stay in Devon? We were happy there."

Beresford went to the end of the corridor to avoid hearing more, hoping that the two of them would sort it out. However, when Jaq came out of the room, his face was pale and upset.

They crept downstairs and slipped out of the house. Aldreda was circling outside, waiting, and she led them back to La Moinerie. Trusting that she had scouted for any danger – really, vampiri were most useful – Beresford and Jaq stole into the ruins.

The old mill churned haltingly in the moonlight, the fir trees throwing long shadows over the stones and water. Aldreda fluttered to the contraption and hung from its side, gesturing with a wing. Beresford saw a thick rope dangling from one of the wooden stakes that framed the mill. It disappeared into the water. He knelt beside it and pulled. The rope tightened, but its burden did not lift. Whatever lay at the end of it was heavy enough to be full of rocks.

Beresford heaved it up slowly. It must have been easier to drop down than to lift, and Beresford wondered if Sidgemoor would have assistance when he returned for it. Or perhaps he didn't intend to fetch it himself.

A hessian sack rose to the surface, dripping wet. Beresford paused, his muscles straining. The last thing they wanted was to detonate the entire contents of the sack as they retrieved it. Jaq, accustomed to being wet, waded into the water to help lift it onto solid ground.

The sack lay in the mud, ungainly and misshapen. Cautiously, Beresford undid the rope and inspected the contents. The shatterstones looked innocuous, like pebbles smoothed by time. Yet his gut twisted as he stared at them, remembering how one small stone had dashed Elinor against the wall into unconsciousness.

"Pretty," observed Jaq. "But nasty."

Aldreda flickered her wings in agitation, unable to voice her opinions in bat form.

Beresford pulled the sack tightly closed. Now that they had the damn thing, what was he meant to do with it? It was a cursed responsibility. He couldn't move the sack to the *Crescent*, as he didn't particularly want to blow up his ship. He thought for a moment. "The walled gardens are close by. I suspect their walls are from old fortifications, as they are so thick. Let's put this against one, beneath the ivy. That way, if it does explode, we only lose a wall and not a whole house."

Jaq nodded, and when Beresford reached for the sack, he put out a hand. "I'll carry it. I'm stronger."

Beresford twisted his lips wryly. It was true: despite his broad-shouldered form, Jaq's lithe limbs had superior, supernatural strength.

Carefully lifting the sack, Jaq walked beside Beresford as they took a circuitous route to the walled garden on the other side of the Seigneurie, at right angles to the ruins. Aldreda flew above, keeping a lookout.

Beresford could hear crickets chirping, and sensed the movements of night creatures in the trees. He cast a sideways glance at Jaq. The selkie looked preoccupied, his expression glum as he hunched under the heavy sack. Beresford did not think the weight of the rocks was what bothered him.

Eventually, Jaq spoke. "Perry says I don't belong in Devon and he doesn't belong in Skerry." He sighed. "He says I should go back to Skerry and be a prince without him. I don't know what to do."

Beresford kept his voice low in case it carried in the quiet night. "He is new to your world. Give him time."

Jaq grimaced. "I'm trying to protect him. What do you think the selkies will say if I arrive at Skerry with him?"

"Perhaps what you already insinuated: that he is unwelcome."

Jaq shifted the sack. "I thought I could be honest with Perry. I don't want to lie. Selkies distrust land folk, and they will distrust him."

"Seraphine will accept him," said Beresford. "And surely your sister isn't the only selkie fascinated by humans."

Jaq frowned. "Fascination does not equal respect."

Beresford smiled in the dark. It was good to see Jaq's usual suavity undone; he was so devil-may-care about everything else. Perhaps he wasn't accustomed to such delicate conversations. "I'm sure you can talk him round, or convince your people to accept him. You just have to decide what you want first."

Jaq was silent, which was probably a good thing. They had reached the far wall. The grey stones were piled close together in a thick, imposing structure that Beresford suspected dated from the twelfth century. It was patterned with lichen and moss, and partly covered in a thick tangle of ivy along the eastern edge.

Beresford parted some trailing stems and Jaq carefully put the sack down. They spent a few minutes arranging the ivy to cover it, then backed away. In the thin light of the moon it was hard to see the sack, but Beresford vowed to check on it in the morning.

"There." Jaq brushed his hands together. "I'm off to bed."

"Wait," said Beresford, as Jaq turned towards the house. "You'd better sleep on the ship. If you are discovered in Perry's room again it will only make things worse."

Jaq's chiselled jaw thrust out in a hint of rebellion, then his shoulders dropped. "You're right, of course."

"You can talk to him tomorrow," said Beresford. "In the meantime, you have Elinor's idea to occupy you. The selkies might know something about Sark."

Jaq nodded. "I'll leave tonight." He turned and vanished into the dark.

22

IN WHICH DANGER HEIGHTENS
ZEST

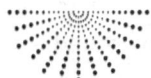

*E*linor lay waiting for Beresford to return; she would certainly be unable to sleep until he was back safely. Unfortunately, this gave her plenty of time to mull over the mysteries that still remained on the island, and to speculate on what awaited them in the caves below Little Sark.

It seemed like an age before Beresford crept in and shut the bedroom door soundlessly behind him.

"James!" she murmured gladly. Then she saw that Aldreda was hanging off his coat as a bat.

Aldreda lifted into the air and flapped over to the bed, landing in a pointed fashion above Elinor's head.

Beresford tiptoed over and leaned down to give Elinor a chaste kiss on the cheek. "All done. The shatterstones are behind the walled gardens on the eastern side, hidden under ivy. I only hope no one stumbles across them."

"Better there than in Sidgemoor's hiding place," she said, and yawned. "Why don't we sleep now?" She patted her bed, but it was a half-hearted invitation: she knew he would ignore it.

He smiled and retreated to his corner of the room. Quickly, he changed into his nightshirt, lay down on the rug, and pulled a blanket over himself. "By the way," he said, as he settled down, "maybe don't mention going to Skerry again to your brother."

"Oh, why not?"

"Jaq seems to think that it might not be a good idea."

Elinor digested this. "Poor Perry." Then she yawned again. She was too exhausted to think much on it, and her head ached. Relieved that Beresford and Aldreda were with her once more, she quickly fell into a deep sleep.

Some hours later, the sound of scraping on the ground outside broke into her consciousness and pulled her awake.

She lay still, eyes wide, listening. The sound came again: a long scrape, like a shovel being dragged over the ground. That must be the sound Perry had heard, like a grave being dug. Elinor shivered, debating whether to leave her warm bed and look out of the window to see what was causing it.

That was when she saw the cloaked figure at the foot of her bed.

It loomed between the bedposts, a silhouette framed by the canopy. Elinor's blood froze. She stopped breathing, her eyes like saucers in the dark.

The figure glided around the bed until it stood next to her. Elinor's heart stuttered.

A hand lifted from within the cloak and moved towards her.

She gasped a breath and tried to scream, but could not. Yet even her quick intake of breath and croak must have warned the intruder that she was awake, for the figure took a step back. Before Elinor could say a word, the black shape turned and retreated, sliding out the door with a whisper of cloth.

Elinor sat up, her heart pounding. "James!" she said urgently, and was dismayed to find her voice faint. "Beresford!"

He did not stir. Elinor looked above her head, belatedly remembering her chaperone. Aldreda's form was not hanging against the frills.

"Blasted bat," muttered Elinor. "What is the point of a chaperone if she's not there when you need her?" The bitter remark gave her enough courage to swing her legs out of her bed and rush over to her recumbent protector.

Beresford stirred and batted her away. "No, Elinor," he murmured thickly, "you must not!"

Elinor huffed with impatience. "Someone was in the room, James! I'm not trying to seduce you, I'm trying to wake you!"

Beresford sat up with a start and blinked blearily at her. "Someone was in the room?"

Elinor nodded shakily. "Near my bed."

Suddenly, he was fully present. He threw off his blankets and leapt to his feet. "What happened?"

"He left when he saw I was awake." Elinor pointed a trembling finger at the door. "I think it was a he." She realised she couldn't be sure; the cloak had disguised the shape of the interloper.

Beresford, clad in his nightshirt, left the room, and Elinor was left biting her knuckles. Oh, why had she woken Beresford? Curse her feminine weakness. She could have followed the cloaked figure just as easily, even if Beresford would have been furious about it later. She would be furious with *him*, if anything awful happened. Impatiently, she wrenched off the bandage that adorned her brow, though her head still hurt.

She lit a candle and paced in her shift, cursing Aldreda, Beresford, and all Sarkees. The room had never felt so oppressive, and she flung the window open, searching the night sky in vain for Aldreda.

Where, oh *where* was Beresford? She would do anything to see him safe, warm, and alive. What if he were hurt? Would she become a widow without ever having been a wife? She wrung her hands with impatience and worry.

Finally, over half an hour later, the door swung open to reveal Beresford, chest heaving with exertion.

She threw herself into his arms and he embraced her roughly. "I couldn't find him," he panted. "I looked everywhere, and then thought I should return and see if you were safe. Did he... do anything to you?"

Elinor clung to him. "No, he just loomed over the bed." She shivered. "Don't rush off like that again – I thought you were dead! Don't leave me to worry!"

Beresford's grasp tightened. "He could have hurt you as I slept."

Elinor shuddered and lifted her face for a kiss. Beresford's lips came down hungrily and, giddy with relief, Elinor felt desire like a rushing tide within her. She pulled him to the bed and they fell upon it, kissing greedily, his hands warm through her shift. She rolled on top of him, heedless of anything except the need to be as close to him as possible. His arms wrapped around her and she revelled in his long body, warm and strong beneath her.

Endless moments passed until she was dizzy with passion from his kisses. Her heart beat wildly and her skin ached and shivered with delight. Beresford rolled her over so that he now lay above her, his thigh between her legs, his mouth on her neck, and his hand moving to a most improper place.

"My Lord Beresford!"

Aldreda's voice was sharp in the dark. Beresford's hand stopped, and so did his lips. Slowly, he withdrew both.

"Elinor!" Aldreda's voice was scandalised. "Stop that at once!"

Elinor blinked hazily, and realised that she was still arching up under her fiancé. "Aldreda?"

"*What* do you think you are doing?" Aldreda snapped. She was standing on the bedside table, completely naked, hands on hips. "I leave for one hour and this is what happens! You ought to be ashamed of yourselves!"

Beresford sat up. It was difficult to see in the candlelight, but Elinor suspected his face was red. Her own body was still tingling, bereft of his touch. Suddenly, she felt very cross indeed. "Leave for an hour?" She struggled to a sitting position, her voice rising. "*You* should be ashamed of yourself! While you were gone, I was almost murdered in my bed!"

"Pardon?"

"I woke up to find a man looming over me," said Elinor. "He ran off and I woke Beresford, who bravely chased after him, seeing as *you* weren't there to do it. He was gone a while; I was sick with apprehension. So you cannot blame us if we succumbed to our inclinations, in the sheer relief of finding each other safe."

"Hm," said Aldreda, but her tone was quieter. "I am sorry for my absence; I went out to find Pags. He didn't return from his hunt for Raddle, so I wanted to give him all the news. I couldn't find him, though I flew all over the island."

Beresford had removed himself from the bed. He now stood several feet away, his hair adorably tousled and his hands clasped in front of him. "I apologise too; I allowed myself to be carried away. I can only blame the fear which overtook me, that I might never hold Elinor close again."

Aldreda coughed gently. "Well, never mind." She turned back to Elinor. "Who do you think was in your bedroom?"

"I don't know," said Elinor crossly. "It could have been anyone. It was too dark to tell."

Beresford's expression became stony. "It is a good reminder that we still have no explanation for the accidents that have befallen us, or for Lieutenant Chaboot's death." He went over to the window and shut it, drawing the curtains tightly across.

Aldreda looked thoughtful. "Quite apart from that, it also means that now someone knows that you two keep separate beds, and the marriage is a sham."

Elinor folded her arms. "There is an easy solution to that."

"You can't be married tomorrow," said Aldreda, "if that is what you are thinking."

"No: Beresford must sleep in this bed with me, in case the intruder returns."

Aldreda sighed and looked from one to the other. Perhaps

Beresford's alarmed look reassured her, for she nodded. "You are right, Elinor. Get into the bed, my lord. I remind you, I shall be watching."

Beresford visibly swallowed, then returned to the four-poster, clambered under the blankets, and gave Elinor a wry look.

Elinor smiled, triumphant, then slipped under the blankets and snuggled up to him. Aldreda tutted but said no more. She merely transformed into a bat and flew to hang above Elinor's head.

Beresford gathered Elinor close. "Goodnight, my dear. We'll keep you safe."

She didn't say it, but she was determined to keep him safe, too. At least now she had him well within arm's reach.

It took her a long time to fall asleep. Her triumph soon faded when she realised she had done the equivalent of stealing a cake she was not allowed to eat. It was an exquisite kind of torture to be so close to Beresford, yet unable to let her hands and her lips roam all over him. With Aldreda's gimlet eye upon them, however, she dared do no more than slight nuzzling. Really, Aldreda was starting to remind her of a gargoyle.

Eventually, she drifted off into sleep, cocooned in Beresford's arms.

23

IN WHICH EFFORTS AT COURTESY
FAIL

*A*ldreda watched the two lovers sleep, feeling rather dispirited. Out of the kindness of her heart she had gone out into the night to find Pags and inform him of the new developments, especially the revelation about Durl and Raddle's discovery of the sack of shatterstones. She had flown all over the island carrying this interesting news, but Pags had proved annoyingly elusive. Where was he? Why was he not waiting for her? If he had left, he should have told her of his intentions.

Could he have flown off the island and left them to it? Aldreda realised with a stab of guilt that she had been less than courteous to Pags lately. He had invited it, with his outrageous comments and aggravating behaviour. Still, a lady shouldn't allow a man's conduct to lower her own comportment. With a sigh, she resolved to treat Pags more politely if he deigned to show up again. That is, if he wasn't already back in Dartmoor.

She was more worried than she liked to admit, and when she heard a tap at the window her heart leapt with relief. She flew with all haste past the curtains.

It was Pags. Her relief was quickly superseded by anger at seeing his human figure clinging to the vines on the side of the house. He was dressed, at least, but it was annoying that their meeting was on his terms, not hers.

Fetching a gown, she dressed behind the curtain, taking her time and keeping an eye on the slumbering forms of Beresford and Elinor. Tucking her hair behind her ears, she opened the window.

The sea breeze nipped its way inside, so she kept the gap narrow and slipped out. "Shh," she admonished, as she sat down on the sill. "Elinor and Beresford are sleeping."

Pags swung himself up and peered over her shoulder. "I won't disturb them, the sweet things." Aldreda looked too; they had not moved an inch.

Pags observed her dryly. "Still playing chaperone, I see. You make a faithful servant."

"I am not a servant!"

"Oh?" Pags looked quizzical. "Miss Avely has a commanding cast of character, I have noticed. And you also follow her mother's decrees."

Aldreda frowned. "Mrs Avely and I are of accord on the matter of propriety before a wedding night."

"Then you are both faithful servants to propriety."

"Better than outlaws to it," retorted Aldreda. Belatedly, she recalled her resolution to remain courteous. "What brings you here tonight, my lord dukel?" she said, in an exceedingly polite tone.

Pags cocked his head. "I thought you sought my company, Miss Zooth. Durl told me you flew all over the island searching for me."

"Durl was mistaken," said Aldreda coldly. "I was looking for Raddle."

"You found him."

"I did," she replied.

"So why the second tour?"

Aldreda scowled. "If you must know, I wanted to tell you

about Durl. It turns out he is a royal guard to the roost and has been guarding them all these years. So you were right," she added reluctantly. "He *was* keeping something from us."

"Oh, yes, I know that," said Pags, grinning. "Durl told me himself."

"When?" she demanded.

"Earlier this evening, over some sloe gin." Pags paused. "He says he is looking forward to going to England after his long vigil."

"Oh!" Aldreda forgot to be icily civil. "Truly? I thought he might want to stay on Sark with Lilian."

"I don't know if I believe him," said Pags. "I think he likes the wild, despite his apparent courtship of Lilian. And also despite his pleasant remarks to you. He is trying to charm you both."

Aldreda bristled. "Nonsense. Durl will *appreciate* civilisation. He probably misses the company of Musors." She considered. "Perhaps, if he comes to England, he can become Perry's companion."

Pags laughed derisively, crossing his legs and staring out into the night. "You won't convince him to do that, my dear."

Aldreda stiffened. "And why not?"

"I told you: Durl has Rofanite tendencies. In his heart of hearts, he believes a vampiri is better off without a Musor. That is probably why he was chosen as a guard, because he is happy to live apart. He will not wish to abide by the dictates of Musor companionships, let alone the Edicts. And like me, he probably finds the laws of decorum a trifle restrictive."

Aldreda sniffed. "It seems you are not suited to be Mrs Avely's companion either, my lord dukel, if you find the laws of decorum so onerous." Her breathing constricted as she waited for his answer. Now he would confirm or refute his intention to leave them.

Pags stared over the dark gardens, the wind ruffling his thick hair. His eyes were fixed on the distant fields and the sea beyond.

"I can bend, my dear, but has it occurred to you that Mrs Avely, as future Marchioness of Lanyon, should offer her bond to the queen?"

Aldreda blinked. "Oh." She thought for a moment. "You mean when Her Majesty comes to Cornwall with us? I see your point: the queen of the roost should be companion to the highest in title, even if a marchioness is not a royal." She paused. "A wonderful excuse for you to step down, but I do not think the queen will mind if things are a little irregular when we reach Cornwall. She will simply be glad to be in civilised society again."

"For such a slave to propriety, I am surprised you do not see the truth of what I say," said Pags. "I cannot rock roost hierarchy by claiming precedence, especially when they are vulnerable and re-establishing themselves. The queen will need a respectable, eminent companion like Mrs Avely, far more than I shall."

"Far more than *you* want one, you mean," snapped Aldreda.

"Wants do not come into it, my dear," said Pags, casting her a sidelong glance. "There is nothing for it; I shall have to return to a life of savagery."

"Don't pretend you aren't pleased!"

"Well," he said with a confiding air, "I do find the Avely women a bit overbearing sometimes, but I suppose you and Elinor are well matched in that respect."

"Well!" breathed Aldreda. "Sark has plenty of sheep. If Durl comes to England, you can take up residence here instead."

She regretted the comment as soon as it left her lips. Pags leaned against the window pane, his dark eyes narrowing. "I might just do that," he said. "The sheep will be better company than a shrew."

Aldreda's mouth fell open. "How dare you!"

"Yes." His tone was coldly thoughtful. "Sheep are quiet, pleasant creatures, and I admit to a fondness for the puffins. They, at least, do not behave in a waspish manner that is designed to put a bat on the back foot."

"Waspish!"

"Always believing the worst and being afraid of the best," Pags continued, his gaze hard. "You are so willing to consign me to the wild that I wonder what scares you, Aldreda."

Her mouth was suddenly dry. "I suppose you think that *you* are the best? Of course, as a dukel, you are accustomed to thinking of yourself in such a light. It must be such a shock when not everyone agrees with you."

"Not *me*," said Pags. "What you and I could have together. That it could be a surpassing delight if only you would stop being such a harridan, Aldreda."

Aldreda gasped. "A fine declaration, indeed!"

"You forgot to add 'my lord dukel'," Pags said dryly. "Never mind, I quite understand. You are too high and mighty to lower yourself to a mere dukel, especially one with such a spotted history. I am disconsolate, but at least I shall have the puffins to cheer my solitude." He stood up and brushed down his coat, his lips pressed tightly together, then looked at her with an unreadable expression. "Goodbye, Aldreda."

Aldreda lifted her chin and held his gaze, though her heart felt like a bucket plummeting down a deep, dark well.

He shrugged. "Enjoy England. I am certain the roost will love you as headmistress. Unfortunately, I can't stomach all the disapproval."

Aldreda spluttered, but before she could answer, Pags had swung himself over the windowsill. She peered over to see him climbing down the ivy with barely a glance upwards.

She ground her teeth to stop them chattering. What a repellent bat. How *dare* he say such things to her? She could wring his thick neck! She was *not* headmistressly. Or headmistress-like. Or anything like a headmistress!

Shivering in the biting sea wind, Aldreda watched as he reached the ground and strode off. Most likely he would drink himself senseless on sloe gin and horse blood. She was glad he was staying on Sark. He could *have* the puffins.

Blinking sudden tears out of her eyes, she slid into the room. She pulled the latch and curtains shut, all the while trying to maintain her composure. She would be damned if that damned bat brought her to damned tears.

All the inward cursing bolstered her spirits: after all, a head-mistress would not curse. Then she saw Beresford and Elinor curled up together, peacefully asleep. Elinor's head lay upon his chest, his arm held her close, and their faces were turned towards each other. Elinor was smiling faintly in her sleep.

Aldreda sat, a tear coursing down her cheek.

IN WHICH MUTUAL BLACKMAIL IS EFFICACIOUS

hen Elinor awoke, her headache was much improved. She looked up to see Aldreda still awake and hanging over her even though light was filtering over the top of the curtains. Beresford had already risen and left the room; the bedclothes were cold next to her.

She slipped out of bed, feeling a little tired still, after the previous night's activity. Aldreda also seemed ill-disposed to talk, so Elinor quietly carried her up to the attic and her basket with its paisley shawl. Then she went downstairs to breakfast.

The atmosphere in the breakfast room was chilly. Lady Orlend treated Elinor with cold civility that bordered on rudeness, and she looked pale and gaunt. When Perry limped in, she barely looked at him, though she did direct Sidgemoor to assist with his chair. Even when Beresford appeared after his early morning walk, the Dame of Sark simply sniffed and did not enquire as to his well-being.

Chester muttered something about a good day for walking and began shovelling food into his mouth. Elinor hoped he wasn't going to traipse around the back of the walled gardens.

Lady Orlend dismissed Sidgemoor and looked around the room with haughtily arched brows. "It seems an appropriate course of action, Lord Beresford, for me to throw you all off Sark without delay. I am aware now that Mr Avely is not what he claims to be, and neither is your wife. I do not appreciate such trickery being perpetuated upon me."

Elinor's eyes widened. Thankfully, it seemed the 'wife' part was not under question – but they simply could not be escorted off the island today! Tomorrow, perhaps, but not before tonight!

She began to speak, but Beresford held up a hand. He was right: their host had not finished.

"Yet I find that I am also in rather a delicate position," Lady Orlend continued coolly. "The explosion of a shatterstone, unaccounted for in La Moinerie, would not look well in your report to King George." She paused. "Therefore, if you leave out mention of that little accident, I shall allow you to stay – and I shall not write to King George with any pertinent information about Mr Avely."

Elinor bit her lip, taken aback by this plain dealing. But Lady Orlend had hit a nerve. King George knew Elinor for the Discernor, but he did not know that Perry was a Travellor, or of his relationship with Jaq. He might not take kindly to being informed of these matters by a distant subject rather than the Avelys themselves. He might, in fact, withdraw his offer of castle and lands and leave them as plain Avelys with a roost of bats on their hands.

A blush stained Perry's cheeks and he stared at his egg. "My intimate friendships are of no concern to the king, and they are no concern of yours."

Lady Orlend raised an eyebrow. "Your Gift might be, however, and the fact that you have lied about it – or at least, failed to declare it. As I say, I am willing to keep my silence in return for yours. You will excuse my speaking so frankly."

Elinor looked to Beresford, wondering what he would say, and hoping he would remember their discussion from the evening before. Lady Orlend's little indiscretion was not limited to one shatterstone in La Moinerie: a whole sackful of them now lay unaccounted for. Still, they had agreed it was best not to reveal any knowledge of this yet.

Beresford cleared his throat. "Very well, Lady Orlend. That seems a suitable arrangement."

Elinor nodded reluctantly. "I am happy if you will let us continue our work uninterrupted. That is very forbearing of you."

Lady Orlend ignored her and glared at Beresford. "You, my lord, I did not expect to be party to such trickery. As His Majesty's emissary, I expected better conduct from you than to permit such a masquerade on your wife's part."

Beresford took a cautious sip of his coffee before answering, and wisely refrained from mentioning that even the wifely part was a facade. "You must excuse the devotion of a fond husband," he said, at length. "I was too easily convinced that my wife's talents should serve the king's interests, and that her brother should take the credit."

The pompous, diplomatic answer worked. Lady Orlend frowned and stood up. "I shall give you two more days," she said. "That should be sufficient for your wife to finish her tour of the island and find any minerals, though I strongly suggest that there are none to be found upon my island. Come, Chester, I need your help in the book room."

Chester stood up hastily and trotted after his mother.

After they left, Elinor morosely stirred her hot chocolate. "At least she thinks I am your wife."

Perry let out a sigh. "I barely merited a glance now that I am no longer Chief Mineral Discernor."

"Chief Travelling Nuisance, more like," said Elinor crossly. "If only we had not been discovered!"

"Well, no harm done yet," said Beresford, putting down his coffee cup. "We must continue. Loath as I am to condone an expedition today, Elinor, perhaps you should go Discerning as if you are still looking for minerals. We don't want to raise any more suspicions – though I *would* prefer it if you stayed abed."

Elinor sat up. "Stuff and nonsense, husband dear. I know just the place to investigate for minerals." She turned to Perry. "Can you remember where you were shot, brother? I think we should pay a visit to that hut."

Beresford sighed.

Perry grimaced. "I'm afraid I don't know where it was. It could be east, north, or anywhere in between."

"But Perry, you were right there!" objected Elinor.

Perry's brow furrowed. "I left in rather a hurry, if you recall. And I arrived there simply by imagining a lonely Sarkian hilltop."

"Could you return by the same means? Imagine the same hill-top?" asked Elinor. "I don't like to ask it of you, being so injured …"

As she hoped, that was enough to straighten Perry's spine. "I can do it right now. A mere twisted ankle cannot hold back a Travellor."

"Be careful," said Beresford wearily. "It is daytime, so surely those men will be less nervous with their firearms, but please arrive at some distance from the hut."

"Though not on a sheep," added Elinor. "Where is Jaq, by the way?"

Perry's expression shuttered. "I am sure I do not know."

Elinor raised an eyebrow. Had Perry and Jaq quarrelled last night?

Beresford cleared his throat. "Jaq has gone to visit Skerry."

Perry paled, and Beresford hurried to explain. "Elinor asked him to do so, to enquire about Sark. He left last night and he will be back soon enough."

Perry's jaw tightened. "Then I suppose I had better do my part too, and find this hut." He pushed his chair back, closed his eyes for a moment, and vanished.

Elinor gasped. "It still unnerves me."

Beresford put his head in his hands. "I just hope he isn't shot again."

Beresford's fears turned out to be unfounded. Perry managed the trip there and back without incident, unless one counted frightening a flock of sheep into a skelter – though not due to landing on one, as he acidly informed Elinor. He observed the sun and the land, limped along the nearest road until he found a signpost, and returned with a direction.

Accordingly, Elinor announced her intention of Discerning for minerals on the western side of Sark. Lady Orlend once more insisted that Hedley accompany them and Elinor meekly agreed, though she chafed at the company.

The party set out, with Elinor, Beresford, Perry, and Hedley once more crowded into the cart. The day was overcast, with a chill wind blowing from the north, and Elinor tied her bonnet close. The fields this time seemed windswept and empty, the sky grey and gloomy. She did not even bother with a Discernment as they drove; she was too occupied with troubling thoughts.

Enough was enough, she decided. For someone to intrude upon her bedchamber was beyond the pale. It was all very well to rescue the roost that night, but unexplained incidents remained. The shatterstone that had thrown her into the wall was possibly an unfortunate accident, a leftover from the Orlend boys' practice, but the soap that had sent Perry off the cliff was a cruel trick that could have ended in his death. She shivered when she thought of him falling among the sharp rocks and slamming waves. If Jaq had not rescued him, Perry could well have ended up with much worse than a twisted ankle.

She could not, however, imagine Lady Orlend stalking out to the cliff with her soap. If the Dame were responsible, she would have sent Hedley. Elinor cast a sideways glance at the farmer. His saturnine face was turned to the road, his hat shading his eyes, and his hands relaxed on the reins. He did not look as if he had been sneaking around with a bar of soap. Nor could she imagine him standing at the foot of her bed, mysteriously cloaked. Still, he might have done it, on orders from his mistress. He was loyal to a fault. Or perhaps Sidgemoor had done it, obedient and unquestioning, just as he had hidden the sack of shatterstones at her direction. Elinor shuddered at the thought of anyone watching her as she slept. Had she been deliberately woken, so that she would see the figure and be frightened?

The question remained: why? Why was Lady Orlend so determined to scare them off? And as she was so fixed on that aim, why had she not banished them from the island when they had given her a good excuse to do so? Was she afraid that they already had too much information to report to King George?

The sea winds blew Elinor's hair across her cheek and impatiently she tucked a curl back. Perhaps Lady Orlend was innocent. Could Hedley have placed the shatterstone in La Moinerie for his own, unguessed-at reasons? Or the Sidgemoors, playing their own deep game? Or even young Chester?

Elinor chewed on her lip, her hands cold in her gloves. Beresford, next to her, wore a grim expression, and Perry was unusually silent, a newly fashioned walking stick at his feet. Elinor had found a moment to tell him about her midnight intruder, and he said the stick could serve as a weapon as well.

Soon enough, they arrived at the tenement in the far west, belonging to the Mr Fitten they had met before. He was tending a field near the farmhouse. His sheep were stolidly ignoring the wind and chewing the grass. They raised their heads at the approach of the cart but did not seem much interested, and fortunately did not recognise Perry from his persecution of them earlier that morning.

Mr Fitten came over and tipped his hat to them, acquiescing to Hedley's explanation that the Royal Mineral Geologist wished to tour the western tenements. Hedley did not explain that Elinor now occupied that lofty position, and Elinor did not enlighten Mr Fitten.

While Hedley was busy talking, Perry jerked his head significantly and Elinor saw the suspect hut, silhouetted upon a hill in the distance. It stood sturdy and grey against the sky, a squat little structure, and she could not guess its purpose. However, she was not cognisant of the ways of farmers. Perhaps it was very necessary: a shepherd's hut, or some such. She would soon find out.

She clambered down from the cart with Beresford's help and nodded a greeting to Mr Fitten.

"Good morning." He bobbed a bow in return. "I'll let my missus know about your arrival, so you can have some refreshment when you are ready."

Elinor professed herself delighted at the prospect, and Mr Fitten strode off.

It was best not to show too much interest in the hut at once. She set off, taking a roundabout route towards it.

She tried a divination while she walked, for the sake of it. This time she searched for gold, out of a passing curiosity. Then she sighed: she probably wouldn't be able to sense a hoard of pirate's gold if it were right beneath her feet. However, she might as well play the part of Chief Mineral Discernor with thoroughness.

Only the brisk wind blowing off the ocean met her senses, and the scent of gorse and bracken. Birds called overhead. She quickened her pace, Beresford walking a few steps behind her, Perry limping at a slower rate with his stick, and Hedley herding them at the rear. As she approached the peak of a hill, the sea came into view, tumultuous and grey. Gulls cried on the wind, high and shrieking.

Out of habit, Elinor sent her inner sense searching for the vampiri. It was a reflexive motion, born of her constant searching over the last few days. So when an answer came she almost didn't hear it, it was so unexpected.

A whisper called from behind her.

Her step faltered and she turned, seeking the source of it. To the right she could see a dip between the dunes. The whisper emanated from there, a dell between the fields. Fir trees grew there, and a hawthorn hedge marked a path to it. She couldn't see it clearly, as the curve of the hill obscured everything but the towering firs.

Elinor narrowed her eyes, listening. The call seemed to come from below the ground. Casting her mind out, she felt confused. Was it vampiri, or gold? What had she been looking for? Her mind swooned a little. She must already be Bemused.

Beresford caught her up. "You've found something?"

She nodded. "Down there, in that dell. I'm not sure what, though." She walked towards it, unable to contain her curiosity. At the breast of the hill she stopped, not wanting to show undue interest under Hedley's watchful gaze.

Shading her eyes, she examined the dell. It was unremarkable save for a large gorse bush thick with flowers, and the majestic fir trees, bowed slightly by the wind. A granite rock jutted out below one of them like the prow of a ship.

She tilted her head, listening, gripping her lapis. It was hard to say how far below the surface the whisper had originated. An image of a large pirate chest full of gold came to mind, but she couldn't tell if it was fantasy or reality.

Elinor turned to Beresford eagerly. "Do you think it may be pirate gold? Perhaps that rock marks the spot!"

"It seems an odd place to bury gold. I suppose the sand is softer here by the sea." He scuffed the soil with his boot. "Perhaps you really *are* sensing mineral deposits. What were you trying to Discern?"

Elinor sighed. "The vampiri roost, out of habit. However, I was also wondering about the gold. I'm afraid I cannot say with certainty."

Beresford looked around. "Well, don't mention it to anyone," he muttered, as Hedley and Perry approached. "It is safer not to cause a fuss, especially if you have stumbled upon gold. We came to look at the hut, remember."

Elinor turned, aware of Hedley watching her. She couldn't very well give in to her impulse to dash down there and start digging, or tie a strip of her petticoat to the gorse to mark the spot. She walked on, ignoring the insistent tug at her senses. She would know the place again, anyway. That rock jutted out just as if a pirate had stood upon it once and decided it was a good place to bury treasure.

"False alarm!" she said cheerily to Hedley. "I thought I sensed silver, but no such luck." Hedley put his hands behind his back and stood by as she trotted towards the hut with Beresford in pursuit.

The hut stood on the ridge: a slate roof, a wooden door, and two small windows dark in the granite rock. She grimaced as she imagined Perry peering through a window only to hear a bullet whistle past him.

Squaring her shoulders, she marched up and entered the hut.

2 5

IN WHICH THERE IS A GHOST
STORY

*T*he hut was empty: swept clean, and recently, too. Even the fireplace looked as if it had been swept out. The walls were bare of ornament or furniture. There was not a rifle in sight, and certainly no sign of the men Perry had seen playing cards.

Elinor turned a slow circle, divining for a secret. The returning silence was loud.

Beresford appeared in the doorway. "Anything?"

"No," she said, frowning as Perry and Hedley came up behind him. "No minerals that I can sense. I might rest here for a moment, though, out of the wind."

However, ten minutes standing quietly in the hut and trying various divinations did not reveal anything other than the pull from the dell further down the hill. Sighing, Elinor stepped outside and continued her walk along the ridge, casting about her desultorily for minerals and feeling rather woolly-headed.

As they returned to their cart, Fitten hurried out and invited them inside the farmhouse for a cup of tea. Beresford accepted and they walked there together, leaving Hedley with the Pumpkin-Pie.

The farmhouse was a low building, pretty enough, but simple

compared to the Seigneurie. Fitten's gait slowed and his face creased in a frown. He cast a furtive glance back at Hedley and lowered his voice. "I saw you come out of the sentry hut, honoured folks. I hope you did not dwell in it long."

Beresford raised an eyebrow. "Why is that?"

Fitten thrust out his chest. "It is haunted. I know that for myself, even if Hedley does not believe me."

"Oh?" said Elinor curiously. She had not thought to divine for ghosts – if that were possible, which she doubted.

"Yes, indeed," said Fitten. "Last Sunday night I was out on patrol when I saw a figure drifting against the hut, peering in at the windows like a lost soul." He paused dramatically, but Elinor blinked at him, her muddled mind slow to grasp his meaning. Fitten continued, lowering his voice. "I thought it was a Frenchy invading our island, so I raised my rifle and shot him. But instead of falling over dead, the man vanished into thin air!" He raised his voice at the last revelation, looking around with his eyes as wide as they would stretch.

Elinor suspected that she was not reacting with a proper degree of horror, since she was fighting back a giggle. She cast a glance at Perry, who did indeed look horrified. "Oh dear," she said, a quiver in her voice. "Can you be certain? Did the Frenchman perhaps hide after you shot him? Sneaky things, Frenchmen, you know."

Fitten shook his head vehemently. "No, for I shot him well and good. And how could he hide?" Perry looked as if he might object, but Beresford narrowed his eyes in warning. "I know what I saw, and what I saw was him go up like a puff of smoke! And besides, the sheep have been behaving strangely – they're nervous near that hut."

Elinor clasped a hand to her mouth to stop a laugh escaping. Fitten took it as a suitable expression of terror and nodded with approval. He opened his front door. "Yes, indeed. The ghost of Sark. Seen him with my own eyes."

He led them through the house, which had low ceilings and neat floors and smelled deliciously of something savoury cooking.

"Hmm," said Beresford, expressionless. "Did anyone else see this ghost?"

"No," said Fitten proudly. "My son and the young man from the next tenement were inside, playing games, but they had no knowledge that the ghost was there." He paused. "They don't go in that hut anymore, of course."

He showed them into the kitchen, a bright room dominated by a large wooden table. Herbs hung in bunches by the window, and a large vase of blackthorn flowers stood on the table. A thin, wiry woman paused in her bustle and dipped a curtsy, her brown hair curled tightly against her head and her apron a vivid red-and-white patchwork.

"Mr Fitten!" she said, in a rich voice which did not match her skinny frame. "Are you blathering on about that ghost again? For my part I think it nonsense, and the boys should not be afraid to go into the hut." She shook her head in censure, wiping her hands on her apron.

"What is the purpose of that building?" asked Beresford. "Is it a sentry station?"

"Aye," said Fitten, pulling out a chair for Elinor. She sat with a swish of skirts, still hiding her amusement. "We were only given a tenement when we swore we would guard the island. It is part of our duty to patrol the cliffs at night, especially with a war on."

"Aye, and a noble duty it is," said Mrs Fitten, untying her apron and hanging it over a chair. "You ought not to be put off by ghosts. Would you folk like some tea and *soufflé au fromage de chèvre*? I am about to bring them out of the oven."

Elinor clasped her hands together in delight. "Is that the wonderful smell? How glorious! I've been aching to try some soufflés!"

Mrs Fitten set a small round dish on the table, the contents puffing over the rim. "Ah yes, Mrs Sidgemoor can never manage them, poor soul."

"A tricky art, I gather," said Elinor solemnly.

Mrs Fitten sniffed. "Only if you don't know how to treat an egg. Begging your pardon, my lady."

Elinor admitted that she did not know how to treat an egg, and she was served a delicious, hot cup of tea, and the lightest dish she had ever experienced. The goat's cheese and fresh herbs gave it a tangy flavour, and the fluffy texture was delightful.

She sighed with satisfaction as she ran her spoon around the bottom of the dish. At least one quest had been completed, and they also had an explanation for the gunshot at Perry. It was as Beresford had supposed: an overzealous Sarkee guarding the island from French invaders. Amusingly, it had resulted in a ghost story.

Elinor took another sip of tea and smiled at Mrs Fitten. "*You* certainly have a knack with eggs, Mrs Fitten."

Mrs Fitten nodded, and took another dish out of the oven, a pie this time. "You can take this rhubarb pie for Lady Orlend, if you like. She needs it, being ill as she is."

Elinor's hand paused in mid-air. "Oh, is Lady Orlend unwell?"

Mrs Fitten placed the pie carefully on the table. "Yes, though she doesn't like to talk about it. Wasting away slowly through some sickness."

"Oh dear," said Elinor, inadequately. "I didn't know." She frowned into her cup. Somehow, this was unsettling news. Why hadn't Lady Orlend told them she was ill? Elinor supposed it was a private matter, understandably not announced to every newcomer. However, it might go some way to explaining why her sons had left so many safeguards on the house.

"Ay," said Mr Fitten, after finishing a mouthful of soufflé. "Rumour has it her ladyship is dying, though I can't see her standing for it."

Elinor took a sip from her cup, feeling rather subdued. She

did not like to think of Lady Orlend dying, even if she was an autocratic old lady who was blackmailing them.

Mrs Fitten wiped crumbs from the table. "Don't worry your head about her ladyship; she has her own to look after her. Why don't you have a sip of sloe gin to send you on your way? It's our local speciality and it will raise your spirits."

"Sloe gin?" asked Elinor. Pags had spoken of it, she recalled, in the hospitality of Thomas Durl. "Yes, I believe I have heard of it. We would be delighted to sample some."

Perry nodded eagerly too, so Mrs Fitten fetched a bottle from a cupboard and poured ruby-coloured liquid into small glasses. Mr Fitten handed them around proudly. "Made from our finest blackthorn berries," he said. "You can't visit Sark without trying it."

The sloe gin was sweet, rich and potent. Elinor widened her eyes, wondering how much Pags and Durl could consume before becoming comatose.

Beresford, drinking his, remarked that they also made sloe gin in Devonshire, and used the remaining sloes to make a flavoursome cider.

Mrs Fitten sipped contentedly. "Ah, a fine idea! We use our gin sloes to make chutney. Both are a favourite with the wild faery who lives in the woods nearby. Thankfully, he doesn't require much to keep him in stock, small as he is."

Elinor pricked up her ears. "A faery?" Could they mean Durl? He wasn't as wild as she had first thought if he was calling on the Fittens for chutney and gin. "Do you mean a small person by the name of Thomas Durl?" She was surprised that he had made himself known so freely to humans; but perhaps it wasn't so strange this close to France, where the vampiri had mingled freely and openly before the Troubles.

Mr Fitten nodded. "Odd fellow. He likes to chat with me on the hill and hear the local news. I haven't seen him lately; he must have enough sloe gin in his supplies."

Elinor reflected that Durl had probably found Lilian more alluring company recently. She finished the last of her drink, relishing the tart, aromatic flavour, and Perry and Beresford joined her in thanking the Fittens for their hospitality.

Mr Fitten escorted them outside, tenderly carrying the gift pie. As Elinor was handed onto the cart, she couldn't help asking him what the ghost had looked like. Perry glared at her, shoved his hat further onto his head, and leaned on his cane.

Fitten considered. "He was dressed as a gentleman, but a tall, wispy thing he was. Nothing to be frightened of, really."

Elinor bit her lip and Perry looked outraged. Beresford hustled him onto the cart. Hedley climbed aboard and set the horse to a walk.

"Thank you for the soufflé and your lovely ghost story!" called Elinor as she waved her farewell.

They were halfway back to the Seigneurie when they saw Jaq walking along the road towards them. His pace was weary, but became more sprightly when he spotted them.

"Beresford!" he called as they drew near. "Walk with me. I have news."

Elinor sat up straight; she did not want to miss Jaq's confidences. "I shall walk too," she announced.

"And I," said Perry coldly.

Elinor eyed his walking stick. "You should stay in the cart, brother dear."

Perry frowned at her. "No, sister dear; I need to stretch my legs."

Elinor sighed. She did not want to keep Perry from Jaq's side, and he would wish to know how Jaq had fared more than any of them.

Hedley pulled the Pumpkin-Pie to a halt. He did not look

pleased to have his charges all leap out, but there was nothing he could do. Beresford politely dismissed him, saying that they wished to enjoy the walk back to the house and that Hedley must deliver the rhubarb pie before it was ruined.

They stood in a circle, watching the cart trundle out of sight. Around them, fields rippled in the wind and goats bleated.

Beresford shoved his hands in his pockets. "I'm glad to see the back of that ubiquitous fellow, I must say. What's your news, Jaq?"

Perry looked on silently, leaning on his stick. He and Jaq had only exchanged nods in greeting.

Jaq rocked back on his heels. "As you know, I went to find some of my selkie friends and see what they knew of Sark. On Miss Avely's request," he added hastily, eyeing Perry.

Perry merely raised his eyebrows.

"Do tell," said Elinor. She took Beresford's arm and prepared to stroll along the road, ignoring the strands of hair that had escaped her bonnet to blow in the insistent wind. After a moment Jaq offered his arm to Perry, who took it hesitantly, and they all promenaded down the deserted lane.

"Well," said Jaq, looking rather pleased with himself, which was nothing new. "By dint of questioning and gossiping – which I do rather well – I found out that Little Sark used to be a haunt for the merfolk."

Elinor drew in a breath, her eyes widening. "Merfolk?"

Beresford was frowning. "A haunt? Do you mean a mer-lure?"

"Yes," said Jaq. "A place where they called in human ships with their song. It explains why there are so many tales of ship-wrecks here. The merfolk occupied the place hundreds of years ago."

Perry limped beside him, leaning on his arm. "Ah yes, that cliff is called Triton's Wall, isn't it? So it wasn't pirates causing all the trouble, but mermaids?"

"Merfolk," corrected Jaq. "Usually mermen."

A confused rooster could be heard crowing nearby as they all considered this.

"But why not recently?" asked Elinor. "What happened?"

"I tracked down some merfolk and asked them. I have a few, er, acquaintances among them."

Beresford gave him a wry look and Jaq grinned back. Elinor resolved to ask them about their encounters with merfolk – later. Now she waited impatiently for Jaq to tell his news.

Jaq looked even more smug. "My acquaintance told me about the cave below the cliffs. There is indeed a cavern below Little Sark. The entrance I attempted is only accessible to the merfolk at high tide, for of course they can only swim. They had another way in, but a rock fall destroyed it two hundred years ago or thereabouts. So they abandoned it, for the cliff entrance was too dangerous and might leave them stranded in the cave."

Elinor was riveted. "And then the vampiri found it."

"A perfect hiding place for them," said Beresford. "Though its inaccessibility means it will be difficult for us too."

"Fortunately, we have Durl to lead us in," remarked Elinor.

Jaq looked a question.

"We have news, too," explained Perry. "We have discovered that Durl is a royal guard. He has agreed to lead us to the roost tonight when the tide is low."

Jaq frowned. "I hope you are not going to attempt it, with your leg."

Beresford cleared his throat. "I hope Perry and Elinor will for once be sensible and stay behind."

It was like putting a match to dry tinder. There was an aghast silence, then Elinor and Perry both began shouting, stepping away from their escorts in affront. Soon everyone was talking and gesticulating furiously at each other, and loud statements about endangering others, patronising pomposity, and the reck-lessness of fools abounded.

Beresford finally bellowed. "Enough!"

Everyone stared at him. The wind ruffled his brown hair and his grey eyes were hard as the granite rocks.

"I am the leader of this expedition," he said. "I command that Elinor and Perry stay behind. Jaq and I are accustomed to dangerous missions, and we shall be accompanied by Durl, Pags, and Aldreda. It would be beyond foolish for us all to traipse down the cliff and into the cave."

"James—"

He held up a hand. "We need someone to stay at the house and ensure that Hedley does not follow us. Also, we must allay Lady Orlend's suspicions. The tide starts receding around dinner time; we can't all excuse ourselves early. Someone has to stay back to keep an eye on her and Chester."

Elinor frowned at this irrefutable logic. "But James—"

"We don't know if we can trust them," said Beresford firmly. "It is integral to the success of tonight's venture that you and Perry stay behind for dinner, Elinor, so that we can reach the cave unobserved."

Elinor's gaze sharpened on him. A faint tinny sound had echoed in his voice. She opened her mouth to speak, then shut it; opened her lips once more, then closed them again. She no doubt resembled a fish. Yet she was in an impossible position. It had almost sounded as if he were lying, but she had promised not to use her Truth Discernment on Beresford. She had said she would trust him implicitly.

She pressed her lips together in a thin line. She did not want to accuse him of deception now, not when tensions were already running so high. And perhaps she had been mistaken. "James, are you certain—"

"Furthermore," he continued inexorably, "we need food for the roost. When we bring them out of the cave, we shall have a hungry queen on our hands."

This was true, and there was no hint of tinniness in his voice this time. Elinor folded her arms crossly. "The queen can feed from Perry."

"Hold on a dashed minute!" said Perry. "I said I wanted to come along, not be a vampiri's dinner!"

"So?" said Elinor. "You were prepared to be a snack for Raddle; a queen's meal is an advance in status."

"A high connection," Jaq grinned. "I think I might get jealous."

Beresford persevered. "Not only a hungry queen, but a whole starving roost. Perry, willing or not, cannot feed them all. Therefore, after dinner he must gather a flock of sheep for the purpose."

Perry's mouth fell open. "You want me to herd sheep?"

Beresford stared back at him stonily. "It is an important task. We don't want the vampiri disturbing a farmer or descending on the village. We need the flock gathered somewhere out of sight."

"But I'm injured!" said Perry, rather contradicting his earlier insistence that he was perfectly able to walk through a cliff tunnel.

"You can Travel," said Beresford callously. "I'm sure you will make an excellent shepherd; perhaps the best the world has seen."

Perry gaped at him. That made two Avelys looking like fish, thought Elinor irritably.

She put her hands on her hips. "My lord, I am quite certain you do not mean to leave me alone in the house while you are all out with the sheep and the bats. Not when there was a strange person in my room last night."

Beresford scowled at the reminder, and she pressed her advantage. "I must at least go with Perry. Once we have ascertained that Hedley and the Orlends are accounted for, he can guard me. And the sheep," she added, as an afterthought.

"Charmed, I'm sure," said Perry bitterly.

"Come, Perry," said Jaq, grinning. "It won't be so baaaad, will it?"

Jaq's joke succeeded in easing the strain. They all groaned, and Elinor convinced herself that she had gained a concession. Beresford's arguments were not without merit, and she supposed she would have to stay behind for dinner and distraction purposes, and to keep an eye on the Orleans. Yet she gnawed on her lower lip, wondering if he could be concealing something from her. She cast him a sideways glance and he smiled, his grey eyes softening as he held out his arm once more. "Come, Elinor, I suppose you may go with Perry, if you must. But only after everyone has retired for the night, and *please* be careful."

His voice was warm and conciliatory. The lie must have been in her imagination, conjured by the hostility of the moment. She took his arm. Even if she had heard right, she couldn't confront him with it now, not when she had promised not to use her Gift on him. And at least she had convinced him that she could not stay in bed all night, while everyone else was adventuring.

Furthermore, she had her own ideas about where to gather the sheep: in the western dell, where she had sensed something hidden below the ground. A shovel might be an advantageous accessory for the evening. There was no need to mention that to Beresford; she could keep something concealed as well.

"Very well," she said. "Perry already has a shepherd's crook." She indicated his walking stick. "He can baaaandy that about."

She grinned at the second chorus of groans, and they resumed their walk to the Seigneurie.

IN WHICH A HORSE'S
SENSIBILITIES ARE DISREGARDED

$\mathcal{A}$ ldreda, asleep in her basket under the attic table, was awakened by the sound of gentle tapping. It took her a moment to realise that it came from the small attic window. No light showed above the curtain, so dusk must have fallen.

Memories surfaced of her fight with Pags the night before, and she hurriedly threw back her blanket. Sleep left her limbs as she changed into her black silk gown, pulling her ties tight and hoping that he had come to apologise. Would he retract his rude comments about headmistresses? Perhaps she would even apologise, too. It was better for them to be friends, especially if they were to meet the queen tonight together. She climbed up the chest by the window, her heart beating rapidly.

However, when she twitched the heavy green cloth aside, she saw Durl clinging to the windowpane. Repressing a pang of disappointment, Aldreda pushed the window open.

"Good evening, Miss Zooth," Durl said, edging into the gap. "May I have a word, if it is not too much trouble?"

He had made some effort to look presentable, wearing perhaps all the clothes he possessed and tying back his brown curls with a ribbon. His expression was serious, and the knuckles gripping the window were white.

"Certainly," Aldreda replied, though with a slight hesitation. "Do come in."

Durl swung himself onto the sill. "This window was locked before, was it not? I am sorry you have to sleep in here, where your compatriot died."

Aldreda did not let her eyes stray to the place where she had found the lieutenant. "I have slept in worse." She gestured to the wooden chest. "Shall we talk here?"

Durl leapt down and stood there, ill at ease, his hands clasped behind his back.

Aldreda raised her eyebrows. "I am listening."

"As I left you last night," he began slowly, "I saw someone behaving strangely."

"Oh?"

"The maid named Dinah was standing outside the window below Lady Beresford's room. She appeared to be listening to our consultation."

Aldreda frowned. "Are you sure?"

"I cannot be certain, but I circled with Raddle, and a few minutes later she was at a different window, rubbing it with a cloth. However, I suspect that was a ruse."

"Hmm," said Aldreda. "So she may know of our plans for this evening. I wonder if she will inform anyone."

"We could change the plan," said Durl. "You and I could fly ahead to wake the roost. After all, we have no need of the humans."

Aldreda stared at him, trying to make sense of his proposition. She rather suspected this might be about Durl's preferences, rather than fear that Dinah might thwart their plans. Perhaps he did not want Beresford and Jaq to witness the vulnerable moment of the roost's awakening.

"What of Pags?" she asked. "Would he join us?"

"I do not think it is necessary," he said, and smiled. "Pags is not the most tactful vampiri I've had the pleasure of meeting. We only need you to play the flute and explain the case. We can be back before the moon is high and avoid any trouble."

Aldreda chewed her lip thoughtfully. Part of her wanted to claim the honour ahead of everyone else. Selkies and humans did not belong at a vampiri hibernation; she agreed with Durl on that point. Furthermore, she felt she had the necessary diplomacy and grace to put their proposition to the queen. She and Durl could do the job while Beresford was still at dinner.

Sensing her interest, Durl held out his hand. "I confess I am eager to wake them," he said. "I have been without vampiri companionship for too long, and lonely without the roost."

His brown eyes were earnest, his large hand inviting – yet Aldreda paused. She did not want to act without Pags: not after their recent argument. She also knew that Elinor would disapprove of abandoning their plan based on the mere suggestion that Dinah had cleaned a window. Their party represented King George, and spoke for England and its Musors. It was only right that Beresford was present at the roost's awakening to ensure that their mission was completed, in Elinor's place. Furthermore, if Dinah had told someone who then tried to block their progress, the vampiri might need human assistance.

"I think we should adhere to our plans," she said, eventually. "We may need the help of Lord Beresford and Jaq if anyone on Sark disrupts us."

Durl's face fell, as did his hand. "You do not feel the delicacy of the queen's situation? It would be less … confronting for her to wake to only the two of us."

"I do, but I am also in a delicate situation," she replied. "I do not wish to undermine my companion's arrangements when the party is on the brink of success."

Durl's mouth twisted and he took a step back, then bowed. "You are loyal, Miss Zooth: a trait I admire. Very well, we shall proceed to the cave as arranged. I only hope it does not prove dangerous to those larger than us."

Aldreda watched him go, worry snaking up her spine.

～

Elinor clung to Beresford. They were in their room and the sun had set. Aldreda sat on the bed, waiting to leave, having informed them of Dinah's possible eavesdropping.

"Please be careful!" said Elinor. "If Dinah wasn't really cleaning a window, then she was probably trying to find out more about Perry and Jaq's tendency to appear in mid-air, but we don't know *what* she heard. And the merfolk tunnel sounds perilous."

"Oh, so now you admit to the danger?" Beresford teased, but he pulled her into a long embrace. He kissed her deeply and Aldreda didn't even say a word. Perhaps she was anxious too, waiting for Pags and Durl. Elinor herself was still troubled by the thought that Beresford wasn't telling her everything.

She gently freed herself from his arms, and decided that she, at least, must be open. "Aldreda, please bring the roost to the western side of the island. Perry and I promise to have a flock of sheep awaiting you in the dell there, behind the hedgerow."

Beresford frowned. "I do not like you returning to that location. Don't forget that Perry was shot at on that hillside."

"Nonsense," said Elinor staunchly. "It is perfect. The hut is abandoned, and they already think Perry is an apparition. He can pop about, being a ghostly shepherd, and I can hide in the dell." She paused. "Or would you rather I came with you to the cliff?"

Beresford sighed and shook his head.

Aldreda nodded. "Very well, we shall bring the roost there." She smoothed down the black silk gown she had chosen for her meeting with the queen, and Elinor repressed a sigh of envy.

"Off you go, then," she said, and gave Beresford's hand one last squeeze. "Good luck, Aldreda. Play the flute beautifully! I only wish I could hear it myself."

Aldreda curtseyed with a wry smile and hopped onto Beresford's shoulder. As they left to meet Jaq, Elinor felt rather like a general deploying her troops. She was a little apprehensive about directing them into danger while she stayed behind with the sheep. Still, this was the reason why they had come to Sark, and she could not balk at the difficulties now. Besides, she needed to find a shovel.

She gave Beresford a few minutes, straightened her gown, then went downstairs for dinner. They had already informed Lady Orlend and Mrs Sidgemoor that Beresford was dining with Jaq on the ship. They hoped the lady of the house would infer that Beresford was cowed by her disdain and had retreated to a masculine sanctuary.

That left Elinor and Perry to carry the conversation. Once they had sat down, Elinor chatted merrily about London fashions. She observed Lady Orlend closely, seeing her gaunt, closed face in a different light, and having a new patience with her short answers.

Perry wasn't very loquacious either. He was still sulky about being relegated to shepherding duties, and it seemed that he and Jaq still had not resolved their quarrel. Only Beresford's expressed reliance on Perry not deserting Elinor had convinced him to stick to the plan.

After the first course of scalloped oysters, Mr Sidgemoor placed small pie dishes before each of them, much like the soufflé pots that had been served at the Fittens'. These cakes, however, were sunk in the middle, a comical dip in each one.

Lady Orlend frowned at hers. "What are these?"

Mr Sidgemoor's hands trembled as he placed the last dish before Chester. "Soufflés, my lady."

"You know we don't have soufflés here," snapped Lady Orlend.

Sidgemoor backed away hastily. "Yes, my lady. It is only that

Mrs Sidgemoor wanted to try them again, when she heard that Lady Beresford enjoyed them so much."

Elinor bit her lip. "I'm sure they will taste delicious, even if they have not risen perfectly."

Lady Orlend glowered at her dish, then sighed. "It is this house, Lady Beresford. There are too many Impacting spells laid upon it. Impacting draws on the earth and the heaviness sinks the soufflés. That is why Mrs Sidgemoor cannot bake them here, no matter how much she tries."

Elinor's eyes widened. That might explain the sense of oppression she felt in the house. She stared at the sorry dip in her dish. "How tragic!" she said. "Perhaps you should undo the spells, if it means such a sacrifice."

Lady Orlend shook her head. "My sons would be most unhappy if I undid all their hard work. Without them here to protect me, I must rely upon their enchantments. And Chester to look after me, of course," she added, though she did not glance at him and merely helped herself to a spoonful of soufflé.

Chester flushed and looked down at the table, and Elinor felt a stab of anger at Lady Orlend's dismissive way of speaking about him. If she had kept Chester home at her convenience, the least she could do was show some gratitude. Perhaps what Dinah had said was true, though, and it was Chester who wished to stay on the island. Why would that be the case? Was he hoping to find the long-lost gold?

Elinor tucked into the soufflé. It was still delicious, but lacked a certain airiness. Her nerves, too, were starting to intrude upon her enjoyment of the food. How long before Beresford and the others reached the cliff and began the descent? They had to walk, so it would take some time. How long before they found the queen and played the flute? More importantly, how long did she and Perry have to gather the sheep?

Consequently, the meal seemed to go on far too long. Elinor was grateful for her head injury, as it gave her the perfect excuse to claim a headache after the rhubarb pie was served. Lady Orlend nodded her dismissal without argument.

Perry stood up too. "My leg pains me; I shall retire as well." He paused. "Is Hedley around this evening? I wanted to ask him about, um, animal husbandry. For our property, I mean, when we return to England. I thought I should learn more about it."

Lady Orlend frowned. "Hedley has retired to his own tenement. You can ask him tomorrow. Though he knows more about fishing."

Behind Lady Orlend, Elinor winked at Perry, glad he had thought to ascertain the whereabouts of the ever-present Hedley. She was equally glad that Hedley was at home, probably drinking sloe gin and regaling his wife with the oddities of the Avelys.

Briefly colliding with Perry in the corridor, Elinor hissed at him to meet her behind the stables. He nodded and limped away.

Back in her room, Elinor's pulse pounded with impatience. Sure enough, she heard footsteps pause outside her door, then a tentative knock. "Do you need any help, ma'am?" called Dinah. Elinor bade her enter in a weak voice and announced her intention to go to sleep immediately.

As Dinah helped her undress, Elinor coughed gently. "Were you cleaning windows yesterday evening, Dinah? It seems an odd time to undertake such a task."

Dinah's hands paused at her work. "My duties are doubled, my lady. It was the only time I could manage it."

Elinor felt guilty at once. "Of course. I should have brought my own maid with me." She didn't have one, but Lady Beresford, wife of the Earl of Beresford, would certainly do so. "Never mind, soon we will be gone, and your duties will become manageable again."

Dinah smiled, reaching for a hair brush to tend to Elinor's hair. Elinor allowed herself to believe that the maid had simply been washing windows, and if she had heard anything, she would not divulge it to anyone.

Once Elinor was in bed, Dinah closed the curtains and left the room. Elinor waited a few minutes, then leapt out again and threw on a blue riding habit. This was the tricky part. It was easy for Perry: he could Travel to the stables with no one the wiser. She had to sneak past the rest of the household.

Could she use her own Gift? Eschewing a bonnet, she tied her hair back and crept to the door, sending out her senses. This time her query was simple: where was everyone?

After several tries and long, difficult minutes, she admitted her skill was not sufficient for the task. She simply couldn't make out where all the bodies were in the house; the Discernment was too complex. With the mundane sense of her ears, she could hear someone walking up to the attic: probably Dinah. Heaving a sigh, she waited. It was only a few minutes before the maid returned downstairs, but it seemed to take forever.

Finally, she decided to risk it and crept slowly out of the room. Her heart in her mouth, she sneaked down the corridor and the stairs.

The front door creaked as she opened it. She cringed, but there was no time to waste. She ran down the side of the drive, then across to the stables. Her head pounded and she felt a little dizzy from her divination, so she put her hands on her knees and bent her head.

Perry was leaning gloomily against the back wall. He appraised her flushed appearance. "Took your time, didn't you?"

"Don't gloat," snapped Elinor. "I don't have your advantages."

"I'm not gloating about being a sheepdog, I can tell you."

"It's an important job."

Perry scowled. "This is the last time I accompany you on one of your larks. I've had enough."

Elinor perceived that brotherly dignity had been severely impaired. "Please don't say that, Perry." She straightened up, putting a hand against the stable wall, and finally caught her breath. "You're essential to this whole endeavour. I didn't tell Beresford, but I'm bringing a shovel."

He stared. "Why? To wave at the sheep?"

"No, silly, to dig for gold. I sensed something buried in the dell by Fitten's farm." She paused for effect. "I believe it may be a stash of pirate's treasure."

Perry pursed his lips. "You're sure it isn't an old soufflé buried there?"

She ignored that. "Both Chester and Pags have told us stories of gold on Sark. What if I've stumbled across it? Don't you want to help me dig it up?"

Perry frowned. "No."

"What?"

"I said no! If I recall correctly, when I last aided your divination – when you sensed that damn pendant – we ended up ejected from society in disgrace."

"Oh, Perry, that is ancient history. Besides, if we hadn't left London, you wouldn't have met Jaq."

"I'm not sure that was a good thing, after all."

Elinor's eyes widened. "You don't mean that. You will come to some arrangement, I know it. He wants to come to Cornwall, and you can both be safe there. And besides," she added slyly, "Jaq would not hesitate to assist a treasure hunt."

Perry glared at her, then sighed. "All right. It had damn well better be a chest of guineas, though."

"Come on, then, we haven't time to waste. Are you stealing a horse?"

Perry pushed himself off the wall. "I suppose so. Just one, and we can ride together. Find yourself a shovel at the Fittens': we can't carry one on horseback."

"Why don't you Travel there with it?"

"Beresford doesn't want me to leave your side," said Perry. "And I don't want to be too Bemused. As it is, I'll be popping up all over the countryside chasing sheep."

Elinor giggled. "Very well. Can you fetch the horse? You can always vanish if you are caught."

Perry slipped into the stable. They had timed it well, as the groom and stablehand were eating their supper. Soon Elinor heard the soft whicker of a horse. It was the chestnut mare, Pumpkin-Pie, with her beautiful brown mane. She eyed Elinor with interest and allowed her nose to be stroked.

Perry finished adjusting the saddle and helped Elinor mount, then swung up in front. Before she knew it, they were trotting along the road in the dim light.

Elinor held on tightly to Perry's waist. The sky was dark grey and the first stars were starting to show. The northern breeze was blowing again, but softer, though she was glad of her warm riding habit. The fields around them seemed eerie now that it was no longer day. For a moment she missed Aldreda, who was accustomed to the night and would have relieved the tension with her wry observations. Aldreda had seemed subdued this evening, however. Perhaps she was nervous about her flute performance. Elinor sent a pining thought towards the secret cave in the southern cliffs. Well, she would find herself a treasure chest instead. It would be a good thing if she had her own discovery to reveal, if Beresford was indeed keeping something from her.

When they approached closer to Fitten's tenement, Perry slowed the horse to a walk and handed Elinor the reins. "The farmhouse is just after the next two bends," he said. "Now, I shall Travel while moving; it is well that Mother had the foresight to make me practise. I'll meet you at the dell." He took a deep breath, then added testily, "Don't let anyone see you! Tether the horse in the next field and walk across. I'll fetch the damned sheep."

Before Elinor could object, Perry vanished. One moment he was sitting in front of her; one smooth equine stride later, he was gone.

However, his practice from a moving carriage had failed to take into account the feelings of a walking horse. Pumpkin-Pie, feeling one of her riders mysteriously vanish, reared with fright and began galloping as if to catch him.

Elinor barely had time to grasp the reins before she was hanging on for dear life. She shouted dire imprecations which did not help matters, except that they allowed some vent to her pent-up feelings. The hedgerows and fields flashed by in a blur of dim shapes, and the wind whipped her face.

Eventually, though, it sank into Pumpkin-Pie's brain that this new state of affairs was not so bad, and she slowed down. Elinor was able to catch her breath and curse Perry in a more quiet and sedate manner.

Unfortunately, by that time she was in plain view of the Fitten farmhouse. Beyond it lay the sloping fields, the sentry hut, and a herd of sheep. Everything was in place except Elinor, who was supposed to be picking her way round to the dell.

Before she had time to turn the horse around, the door of the cottage opened and the pale oval of Mr Fitten's face peered about. He stared for a moment, then hurried out. "Who goes there?"

Elinor froze, her heart still beating wildly. She pulled Pumpkin-Pie to a halt.

Fitten approached with a lantern. He peered up into her face, then pulled back like a frightened turkey. "Lady Beresford, is that you?"

"Er, yes," confessed Elinor, thinking hard. "I do apologise for this late visit, Mr Fitten. I think I may have left my reticule here today. Could I see if perhaps …" She didn't really want to enter the house; she wanted to be out on the hill. Would Perry see her dilemma and rejoin her?

Mr Fitten looked behind her as if searching for her escort.

"Mr Avely was walking with me," Elinor added airily. "This

excitable animal bolted, I'm afraid. My brother was left far behind."

Pumpkin-Pie blinked stoically, refusing to play her part.

Mr Fitten blinked back. "Oh," he said. "Lady Beresford, I have not seen your reticule."

Elinor stared with hauteur. "Really? Are you certain?"

"I can ask my wife," he said hastily. "Please wait a moment."

As he backed away, Elinor looked around with some anxiety. Where was Perry? He would not be able to see the farmhouse from the dell, so he would not know of her trouble. She needed to think of a plan, and quickly.

When Mr Fitten returned he was accompanied by his wife, who was wiping her hands on her apron and looking sceptical. When she saw Elinor her eyes widened, as if she had not believed her husband's word. "Goodness!" she said, in her warm tones. "I thought Fitten was seeing things again, but you really are here, my lady." She paused and gave Elinor a measuring glance. "I haven't seen your reticule, I'm afraid. Are you certain you left it?"

Elinor leaned forward conspiratorially. "Well, actually, I confess there is another, more frivolous reason for my call. I was hoping to see your ghost."

The Fittens stared at her.

"I thought if I returned after dusk I might catch a glimpse of it." Elinor waved a hand. "Do you mind if I ride up to the hut? I *so* wish to see a ghost; it would be *most* romantic."

She turned to examine the slope and at that moment the sheep, who were gathered there, scattered.

Behind them Perry appeared, waving his hands wildly.

27

IN WHICH SOMETHING
UNEXPECTED IS UNEARTHED

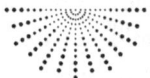

*M*r Fitten gasped. "Look! See that?"

"What?" asked Elinor innocently.

Perry vanished again.

"There!" shouted Fitten. "He's gone again!"

"Where?" His wife peered over his pointing finger. "Oh, those sheep! So nervy lately. I wonder if a feral cat is bothering them."

"Not a cat, the ghost!" cried Fitten. "He appeared behind them with his hands out-flung!"

Mrs Fitten put her own hands on her skinny hips. "Surely the sheep wouldn't notice a ghost, even one flinging out his hands," she said reasonably. "An apparition is made of wisps and air, no?"

"Hands out-flung?" cried Elinor. "Oh, please let me go and look! I wish above all things to see such a dramatic ghost!" She paused. "May I take a shovel with me?"

The Fittens turned and stared at her again. "A shovel?" they said, with one voice.

Mrs Fitten gave her a suspicious look. "You don't mean to hit the ghost over the head, do you?"

"I wouldn't dare," said Elinor, though she rather felt like smacking Perry. She leaned forward with a confiding air. "I didn't want to mention this before, but my brother sensed something buried on the hill. I think it might be the abandoned body of the soul who now haunts you. If we could discover his burial ground and sanctify it, we would put his troubled soul to rest." She paused. "Hence the need for the shovel."

Mr Fitten swallowed. Under Elinor's pious gaze, however, he dared not voice an objection to this outrageous request. "Yes, my lady." He handed the lantern to his wife and hurried off.

Elinor felt pleased with herself: she had managed to turn an obstacle to good account. Mrs Fitten, however, was not so easily swayed. "Do you really mean to dig up a corpse?" she demanded. "What will Lady Orlend say when she hears such a thing? You should be in your bed, madame, if you don't mind me saying so. A corpse is not for the likes of you."

Elinor dismounted and patted her horse. "It may not be a corpse," she pointed out. "My brother might have sensed a chest full of stolen gold. Perhaps the ghost is trying to show you where to find it."

Mrs Fitten looked unconvinced, but the possibility, however vague, of finding treasure seemed to mollify her. "Very well," she said reluctantly. "I'll make us a pot of tea, in case we need to steady our nerves."

"An excellent suggestion."

Mrs Fitten nodded, passed the lantern to Elinor, and withdrew.

Elinor led Pumpkin-Pie to a field and tethered her. The chestnut horse was happily munching on the grass when Mr Fitten emerged with a shovel and a gun. "Where's your brother?"

Elinor, gripping the lantern, tried to look unconcerned, for that gun was no doubt the one Mr Fitten had already employed once against Perry. "Mr Avely is no doubt making his way to the spot where he sensed something was buried. Let us hurry, before he begins to worry about me." She hoped fervently that Perry would be waiting for them and that he wouldn't appear out of nowhere.

They fell silent as they walked, Elinor leading the way with the lantern. She moved briskly, glad she didn't have to skulk the long way round. Clouds were streaming across the sky in long banners. The wind nipped at her face, and her cheeks and nose were cold.

Soon they were out of sight of the house and following the hedgerow to the dell. Elinor looked around but could not see Perry. Nor did she see any sheep. Ahead, the fir trees shivered in the wind.

Never mind if Perry is still shepherding, she told herself. It gives me time to dig.

Reaching the trees, she followed her Discernment to the jutting granite rock, Mr Fitten trailing behind. She paused, listening to the insistent whisper calling her. It was still impossible to say what it was; she only knew that it demanded to be uncovered. She put a booted foot on the rock and pointed. "There. Let us dig!"

Mr Fitten, however, hung back, looking over his shoulder. "Are you certain this is a good idea, Lady Beresford? What if we bring down the wrath of the spirit for disturbing his grave? I tell you, his hands were out-flung, as if in warning!"

"Nonsense," said Elinor impatiently. "We are trying to put the spirit to rest, and we should do it before he worries your sheep to death. If you won't dig, I'll do it myself." She put her lantern down on the rock in a businesslike fashion. However, her scandalous suggestion was enough to goad Mr Fitten into action. He leaned his rifle against a tree and tentatively thrust the shovel into the earth.

Elinor looked at the tall firs with their rustling needles, and heard the distant bleating of sheep. She rubbed her arms in the cold, wishing Perry would hurry up and show himself in a respectable fashion. Surely they were running short of time before the vampiri roost turned up.

After a few reluctant shovelfuls, Fitten suddenly shrieked,

quite in the manner of a maid seeing a mouse. Elinor jumped, expecting to see Perry, but Fitten stumbled back, the spade falling from his hand. "I hit something!" he declared. "A bone, or a coffin!" He backed away, trembling.

Elinor hurried forward. "Surely not. You've barely started!"

Yet as she knelt by the disturbed earth, she saw he was right. In a few strokes he had uncovered a box. It was small, though: only the size of two hand spans.

Elinor brushed the dirt away and pulled a wooden box into her lap. It hummed to her inner senses. She could smell the scent of fir trees and the faint tang of the sea, but when she scanned with her Discernment she realised that nothing else murmured from the earth. Was this all? It was not the pirate's chest she had fondly imagined. She made a wry face, knowing that Perry would be none too pleased.

Her fingers brushed the dirt away carefully, and for some reason she felt a stab of disquiet.

Hesitantly, she worked at opening the box. It was the size of a small tea chest, though plain and unadorned. It was the size that gave her the first clue as to what might lie within. For she had seen Aldreda put in such a small wooden box once before.

She lifted the lid, the hinge opening with a faint creak.

A dead vampiri lay inside.

Elinor stared at the remains of the tiny body, a shiver running through her. With all her talk of corpses, she had not expected to find one.

The vampiri lay ramrod straight, arms folded over his chest. A cloak covered the rest of him, but the hair was cut in a masculine style, cropped close to his head. Under the body lay a scrap of cloth, faded and old. No other token or ornament graced the coffin.

Elinor stared, dumbfounded. Who was this? It could not be Lieutenant Chaboot, who had died in his bat form and had a distinctive streak of grey on his head. Chaboot had been found curled up and dried out: it was impossible that this carefully tended corpse could be his.

Was it a member of the hidden roost, who had died? If so, how had he come to be buried so far from their cave, in a hidden dell on the western side of the island?

She looked up. Fitten was several feet away, staring. "What is it?" he asked, his voice shaky.

Elinor closed the box. "A trifle, probably hidden by a young boy. Not gold, unfortunately." She spoke stiffly. "I am sorry to have misled you."

Fitten stared at her suspiciously. "Can I see, then?"

"Er ... um ..." Elinor's mind had gone blank.

She was saved by the sheep, who came thundering into the dell, bleating with fright. Elinor looked around gratefully, for once applauding Perry's timing. He had managed it! Somehow, popping up like a sprite all over the hill, he had herded the sheep into the dell.

The sheep swerved around Elinor and Fitten and scattered to the far end of the clearing. When the hedgerow kept them from going further, they milled around in agitation. However, when Perry failed to reappear with his hands outflung, they gradually calmed down and huddled together.

Elinor smiled at them. One flock, ready for a roost's dinner! Now they simply had to await Aldreda's arrival with the queen and her people. Yet the strange, small coffin in her hands pulled at her. Elinor looked down, worry tugging at her heart.

Fitten was unnerved by the sudden appearance of his sheep. He moved closer to Elinor, staring at the flock. "Do you think the ghost is about? Why have the sheep come here? Surely they should avoid a cursed place like this?"

Elinor shrugged, then remembered her role and stood up, brushing her habit down with her free hand. "Oh, I hope the ghost is about! Perhaps we should go up to the hut to see?"

Fitten gave her an appalled look and picked up his gun. "Where's your brother? Shouldn't he be here by now?"

Perry chose that moment to appear at the edge of the dell. He paused, surveying the scene as if he were out for an afternoon walk.

The sheep shuffled nervously and Fitten clutched at his rifle.

"Perry!" exclaimed Elinor, gladly. "You're late!"

"Good God!" cried Fitten, at the same time. "It is the ghost!" He raised his gun shakily.

Perry looked at them and did the only sensible thing. He vanished.

"The ghost!" spluttered Fitten again. Then he frowned at Elinor, lowering the rifle. "Did you *say* something to him?"

Perry reappeared, this time directly behind Fitten. "Boo!"

Fitten jumped as if Napoleon himself had crept up on him. He spun round, eyes as wide as a soufflé dish. "Ahhhk!"

He raised the rifle again, but Perry plucked it out of his grasp. "I'll have that, thank you." Elinor realised that her brother was Bemused. His blond hair stood on end, bits of grass were scattered over his person, and his eyes were over-bright. He waved the gun at Elinor. "Those sheep are cursed stupid, I can tell you. Maybe they'll listen to me now."

Fitten shook like a pine needle in the wind.

"Don't frighten the poor fellow," reproved Elinor. "Mr Fitten, I assure you that my brother is no ghost; he is as much flesh and blood as you are. He merely has a little trick of dislocating himself, which I also find a little agitating." She frowned at Perry. "You're late, Perry."

Perry scoffed. "That's rich! Where have *you* been, sister dear?"

"Pumpkin-pie bolted," said Elinor testily. "When *you* disappeared. I had to find another escort."

"Perry?" quavered Fitten. "You're the brother?"

"Unfortunately, yes," replied Perry. "Ha, I see you got hold of a shovel, Ellie. Any luck with it?"

Perhaps it was Perry's use of her childhood name, but slowly Fitten's shoulders relaxed. His expression indicated that the night-time excursions of the pair of siblings left him in the need of a strong drink.

Elinor smiled brightly. "I'm afraid Mr Fitten already dug up the gold and it isn't gold at all, just an old box with dead beetles in it. Buried by a boy, most likely."

"Dead beetles?" said Perry. "Curse it, Elinor, you promised me a pirate's chest." He thrust the rifle back at Fitten. "Here, you can have it back if you promise not to shoot at me. Keep it trained on those pesky sheep." Fitten nodded feebly and took the gun.

"Sorry, only dead beetles," Elinor affirmed. "Or maybe it is a dead bat. Or a caterpillar. I can't really tell."

She was pleased to see comprehension cross Perry's face, but not so pleased when he blurted out his conclusion. "A dead bat? How can there be a dead bat?"

"Indeed, I cannot say!" she snapped.

"A dead bat?" said Fitten, looking from one to the other. "Do you mean a fae bat?"

Perry and Elinor turned to regard him. "Yes," Elinor said, eventually. "Do you know of many on Sark?"

"Only Durl," said Fitten. "The wild one, who takes our chutney. I haven't seen him for a few months."

"It can't be Durl," said Perry. "We saw him last night, and he definitely wasn't dead."

Elinor, however, shivered. She held out the box and lifted the lid. "Mr Fitten, do you know this fae bat?"

Fitten took a step closer, stared for a long moment, then raised his eyes. "That would be Durl," he said. "I recognise the cloak, and the hair. What's Durl doing in this box, poor old fellow? I didn't know he could die; I thought he belonged to Lord Blackthorn, of the fae."

Perry shook his head vehemently. "It can't be Durl," he

repeated. "We saw him last night. I tell you, he wasn't dead. It can't be him in that box."

Elinor's skin prickled. "What if the vampiri we met is not Durl, Perry? He only *told* us he was Durl – no one but Lilian confirmed it."

"But you Truth Discerned him!" cried Perry. "You would have realised if he wasn't Durl!"

"I didn't ask about his name!" snapped Elinor. "And I said something was off; I knew he wasn't telling us the whole truth. I thought that was because he was hiding his role as a royal guard."

"But he isn't one?" said Perry, rubbing his head as if it hurt. "Who is he, then?"

Elinor's hands tightened on the box. "I don't know – it makes no sense!" She recalled something else. "Lilian said she only made Durl's acquaintance recently, so she must have only known the imposter. Who has arrived on Sark recently? It could be someone like us, looking for the roost."

Perry leaned in and examined the dead figure. Then he looked up, his expression sharpening into lucidity. "Look, Ellie. His death wasn't an accident. There's a rope around his neck."

Elinor looked again. Perry was right. What she had taken to be the ties of the cloak was a thin rope wrapped around the throat of the dead vampiri.

Around them, the wind moaned in the tree branches. Elinor felt her heart thud and she swallowed. "Durl murdered him."

Perry frowned and Fitten stared at her, his hands slack on the rifle. "What?"

Elinor wet her lips. "The pretend Durl murdered the real Durl. I've seen him wearing a rope like that, tied at his waist."

Perry rubbed his forehead again. "But why, Elinor? Why?"

She shut the box with a click. "I don't know. He must have killed Chaboot, too. I presume it's something to do with the roost. We have to warn the others; he could be leading them into a trap."

The sea whispered in the distance. Elinor bent and put the box back in the ground, then straightened up. "We have to go to the cave."

Perry blinked foolishly at her. "I'll be off, then," he said. "Won't Jaq be surprised to see me!"

Elinor flung out her hands, much in the manner of a dramatic ghost. "Wait! Take me with you!"

Fitten looked from one to the other. "Do you need your horse?"

Perry ignored him. "Are you crazy, Elinor? We've never tried that before. Besides, Beresford would kill me," he added. "I don't fancy that much."

"You've managed it with Jaq," she retorted. "You've carried him from one side of the island to the other."

"Even so, Beresford would still kill me," repeated Perry. "I might be Bemused, but I know I can't take you straight into danger."

Elinor stamped her foot. "I can't send *you* into danger, especially when you are so Bemused. I should never have told you! And Beresford doesn't even *know* the danger," she cried. Then she paused, arrested by a new thought. Could this be the thing Beresford had concealed from her? She could not believe that he could have discovered something of this magnitude and kept it from all of them. And how could he have possibly uncovered Durl's deception?

She shook her head vehemently. "Both of us must go," she said to Perry. "We must warn everyone and rescue the roost. You can grab the queen and bring her back here while I distract Durl – I mean, not-Durl. What if he tries to kill the queen?"

"The queen?" said Fitten. "What queen?"

Perry groaned quietly. "I don't like it. Lord, Elinor, what if I make a mistake and we end up buried in the cliff instead of the cave?" He paused. "At least I won't have to explain anything to Lord Bossyford if I am petrified."

Elinor huffed crossly. "Take us to the ledge," she said. "We can go in from there."

"What about the soap?" asked Perry. "Although I suppose that if we are both dashed against the rocks, I won't have to explain that, either!"

Fitten looked at them as if they had both gone mad. "Soap?"

Elinor put her hands on her hips. "You know about the soap now, and we can watch out for it."

Fitten shook his head sadly.

"And the danger?" demanded Perry. "This reminds me of what Mother said. Once you know of the peril, you run straight towards it! It's like Father all over again, warning of the ambush and dying in the attempt. How could I possibly tell Mother I allowed you to repeat his mistake?"

Elinor glared impatiently. "A murderous vampiri will be no danger to me, when I am so much bigger than him. I am worried about the queen, and Aldreda, and Pags. How can I possibly stay back here when we might save them?"

Perry sighed and threw up a hand. Nearby, a sheep bleated nervously. "Very well," he grumbled. "Embrace me tightly, and watch your step for the soap."

Under Fitten's bewildered gaze, Elinor moved closer and put her arms around Perry's waist. Perry returned the hug, both arms fast around her.

Elinor looked over her shoulder. "Mr Fitten, may we borrow your lantern? It is a matter of life and death."

Wordlessly, Fitten handed her the light. Elinor took it with some apprehension; it was difficult to hold on to both that and Perry. However, she didn't want to make any comments about Perry catching on fire, as he was already anxious enough. "Please tell your wife to keep the kettle warm, Mr Fitten," she said instead. "We hope to return soon."

Fitten nodded doubtfully. "Shall we go back now? She was

baking *soufflés aux framboises* this evening," he added, as if offering an apple to a recalcitrant horse.

Elinor contemplated the raspberry soufflés wistfully only for a moment. Then she strengthened her resolve. "Later," she promised. "Now we have to visit Little Sark." She tightened her grip on Perry. "I'm ready. Watch out for the puffins, and the soap."

"Right," he said, a lock of blond hair falling into his eyes. "To the ledge. Hold on!"

Elinor drew in a breath. Something yanked at her innards and the world went white.

28

IN WHICH PARTIES RECONVENE

*L*ightness filled Elinor's being for several moments, then a jolt ran through her and heaviness returned to her limbs. Her eyes were still open, but she heard more than saw their new location. Waves crashed nearby, the spray wetting her face.

She exhaled and peered into the darkness. Her lantern showed the steep rise of the cliff alongside them. Starlight showed the swirling, turbulent waves below.

"Thank God," murmured Perry devoutly. "No puffins."

"Not yet. And we didn't slip."

"I wish I could have seen Fitten's face when we disappeared."

Elinor giggled and carefully extricated herself from Perry's grip, holding the lantern firmly. "You're right," she said. "There's a faint scent of lavender. How incongruous."

"I like the lavender," said Perry conversationally. "Might obtain some of that soap myself."

"Never mind that now. Where's the entrance?"

"Behind you. Carefully."

Elinor turned. Within the grey of the cliffs, she could make out a scoop of black. She edged towards it, holding the lantern aloft. Once her foot slid along the rock, but Perry caught her arm before she could lose her balance.

She glanced back. His face was pale, his hair windswept and damp. He jerked his head forward. "On we go."

"You don't want to go back to the sheep?"

Perry shook his head, a faint smile upon his lips. Clearly, he had decided to embrace the adventure. Elinor sighed and crept into the cave, bending as the roof curved low. She had been so eager to see this tunnel, but she couldn't bring herself to be glad of the circumstances that had brought them there.

She edged forward, and all around her was impenetrable stone, glimmering in the weak lantern light and green with slime. The smell of seaweed was sharp on the air. Water trickled at her feet, the first hint that this passageway would become a rushing vortex of water at high tide.

The noise of the waves outside seemed hugely magnified within the confines of the tunnel. Elinor gripped the lantern tightly and kept a trembling hand on the clammy stone wall, taking small steps. She cursed that she had brought Perry, with his limp, into these slippery, crouched conditions, but how else could she have reached her destination so quickly? And they would need his help again before the night was out.

The cave seemed likely to muffle any sound, but Elinor wondered if she would be heard over the trickling of water and the boom of the waves. "Aldreda!" she called. "Aldreda!" It was a faint hope, but Aldreda's ears were very good. She might hear, if Elinor's voice echoed into the cavern beyond. The only problem was that not-Durl might hear too.

They inched forward, Elinor calling every so often and feeling cramped in the narrow, low tunnel. She ached to move faster, but haste would not be served by two Avelys with a twisted ankle. As she eyed the water at her feet, she saw it now covered the floor and lapped at her boots. The tunnel must angle downwards, as Jaq had said, and the tide was slowly rising.

~

Aldreda had first entered the cave in Beresford's coat pocket. Durl had ridden in the other pocket, wearing only a cloak and his usual rope around his waist. Aldreda, in her black silk, thought it strangely informal garb to meet his queen, but it would allow Durl to change into bat form quickly if needed and perhaps it was de rigueur attire for a royal guard. He also carried a sack with clothes for Her Majesty, which was why he had deigned to be carried by a human.

Pags flew ahead, his black form a quick shadow. Aldreda only hoped he did not intend to transform into human nakedness for the forthcoming royal audience – not after the argument that had broken out on the southern cliffs.

They had been held up by Jaq's choice of clothing. He had originally appeared at their rendezvous point in only a cloak and boots, ready, like Durl, to transform at a moment's notice. However, Lord Beresford had balked. He refused, he said, to appear before the vampiri queen with a naked selkie at his side, wearing riding boots and not much else – it offended his English sensibilities, and would offend the queen. He had made several biting comments on the vulgar habits of selkies and sent Jaq back to the *Crescent* to find more suitable attire.

This quest had delayed them for almost an hour. Durl, impatient, had suggested they move forward without Jaq, but Beresford had said that with the tide out, they could wait for decent clothing. They had loitered on the cliffs until Jaq reappeared, now royally (if sulkily) garbed, then begun the careful crossing over La Coupee and the perilous descent down the rock face.

Peeking out of Beresford's pocket, Aldreda was glad not to have to walk the narrow, low tunnel that Jaq had discovered. The floor and walls were damp and slimy, and her black slippers would have been soaked. Beresford's lantern set shadows looming, and pungent oil mixed with the stench of seaweed. They walked in silence, though chatter would not have disturbed a roost so deep in hibernation.

When Beresford finally straightened up, Aldreda saw that the roof opened into a large natural cavern, stretching about fifteen yards high and twice as wide. The tunnel floor also rose in shallow stone steps, which Beresford cautiously climbed. To their left, water trickled from the tunnel into a large black lagoon.

Above them, stone icicles hung from the ceiling, glittering in the light of the lantern. And heaped in the back corner was gold, on a rock ledge that curved like a half moon. Piles and piles of gold, glimmering like dappled sunlight, spilling over the cavern floor.

Aldreda had no eyes for treasure, however. Her gaze was drawn to the ledges above. A roost of bats hung fast asleep, motionless in the still air. They looked like a patch of strange blooms yet to flower, the wings curled around each small body like an unopened bud. They did not stir as Beresford and Jaq walked closer.

At her insistent tug, Beresford set Aldreda on the cold floor. He put the lantern on a flat rock, and helped Durl from his other pocket. Pags flew up and hung from a stone icicle at some distance from the roost, and Jaq strode around the cavern, looking every inch a royal prince. Aldreda had to admit that he added a certain dignity to their party.

While Beresford and Jaq slowly circled the cave, Aldreda stayed by the tunnel entrance, observing. That meant she was well positioned to hear Elinor's voice calling her name. The sound was faint above the trickling water, like a ghost.

Aldreda looked around the cavern. No one else had heard the eerie cry. Doubting her own ears, and suspecting trouble, Aldreda said nothing. With a glance at Beresford, she slipped into the darkness, following Elinor's voice through the tunnel.

She walked briskly in her human form, grimacing. The hem of her gown was getting soaked by the rising waters that snaked along the tunnel floor. What was Elinor doing to delay proceedings even further? It had better not be a matter involving apparel.

Halfway along the passage, she found Elinor. Perry limped behind, shoulders hunched and head bowed against the low rock. Aldreda felt a chill of premonition run down her spine, but she was too cross to give it much credence. She stalked forward, swishing her dampening silk skirts. "What are you doing here?" she demanded, her voice echoing around the tunnel.

Elinor let out a gusty breath. "Oh, I am so glad to see you!"

"Well, I cannot say the same! Can you not follow instructions for once in your life?"

Elinor crouched on the tunnel floor. Then Aldreda realised for certain that something must be wrong, for Elinor would not spoil her gown without good purpose. There was dirt on her habit, and her face was drawn.

"Durl is not Durl!" she said, in a low, urgent voice. "I found a dead vampiri. We think Durl killed him – not Durl, but whoever he is."

Aldreda blinked. Elinor wasn't making sense, but her tone was deadly serious. "Pardon me, but did you say that Durl is not Durl?"

"I can't explain it all now," said Elinor. "We must stop him from waking the queen: I fear for her life. You must fly back and halt proceedings, and quickly!"

Perry, looming over Elinor's shoulder, nodded. "We'll follow. I'll grab the queen, and Elinor can grab not-Durl."

"Grab the queen?" said Aldreda, drawing back. "I should hope not!"

Elinor leaned closer. "Would you prefer her to be grabbed by Perry or strangled by Durl?"

Aldreda shook her head dazedly. "Very well. If you are quite certain—"

"I am," said Elinor.

Aldreda drew herself up. "Then I shall disrobe, as I may need to be agile." It was a marker of the crisis that Perry did not even object: he merely raised his eyes to the ceiling and sighed. Aldreda untied her gown and stepped out briskly, feeling cold air on her bare skin.

Elinor took the dress but held up her hand before Aldreda could transform. "Wait! Don't go near Durl. He is a danger to you, Aldreda – you are smaller than him. Promise me!"

Aldreda nodded. Elinor picked her up and Aldreda used the height to jump, turning into a bat as she flew through the air. Her return to the cavern was swift, for she was dexterous in the dark. She swept into the cavern without hesitation.

The scene was much as she had left it. After all, only minutes had passed since she had left, though it seemed like the whole world had shifted. The group in the cave had barely moved. Beresford still stared at the gold on the bank of the lagoon, and Jaq ran his fingers through it. Durl – or Not-Durl – was standing under the roost, looking up. The bag on his shoulder seemed heavy now to Aldreda's suspicious gaze. He turned to Aldreda as she tumbled to the ground, and his eyes were hard.

Aldreda had no time to worry about her lack of clothing. She stood a little shakily and held up both her hands. "Stop!"

"Where did you go?" demanded Not-Durl. "We need you to play the flute." He pulled it from his bag and the tiny sliver of gold glinted in the lantern light.

"Not yet," said Aldreda. "Lady Beresford is on her way."

Beresford closed his eyes and groaned. "Elinor? Why, for God's sake?"

Aldreda folded her arms. "And Perry."

Jaq smacked his forehead. "Oh, Triton."

Aldreda managed a small smile. "They have news. I suggest that we wait until they join us."

"No need to wait," snapped Not-Durl, and marched over to Aldreda. She fought the urge to flinch, but he only thrust the flute in her face. "The tide is rising; we must hurry. Play the Viveroust. You don't need clothes for that."

Aldreda took the flute and held it up to the light. "This looks remarkably like the one I lost," she observed mildly. As she examined the golden swirls and tiny winking stars, she realised that it was the very flute Elinor had brought to Sark. Not-Durl must have stolen it out of her reticule on that first evening. Lord knows, he could sneak into the house unnoticed.

Not-Durl folded his arms. "All Viveroust flutes are styled the same," he said. "This one belongs to the roost, and it will wake the queen. Now play it."

Aldreda lowered the flute, grasping it tight, the engravings pressing into her palm. "They have slept so long; another few minutes will not matter."

Not-Durl glared at her.

Observing this, Beresford strode to the place where the corridor entered the cavern. Pags flapped slowly after him.

They could all hear Elinor's light, airy voice echoing into the space. "Oh, I do hope she is lovely. I've never met vampiri royalty, of course. I'm certain she will be all that is gracious."

Perry muttered something about the likelihood that the queen might need a gown, and the brother and sister entered the cave.

Elinor gasped at the size of it. "Oh!" she exclaimed. "How wondrous!" She surveyed the company as she mounted the shallow stairs. "And gold, too! Mr Orlend will be so pleased." She went to Beresford and stood on tiptoe to give him a kiss on the cheek, choosing the side furthest from Not-Durl. Aldreda could not hear what she whispered, but she could imagine. Beresford's eyebrows rose.

"Greetings!" said Perry loudly, smiling around at everyone. "So this is the secret cave! Charming!"

Beresford schooled his expression and returned Elinor's chaste kiss. "Delighted you could join us, dear wife. You couldn't resist, could you?"

Elinor waved a hand and turned to smile brightly at everyone. "I did not want to miss all the fun. However, we have a small problem."

"What would that be, dear?" inquired Beresford.

Not-Durl was standing stiff and alert, watching Elinor, his impatience and suspicion plain to see.

Elinor sighed. "Perry could only find one sheep."

"One sheep?" repeated Beresford obligingly.

Perry scuffed his boot along the floor, head down. "I did warn you that I am not cut out for shepherding duties."

"But only one sheep?" cried Jaq, getting into the spirit of the thing. "Surely you could do better than that, my dear fellow."

Perry sighed. "I did land on one, which is how I collared him. The rest took an aversion to me after that."

Aldreda cast him a sharp glance, wondering if this part was true. Perry gave her a broad wink and she looked away hastily. He was clearly Bemused.

"Yes," said Elinor sharply. "My poor brother did his best, but the sheep did not co-operate. Indeed, the silly creatures became quite unnerved by Perry bursting in all over the place. So we thought we should inform you that we do not have a whole flock awaiting the roost. Therefore, Perry will offer himself as the queen's dinner. Since he failed to catch the sheep," she added, in needless explanation.

Perry nodded and shuffled over to the roost. He stood below the hanging bats, staring up in apparent wonder at their delicate shapes. Then he cast a glance at Elinor. Aldreda saw the desperation in his eyes and hoped that Not-Durl did not notice – or that if he did, he put it down to Perry's reluctance to serve as dinner.

Not-Durl stalked away from Aldreda. "We don't need Perry. One sheep will suffice."

Elinor looked shocked. "How can you say that, Mr Durl? Your roost would drain a poor sheep of all its blood. I refuse to allow such cruelty. How many vampiri are there?" She, too, walked over to the roost and fell silent, gazing up at it. Aldreda could see that she was holding her lapis lazuli.

"Keep your distance from Her Majesty," said Not-Durl. "Let Miss Zooth play the flute and wake the queen before the tide rises – unless you all want to be trapped here?"

Beresford spoke. "Haste does seem advisable, wife. The tide waits for no woman or bat."

"Just my clothes," said Jaq, with a grin. "Or a selkie, I suppose."

Elinor raised an eyebrow. "Yes, husband, but I count at least twenty bats here. You certainly cannot foist all that upon one poor sheep. I wonder which is the queen. Perhaps that large one?" She pointed to a bat bigger than the others, hanging on the outer edge. "Or the little one up high? Or perhaps that one in the very middle, with the delicate feet? She could be any one of them! How shall we know which one Perry must feed?"

She strolled away, looking thoughtful. Perry bit his lip, kept his gaze upon the vampiri, and edged closer.

Not-Durl bared his teeth. "There will be no need to give your brother to the queen; she can find a sheep with the rest of them. There are plenty on the island, even if Mr Avely is unable to collect them." He turned to Aldreda and gestured at the flute. "Now, play!"

The lantern light flickered, and only swirling water broke the silence.

Elinor took up a position beside Aldreda. "Yes, do play, Aldreda. What on earth are you waiting for?"

Aldreda gave her a dry look. "Merely for you to stop pontificating, my dear."

"I have finished now." Elinor folded her arms.

Aldreda raised the flute to her lips. The gold was warm to touch. She placed her fingers over the apertures, feeling the instrument come alive. It was as though it had been made for her, the engravings delicately framing her fingertips. She put her lips to the slender mouthpiece and blew.

A sound came forth: soft, sweet, and very high.

Elinor tilted her head. "Is it working? I can't hear anything."

"Shhh," hissed Not-Durl, staring intently at Aldreda.

Aldreda blew again, moving her fingers in a tentative melody that she had practised on the ship. The flute sang with a pure sound, amplified as it arced through the cave. It sang of the night sky, moonlight, and a soft breeze on a bat's wing. The golden flute seemed to brighten under her fingers.

Perry frowned. "Shall I whistle?" he asked in a stage whisper.

Aldreda ignored him; clearly humans could not hear the Viveroust, though the sound was achingly insistent to her own ears. She was aware of Pags' gaze on her from above. She played with more vigour, revelling in the rise and sweep of the music, mimicking the dip and soar of flight.

Everyone craned their necks to look at the roost. The vampiri hung motionless, seemingly unaffected.

Jaq equalled Perry with his stage whisper. "It doesn't seem to be working."

"No," Perry hissed back. "Is the flute broken? Beresford, perhaps *you* could whistle?"

Not-Durl gave them all a scathing glance. He put down his bag and crept towards the roost, his hand going to the rope that hung round his waist.

High above him, a wing fluttered.

Aldreda blinked. The queen was awakening. She dared not stop playing, but she simplified her tune so that she could watch the roost.

A tiny figure, one of those that Elinor had pointed out, twitched and fluttered against the ceiling.

The flute continued in its high, small voice, singing of the night.

The queen's head emerged from her curled wings. Two dark eyes winked open.

The flute seemed to sing louder of its own accord, a note

swelling sharply. Aldreda's fingers faltered and she glanced down to find her place. She heard a gasp, and when she looked up again, her own eyes widened.

The queen was now half woman, half bat. She clung to the roof with bat claws and wings, but a human head was on her shoulders. Red hair fell down in a cloud and her eyes were bright above a small nose. Her lips looked large in her tiny face – or perhaps that was the effect of being upside down, and of the human features contrasted with the bat.

A small gasp escaped Elinor. Perry let out a murmured curse and backed away hastily. Neither of them had seen the Duum form before, but that was scarcely an excuse for bad manners. Aldreda herself had only seen it once, and she quelled the unease that rose in her even as her music skittered to a halt. It was only right that the queen should demonstrate her superior control thus, and perhaps it was also assisted by the magic of the Viveroust.

The queen spoke in French, her voice richly aristocratic and somewhat sleepy. "Dear me, is it time to wake up?"

Everyone stared. Her Majesty blinked and wrinkled her nose. "What is wrong with you all? Am I late to rise?" She yawned, white teeth sharp. "I *am* rather hungry."

Aldreda saw that Not-Durl was moving, even as the rest of them stood transfixed. He stepped forward, swinging his now-untied rope casually. "Your Majesty." He bowed deeply. "We welcome you back to the world of the risen. Let me assist you to descend, and we can find you sustenance."

"Hm," said the queen. She sniffed delicately. "Can I smell *selkie*?"

Jaq sidled backwards.

Meanwhile, Not-Durl stripped off his cloak with one hand. Then he launched himself into the air, turning into a bat. Holding the rope in his claws, he flew towards the queen.

She watched him curiously, half-asleep, hanging upside-down

and vulnerable, her red hair swinging loose, her long white throat exposed.

Aldreda drew in a breath to shout and the flute squawked. Durl swooped closer, the rope tightening to a sharp line in his grasp.

"Now, Perry!" shouted Elinor.

Perry cast her an agonised glance and stepped forward. Reaching up with a grimace, he plucked the tiny queen from the roof. Her face twisted in surprise. Gulping, Perry plucked another vampiri from the ledge with his other hand. Then, hands full and looking rather guilty, he vanished. A pebble rolled along the ground in the silent cave.

Elinor let out a sigh of relief. "Thank goodness for that. I must say that I had not expected Her Majesty to be so ... flexible."

Aldreda lowered the flute. "That was the Duum form; only a few vampiri are capable of it."

Jaq raised an eyebrow. "Very impressive."

Aldreda frowned. "Nonetheless, Her Majesty has probably received a terrible shock. Where do you suppose Perry has taken her? I'm glad he thought to take a chaperone as well."

Not-Durl tumbled to the floor, snapping into his human body. "Damn him! What is he doing? Where has he gone?"

Elinor shrugged. "As far from here as possible, I hope."

Not-Durl's face was livid with rage. "You planned this!" he spluttered. "You want the queen to feed on his Musor blood!"

"And why not?" asked Elinor. "She said she was hungry. It will help her mind clear after a long sleep."

"No!" hissed Not-Durl. "It will cloud her judgement. You want her to go with you, so you have sought to bond her from the start."

"Nonsense," said Elinor. "It will be entirely the queen's decision. You are the one who wishes to prevent her going anywhere. In fact," she added, "I believe you want to dispose of her entirely.

You want the roost to stay on Sark, unbonded and living apart from Musors."

Not-Durl's knuckles showed white around the rope. "What?"

"You are not Durl," stated Elinor. "I just found Durl's body, buried in the western dunes. You killed him and Chaboot because you wanted to find the roost and make it wild. You are a Rofanite, after all. You cannot bear the thought of the last French roost being civilised."

Not-Durl stalked forward. "How dare you insult a royal guard with such accusations!"

"You are no royal guard," Elinor replied. "Are you Rofan's successor? What is your real name?" She paused. "We shall call you Rofan if you do not tell us."

Not-Durl's eyes bulged.

"I suppose it was you who stole the soap and put it on the ledge outside, endangering my brother," continued Elinor. "Did you think you could wake the roost yourself with the flute you stole from my reticule? That must have been very frustrating for you."

"You are deranged," asserted Not-Durl, folding his arms. "The queen will want nothing to do with such insanity."

Aldreda could hear the bluster in his voice. "So that is what you wanted," she said. "Your own roost, away from Musors and their problems."

Not-Durl said nothing, but narrowed his eyes.

Elinor shook her head. "You are prejudiced against Musors. You planted the shatterstone for Perry to find, didn't you? A neat way to dispose of a Mineral Discernor, I must say, but cruel if it had worked."

"Nonsense," replied Not-Durl, picking up his cloak and tying it around his shoulders. "I put it there for you to find, I will admit that. Lady Orlend shouldn't have a private collection of shatterstones. She is afraid, being sick and alone, but you should concern yourself with her misdemeanours instead of persecuting me."

Around them, the stone icicles glinted in the lamplight, and the rush of water into the cave seemed to grow louder. The tide was still rising. Aldreda eyed the lagoon uneasily. What was Not-Durl – Rofan, rather – planning? Had he intended to trap them here all along?

Jaq spoke, voicing her own question. "But why did you bring us all with you? You knew the roost was here."

"No, he didn't," said Elinor. "You found it, Jaq; he simply pretended he already knew about it."

"But why cart us all with him?" insisted Jaq.

Aldreda bit her lip. "He needed me to play the flute, and I wouldn't go alone with him."

Pags tilted his head with interest above them, his eyes watchful.

"Aldreda," said Beresford, "you said that after she awakens, the queen must play the flute to rouse her people. If the queen is killed, what happens? Does the roost stay sleeping?"

Aldreda passed a hand over her brow, the flute still warm in her grasp. "In the queen's absence, the next highest-ranking vampiri ascends to rule. On Sark this would be Lilian, as she is companion to Lady Orlend, the Seigneuresse who owns the island. Indeed, she is the only bonded vampiri on the island at all." She turned to Rofan. "Very clever to see that Lilian could be used that way. I suppose you were going to bring her here to claim the roost."

Rofan gave an ironic bow. "A delightful story, Miss Zooth. I did not know you were as mad as your Musor, or I would never have invited you here." He picked up his bag and hefted it over his shoulder. "I beg you not to repeat your ravings to anyone else, for your own sake."

"So Lilian doesn't know," said Elinor. "She doesn't know that you are a killer. You were going to spin her some tale and beg her to be queen."

Behind Beresford, the lagoon waters lapped higher on the rocky shore, touching the edges of the strewn gold.

"If you insist, Lady Beresford, and who would refuse a chance to be queen?" asked Rofan, with another bow. "Now, I have much to accomplish this evening, as Mr Avely has been so vexatious. It is time for me to leave." He backed away slowly, sliding a hand into the bag by his side.

Beresford, Jaq, and Elinor all stepped forward. Before all of them, though, Pags dropped into flight, going straight for the other vampiri. Pags was like a black arrow, but Rofan was faster. He withdrew his hand from the bag and held up a shatterstone.

Pags veered upwards suddenly, missing Rofan by a wingspan.

Everyone else froze.

Aldreda caught her breath. The dark sphere was pale grey in the dim light of the cave. She recalled what Elinor had said about the grey stones carrying more power than the black. The shatterstone was the size of a small egg: smooth, heavy, and ominous.

Rofan backed towards the entrance, keeping the pale stone firm in his grasp as he watched them. "Follow me, and I shall fling this stone in your face. Don't be fooled by its size. This is more powerful than the one I left in La Moinerie, and I have more here. It was good of you to leave the sack by the wall for me to help myself. Far harder to fetch them out of the water." He smiled at their aghast expressions. "I fear you have no choice but to stay in this cave, where you will be tragically lost in your mineral explorations." His smile broadened, becoming frightful. "In the meantime, I shall visit the queen: a visit which is long overdue."

29
IN WHICH A SACRIFICE IS MADE

*E*linor knew it was hopeless. This dreadful Rofan would use the shatterstone anyway, once he was in the tunnel. It would be easy enough to trap them all inside the cavern while leaving a space for the roost to escape.

It was pointless to wait. She sighed, and edged forward.

Unfortunately, Beresford's brain was rather acute. He must have reached the same conclusion – or perhaps realised what her conclusion might be – for he started forward at the same time.

Jaq was a step behind Beresford. But Elinor was ahead of both of them. "I'm afraid that your manners are sadly lacking, Mr Rofan," she said loudly. "Why don't you simply *ask* the queen whether she would like to join your cause? She might wish to live on Sark for a while, partaking of sloe gin at your expense."

"Keep away," hissed Rofan. When Elinor took another step, he shook the shatterstone at her. "I won't hesitate!"

"Get back, Elinor," said Beresford grimly behind her. "For God's sake, let me talk to him."

Elinor advanced in small, mincing steps. "The queen might like sloe gin. You could at least try it, rather than resorting to even more uncouth methods."

Insulting his beverages was the final straw. Rofan drew back his arm and flung the stone at Elinor.

At the same time, she dived for him.

She knew it might be the end of her. It was a risk she was willing to take, given that Beresford was right behind her, as well as Aldreda and Jaq, and she'd much rather she took the Impact herself. But she had forgotten about Pags. Quicker than lightning, Pags dived to intercept the shatterstone and knocked it away from her.

With a whoosh, first the shatterstone, then Pags, hit the floor of the cave.

This time Elinor saw the explosion as well as felt it. The smooth egg burst open with a flash of light. Power like an unseen wave of aggression shot out. Flecks of stone and metal pelted towards her, but that was minor compared to the Impact itself, which tossed her backwards like a sack of wheat, spinning her around.

She saw Beresford and Jaq thrown back, and Pags flung like a pebble on a wave. Even Aldreda, much further away, was pushed like a feather in a gust of wind.

Aldreda gave a sharp, wounded cry, and Elinor's gaze found Pags. His black figure was inert on the hard floor, close to Aldreda. The golden flute fell from her hands, a tiny clink on the stone, and rolled towards Pags' motionless body.

Elinor's heart clenched in fear, but she wrenched her attention to what Rofan was doing. He too had been thrown backwards, but it had brought him closer to the entrance. He scuttled to it, his hand reaching for another stone.

Elinor scrambled to her feet, but she was too late. With one last vicious glare, Rofan vanished into the tunnel.

She hurried after him, though her body was bruised and battered. Just as she reached the entrance, another explosion rocked the cavern. She was thrown back, landing on her side and jarring her elbow. Pain wrenched through her.

The roof of the tunnel erupted, and rocks rained down on them.

She turned, fear and anger loud within her. Another boom echoed and a huge slab of rock shivered and collapsed in the tunnel entrance.

Beresford grasped her and pulled her away. "Watch out!" he shouted. "Everyone down!"

Aldreda was at Pags' side, bent over him, ignoring the destruction around her. Jaq threw himself in front of them, and Elinor realised that he was using his body to protect the vampiri from falling rocks.

However, the next boom seemed quieter. They waited, listening. Perhaps the sound was blocked by the fallen stones, or perhaps Rofan had retreated further. When the next crash came, it had a different resonance.

In the cavern, another rock slid down like an afterthought. Dust rose around Elinor, obscuring her view.

Silence came – if one counted silence as the absence of explosions. Before them, water rushed into the lagoon, pouring out of the tunnel from a more restricted aperture and frothing. So perhaps there was still a way out, if any of them would brave it.

Elinor realised she was in Beresford's arms and turned to cling to him. "Are you all right?"

"Fine," he said, wiping dust from his brow. "What about you? You were closer."

"Just a bit sore. What of Pags?" She twisted out of his embrace. "He saved me."

Jaq slowly got to his feet. He took a step back and Elinor hurried forward, her heart catching in her throat. Now she could see that Aldreda was lying against Pags' bat body, careless of her own nakedness. Elinor swallowed. Pags' form was limp, his black torso awkwardly twisted.

"Don't you dare die, you wretch," Aldreda said, tearfully. "Don't you dare!"

"He can't be dead," Elinor said, kneeling next to Aldreda. "He's so strong. He has supernatural strength. Doesn't he, Aldreda?"

Jaq answered for her. "Supernatural, not immortal. Can't revive a stopped heart."

Aldreda choked back a sob and Elinor gave Jaq a reproachful look. She examined the roost, but the gathering of black flags remained furled and motionless above the gold. How could they have slept through that racket? It was just as well, however, as Elinor did not like to think what might happen if the roost awoke without their queen to guide them.

Beresford approached her. "I am concerned for Pags, but also for us. Jaq, how much time do you think we have? Will the tide fill this cave?"

"No," Jaq replied. "You will have space and air, as the cavern is higher than the tunnel, but the tide will make it damn difficult for me to swim against that rushing water."

Elinor listened to what now sounded like a roaring river, emptying tumultuous currents into the lagoon. "Must you, Jaq? I do not like your chances, with so many rocks fallen and the tide rising."

Jaq shrugged and took off his velvet jacket. "It is the only way out. I'm the best swimmer, and Perry might need me. I can wade in human form, and if it becomes too rough then I can become a seal." He stepped out of his breeches and Elinor hastily looked away. "See, Captain, I said these clothes would only slow me down."

Beresford shook his head. "You want to swim *up* a horizontal waterfall this time?" He pressed his lips together then expelled a sharp breath. "I wish there was another way, Jaq."

Jaq ignored him and strode to the edge of the steps. He paused, naked, hands on hips. "Where do you think Perry took the queen?"

Elinor stared, unseeing, trying to think. She hadn't discussed that detail with Perry in the hurry to reach the cavern, merely trusting that he would take the queen out of harm's way. "The *Crescent?*" she suggested. "Though he might try to find a sheep first."

"I hope he doesn't bring a sheep onto my ship," said Beresford.

Elinor smiled weakly. "He will find the sheep first, I suppose."

"The western dell?" asked Jaq.

"No," she replied. "Rofan knew of that plan. Surely Perry will avoid it."

"Perry will be Bemused," Beresford said, grimly.

Elinor sighed. Then a thought occurred to her and she winced. "Try his room, perhaps."

Jaq sighed. "I'll have to explore the whole island."

"If you make it through the tunnel," said Beresford.

"I can but try." Jaq waded down the steps into the tunnel. He had to bend almost double to fit into the gap remaining in the jagged rocks. Water rushed against his legs, reaching to his thighs.

Elinor turned away, not wanting to watch Jaq thrust his body into that dark space, made treacherous by the rushing tide. In the cave, Aldreda still clung to Pags. The air seemed colder and danker than before, and smoke from the lantern clogged Elinor's lungs.

Beresford turned abruptly. "I'll give Jaq ten minutes, then see if I can clear a way through behind him."

"Be careful," said Elinor wearily. "The rocks might shift again." She returned to Aldreda's side and bent down. "Can you hear a heartbeat, my dear?"

Aldreda sniffed and pressed her tiny ear closer to Pags' heart. "Yes," she said at last, with a sigh. "Very faint. It is his head I am worried about. His thick head! He fell on the rock like a stone."

Elinor bit her lip; she had seen the strong impact on Pags' small form. "He has a thick skull," she said. "Don't give up yet, Aldreda. Once we get out of here, we can find help."

She looked around. The dust had settled and the cave looked

much as it had before: the golden crescent of piled treasure, the quiet, sleeping bats, and the sharp cones of rock hanging above her head. But the lagoon had risen higher.

The Viveroust flute lay abandoned on the floor. Cautiously, Elinor picked it up and put it in her reticule. The metal was dull and cold to her touch, though it had seemed to glow in Aldreda's hands.

Beresford was gingerly poking around in the rocks. As he did so, another fell. Elinor started nervously, then left Aldreda to her vigil and approached Beresford.

"Did you guess?" she asked him. "Did you know that Durl was not Durl?"

Beresford turned. "God, no. I'm glad you warned us, though I wish you weren't stuck here now with us."

Elinor dropped her gaze. Of course he hadn't known. She realised she was shivering, and rubbed her hands briskly on her arms.

Beresford glowered at the wall of rock where the tunnel had been. "He did a pretty good job, curse him. He must have thrown the shatterstone into the roof. The tide is covering three steps now."

She looked down and saw that Beresford was right. Water lapped at his boots.

Beresford examined the rubble. "I don't know if even Aldreda could find a way through now."

Elinor glanced back at her. "She won't want to leave Pags."

"She may have to."

"Perry knows where we are."

"He doesn't know that Rofan has bombs."

Elinor twisted her hands together. "You think he will attack Perry?"

"It is a possibility," he admitted reluctantly. "One hopes that Perry is far away or well hidden. Or that he sees Rofan in time and Travels out of harm's way."

Elinor brushed the dust off her habit roughly. "We need to climb out and find him before Rofan does. Save the queen, and so forth."

Beresford smiled at her in the gloom. "How do you propose we do that?"

"Move some rocks," she replied, and sidled around the water to reach for a stone.

Ten minutes passed in silence, except for the scuff and clang of shifting stones and the splashing of water. Elinor did not want to discuss possibilities or make small talk – not when Aldreda was still desperately waiting for a sign of life from Pags.

The possibilities were uncomfortable to contemplate. Rofan had a head start on Jaq, and the benefit of wings. He could circle the island faster than the selkie, and he would most likely find Perry sooner.

Perry knew he should be wary of Rofan, but he was injured, Bemused, and looking after two bats. A shatterstone could easily take him by surprise, and Rofan had already shown no hesitation at using one on a Musor. With Perry disposed of, his way would be clear to kill the queen, or he might even kill them both together.

Elinor wished to avoid dwelling on the possibility that she had corralled Perry into his death and caused Pags' passing, so she focused on moving rocks. The aching in her muscles was a welcome distraction. The water soaking her shoes and skirts, however, was a damned hindrance.

Beresford worked in silence alongside her. Sweat beaded his brow, and after a few minutes he took off his coat. His muscles tightened as he grappled with the larger boulders, trying to push them aside.

Aldreda stayed by Pags' side without a word.

When a voice finally spoke in the dim cavern, it was none of theirs. It was small and high, floating down from above their heads, and it sparked hope in all their hearts. "Can I help, madame?"

Elinor looked around sharply. Her first thought was that it must be one of the roost, awakening – yet the voice was familiar. Eventually, her eyes found a tiny, naked boy, sitting on a ledge that jutted from the rocks above.

Raddle swung a leg over and stared down at them with curiosity. "What happened? Are you stuck?"

"Raddle!" Aldreda craned to look at him. "How did you get in here?"

"Yes, how *did* you get in here?" echoed Elinor. If there was a way in for the vampiri child, there was hope that Aldreda and the roost could escape the same way. And Pags too, if only he could fly again.

Raddle blinked down at them and pointed to a dark, shadowy corner above. "The same way I went out."

"The same way you went out?" repeated Elinor, feeling like a child at lessons.

Raddle nodded. "There is a passageway to the surface. When I told Durl about it, he assumed I meant the tunnel from the cliffs. I didn't correct him."

Elinor cleared her throat. "He isn't Durl."

"Yes, I know," said Raddle. "He told me you wanted to hurt my queen, but now I think *he's* the one who wants to hurt her. So I came tonight, just in case. You don't want to kill Her Majesty, do you?"

Elinor shook her head. "No, Durl does – I mean Rofan. That is what we are calling him."

Raddle's eyes were wide in his small face. "Is she safe?"

Elinor didn't know what to say. She looked at Aldreda, who gnawed her bottom lip, her hand still resting on Pags.

Finally, Beresford spoke. "For now, perhaps. Mr Avely took her away, but Rofan is after them."

The rushing and lapping of the water was loud. Raddle stood

up on the ledge. "Where is she?" he asked, drawing himself up. "I shall save her."

Elinor sighed. "We don't know where Perry and the queen went."

Raddle blinked. "Then I shall find her."

"Wait," said Aldreda, a faint tremor in her voice. "I shall come with you."

Elinor wiped her hands on her dirty habit and walked over to her. "Aldreda, you can't leave. What chance do you and Raddle have against Rofan? We must trust Perry and Jaq to it."

"I want to stay with Pags, the stupid, brave, noble idiot that he is," said Aldreda. "But Jaq may be stuck in the tunnel, and Perry is vulnerable wherever he is. Raddle must show me the way out. We can both search for Perry."

Elinor wrung her hands, knowing that Aldreda was right. The more chances they had, the better. Rofan might still be hunting for Perry, and Aldreda might somehow reach him first.

Aldreda turned back to Pags. She lay her head on his chest and a tear trickled down her white face. "Goodbye, Pags, dearest," she murmured. "Stay here and wait for me, dear brave one. I'll be back soon." She paused. "Don't you *dare* leave me."

The tear slid off her cheek and onto Pags.

It was like the tear of true love that woke a sleeping princess. Pags' twisted bat body shivered – but he was no princess. Before Elinor's anxious gaze, he transformed into shaggy, masculine, miniature humanity. His black hair lay tangled against the rocks, and Aldreda found herself leaning on a hairy chest with Pags' arm tightly curled around her. Her eyes widened.

Pags gave a weak smile. "Leaving me so soon, Miss Zooth?"

30

IN WHICH CHAPERONES ARE ABSENT

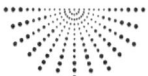

*A*ldreda started back, her expression both disbelieving and hopeful.

Elinor sighed with relief. "Thank God. Are you all right, Pags?"

Pags grimaced, shifting a little. Then he grinned and pulled Aldreda closer again. "Never been better."

Aldreda broke from his grasp with a huff. "How dare you throw yourself at a bomb! I'll never forgive you!" Her voice quivered.

Elinor shook her head. "Yes, that was most ill-advised. However, thank you for saving my life, dear Pags."

Pags put his hands down on the rock to support himself. "Well, if it demonstrated my noble heart to a sceptical audience, it was worth the pain."

"Are you in pain? Is it bearable?" Then Aldreda scooted back on her heels. "You deserve it, you wretch. I thought you were dead!"

"Merely resting," said Pags, with dignity.

Aldreda's lips pinched together. "Could you hear us talking while you were lying there?"

Pags widened his eyes. "I couldn't move, but I could hear a little. Something about my nobility and courage, I believe?"

Elinor bit back a grin and shared a glance with Beresford, who had left his efforts by the tunnel to see what the fuss was about.

Aldreda's voice lost its quiver and developed an edge. "Something about you being a fool and an idiot, perhaps. I must apologise: my nerves were overcome by the extremity of the situation. I may have said things that I didn't mean."

"So you don't want me to wait for you?" said Pags.

"Er." Aldreda was momentarily flustered. "Yes, you wait here."

"Where are you going?" he enquired.

Aldreda stood up. "I'm going with Raddle."

"Why?"

"To eat soufflé!" retorted Aldreda.

"To stop Rofan," explained Elinor.

Aldreda glared at her.

Gingerly, Pags pushed himself to his knees. "I'll come with you, my angel of the night."

"You most certainly will not!" exclaimed his angel of the night sharply.

"I shall," said Pags, wincing. "I'll be fine in a minute."

"You will *not* be fine, and you will rest, or I shall have nothing to do with you!" snapped Aldreda.

"You have nothing to do with me already," pointed out Pags. He stood up shakily. Closing his eyes, he pressed his hands against his temples, the veins standing out.

Aldreda turned to Elinor. "Tell him!" she demanded. "Make him lie down! It is outrageous that he should accompany me!"

"Pags, please rest. You have done enough for today."

Pags opened his eyes. "I'm not staying in this cave while Aldreda chases Rofan about the island."

"I won't be chasing Rofan about the island!"

"Well, you will," said Elinor.

"Not like that!"

Elinor sighed, feeling that the conversation was getting beyond her. "Aldreda, you cannot stop Pags if he truly wishes to go. Perhaps you will be glad of the company."

"There," said Pags. "I always knew Miss Avely was a sensible woman. This is one instance where I approve of her commanding manner."

Aldreda ground her teeth.

Raddle spoke from his ledge. "If you don't hurry up, I shall leave without either of you. The queen is in peril, and you two are quarrelling like an old married couple."

Pags waggled his eyebrows at Aldreda and she scowled back. He straightened up. "No time to waste, my angel. Rofan might return with Lilian and claim the roost."

Aldreda turned to Elinor. "Lift me up," she demanded.

Elinor put a hand out for Aldreda then raised her off the ground. In a flash Aldreda jumped off, becoming a bat and twisting through the air towards Raddle.

"Me too," said Pags.

Reluctantly, Elinor held out her hand. She did not want him to launch from the ground, though she knew he could when he was not weak and in pain.

Once Pags was several feet above the floor, he too leapt off with a wince and became a bat.

"Hurrah!" said Raddle. He jumped off his ledge, also changing form. Then he led the other vampiri up to the dark recesses of the cavern.

Alone with Beresford and the roost, Elinor felt her shoulders droop. Around her the cave seemed cold and empty, and her legs suddenly felt very tired.

Beresford came over and put an arm around her. "Just us now, my love," he said.

Elinor nodded dully, aware that her wet skirts were clinging to her calves and her body was bruised. Worst of all, her heart was sick with worry.

"I think I need a rest," said Beresford. "I'm a bit tired of moving rocks and watching dramatic scenes. Shall we sit together for a while?"

"We may as well, while we wait to be rescued," said Elinor despondently.

She allowed him to lead her to a large boulder. He spread his coat upon the floor and they sat down with their backs against the rock, Elinor tucked under his arm.

She blinked back her sudden tears. "They are all out there without us! I hate not knowing what is happening. They are facing the danger, while we are stuck in this wretched cavern."

"We have the worst of it," agreed Beresford, running his hand down her arm. "Yet even if the tunnel *was* clear of debris, the tide is now heading towards its height. We are stuck here for the next six hours at least, my love."

Elinor looked around and saw that he was right. The lagoon had grown higher, its black waters lapping over most of the steps. The cavern had shrunk with the rising water, and the hole of the tunnel was now more than half obscured.

"But what if Jaq has been crushed against the rocks?" she wailed. "What if Rofan creeps up on Perry and throws a shatter-stone at his head? What if Pags is too weak to fly and plummets to the ground?"

Beresford cupped her cheek, turning her face to his. "There is one advantage to this situation, my dear. We are now without a single pesky chaperone."

Elinor smiled feebly. "Unless you count a sleeping roost."

Beresford cast the roost a disparaging glance. "I do not, and I intend to take advantage of our solitude." He brought his lips to hers and kissed her gently.

At first Elinor could not understand how he could be thinking of such things at a time like this, but as his lips warmed hers, she let out a sigh and surrendered to it. He kept kissing her, slowly and sweetly, and she let herself be relax into his embrace.

After a while, however, she pushed him away. An earlier vexation had returned to her mind, and in the darkness and the extremity of their situation, it seemed silly not to say something now. She spoke tentatively. "James - there is something I must tell you."

"Oh?" Beresford leaned back with a smile, his hand still resting on her waist.

She drew a breath. "I heard a lie in your voice yesterday. When we were arguing." She paused nervously, and sat back on her heels. "I know I said I would not Truth Discern you, but I could not help it."

Beresford's expression darkened and his arm fell. "Elinor! You promised you would not."

"I know, but it is difficult for me to control!" She stood up in agitation. "It is because I know you so well, I think, that I can hear the lie in your voice without even trying." He was silent and she hurried on. "You must understand that my Discernment is part of me, and our marriage will have to accommodate it. You simply *must* accept that we cannot have any secrets from each other."

Beresford twisted his lips under her accusing expression. "It was only a white lie."

"But it eats away at me when I suspect you are keeping something from me!" She put her hands on her hips. "What was it?"

Beresford sighed. "Merely that Pags eavesdropped on Lady Orlend and Chester and discovered them to be innocent. So there was no real need for you to keep watch on them. I didn't want you to know, because I wanted you to stay safe at the Seigneurie." He paused. "You wouldn't listen to me otherwise."

Elinor was silent a moment with outrage. "Well! That is *extremely* annoying. I deserve to be told all that Pags discovered! What if I made the wrong decision based on false information?"

"But you don't listen to me and you won't stay out of harm's way," he snapped. "I'm your husband, I have a responsibility to protect you."

"Nonsense! I *do* listen to you. I stayed behind tonight, did I not?"

"And yet, here you are!"

"I had to come," she shouted, her voice magnified by the cavern's echo. "What is more, I might have determined the danger earlier, if you had not concealed your knowledge. We must decide these things together! It is not for you to autocratically decide them for yourself!"

Beresford rubbed both his hands over his face, his shoulders braced against the stone wall. After a moment, he sighed and dropped his hands. "Yes, you are right."

"Of course I am!"

A reluctant smile tugged at his lips. "I suppose if I am to marry you, I must accept that ours will be an extraordinary marriage." He looked at her, held out a hand, and drew a deep breath. "No secrets anymore. I promise."

Elinor's eyes welled up and she threw herself at him. He caught her in his arms and held her tight. Sniffling into his damp shirt, she felt relief sweep through her, and a new warmth; a sense that their love could grow deeper and stronger. She turned her face up towards him again, her hesitations dispelled.

31

IN WHICH ALDREDA ADOPTS A
COSTUME

*A*ldreda followed Raddle through the aperture in the ceiling. The passage was so narrow that it brushed her wings as it twisted and turned to the surface. One point was so tight that she had to stop flying and claw her way through, the rocks scratching at the delicate membrane of her wings. She turned to help Pags, for whom it was an even tighter squeeze, though Raddle must have slipped through easily. She winced at the pain Pags must feel; curse his stubbornness! Making certain he was through safely, she followed the sound of Raddle's progress.

The tunnel turned once more, and rose. When she emerged into the night air, Aldreda could see that they were far back from the cliff's edge, sheltered by an overhanging rock in a field. Above them, the clouds had been swept away by the wind, leaving the stars twinkling brightly above them like a map of diamonds.

She became human, and Raddle dropped reluctantly to the earth beside her in a sprawl of childish limbs.

"How did you smell the blood from here?" she asked, as they waited for Pags.

"I didn't," replied Raddle. "Durl woke me the first time he visited us. I suppose he tried to play the flute but it didn't work.

He crawled along the roof, trying to find the queen, and he must have dislodged a stone, for it fell on my chin."

"He didn't see you wake?"

"No. I was still sleepy; I saw him leave not long after. I waited a while, then I became hungry and found my own way out when the tide was high." He nodded proudly to the hole in the ground, which looked like an abandoned rabbit burrow below the jut of the rock.

Pags hauled himself out and became human in a shudder. His face was pale but alert as he looked up at the vast sky. Aldreda could hear the crash of waves; the noise echoed the insistent worry in her own heart. Perry had the queen, and Rofan was after them both.

"We'll fly high," she said, "if you can both manage it."

Raddle and Pags gave her identical looks of disdain.

"High up, we might see Rofan," she added. "We should look for him, not Perry. God knows where Perry is, but I suspect Rofan has heard the infamous story of Perry arriving in his room with Jaq. He will try there at some point, and if we hurry we might catch him as he approaches the Seigneurie."

Pags nodded. "He might also check on Lilian." He paused. "I have an idea, Aldreda."

"Yes?"

"I would offer to enact it myself, but I fear I am too large and uncouth to play the queen."

Aldreda's eyes widened. She moved closer to listen and Raddle sidled up. As Pags talked, Raddle snorted with amusement.

"I am not a teapot!" said Aldreda, glaring at Pags.

Pags smiled. "I think it will suit you very well. Only you could carry it off with the requisite dignity."

"How do we know we can trust Lady Orlend?"

"I heard her talking with Chester last night," said Pags. "When you were searching for me, I was hanging in the Dame's curtains. I thought it was time to make use of our natural advantages."

"By eavesdropping?" Aldreda's eyebrows rose. "What did you hear?"

"She told Chester she had arranged for the shatterstones to be hidden, and asked if he knew who had put one in La Moinerie. She sounded worried, and concerned for the safety of our party. And she told him to confess to his own Gift, and use it to help us."

"But we know he is Gifted now."

"I gather that Miss Avely rather jumped to conclusions in assuming he is an Impactor."

Aldreda bit her lip. That was certainly a possibility, and no one had thought to question Elinor's conclusions. "So what Gift *does* he possess?"

Pags rolled his shoulders gingerly, testing the pain. "They didn't say. But the Dame expressed a wish to know what we are really seeking. Chester said he thought it might be the pirate gold, but they both seemed to be in the dark. They were worried that someone on Sark meant Elinor or Perry harm."

Aldreda chewed her lip, considering, then she looked at Pags accusingly. "Why didn't you tell us this before?"

Pags' eyes dropped. "I did. I told Lord Beresford that night, just before dawn. He said not to say anything to anyone else. He wanted an excuse to keep Elinor at the Seigneurie this evening, watching the Orlends."

Aldreda let out an exasperated huff. "Beresford can be damned dictatorial sometimes."

Pags shrugged, then winced. "I could sympathise. One less body to worry about. I thought you would want Elinor kept safe."

Aldreda sighed. "I thank you for protecting her. But she is not the only one whom I want kept safe." She let her eyes rest on him meaningfully, and his hand lifted to grasp her arm warmly.

Raddle looked from one to the other, not following all the revelations. "Can we go now? Will you do it, Miss Zooth?"

Aldreda nodded.

"I won't fail you," said Pags.

"I know," replied Aldreda.

His hand dropped again and they smiled at each other. She stepped onto the overhanging rock then off again, becoming a bat. Pags and Raddle followed and they all lifted high into the air, heading straight across the middle of the island to the Seigneurie.

Aldreda let herself into the attic, pushing open the very same window that Rofan had knocked at earlier that evening. Fortunately, she had thought to leave it ajar. The window swung back without a sound, showing the room to be empty and quiet, just as she had left it.

Raddle was on the roof behind the top cornice, peeping over to keep watch on the window. Pags had gone ahead to scout the other rooms and had not given any warning whistle, so Rofan must still be scouring the island. It would not be long before he came to the Seigneurie.

I must hurry, thought Aldreda. She had to set the scene.

The first thing was to fetch light. She flew to the door and felt a moment's terrible shock when it failed to move. With an extra shove, though, the door handle turned and she pulled it open.

She flew downstairs to the drawing room. She checked to see that it was empty, then edged in, keeping low in the dark room. Candles stood upon the cabinet in silver candelabras. They were all extinguished, but she had expected that. She wrenched one out with her claws and flew to the fireplace. The fire still glowed, easy for Mrs Sidgemoor to reinvigorate when she came to light it in the morning.

This was the tricky bit. Fluttering above the fire, Aldreda held the wick of the candle to the hot coals, praying it would light quickly and Rofan would not surprise her in the act.

The heat felt as if it would sear her wings. After a few moments she backed away, then returned. Just when she thought she could bear it no longer, the wick flared to life.

Cautiously, she lifted the candle into the air, now carrying a wavering flame. It gained in strength, becoming a long tongue of yellow. Slowly, very slowly, she flew out of the room, watching the vacillating light with her heart in her mouth.

It was wrenchingly hard work to fly so slowly while holding the weight of the wax and avoiding the fire with her wings. She dared not stop, however, and continued up the two flights of stairs to the attic.

Once there, she edged the candle into the room and used the flame to light the candelabra on the table. Three candles in all, plus the one which she now let fall on the table. She smothered it by pulling the tablecloth over it, as it was simply too difficult for her to insert it in a holder. The cream fabric blackened and stained as the flame snuffed out.

Next, she went under the table to her basket. As Pags had observed, her new paisley shawl, with its swirls of deep blue and burgundy, was finished with red tassels. She sighed, then used her sharp bat teeth to bite one off. Mrs Avely would not mind too much if her shawl was desecrated in the name of the queen.

Aldreda carried the red tassel up to the table, along with her silk robe. She rested only a moment before flying to the window. Dropping to the windowsill, she became human. Quickly she heaved the curtains open, pushing the heavy green fabric back to show a glimpse of the gardens. The sea breeze swept through and nipped at her bare skin.

Outside, the sky was still clear and starlit, and the sea was a dark shimmer in the distance. The candles behind her would be like a beacon over Sark, a lone spark in the night.

She took a deep breath. The props were in place: candles lit as if by human hand, curtains open. Now for the performance.

Gritting her teeth together, she became a bat again and flew to the table and the tassel. Now for the ridiculous part. Becoming human once more, she slipped on her robe and flung the red tassel over her head. She looped it over her ears, feeling like a fool. She must look like a doll, or a medusa. This would only trick Rofan at a distance, but they were hoping that a glimpse of red hair would mislead him. Moreover, he thought Aldreda was trapped in the cavern; he did not know of Raddle's secret way out.

Her limbs were weary, but she began pacing the length of the tabletop, showing herself briefly in the gap of the curtains. Like a queen stretching her legs after long hibernation.

Like a hungry queen, waiting for her dinner.

As she walked, she hoped devoutly that Raddle was still in his place and that Pags was doing his part. She did not much like the role of bait, but Pags had assured her that he would not fail her. And it was the best plan they could think of at such short notice – as well as having the charm of poetic justice.

She walked and walked, keeping her pace brisk and her bearing regal. The damn tassel twitched around her ears and kept falling into her eyes. She tried to ignore it, keeping her hands loose by her sides. It was hard to remain calm when she seemed to be walking on gorse prickles. How was she supposed to look like a queen when she felt like a mouse in the sights of an owl?

It helped to imagine that Pags was in front of her and that she was scolding him for almost dying. The impertinence of it! Her stride became positively a stalk. She would have to have strong words with him later. Under the cursed tassel she stuck her chin in the air.

Despite her mutterings, Aldreda kept her eyes on the window as she paced. So she saw when the curtain twitched once.

Her heart stuttered. She slithered off the table, transforming into a bat as she fell. Her silk robe fluttered away, but she wrenched the tassel to stay on her head. Rofan must not see her up close, but if he did, the sight of it might confound him for a crucial second.

The silence in the attic was absolute; she could feel her heart pounding. She strained to hear whether he had entered the room.

Silence. She edged towards the door, keeping in line with the table. The attic door was open a fraction, the stairwell dark beyond it.

"Your Majesty?" Rofan's voice came at last, his tone mild and pleasant once more. He sounded as if he was speaking from the chest below the window, or perhaps the floor. "Your Majesty, are you there? I have come to give you proper greetings after the ill-mannered treatment you received. I hope you will accept my apologies for the barbaric behaviour of the humans."

Aldreda wished she could wrench the tassel off her head, but she dared not. She crept closer to the door, keeping in the shadow of the table.

"Your Majesty?" said Rofan again. His voice was closer, and sounded suspicious. "You can trust me. Where are you?"

The click of the window was loud in the silence. It must be Raddle slipping into place, closing the window as if the wind had blown it shut.

That sound was her signal. However, it also alerted Rofan that something was amiss. He darted around the table and saw Aldreda creeping along the floor.

Whether or not he knew it was her, it didn't matter. He lunged at her, his face distorting in a snarl, the rope in his hands.

Aldreda, heart thumping, stretched her wings and flew for the door.

Rofan surprised her with his quickness – he transformed mid-air into a bat and surged forward. The rope brushed the tip of her wing.

"Now!" Pags' voice shouted from the dark corridor. The door

began to close, the gap slowly reducing with terrible implacability.

Tired and scared, Aldreda was still fast. She crossed the final stretch with the speed of a hunted mouse and slipped through the last, tiny gap.

The door closed with a click, and a low clatter signalled Rofan's collision with the wood. Aldreda let her breath out in a whoosh of gratitude.

Then she looked up. In the stairwell stood Lady Orlend, sleepy and frowning, hidden in the dark. She was clothed in a voluminous dressing gown. Lilian was sitting on one shoulder, dressed, while Pags sat on the other, stark naked.

He smiled down at her, his face still drawn, and wiped a hand across his brow. "A close run, my dear."

The Dame of Sark's hand remained on the doorknob. She lifted her hand to the key and turned it in the lock. Aldreda, panting, saw Lady Orlend's lips moving and heard soft words. She felt heaviness press on her wings as the Defence spell took hold.

"There," said the Dame of Sark. "That should lock the window as well. Now, please explain to me what is going on!"

In the cavern, the lantern finally guttered. At first the darkness seemed absolute, and Elinor and Beresford blinked, unable to see each other's faces even though they sat so close together. Then their eyes adjusted to the gloom, able to see by the faint luminescence on the walls.

"Still no chaperone," he murmured into her hair.

She smiled back, and eagerly pressed her lips to his. They kissed, long and deeply, and she pulled him closer, the dark wrapping them together in a strange intimacy. Pressing her body against him, she followed the dictates of the liquid demand within her.

She could not say how long this continued, or how quickly things escalated. Yet somehow she found herself on top of Beresford, her skirts bunched up and her habit undone. The cave now felt warm and her face flushed.

Beresford's hands held her under her skirts. In the dim light she could see that his eyes were wild with desire. Her body was pressed tight against him and she could feel the most exquisite sensations spinning from where they were joined.

"May I ravish you, Elinor?" he asked, his voice thick.

Elinor blinked, feeling hazy and desperately incomplete. There was nothing she wanted more than for Beresford to ravish her, thoroughly and utterly. Yet another thought rose up, unwanted but somehow insistent.

"What about our wedding night?" she whispered.

"Forget the wedding night," said Beresford huskily. "I want you now. What is a wedding night, after all? You were right: it is all nonsense."

Elinor longed to agree, but something held her back. "A wedding night is important to you," she said, reluctantly enunciating the words. "You've been so determined. I would not want to be the cause of you abandoning your principles at this late hour."

Beresford groaned, letting his head fall against the rock with a clunk.

Elinor bit the inside of her cheek, humour bubbling up inside her. "You might regret it later, my dear. I think it is my turn to be strong."

"Curse my principles," moaned Beresford.

"I love you for them," she replied, and put a last chaste kiss on his cheek.

She slowly extricated herself, pushing her skirts down, straightening her bodice, and refastening her habit. She almost flung herself back onto him when she saw his eyes, dark with lust and staring at her, bereft. But she knew he would chastise himself for it later. The last thing she wanted was for him to have cause for regret after such an act.

"Later," she promised. "When we are married. In a proper bed, without frills."

Beresford put a hand over his eyes. "Not on the rocks?"

"No. After a bath and some food. I'm quite hungry, actually."

Beresford groaned again. "If you start prattling on about soufflé, I shall explode."

"Why?" She bit back a smile. "Soufflé is a ravishing dish. I do hope that I can take the recipe home. It will give me lots of energy for our conjugal activities."

Beresford rubbed his eyes. "At least your usual indomitable spirit has returned."

"Indeed," she replied, brushing down her skirts matter-of-factly, trying to quietly dispel her own desire. "Perhaps we should return to our work." She paused. "I cannot guarantee to prop up our fortitude if we remain here too long."

Beresford heaved a sigh and climbed to his feet. "To the rocks then, my love."

But by now the tunnel was completely obscured with a wall of frothing water. They stared at it, realising that the tide was too high: it was impossible to work with the steps covered and the tunnel impassable.

Beresford turned, taking her hand. "Perhaps we should try to sleep instead, while we can." He cleared his throat. "You may rely on my fortitude from now on."

Elinor smiled at him, and they laid down upon Beresford's coat once more. She put her head on his chest this time, trying to ignore the worries that rose to circle her like sharks. He tightened his arms around her, and she closed her eyes.

Strangely, sleep crept upon her. As she drifted off, Elinor couldn't help but wonder if she would slumber here for years like the bats, but she couldn't bring herself to care overmuch. She slept the chaste sleep of the exhausted, lulled to rest by the water swirling and lapping against stone.

She awoke sometime later. Turning to examine the tide, she saw it had receded a little, and the first two steps were now visible again.

Beresford's arm was still under her head, and he was staring at the cones of rock hanging from the ceiling. "Awake, my love?" he asked.

Elinor nodded, snuggling against him. Then all her worries came rushing back, making her stomach twist with anxiety. Perry, Aldreda, Pags, Jaq, the queen, Raddle – all of them were above ground, trying to evade or hunt down a merciless killer. For all she knew, something terrible had happened while she slept. "Oh, how I wish I was a Travellor," she whispered. "Why did I have to be born a Discernor?"

Beresford squeezed her reassuringly. "If you hadn't found the real Durl, the queen would be dead already. You have done your part. Now we must trust to our companions while we wait for the tide to recede."

"I do not think I have the patience!" exclaimed Elinor wretchedly, and hauled herself to a sitting position. "Let us work again, or I shall ravish *you* this time."

Beresford got up hastily. "Work it is."

They began in silence, moving what little stones they could, but soon they began talking. They talked of what might be happening on the surface, of how they would transport the roost to England, of the wedding, of their honeymoon.

"We must travel to Devon," said Beresford. "Immediately after the wedding."

"That sounds lovely, but I may be needed to help settle the roost in Cornwall."

"Your mother can do that," said Beresford, carrying rocks. "We need time alone without any bats, selkies, or murderers."

Elinor nodded, rolling a particularly large rock away from the tunnel. "I quite agree. Shall we be allowed to consume plum jam once more? I have a sudden craving for chudleighs and cream, but it won't be the same without the Beresford plum jam."

He grinned at her. "Well, if you think it wise…"

She looked coquettishly over her shoulder, about to make a remark about the likely effect on their vital forces. But Beresford held up a hand for silence.

She froze, her hands on the rock, as the faint sound of voices came through the rubble. Beresford stepped forward, putting his ear against a gap in the stones.

The voices sounded as if a woman and a man were speaking. Surely, at that volume, they must be human voices, not vampiri. She let out a sigh of relief: not Rofan with Lilian, then. But who? The female voice was speaking in what sounded like French. Lady Orlend? Had someone managed to bring help?

"It is Lady Orlend," Beresford whispered, his ear still against the wall.

Elinor hurried over. "With Perry, or Jaq?"

The female voice came more clearly. "Lord Beresford? Are you there?" It was unmistakably Lady Orlend, her voice imperious. She must have been hauled from her bed.

"I'm here with my wife," said Beresford, and Elinor allowed herself a small smile. "We are stuck."

"I can see that," said Lady Orlend peevishly. "Please move back: I shall use a shatterstone to clear the way. I shall use my Gift to guide the Impact through the blockage, so that the roof doesn't come down."

Elinor's eyes widened. "Are you sure that is wise, Lady Orlend?"

She was relieved when she heard Jaq's voice through the rocks. "You can trust her. It is the only way to clear the rubble for you – another slab has fallen since I went through. If we don't blow it up, you'll be stuck there forever."

Beresford backed away hurriedly. "Elinor, back!"

Elinor walked briskly towards the lagoon, with Beresford two steps behind her. When they reached the lapping waters, they turned and joined hands. Elinor could feel the waves touching the back of her boots.

Beresford called out, "We are ready, Lady Orlend." His voice echoed hollowly round the cavern.

Elinor tensed, waiting for the Impact. Would Lady Orlend truly be able to guide the shatterstone's Impact through the rock? She cast an anxious glance at the sleeping roost, still furled and quiet, and hoped they would not be disturbed.

The Dame's voice filtered through, calm and confident. "Ready."

When the explosion came, a round hole showed: a black wound in the rubble. It was all Elinor saw before Beresford let go of her hand and stepped in front of her.

She had time for one cross thought before the Impact hit: how could he decide who was to take the blow? Then the wave of power hit, sharp and forceful. It slammed into him as if he were its target.

He was braced against it, so he didn't fall backwards onto Elinor. Instead, he fell sideways. As he hit the rock, the force continued to push him, rolling his body into the swirling waters of the lagoon. With an awful sucking sound, the waters closed around him.

Elinor let out an unearthly shriek, her voice echoing in the cave. She waded into the water, her heart beating so rapidly that her vision seemed to blur. All she could see was the black, empty lagoon. It was unexpectedly deep, and soon she was floundering as she tried in vain to locate him. Taking in mouthfuls of the inky water, she spluttered in fury and fear. "Beresford! James! No!"

Dimly she saw more light spilling into the cave as the new occupants entered. Fresh lantern light glimmered on the gold across the lagoon, casting ripples of yellow.

Someone pulled at her shoulder, heaving her out. It was Jaq, his expression grim as he thrust her back on the rocks. Then he leapt in, becoming a seal even as he hit the water.

She watched the black and gold waves, too taut with anxiety to look away.

A minute later, Jaq pulled a limp body onto the cavern floor. It was Beresford, his face very pale and covered in gashes, his arms slack, his eyes closed.

It was Elinor's turn now to throw herself on her beloved's chest, like Aldreda, and weep. But unlike Pags, Beresford had no supernatural strength to rely on.

He was human, and mortal.

32
IN WHICH A MARRIAGE IS KNOWN
TO BE A SHAM

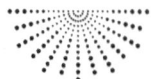

*E*linor lay beside Beresford's soaked body and choked back her tears to listen. Surely he would not leave her now; not when they were about to embark on a life of happiness together.

Hoping against hope, she laid a trembling hand on his stomach, put her ear to his chest, and strained all her senses for the rise and fall of his breath.

It was there, weak and unsteady. Tears pooled in her eyes again as she felt its faint, valiant progress. But she sensed, despite herself, that it was unreliable and faltering. Perhaps an internal injury made breathing difficult for him, or he had swallowed too much water. She almost shook him. His strength and his autocratic nature should balk at being undone by a tiny bomb and a dip in a lagoon.

"Come, James," she whispered. "Come back to me. I insist upon it." Tears leaked out of her eyes even as she tried to speak firmly. Beresford's face was white, his flesh clammy.

"May I help?" said a voice beside her.

She glanced up to see Chester, his face worried. His mother was two steps behind him, frowning and pale. Lilian stood on

Chester's shoulder, clinging to his ear, her face white and determined.

"What can you do?" Elinor demanded, her voice trembling. "You've done enough. He is badly injured, I can tell. He is close to death." Her voice cracked on the last words.

"I'm a Healor," said Chester. "Let me help."

Elinor blinked, a sudden jolt of hope shooting through her like sunlight in sodden skies. She backed away from Beresford and gestured for Chester to step forward, her hand shaking. As he knelt down, Lilian jumped to the ground and took her place at his side. Elinor barely noticed: her gaze was fixed on Beresford's face.

Chester worked on Beresford for an hour, with intervals of rest. Jaq retreated to the far wall with Chester's cloak around him, watching with lips in a grim line. Elinor, freezing and shivering with cold, refused to leave the cave, despite Lady Orlend's pleas. The Dame of Sark looked unwell herself, huddled in a heap on a rock, and Elinor told her to leave without them. But Lady Orlend did not go, and they both kept watch while Chester worked. Lady Orlend's eyes occasionally drifted to the vampiri and the gold, but Elinor looked only at Beresford, urging him to return with all her might, her world narrowed to a single imperative.

When at last Beresford rose into consciousness she wept with relief, sweeping Chester and Lilian out of the way and embracing her beloved tightly.

Beresford ran a tentative hand down her quivering back. "Are we still in this damn cave, my dear?"

"Oh, James!" said Elinor, and started crying again.

"How did you all get here?" Beresford asked, looking around at Lady Orlend, Lilian, and Chester.

"A vampiri by the name of Pagrilliard woke us," replied Chester, wiping his brow. "Well, he woke Mother, and she thought I might be needed, so she roused me too. Jaq guided us."

"So Pags is all right?" breathed Elinor, clinging tightly to Beresford. "Aldreda? Perry?"

Jaq stepped forward, pulling Chester's coat closer. "Everyone's all right," he said, soothingly. "Rofan is contained. I'll tell you all about it later, but I suggest we leave this cave as soon as possible. We don't want to be stuck here for another nine hours."

Beresford propped himself up to a sitting position. "We have been here long enough, believe me."

Chester stood. "Ordinarily, I would suggest that you rest, my lord, but Jaq is right." He turned to Lilian, concern furrowing his brow. "The sun is rising, Lilian, so perhaps you should stay here, where it is dark."

Lilian sat down on the stone floor, her primness undone: shoulders slumped, legs crossed, her face weary. "I shall stay with the roost."

Elinor stared at her. "You are Chester's companion, not Lady Orlend's?"

Lilian dipped her head in acknowledgement, folding her little hands in front of her. "I am, though I do not mind helping Lady Orlend with the needlework."

Elinor put a hand to her head. "So that is why you sleep in the cellar!" It would be awkward for a lady vampiri, so often unclothed, to sleep in the same room as a young man like Chester. "We thought you were Lady Orlend's slave!"

Lilian smiled guiltily. "Perhaps I overdid it in my efforts to pretend I was her companion."

Chester dusted off his shirt and helped his mother rise. "I didn't want the king to know of my Healing and send me to serve in the army. We thought it better to pretend that my mother was the practising Musor — a deception I'm sure you can understand, Lady Beresford."

"Hm," said Elinor.

Lady Orlend stood up, her spine as stiff as the stone wall behind her. She shook off her son's arm. "I am an old lady, not a child. I do not think it necessary for Chester to stay behind, but he insists."

Elinor frowned. "I thought you demanded it."

"Not I," snapped the Dame of Sark. "I think Chester should leave this island and strike out in the world, not stay behind like a nursemaid."

Chester sighed. "I shall not leave my own mother to die alone."

"I am not alone," retorted Lady Orlend. "I have the Sidgemoors and Hedley." She gestured upwards. "And who, may I ask, are all these bats?"

Elinor decided it was safe for the truth to emerge now. "That is the last remaining French vampiri roost. It is the real reason we came to Sark." She pulled Beresford to his feet, brushed the hair from his brow, and stood on tiptoe to place a kiss on his mouth.

"Thank God for that," said Lady Orlend irritably. "You can leave now, and put an end to your licentious behaviour." She sniffed. "I am quite aware that you have been living in sin."

Elinor looked across defiantly. "We have not!"

Lady Orlend sighed. "I suppose you *have* been sleeping separately. Chester visited you the other night, to see if he could Heal you after your brush with that shatterstone. He had some very interesting things to tell me about your sleeping arrangements."

"How dare you, Mr Orlend!" exclaimed Elinor. "Sneaking into our room like that! I thought you were a ghoul about to murder me!"

"I apologise," said Chester. "I was only trying to help. We felt terribly guilty about leaving the shatterstones in the cellar for anyone to misuse."

"Yes," said Lilian softly from the floor. "Especially I, as I sleep there. I should have kept better watch. I came with Chester that night to see what we could do."

Elinor, who had her arm tucked around Beresford's waist,

blushed. "Plenty of married couples sleep in separate beds. I don't know what you are talking about."

Lady Orlend sniffed again. "Not couples who look at each other in the way that you two do," she observed. "It is enough to tell anyone that you are still unwedded."

Beresford cleared his throat. "Not for long. Our wedding breakfast is to be attended by Prince George himself in a few weeks."

"I am glad to hear it," said Lady Orlend, severely. "Now let us go home. I am rather weary of the dark."

"Poor Mother," said Chester anxiously. "You must be exhausted after using your Gift."

Elinor pursed her lips. "You are a powerful Musor, Lady Orlend, if you can practice without a vampiri."

"Nonsense," said Lady Orlend dismissively. "I merely directed the stone, I didn't conjure the Impact myself."

Elinor was not convinced but Chester changed the subject. "Look at all that gold! Thank you for finding it, Lady Beresford – er, Miss Avely." He cast a longing look at the treasure. "You must take your fair share, of course."

"There is plenty of time for that later," said Elinor, who was currently vastly uninterested in gold. "James, do you think you can walk?"

She insisted that Beresford lean on her, and he insisted that he wouldn't. Wet and bedraggled, they crawled through the dark tunnel bickering, seawater still swirling around them, followed by Lady Orlend, Jaq, and Chester, clutching a gold slab. Lilian stayed behind to tend to the roost should they wake, and to stay out of the rising sun.

Elinor felt strange as she emerged from the tunnel into the dawn: as if she had lived the longest night of her life and yet daylight was still surprising. Soft pink spread through the sky, and the wind's fresh touch was a delight after the smoky darkness of the cave. She looked over the vast ocean and felt a sudden, deep gratitude for her own life, and an awareness of every particle of her being.

She had never seen this part of the island in daylight, and she looked around with curiosity at the wild landscape. Jewel-like pools were exposed by the low tide, gleaming between the rough granite outcrops. The puffins were stirring, and gulls greeted the day with their high, keening cries. She smiled at them in benediction and gripped Beresford's hand tightly, revelling in his warmth.

The waves continued their insistent roiling and Elinor turned to ascend. It was not so easy without Perry to Travel her wherever she liked, but Chester had strung two ropes to assist their climb. She heaved herself up, her hands burning on the rope.

In the shock of almost losing Beresford, she had been happy to gloss over what had happened to the rest of her companions. Now she began to be impatient for news. "Lady Orlend," she said, turning to help Chester hand his mother up the final rock. "Did you happen to see Peregrine on your way here?"

Lady Orlend tottered to the cart that awaited them and leaned heavily on it. "Your brother? No. Is he not in bed?" She sighed. "Of course he isn't."

"Jaq, where is Perry?"

Jaq grinned. "He probably *is* in bed by now, but not his own. He had a midnight feast of raspberry soufflés, so he won't need breakfast."

Elinor's eyes widened. "He went back to the Fittens'?"

Jaq shrugged. "Mr Fitten had mentioned raspberry soufflés, and that came back to his panicked mind as he clutched the vampiri. Mrs Fitten was expecting company, and she was kind enough to take the bats in, too. Mr Fitten even offered up some of his sheep, and he did a better job than Perry at fetching them."

"To be fair, Perry did do a good job," said Elinor loyally. "We were just prevaricating to hold off Rofan."

"And what of him?" asked Beresford, as Jaq pulled him to the top of the cliff. "Where is Rofan?"

"Ah, you'll like this," said Jaq. "Pags and Aldreda locked him in the attic. Aldreda lured Rofan in by pretending to be the queen while Pags woke Lady Orlend, who was gracious enough to lock the attic door and put a Defence spell on the window. So Rofan is hoist with his own petard."

Elinor shuddered. "We can't leave him there."

Chester helped his mother into the cart. "What will you do with him? I believe he has caused quite a lot of trouble."

Beresford climbed into the back. "We'll take him to England with us, so that he can be tried for murder in London. I believe King George has set up a Musor court to deal with such crimes."

There was plenty more to discuss – such as what the queen had made of her rescue by Perry. Elinor did not want to expose all the details before Lady Orlend, however, so she curbed her curiosity.

"Now," said Beresford, "I think I should lie down, with my head supported."

"Your turn," said Jaq, grinning, and he handed Elinor into the cart. Elinor promptly sat down and patted her lap, inviting Beresford to lay his head there.

He did so with a sigh. "There are some advantages to being a hero."

"Indeed," said Elinor, stroking his brow and holding his hand tightly once more. Then she frowned. "You do realise that while we were heaving rocks in the dark, drenched, bombed, and sick with worry, Perry was having a pot of tea and raspberry soufflé!"

"Sloe gin, too," remarked Jaq. "It was a merry party. Aldreda and Pags joined him, while I went to rescue you."

"We must go to the Fittens' at once!" announced Elinor.

33

IN WHICH ONLY THE QUEEN IS NOT WEARY

*T*hey delivered Lady Orlend and Chester to the Seigneurie first, with many thanks, and changed out of their soaked, dirty clothes. Mrs Sidgemoor even produced a basket of cheese, rolls, and ham to take with them to the Fittens.

As Mrs Sidgemoor handed the basket up to the party in the cart, she cleared her throat. "I heard your real purpose on Sark is to fetch some vampiri," she said tentatively. "I found one in the attic – dead, poor fellow. Were you looking for him, perhaps?"

"Why, yes," said Elinor, her eyes narrowing. "He is Lieutenant Chaboot, and we hope to give him a proper burial. Where have you put him, may I ask?"

Mrs Sidgemoor's gaze dropped to the ground. "Mr Sidgemoor cremated him. I didn't want to bother Lady Orlend with the matter, so I told Sidgemoor to make him a funeral pyre in La Moinerie. I am very sorry if we did wrong."

Elinor remembered the old ashes she had seen in the ruins. "You should have told us, though I suppose you weren't to know that we were looking for him." At least the lieutenant had received something approaching funeral rites. She resolved to build a small cairn for him in the ashes, and one for Thomas Durl on the granite rock where she had found his coffin. "What were those scraping sounds at night, then? I thought someone was digging a grave."

"That was me too, but only at the gates." Mrs Sidgemoor blushed. "I've been trying to undo some of the protections on this house, for I believe they are too heavy and make Lady Orlend ill. So in the night I open the gates, which weakens the spells somewhat."

"That was the sound of the gates?" Elinor recalled the heavy gates at the end of the drive. The sound must have travelled in the night, winding its way to their windows and becoming distorted in the process. Or perhaps she and Perry simply had nervous imaginations.

"It seems you and your husband often undertake night-time activities," she said wryly. "What of Dinah – does she also do your bidding? She was seen lurking outside our window yesterday evening."

Mrs Sidgemoor drew in her chin. "Nothing untoward, madame, I assure you. I gave Dinah the key that undoes the Defences; she was merely unlocking the windows. I was busy in the kitchen that evening."

"I see," said Elinor. "And did Mr Sidgemoor take the shatterstones to La Moinerie to reduce the spellwork in the house?"

Mrs Sidgemoor looked a little surprised. "No, Lady Orlend ordered us to move them out of harm's way. We thought that if they were underwater it would be more difficult for anyone to help themselves."

Elinor's lips twisted at the irony. If Beresford and Jaq hadn't moved the sack, Rofan wouldn't have been able to throw bombs at them.

"Actually," confessed Beresford, "we moved the sack of shatterstones to behind the walled garden. What will Lady Orlend do with them now?"

Mrs Sidgemoor's expression lightened. "The Dame says that

she agrees with me, and that you may take the sack with you, if you please – perhaps for your castle."

Beresford raised his eyebrows, perhaps thinking, like Elinor, that the Dame of Sark was trying to avoid royal chastisement. All he remarked, however, was that it was good of Lady Orlend to forego some of her Defences.

"The spells are excessive," replied Mrs Sidgemoor severely. "And I can't bake soufflés while they hang over the house so!"

"An onerous encumbrance," agreed Elinor, surveying the fine old house and wondering if it felt lighter now. The sunlight glinted on the mullioned windows and made the white frames gleam. "I hope you are right and Lady Orlend's health improves."

"You look a little peaky yourself," admonished Mrs Sidgemoor. "You must eat some of that food, madame, when you share it with the Fittens."

Elinor settled the basket on her lap: a tricky feat, as she was once again holding Beresford's hand. "I shall do so gladly."

Lady Orlend stepped out of the house and into the sunlight, her face drawn with tiredness. She nodded cordially at Elinor and Beresford. "I hope you find Mr Avely safe and sound. Let me know what assistance you need tonight." She paused. "And what you plan to tell King George."

Elinor leaned forward. "Do not worry; we shall not inform on Mr Orlend. He is free to come and go as he pleases, just as Perry does."

Lady Orlend inclined her head and lifted a wrinkled hand in salute. "I am glad you prevented regicide. I would not want that on Sark's conscience."

Elinor smiled and saluted in return. She felt that they both understood each other rather well now.

The cart trundled off in the morning sunshine with Jaq driving, heading west. Elinor held Beresford's hand and drank in the scene, her eyes feasting on the green fields and waving white flowers. The scent of gorse and blackthorn hung in the air and white clouds piled high in the sky. She felt a tired happiness, though it was tempered by remnants of anxiety from the night's adventures and the fact that she still had not laid eyes on Perry or Aldreda.

Soon they pulled up at the Fittens'. The lady of the house hurried out to greet them, wiping her hands on her bright apron. "Ah!" Mrs Fitten cooed. "Your brother just awoke. Do join us for breakfast in the kitchen, though I'm not certain if he wants any."

Elinor handed her the basket of food and they were taken inside. There, at the familiar kitchen table, sat Perry, his long legs stretched out and his head in his hands.

He looked up as they entered, and Elinor saw that he was a little pale. "Oh, you made it, did you? Glad to see you all."

"What's wrong?" asked Elinor anxiously. "Where are the queen and Aldreda?"

Perry waved a negligent hand. "Oh, they're asleep in the cellar with Pags, Raddle, and the other one." At their expectant looks, he continued. "I explained the situation to Her Majesty, with some difficulty given my execrable French. Fortunately, she has accepted our offer of castle quarters. She plans to wake the roost tonight, and then we can all leave this sheep-ridden island behind us."

"So why the despondent attitude?" queried Beresford.

Jaq went to Perry. Elinor could tell that he wanted to take Perry's hand, just as she had been holding Beresford's all morning, but the Fittens' presence meant that he could only grip the chair. "Are you all right, Perry?" he asked, bending over him.

Perry rubbed his head. "Just a bit under the weather. Sloe gin is potent stuff, and bat herding is even more arduous than sheep herding. When I Travelled here, the vampiri took exception to the sudden dislocation and became fully human in order to voice their opinions. Mr Fitten's nerves were then overcome by the sight of me with two tiny naked ladies. It took some time to calm everyone down and explain that we weren't ghosts or faeries."

Jaq stifled a laugh, and Elinor thought that perhaps she hadn't had such a bad time of it after all, in comparison to Perry's trials.

Beresford pulled out a chair and she sat down, gratefully accepting a hot cup of tea from Mrs Fitten. She sipped the fragrant brew and sighed with relief, glad that everyone was safely accounted for.

Once she had drunk two whole cups she felt far more like her old self. Almost, in fact, in a fit state to meet a queen. The rest of the table were discussing the various events of the night, but she stood up. "Might I visit the cellar?" she asked. "Just to check on Aldreda and Her Majesty?"

"Certainly," said Mrs Fitten, and she led the way to the back of the house, lighting a candle for Elinor in the stairwell.

Elinor went downstairs and opened the door cautiously, remembering how Raddle had hated the sunlight. She slipped in and shut the door, holding her candle aloft.

The Fittens' cellar was small, piled with produce, and thick with the smells of herbs, wines, and salted meat. Aldreda hung in her bat form, fast asleep among the lavender bunches dangling from the ceiling. After all, she had experienced a very busy night; she must be exhausted.

Pags, too, hung among the lavender, close to Aldreda but not touching her. Elinor was pleased to see that. She hoped a good sleep would help to heal his battered body, and that he and Aldreda might come to an understanding. She wondered whether Pags would deign to remain as Mrs Avely's companion, or Perry's, and whom the queen would bond with. All those questions, though, might have to wait until they reached Cornwall.

She felt someone watching her, and her gaze found that of a tiny, naked queen. Her Majesty was wide awake, standing on a sack of potatoes, and examining Elinor with great interest. Her dark eyes were as bright as before, and her red hair made a soft cloud around her head.

Hastily, Elinor dropped into a low curtsy. "Your Majesty," she said, keeping her eyes down.

"Qui êtes vous?" demanded the queen.

"I am Miss Zooth's companion," answered Elinor in French, daring to look up. "My name is Elinor Avely, and I am very glad to meet you."

"Ah, Mr Avely's sister."

"Er, yes," said Elinor. "I apologise for any, er, ham-fistedness he may have employed—"

"No need," said the queen graciously. "Mr Avely did what seemed necessary at the time. I believe we must thank *you* for realising the imminent danger."

Elinor demurred, but the queen waved a hand in benediction. "Mr Avely tells me – in his terrible accent – that you have a castle for my roost."

"Yes, indeed," said Elinor. "If you wish to seek asylum in England, you may come to Cornwall with us."

"Ah yes, the Musor school." Her Majesty paused thoughtfully. "I am not averse. We need a place to recover and re-establish ourselves after the persecution we suffered in France. However, I do not know how we shall fly all the way to Cornwall in our current state. It is too long a trip to make in one night."

"We have a ship," explained Elinor. "With plenty of cupboards. We can take out the rations and brandy to make room for you all."

The queen wrinkled her aristocratic nose. "I do not like sea travel."

"Nor do I," agreed Elinor. "I shall be dreadfully sick. However, we may not have any alternative."

The queen sat down on the hessian cloth with a rather un-regal plop and sighed. At that moment, Raddle stuck his head out of a crack in the wall. "Ooh, I've never been on a ship before. Can we hang off the rigging at night?"

"Most certainly," said Elinor, laughing. "Though you might not like the lurching."

Her Majesty wrinkled her nose again. "I suppose I should try to sleep now, while I can."

Elinor took that as her dismissal. "One more thing." She put the candle down, rummaged in her bag and pulled out the golden flute, light and delicate in her hand. "The Viveroust flute, Your Majesty. You can use it to wake your people tonight."

She knelt and presented it to the queen. Tiny, pale fingers took the flute from her palm. "Thank you," said Her Majesty. She admired the scrollwork. "King George is considerate in his assistance. We are most grateful."

Elinor curtsied and backed out of the cellar. As she closed the door, Raddle winked at her.

Smiling, she returned to the kitchen, where bright morning sun streamed through the windows. Jaq was sitting next to Perry now, and Mrs Fitten dished up plates of bacon and toast, while Beresford still nursed a cup of tea.

Elinor took her seat and filled her own cup from the teapot again. "There's one thing I don't know yet." All heads turned towards her. "Did Perry really canter about on a sheep last night?"

Everyone laughed, and Perry gave an enigmatic smile. "You will never know, dear sister. The ghostly shepherd of Sark does not divulge his methods. Suffice to say, I'll be pleased to never see another sheep in my life."

"Sorry," said Beresford, leaning back in his chair. "Cornwall is overrun with the creatures."

The smell of bacon filled the air, but a shadow passed across Perry's face.

Jaq gave a cough. "Skerry is not, however, cursed with sheep. Perry and I shall go there first."

Perry turned to look at him, a tentative smile dawning. "Really?"

Jaq self-consciously pushed a lock of hair behind his ear. "You need a rest from sheep. And besides, I want to introduce you to my mother." Elinor hid a smile, for Perry looked flustered now as well as pleased.

Beresford set down his cup. "Don't forget to attend our wedding."

Jaq grinned. "We won't forget your wedding, my lord, and we're certain *you* haven't. Dare I ask, will there be jam and cream at the wedding breakfast?"

Elinor blushed and answered for Beresford. "Of course. And soufflés, if I have anything to say about it."

Beresford's hand crept under the table and took hers. He smiled across at her, squeezing her hand.

She smiled back. She could hardly wait.

~

THE END

NOTE FROM THE AUTHOR

Thank you for reading *The Golden Flute*, and for making it this far into the series! If you enjoyed it, and want more, please say so in a review. Reviews are essential to the success of independently published books like this one, and I really appreciate any time you take to post them.

To keep up with new releases, book recs, and recipes, you can join my mailing list at rosalieoaks.com/newsletter.

Much love to my readers. You make this whole authorly endeavour even possible.

Happy reading and tea drinking,
Rosalie

ALSO IN THE SERIES...

The Selkie Scandal

Book 1.5, The Selkie Scandal, doesn't always show up in your store's list for the Lady Diviner series, but it exists...

A royal ransom, a dangerous rescue, and the famous Beresford jam...

England, 1804: the Earl of Beresford has his morning interrupted by naked selkie royalty. The seal-woman in question wants Beresford to find her brother, the High Prince of Skerry, who has been taken hostage for two thousand guineas.

Lord Beresford knows the coast better than he knows his own cravat—but his wits alone may not be enough to stop a war and save a selkie prince from death. Thankfully, he *also* has a whole case of the famous Beresford Jam.

Who stole the seal prince? How will Beresford find him? And what *really* happened at the royal birthday party?

The Selkie Scandal is an inter-novella in the Lady Diviner series.

ABOUT THE AUTHOR

Rosalie Oaks writes novels set in a magical Regency England full of manners, mystery, and cream tea. As a child, she loved conducting home-made theatre productions with her three younger brothers. Now she directs her characters instead, but like her brothers, they don't always do what she says.

Rosalie wants to live in a world where scones are good for you, cream is slimming, and she can make the perfect jam. While writing, however, she contents herself with vast quantities of tea and chocolate.

Join Rosalie's newsletter to get bonus scenes, book gossip, as well as your free copy of the prequel novella, *A Pendant for Trouble*. Find out more at rosalieoaks.com.

ALSO BY ROSALIE OAKS

The Lady Diviner series

A Pendant for Trouble (prequel novella)

The Lady Jewel Diviner (Book 1)
The Moria Pearls (Book 2)
The Sapphire Library (Book 3)

The Selkie Scandal (Book 1.5, prequel novella)

www.rosalieoaks.com

www.ingramcontent.com/pod-product-compliance
Lightning Source LLC
Chambersburg PA
CBHW030529120726
47904CB00005B/1686